ONCE THE SKIES FADE

ONCE THE SKIES FADE

IMMORTAL REVERIES
BOOK TWO

VANESSA RASANEN

To those who have loved and lost:
Don't be afraid to love again. It is worth it.

Love is always worth it.

AUTHOR NOTE

This book contains strong language, torture, gore, violence, death of a loved one, depression, and sexual intimacy on page.

A "spice rack" is provided in the back for readers who prefer to know when to expect intimate content.

PRONUNCIATION GUIDE

Calla: KA-lə
Vael: VAYL
Matthias: mə-THY-əs
Orelian: ə-REH-lee-ən
Isa: EE-sə
Brennan: BREH-nen
Graham: GRAM
Lieke: LEE-kə
Connor: KON-er
Durand: der-AND
Sera: SEHR-ə
Lorynne: LOR-in
Oryn: OR-in
Vestiliaga: ves-TIH-lee-ah-gə
Veslane: VES-layn
Vestia: VES-tee-ə
Vranić: VRAH-nich
Nevan: NEH-vən
Emeryn: EH-mer-ən
Arenysen: ə-REH-nə-sehn

Dolobare: do-lo-BAR
Engle: EHN-gəl
Linley: LIN-lee
Shoerda: SHOR-də
Fairden: FAYR-dən

NOVIBEL
CASTLE ARENYSEN
SHOERDA
ENGLE
ARENYSEN
EMERYN PALACE

DOLOBARE
LARABURN SEA
WRENWICK CASTLE
CROWMER
WRENWICK
MINERVA'S COTTAGE
HILLSCHADE
HOLSHAM
LINLEY
GERRALT

DEAR READER

Matthias here.

I've been tasked by the prince, who is apparently too busy on his honeymoon to do this himself, to remind you of what happened before this book you're about to read. He said something about not wanting you to be confused or feel lost or something. I suggested we just let you reread the previous book if you need to, but he insisted on a recap.

Isn't that just like him? Always thinking of others.

That must get exhausting.

Regardless, if he thinks this is worth taking time away from my hunting down the remaining human rebels, then so be it. He's the boss, and this is now part of my duties. I'll try to keep this short, though, because I know you're dying to jump into this next story (which is all about me).

Let's see here. How to make this fun?

There once was a girl at the castle,
Who was quite the frustrating hassle.
She loved the wrong prince,
So his brother stepped in,

And repeatedly saved her ass—um...never mind.

Let's try something different.

Once upon a time...shit, I don't like that either. Fine, I'll just lay it all out there as best I can. Try to keep up, okay?

So you remember my friend, Connor, right? Do-gooder with a heart of gold and the temper of a badger? Yeah, that one. Well, his dad—the king, who is, admittedly, a bit of a dick (and that's putting it lightly, I know)—tasked him with controlling his brother, Brennan, who had been living his best life bedding anyone with breasts. With the humans and fae still not getting along two decades after that stars-damned War of Hearts ended, the king wanted to establish an alliance with the other fae kingdom, Arenysen, using his youngest son as bait. Yes, it's complicated. Politics usually are.

Poor Brennan had to woo a pretty princess and promise to settle down, but like any immature brat, he didn't want to be told what to do and refused to cooperate.

Enter Lieke, our heroine.

Poor girl...uh, woman...made the foolish mistake of falling for the dumbass (Brennan, not the king), and she got it in her head that she should finally make her move and tell him. That went over about as well as you'd expect—worse, actually— as she ended up in the arms of an asshole fae noble. My boy, Connor, *had* to save her—even shifted into his hound form to do so, which is kind of a big deal, because he *loathes* shifting. (How he repeatedly denied having any feelings for her is beyond me, but I digress.)

Long story short...ish—Lieke got sent away to live with her family, who later turned out to be the rebels Connor and I had been failing to hunt down, not that we knew that at the time. All we knew was some humans were killing a bunch of our fae citizens on the roads with some mysterious poison.

For three years Connor babysat his brother. Just when Brennan was finally cooperating, set to announce his engagement to the princess, Lieke came back. Dun dun dun! And yup, she got in the way.

Connor tried to warn her with that scary growl of his—even shoved her against the wall by the throat...which I still think sounded kind of hot, though he didn't agree—but she's a stubborn one for a human. Also an unlucky one. She ended up back in the clutches of that same fae noble, but Connor wasn't there to save her, so she saved herself—sort of—with a pair of poisoned daggers that killed him. I say "sort of," because she got dragged before the king and sentenced to death for killing a fae—which is a crime, if you didn't remember.

Brennan, spineless coward that he is, refused to help her, so Connor did what he does best and saved her (again) in the most ridiculous, surprising way: by pretending she was his fiancée.

Sigh.

That went over about as well as you'd expect, but she agreed to it, albeit reluctantly. Not really sure what she had against having to *pretend* to be engaged to my friend—a prince, even—especially when it wasn't like she actually had to marry him. She just needed to fake it until Brennan sealed the deal with his vows.

Watching the two of them was both frustrating and entertaining. You could have cut the fucking tension with a dagger, but those hard-headed fools. I tried to help them, of course, but not even a room with one bed could get those two to admit their mutual attraction. Still, they did an adequate job playing their parts—enough that some fae tried to avenge that asshole noble's death by attacking Lieke at the inn. Yes, yes, Connor shifted and saved her.

A vicious attack on the road—one of the most gruesome scenes I'd ever seen, even during the war—forced us to split up, which probably wasn't the best idea, but nothing I can do to change that now. I stayed behind to investigate the scene while they rode off down a shortcut to get home faster. An ambush— set up by Lieke's rebel family—got two of our best guards and Connor's favorite horse killed. We didn't know it at the time, but her family set up the ambush to threaten to kill either prince if she didn't somehow stop the alliance with Arenysen.

Sigh.

When they got back to the palace, Connor went and made things complicated by kissing Lieke, and—SNAP!—the mating bond. They were mates all along! Though Lieke didn't realize it, because humans aren't as sensitive to that shit, or something. Now, I'm still iffy on the whole mate mumbo-jumbo, and I certainly don't think there's a mate out there for everyone, but it's hard to deny that it was true for these two.

Both of them were scared, though, for different reasons.

Connor couldn't bear to tell her they were mates and have her reject the bond and him, while Lieke was trying to find a way to stop Brennan's wedding and keep Connor—and his brother— from being killed by her psychotic family.

So, he avoided her, despite my telling him not to be an idiot, and she lied to Connor, making him believe she still loved his brother. The crazy fool believed her. I know what you're think-ing...ew, miscommunication, gross. But hear me out: Lieke lied for a reason, and a stars-damned good one in my opinion, and Connor—after having his fake fiancée demand to be listened to and trusted for months—finally did just that and believed her lies.

Now, I don't know all the details about what happened between the kiss and the final battle at the barn—though, I quite clearly recall Connor getting shit-faced drunk off my favorite brandy and showing up at Lieke's door after insulting one of the staff. There was something about shared dreams—not that Connor would share any details—a retrieved necklace, and more than one of us telling Connor to buck up and just tell her the stars-damned truth about their bond.

Before he could, though, Lieke got lured out to an old farm where her family ambushed her and laid a trap to capture Connor. Which they did. After shooting me in the shoulder with a thankfully un-poisoned arrow. Connor, however, did get poisoned when he shifted and bit one of the humans (whose blood was poisoned) and after we finally managed to kill the humans—all except Lieke's cousin, Raven—Lieke and I took Connor to see the old creepy mage, Minerva, who was the only person who could possibly save him.

Lieke paid with her mother's necklace to have Minerva save him. Raven disappeared—as did Marin, the rebel's presumed spy inside the palace. Brennan married his princess. Lieke and Connor got married in the muddy woods. The kingdom may not have healed completely, but it's as happy an ending as we could hope for.

Okay, now I need to get back to my more pressing duties of tracking these rebels. If Connor asks how I did with this assignment, I'd appreciate a positive word. I'm not encouraging you to lie, but there could be a bottle of brandy in your future if you help me out.

-Matthias Orelian
General of Emeryn

CHAPTER 1

CALLA

Death was a greedy bitch. Taking one life—two, even—could not satisfy her. No, her ravenous darkness craved the hearts of those left to mourn. We still drew breath, sure, but from air rancid with death's foul touch. Forced to live on in a world robbed of love and laughter, we remained behind only to watch everyone else move on. Would our pain ever ease?

I'd been wondering that for the past three months.

That's when Death came for my parents, drowning them in the Laraburn Sea on their voyage back from Dolobare and leaving me to rule my kingdom well before I was ready. The bitch might as well have taken me under those waters too, with how poor a job I was doing as the new Queen of Arenysen.

Three months.

Three months and I still had no answers surrounding their deaths, and no idea how to rule in their absence.

Thank the stars I didn't have to govern alone. Try as they might though, neither my best friend, Isa, nor my husband, Brennan, knew how to help me heal. They'd at least agreed not to have a memorial service, instead instituting an official Day of Mourning for our citizens, but they'd refused to cancel today's festivities. Apparently the day of my birth was something to celebrate no matter how persistent my grief.

I'd agreed, as long as they didn't require me to dance. It was the last thing I wanted to do—aside from stand here surrounded by hundreds of guests—even if Brennan was exceptionally light on his feet. Standing there in my usual corner, watching the crowd as I always had my whole life, I wondered if perhaps twirling around the floor would have been a better alternative to the incessant chatter of near strangers.

My mother had made these parties look easy, greeting each guest—fae and human alike—as if they were the most important in attendance. Not once had she complained about the pain from donning a constant smile, the ache in her feet, or the exhaustion that overcame her after so many hours. She could have shooed everyone out the door promptly at the end of the night, but she never rushed anyone, always listened, and genuinely cared for them. In short, she'd been the type of queen I wanted to be but sorely wasn't...yet.

A glass of wine floated into view, demanding my attention. Isa's smiling face appeared as she shoved the drink into my hand.

"Your mother would have loved this party," she said quietly, drumming her fingers on the pommel of her sword. As general of the Arenysen army, she declined the usual gowns the females wore to these functions, favoring instead her formal uniform. I might have keeled over from the shock alone if she ever attended one of these in something remotely resembling a dress.

"Birthdays were always her favorite," I noted. I took a long sip. If only I could drown myself in the small glass, I could avoid the inevitably awkward farewells. I cringed at the inappropriate thought as an image of a sinking ship flashed into my mind. It disappeared when Isa clinked her glass against mine.

"Happy birthday, by the way."

"Thank you," I muttered half-heartedly.

Brennan slid up beside me and squeezed my hand as he kissed my temple. "Happy birthday," he echoed into my ear. All I could do was hum quietly in response. Isa snatched another glass from a passing server and offered it to Brennan. When he declined it with a wave of his hand, I took it from her instead, ignoring their stares as I downed the wine quickly.

Thankfully, neither of them commented, and instead Isa addressed Brennan. "It's a shame your brother and his wife couldn't be here. It would have been nice to see them again."

Brennan nodded along as she spoke. "Agreed. It's been too long since we've been able to visit, but they've been kept busy, as I'm sure you know."

"Yes, of course," she said. "Their general contacted me months ago with a request to aid in his search."

"Have they still not found the remaining rebels?" I asked. Isa shook her head silently. "I'm still curious why we didn't experience the same sort of attacks here in Arenysen."

Isa pursed her lips. "I've wondered the same, honestly, especially with the rumors of growing animosity toward fae in the southern kingdoms." She pointed a finger at my husband's chest. "I mean, that is why your father pushed so hard for this marriage, is it not?"

"Indeed," Brennan said and lifted our clasped hands so he could kiss the back of mine. "I'm just thankful our Calla, here, chose me out of all her other suitors. Stars know she could have had anyone she wanted."

Isa leaned toward me and loudly whispered, "And still can, by the way."

Mischief flashed in Brennan's eyes as he quirked a brow. "Over my dead body, general."

"Don't say that too loudly, Your Majesty," Isa said, looking around the room suspiciously. "You never know who here might take it as invitation."

My palms itched. I yanked my hand free from Brennan's and squeezed them into fists behind my back. A groan rumbled out of me. "That's enough, you two," I said. "No more talk of death and dying and—"

"Sorry," they said in unison.

Brennan pulled me to him and pressed a kiss to my forehead. "You're right, my queen. Today is to be a happy day, all about you."

"A day I wish would end already," I said. My eyes began to well with tears I did not—could not—dare shed here in front of everyone.

Isa's hand lightly rested between my shoulder blades. "Soon, friend. Soon enough. Just a little longer."

❧

That *little longer* turned out to be another two hours before our guests started to depart. Isa had drifted away to find my head advisor, Graham, to try and discretely usher everyone toward the exit, while Brennan had left my side at some point in search of food. He didn't return until I'd already said farewells to several couples and families.

Sweeping my hair aside, he lightly kissed behind my ear and then said in a voice smoothed by an abundance of wine, "Happy birthday."

"So you've said." I paused and pulled back enough to smirk up at him. "How much wine have you had?"

He lifted a nearly empty glass and scrunched up his face as he examined it. "This would be number...I'm not sure actually," he finally said, downing the last of the drink before giving a light peck to the tip of my nose. "Barely enough to endure listening to Lord Whosits and that advisor of yours prattle on about shipments and orders and what not. They seem to have mistaken your birthday for an assembly meeting."

Stifling my laugh, I cupped his cheek with my hand. "You could have talked to someone else."

"Oh, I did. Lord Hairy Ears entertained me with talk of plans to plant new trees along his property line, and Lady Big Nose excitedly told me how you share a birthday with one of her twelve cats."

This time my attempt to contain my laughter failed, resulting in an undignified snort which earned me a comical stare from not only Brennan, but also the couple who had just joined us. They, of course, recovered from their shock quickly—much more so than Brennan—and bowed their chins in unison.

"Thank you so much for a lovely evening, Your Majesties," the female said, but then her smile faded slightly. "It is a shame your mother and father couldn't be here to celebrate with us."

A familiar sting pricked my chest, but I forced my voice to remain calm as I replied, "Agreed. Mother loved parties."

The male started to say something about the food or the music, I wasn't entirely sure which, as I was more focused on Brennan, who squeezed my hand once more. He tossed his head toward the ballroom exit and the stairs beyond as he whispered, "I think I need to go lie down."

I nodded and watched as he slipped away through the dwindling crowd, wishing I could avoid all of these final farewell conversations myself. At least one of us could be spared, though, and for all Brennan had done for me since my parents' deaths, I wouldn't begrudge him this early escape.

Our guests could not have left any more slowly if they had tried. By the time I was able to leave the ballroom and allow the staff to clean, my feet barely had the strength to climb the four flights of stairs up to our room, and were only mildly relieved by my removing my shoes halfway up. All I wanted to do was to fall into bed beside my husband, who had no doubt fallen asleep an hour ago.

Even with the fire burning low in the grate, our room was dark when I stepped inside. Dropping my shoes beside the door, I opened my mouth to call out for Brennan but decided against it.

If he was asleep, I didn't want to wake him. A breeze rustled my hair, and even though it was unusually warm for spring, it pulled chills up my back. I pushed aside my unease. Brennan loved to spend most nights on the balcony looking out to the front lawn and the enchanted woods below, regardless of the season.

Sure enough, when I stepped into our bedroom, the door to the balcony was wide open, but Brennan wasn't leaning against the rail as he normally did. I glanced to our bed, but it lay untouched and empty. A weak groan pulled my attention back to the balcony, and I raced to it. Panic thundered through me, and my heart hammered against my ribs until I saw him.

Crumpled on the balcony floor, Brennan lay still except for his hand trembling by his side as if he were trying to lift it but couldn't.

"Brennan!" My voice sounded far away and foreign to my ears, and my knees slammed hard against the floor as I dropped beside him. I looked him over as best I could in the low light of the half-moon, but I found no wounds, no blood, no answers. Pulling his chin toward me, I searched his eyes. They were already glazing over, the light in them fading fast.

No, no, no. This can't be happening.

"What happened? Who did this?" I asked, my voice frantic, but he didn't answer except to blink slowly.

I gripped his shoulder and shouted at him.

"Don't leave me!"

My fingers shook as I curled them into his shirt. Tears clouded my vision.

"You can't leave me, Brennan! I can't lose you too."

Throwing my chin over my shoulder, I shouted for help, but no one would make it in time.

My hands trembled, palms tingling, and the power I'd spent so many years hiding unfurled itself. Dark wisps of shadows seeped out of my closed fists and traced over Brennan's body as if looking for a way to heal him.

But shadows couldn't heal.

Brennan shuddered beneath me, and blood trickled out of his mouth as he choked out, "I'm...sorry...Calla."

"Don't leave," I sobbed. "Don't go. Stay with me, Brennan. Please. Don't."

His lips quivered, his eyelids fluttered, and his last breath whispered, "Love...you."

A mournful wail burst from my lungs, and my shadows erupted forth, shrouding my entire world in darkness.

CHAPTER 2

MATTHIAS

Two months, four days, and fourteen hours. That's how long it had been since I'd slept in my own bed. Not that I was counting or anything. Initially I had delighted at the prospect of getting a break from the irritatingly cute displays of affection between Connor—prince of Emeryn and my closest friend—and his new wife, Lieke, but now I was ready to be home.

While the inns around Emeryn provided adequate drink and hot food, the sleeping accommodations left much to be desired. Stars, when had I become such a pampered, pompous prick? I shook my head. Fuck it. If not wanting to sleep on a lumpy straw mattress night after night and wishing my ass didn't hurt from riding in a saddle all stars-damned day made me a jackass, a jackass I would be.

I'm getting too old for this shit.

I might not have cared quite so much about the discomfort had we had any success whatsoever. For the third time since the rebel leaders had been killed a year and a half ago, my guards and I had traversed the entire country, stopping in every city and town and hamlet from Holsham to Shoerda in search of the remaining rebels—or any humans, for that matter. Even with Lieke, a human as well as their future queen, the mortals had refused to reintegrate into Emeryn society.

"Can I ask you a question, sir?" My second in command, Tanner, rode up alongside me but kept his eyes straight ahead.

"Of course," I said, side-eyeing the younger fae. He hadn't served with us in the war, due to being too young. With so many of our force suffering from trauma and injury, it was the younger generation who had stepped up to fill our thinned ranks, and Tanner had quickly set himself apart from the rest with a keen sense of strategy and an unparalleled work ethic.

Tanner dropped his voice low, as if he didn't want the rest of the guard behind us to overhear. "Why do we keep going on these campaigns? It's obvious the rebels are gone."

"Obvious how?" I asked.

"Nearly a year, sir, and no trace of them. No sightings. No scent trails. Nothing. And..." Tanner fidgeted in his seat.

"And what exactly?" Silence. "Spit it out."

"Well, how do we expect to find them now that they've gone dark, when we failed to track them while they were actively attacking our roads? Even with some indication of where they were, we still never found them. Now we have nothing to base our search on, and we blindly fumble about the country."

My mare, Storm, grumbled and shook her head, as if she were agreeing with Tanner's assessment. Roughing a hand over my chin, I hummed thoughtfully.

"What happens if we stop, Tanner?" I asked casually.

He scrunched his face in concentration. "Well, we wouldn't be cold and sore, for one."

"And would we have any hope of finding the rebels by sitting on our asses back at the palace?"

Tanner shrugged. "Maybe."

"Enlighten me."

His earlier discomfort faded away as he straightened up in his saddle with refreshed confidence. "We could utilize local citizens to monitor traffic, or reach out to our counterparts in Arenysen for reinforcements and reconnaissance. What good is an alliance with them if we can't call on them for aid?"

I glanced at him sidelong again and asked, "What makes you think we haven't done that already?"

"Have we?"

I nodded solemnly, fixing my gaze forward again.

"And still nothing?"

Shaking my head, I pulled in a long breath of pine-soaked air. "But we don't give up, not until we're ordered to stop. Like it or not, Tanner, that is the job. We advise and offer council, yes, but ultimately we live to serve the crown. Like it or not, we are duty-bound to the royal family."

"Do you ever wish for more?" Tanner's question might have surprised me if I hadn't been asked this so often by Connor in his odd attempt to play matchmaker and find me a wife of my own.

"This is the life I signed up for. It's the only one I know, and the only one I want." Before Tanner could come back with the same old arguments Connor always had, I gestured ahead of us. "We're almost to Engle. Let's hope our contact there actually has something for us this time."

With that, I spurred Storm gently and rode on ahead.

Leaving the other two guards waiting outside, Tanner and I entered the Garrison Tavern. As expected at this late afternoon hour, it was nearly empty, and the only patron—a male hunched over the bar—quickly slapped two coins on the table and rushed out the door, leaving the barkeep alone with us. Tanner situated himself against one of the support beams, his hand resting lightly on the pommel of his sword while I approached.

"Mr. Marstens. It's good to see you," I said, but the demi-fae didn't appear to share my sentiment.

He bristled as I picked up the departed patron's coin and

proceeded to spin it atop the bar. "I told you last time, general, I haven't seen them."

The coin's whirring filled the room as I contemplated my next move. I'd been in here several times since the rebels had lured us to that barn outside of town, and every time it was the same answer. Despite Lieke and Mrs. Bishop's assertions that Mr. Marstens wouldn't lie and could be trusted, I couldn't ignore my intuition. After all, this male here had known where to take Lieke when she'd been sent away to her family years ago. At the time, Lieke had had no idea her family were the rebels behind the deadly attacks on the fae, but I wasn't convinced this tavern owner was equally clueless.

The coin began to wobble unevenly under my hovering hand. My fingers twitched as if about to drop on top of it, but instead I reached up with my other hand, gripped the big male's head, and slammed his face into the bar. He lurched back, his hands flying up to his nose. Blood seeped between his fingers as he growled.

"You broke my nose!"

I waved my hand dismissively. "Oh, calm down. It will heal soon enough."

His nose made a satisfying crunch as he snapped it back into position. "And you wonder why the humans don't trust the fae," he muttered.

"Oh, but they trust you, Mr. Marstens," I said, reaching over the bar and grabbing a glass and the nearest bottle. Unstopping it, I sniffed the contents and tried to hide my disgust at the cheapness of the liquor. Still, it would do. I poured a dram of the deep amber swill and replaced the stopper before bringing the glass to my lips.

Mr. Marstens watched me defiantly, but when his eyes flicked briefly to Tanner, I tossed the contents in his face. He hissed in pain as the alcohol splashed into his eyes and bloodied nose. Gently, I set the glass back down and cleared my throat.

"Tell me where they went," I said calmly. "Before I lose my patience."

Pulling a towel from behind the bar, the demi-fae wiped his face, but instead of cleaning it, he only managed to smear blood across his cheek and down his chin.

I gestured to my own face and said, "You missed a spot."

He showed absolutely no appreciation for my help, and threw the towel down onto the bar with another growl. "They had a camp, east of here in the—"

"Woods. Yes, we know. We've been there. It was deserted long ago. Now, stop wasting my time, Mr. Marstens, before I have to drag you back to the palace for a more thorough interrogation."

"That's all I know," he said, but his eye twitched ever so slightly as he spoke.

He was lying.

And I was tired.

I clicked my tongue at him. In a flash I had my dagger drawn, its tip at his throat before he could utter another word.

"Are you sure?" I asked, pressing the blade into his skin. "There isn't something you might have forgotten? A little nugget of information you've misplaced in that thick skull of yours?"

He swallowed hard, wincing as the movement caused my dagger to bite into him, but still he said nothing.

Looking about the tavern, I addressed Tanner. "Would be a shame for this town to lose its only tavern, wouldn't it?" On cue, my second produced a bundle of matches from his pocket and held them up for Mr. Marstens to see.

"You can't threaten me," the demi-fae said, a slight tremble in his otherwise confident voice.

I leaned forward slowly, pivoting my blade so that the long edge now lay across his throat. "I believe I just did. Now. Tell me what you know about the humans' whereabouts, before I'm forced to spill *more* of your blood and order young Tanner to burn down your fine establishment here."

Mr. Marstens's glower hardened briefly before he relaxed and lifted his hands in defeat. "They've all left. Left Emeryn, I mean."

"Recently? When did you last see them?"

"The last of them came through a couple weeks back and stopped to bring me this," he said, gingerly reaching one hand into his pocket and retrieving a piece of paper.

I snatched it from his hand and noted the scrawled name on the outside. *Lieke.*

"Who left this?" I bit out as my stomach knotted uncomfortably. While it was possible Lieke had more remaining contacts from the years she spent training with her family, there were only two names I would recognize: one a friend, the other a traitor.

"Her Highness's cousin, sir. Raven?"

Some of my tension eased, and an image of the young woman flashed in my mind. I'd only met her once and under less-than-ideal circumstances, but she had seemed trustworthy enough—at least, until she failed to come to the palace as Lieke had requested.

"And you haven't bothered to send it on to the palace?" I asked.

"Haven't had the time yet, and I didn't want to send it by falcon."

Pulling my blade away from his neck, I quickly sheathed it at my belt. With a quick nod to the door, I gestured for Tanner to prepare to leave, but I didn't turn away from Mr. Marstens yet. Instead, I reached across the bar and retrieved a second glass, pouring a bit of the liquor into each as I asked, "Did Raven happen to say where she was going?"

Reluctantly Mr. Marstens took the drink I nudged in his direction and nodded. "Believe I saw her jot some mention of Holsham down in her note, but I doubt she'd still be there now."

"Convenient," I muttered to myself, before downing the barely adequate drink and setting the glass back down. With a final rap of my fingers atop the blood-splattered bar, I said, "Thank you for your honesty. And for the note. I'll see that Her Highness receives it."

CHAPTER 3

CALLA

The clock still ticked by the loathsome hours of my tormented life. By the second day, my tears no longer spilled. Dried up and gone, just like my husband. And my parents.

Around and around my thoughts swirled in a perpetual tempest of misery and grief.

What had I done to deserve such anguish?

Was I being punished for having darkness in my veins?

Had I somehow angered the stars? Had they cursed me, stolen away everyone I loved?

Not that it mattered why my family had died. These answers —even if I could find them—could never fill the emptiness their deaths had left behind.

Empty.

Broken.

Alone, though not truly.

Isa and Graham tried to console me, as if that was possible. They encouraged me to eat, though my stomach insisted on remaining as empty as my heart. They urged me to describe what had happened, but I couldn't bring myself to say the words—or any others. By the fourth day, they ceased all attempts to coax me into speaking.

For six days I didn't speak at all, because drowning myself in silence seemed fitting after Brennan had drowned in his own blood.

Stars, his blood.

It was all I saw when I closed my eyes. I couldn't picture his smile or the mischievous glint in his hazel eyes. His final ragged breaths were all I heard. I couldn't recall his hearty laugh or his tender voice. Nor could I remember the loving touch of his hands. Mere days had passed, and I was already forgetting him. But maybe that was the one blessing in all of this. Perhaps my mourning wouldn't be so hard or last so long if I forgot the little pieces of him that made him mine.

Isa burst into my room without a word and without a glance toward where I sat on the floor against the wall, my legs stretched out in front of me. I winced with each hammering step of her riding boots against the wooden floors as she made her way to the windows. Brazenly, she yanked open the curtains, and I slammed my eyes closed. Had I the strength, I would have summoned my shadows to block the harsh sunlight that poured in, but the self-imposed lack of movement and sustenance had left me weak.

My general stalked back over to me and nudged my foot with the toe of her boot. Tilting my chin up, I slitted my eyes against the light to look at her as best I could. She wasn't wearing her normal attire, instead having donned her leather armor and traveling cloak.

"You don't have to speak, Calla, but I do expect you to bathe," she said, and as if on cue, two handmaids entered. They didn't meet my gaze as they approached me on either side, knelt down, and hooked their arms around mine. I had no energy to resist them as they gently hoisted me up and guided me to the bathing chamber where they lowered me into a chair before bustling about to prepare the bath.

Isa posted herself at the doorway, and though I didn't look at her—my vision instead remaining unfocused on the floor in front of me—I could sense her studying me. My lips twitched as I tried to force myself to care enough to speak to her, to ask her what was happening, but death had robbed me of all feeling.

I simply didn't care. *Couldn't* care.

"I know you don't want to do this," Isa said, pausing as if waiting to see if I would look at her. I didn't. "But unfortunately, we need you to at least attend. There are already rumors swirling about—rumors that must be put to rest before they get out of hand—and if you are not there, it will only make things worse. It will be hard, I know, but I will be with you every step of the way."

Confusion tightened my chapped lips and drew my brows together as I finally turned to face my friend. Kneeling beside me, she gently gripped my hand in hers and spoke patiently.

"King Durand requested his son be buried on his family's property, so we will ride for Emeryn this morning for the burial in two days."

Burial. Buried. Emeryn. Two days. So soon.

My whole body tensed, and panicked sobs began to build in my chest.

No.

I shoved them back, suffocating them beneath a mask of numb resilience and bitter determination. Breaking down would do no one any good. It was better to seem the cold, distant widow in mourning than appear weak and incapable of ruling my kingdom.

Pulling in a deep breath, I silently pushed to my feet.

The handmaids slipped my nightgown up over my head and helped me into the bath. If only the steaming water could wash away the stain that had marred my soul as easily as it did dirt and grime.

CHAPTER 4

MATTHIAS

I had barely stepped through the palace doors when a page appeared out of nowhere, calling my name.

"Mr. Orelian! Sir!" The poor boy said frantically, and I raised a hand, trying to urge him to slow down and relax. He didn't, continuing to speak breathlessly. "Prince Durand told me to fetch you as soon as you returned. He's in his study, sir."

I muttered my thanks, marched past him, and bounded up the stairs to the king's former office, now Connor's. While the healers didn't expect the king's heart to give out any time soon, his health had taken a decidedly downward turn, and he had insisted on stepping aside to help Connor settle into his future role. That decision had shocked us all, but no one could deny that something in the king had shifted suddenly when Connor and Lieke's bond had formed a year ago, as if their bond had ripped away a mask he'd donned long ago.

Knocking out of courtesy alone, I entered to find Connor sitting at his desk, his head resting in his hands. Lieke stood behind him, staring out the window with her back to me. The mood in the room was notably somber. Neither acknowledged me even when the door shut loudly.

"Who died?" I joked, but Lieke spun around and Connor

snapped his head up to stare at me. That was apparently not the thing to say.

"Are you kidding?" Lieke asked. I shrugged innocently, but Connor angled his chin over his shoulder to speak to his wife.

"He doesn't know, Sapphire. Give him a break."

"Know what?" I asked, noting that Lieke's bottom lip began to tremble as she turned back to the window. I looked to Connor. "It's not the king—"

He shook his head, but didn't bother to explain either.

"Am I supposed to guess?" I asked, trying to keep my mind from jumping to conclusions.

"It's Brennan," Connor said, flatly.

I dropped my head to the side. "What about him?"

Connor closed his eyes for a moment, his lips pressing into a tense line as he drew in a long breath. When he finally looked at me again, a mist had rolled in over his golden eyes.

"He's dead."

"What? When?"

Before he could answer, though, Lieke turned quickly and rushed for the door, refusing to meet my gaze as she passed me. The slam of the door closing echoed through the large room.

"I see she's taking it well," I said, and bit the inside of my cheek as I waited to see how Connor would react to my less-than-proper response.

He showed no irritation, though, only weariness. Running a hand over his mouth before resting his chin in his palm, he remained silent as he shook his head again slowly. After a full minute passed and he still hadn't said anything, I stepped forward and took a seat in one of the chairs in front of his desk.

"How are you? Really?" I asked. Perhaps it was an asinine query. Connor had spent most of his life protecting his brother from their father's rage, and while the males had had their differences and their rivalries, Brennan's death undoubtedly pained him.

Connor lifted his shoulders awkwardly and pushed himself

back in his chair. "I just keep wondering if there was some way this could have been prevented. I shouldn't have forced him to marry—"

I flicked my hand up into the air to cut his answer short.

"Did you kill him?" I asked, and Connor simply stared back at me as if I'd spoken utter gibberish. "Well? Did you?"

"No," he growled.

"Then you don't get to blame yourself for this," I insisted. When he remained quiet, I asked, "How did it happen? When?"

Connor cleared his throat and scratched at the stubble along his jaw. "Nearly a week ago?" He worded it as a question, as if he couldn't quite remember. "We got word from them the day before yesterday, but they don't know what happened yet."

I leaned forward, my brow tightening. "They don't know? Or they're not telling us?" Once again, he lifted a shoulder but said nothing. I huffed out a sigh. "What did the queen say? Can I see the message?"

Connor pointed lazily to a torn envelope on the side of his desk, explaining, "It's not from Calla, but I don't fault her for not writing herself. I can't imagine..." He let the thought trail off and then blinked several times before recovering, explaining, "General Marlowe wrote for her."

General Isa Marlowe.

Solid warrior. Respectable female. While she hadn't been as much help with tracking down the rebels as I'd hoped, she'd been more than cooperative and understanding with my requests.

Her note was brief but warm, formal but caring, and held as little information as Connor had indicated. Their healers had found no conclusive cause of death, yet they seemed hesitant to classify it as a murder.

As I tucked the paper back into the envelope, I peered at my friend cautiously. "What do you think?"

He crossed his arms over his chest. "With the remaining rebels unaccounted for, we can't assume they didn't have some hand in this."

"Agreed. But what can we do about that?"

Connor narrowed his eyes. "No luck on this last trip?"

It was my turn to shrug. "Some, but not as much as I would like."

"What does that mean exactly?"

"Well, after months on the road, I'd prefer to have an actual rebel or two in custody. It's been a long year with little more than shit to show for it. Tanner asked why we keep searching when it's clear the humans have all left."

"And what did you tell him?"

"The truth—this is the job."

"You didn't think to explain beyond that?"

"To be honest, I'm beginning to question the reasons myself." Connor pinched the bridge of his nose, but I continued regardless. "I understand the desire for peace and for the humans to return, but maybe we need to accept their decision not to."

"And the rebels? Do you think it's foolish to keep hunting for them?"

"That's a more complicated matter, which is why I haven't argued against it. Oh, I almost forgot." I paused to reach into my pocket and handed him the letter I'd taken from Mr. Marstens. He raised a brow in question. "It's for Lieke."

His eyes dropped briefly to the paper suspiciously. "From?"

"Raven. Or so I'm told. I didn't read it."

"Who'd you get it from?" Confusion swirled in my friend's features as he appeared to be trying to answer his own question. I might have laughed had the circumstances—his brother, the rebels, everything—not been so dire.

"Tavern owner in Engle."

Connor's shoulders slumped and his head dropped to one side. "Tell me you didn't hurt Marstens."

The corners of my mouth fell as I peered up at the ceiling for a moment before finally replying, "Fine. I didn't hurt Marstens."

I had barely gotten the demi-fae's name out of my mouth

before Connor threw the paper onto his desk and growled. "Seriously?"

Shrugging nonchalantly, I explained, "He lied to me." Connor pressed his fingers to his forehead like a parent exasperated by their child. "You've never taken issue with my methods be—"

"He's Lieke's family!" Connor barked, but recovered quickly, adding, "Or as close to family as she has left."

"Some family, to hold on to that letter for so long," I noted, but Connor's glower only deepened. "He shouldn't have lied to me. Claimed he didn't know where the humans had gone."

"And did he know?"

I pointed to the paper on his desk. "Produced that note and said the last of them had all fled Emeryn months back. Raven left that with him a fortnight ago. He believes she left by way of Holsham."

Slowly Connor opened Raven's note, and I didn't bother to question whether that was entirely proper. Mates shared emotions and dreams. No doubt they didn't mind sharing their private correspondence.

"Well, what does she say?" I asked.

My friend dropped the paper onto his desk. "It's an apology for not coming to the palace as requested."

"Seems odd to apologize over a year later. Does it say where she's heading?"

Connor shook his head. "She says she's *trying to make things right*—whatever that means—and asks Lieke to trust her."

After several breaths of silence, I cleared my throat to get his attention.

"When is Brennan's burial?" I asked quietly, and Connor blinked rapidly as if confused by the sudden change in topic.

"They arrive in a couple days. Why?"

"I would like to pursue this information from Marstens. If you'll allow it, of course."

Connor slowly pushed away from the desk and stood. He

didn't speak or look at me as he went to look out the window. He would soon be shoving his hands in his pockets like he always did when he was uncomfortable.

Sure enough, he did just that.

"It's been a couple weeks since she passed through?"

"So he claims. Regardless, I'd like to verify and see if we can determine which kingdom she may have fled to. I already lost the trail on that Marin woman. I need to at least check this out."

Connor pivoted slowly on his heel. His face wore a blank expression. "But you've been to Holsham already."

"Several times," I conceded. "But this is the best lead we've had in over a year. I can't ignore it."

"Not even for a few days?"

Standing from my chair, I met Connor's hard gaze. A pang of guilt nipped at me for abandoning my friend at such a time, but I ignored it and said, "I'll be back in time."

CHAPTER 5

MATTHIAS

Settling onto a barstool at the only pub in Holsham—The Houndstooth—I lifted a finger, signaling to the pub owner. This was decidedly one of my favorite pubs in our entire country, due in no small part to the pretty female who owned it. Hailee's green eyes lit up with a playful wickedness as she came to stand in front of me, lifting a glass and bottle of whiskey from beneath the bar.

"Two visits in as many months, general? What did I do to deserve such a treat?" she asked, pursing her lips. But the mischievous gleam in her eyes indicated she knew exactly what she'd done the last time.

My gaze lifted lazily to the ceiling—to where her bedroom sat on the second floor—before circling back around to find her leaning across the bar. It was impossible to avoid staring at her breasts, which seemed ready to spill out of her dress at any moment. An accident I would welcome.

I smirked as the memories returned—her hands fisting her blankets, her brown hair cascading down her back, and her moans filling my ears. My body responded immediately to the images playing in my head, and I had to shift in my seat to relieve some of the pressure.

"Unfortunately, I'm not here for you—or me, for that matter," I said.

"So, all business this time?" she asked, dropping her chin. Some of her hair fell from behind her shoulder, and I caught a lock of it in my hand. Rolling it between my thumb and forefinger, I pulled the corners of my mouth down and released a long exhale.

"I am in a bit of a rush."

Hailee peered up from beneath thick lashes. "Some things don't take too long, you know."

Her tongue slid out to wet her bottom lip seductively before she bit down on it, flooding my mind with memories of all that mouth of hers could do.

Fuck.

I shifted again on the stool and shook my head, as much at her as at my own growing need for release. Connor might forgive my tardiness for business reasons, but this wasn't likely on his list of acceptable excuses.

Finally, I said, "Maybe another time."

Hailee rolled her eyes, exaggerating her sigh as she straightened and pulled her hair free from my fingers. "If you say so, general. What *can* I do for you then?"

I downed the whiskey in one gulp and set the glass back down on the bar before answering her. "Word is you've had a human in here recently."

Her expression froze as if I'd just accused her of murder, but she quickly recovered, raising her chin slightly. "When did that become a crime?"

I narrowed my eyes at her. "It hasn't, but this woman might be of particular interest to the crown."

"What did she do?" When I didn't respond, she huffed out an annoyed breath. "What does the king want with her?"

"Not your concern," I said.

Hailee crossed her arms. "Then her whereabouts are none of yours either," she said coldly.

Rubbing my hands together slowly, I pretended to be searching for my next word. Finally, I let my shoulders slump in defeat. I gestured for her to come closer, thankful when she obliged, until she hovered so close to me that I nearly forgot why I was really here. Swallowing hard, I forced myself to focus. "Thank you for confirming she's been here. That's all I needed."

At this, Hailee pulled away and angled her head as she scrutinized me for a brief moment.

"We both know that's not *all* you need," she said bitterly.

"Perhaps, but duty calls."

Hailee's gaze briefly softened with pity, but she then pressed her lips together and shook her head at me. "If you aren't careful, general, you're going to put your work before your heart for so long you'll eventually forget you even have one."

I nodded slowly, letting my eyes drift closed as if I were seriously considering her warning. When I looked at her again, I pushed my lips into my favorite nonchalant frown and said, "That happened a long time ago."

"Get what you needed?" Tanner asked, holding my mare's reins to me.

"Nearly," I said, and he gave a short, quiet laugh. "But she was here," I clarified, as I mounted.

"Did Hailee say where she went? And are we sure it was this Raven woman?"

I shook my head with a sigh. My conscience snagged as I wheeled Storm's head down the road that led south out of town, the opposite direction of the palace.

"So where are we going then?" Tanner asked as he trotted up beside me.

"I know someone in the area who might have heard something. It's a long shot, but worth a try. At this point, I'll try just about anything."

In silence we traveled down the road for nearly an hour before reaching the blackened tree that marked the hidden path we needed. Without a word, I turned Storm into the forest and started down the barely visible trail, ducking to avoid the low-hanging branches. Tanner followed silently.

The air around us grew colder as the thick canopy overhead blocked out the afternoon sunlight. After another hour of navigating the dense woods, the small house came into view up ahead. It was a stout little building covered in moss and ivy, helping it blend in with its surroundings. A small veranda ran along the front of it with two rocking chairs sitting beside the door.

No sooner had I dismounted than the door opened, and a slender woman stepped out. She planted her hands firmly on her hips as she glared at me. Her eyes darted to Tanner, still atop his mount, before landing squarely back on me.

"Must be serious if you take this risk, brother," she said, tossing her head toward him. When I didn't respond, she addressed Tanner directly in a stern, yet teasing, voice. "You can come down. I'm not going to bite you, you know."

Tanner made no move to comply, so I turned to him, shrugging. "Sera does actually bite, but only if you make her mad."

Sera scoffed. "That was *one* time, and you deserved it."

"She's your sister?" Tanner asked quietly, still refusing to dismount.

"Half-sister, actually," she explained before I could answer, tucking her long brown hair behind her rounded ears. "Unfortunately, I didn't inherit the outward fae traits from our father."

"Hence why she lives out here away from town," I further explained to Tanner, but it still wasn't until I gave him a quick nod that he actually stepped down, sliding the reins over his gelding's head.

Sera laughed once before spinning around and waving us to follow her inside while speaking over her shoulder, "Tie the horses to the rail and come on."

The house was simple with one large main room containing

the kitchen and a living area. Four doorways at the back led to two small bedrooms, a privy, and out back to the garden. The room was sparsely furnished, but cozy and inviting as it had always been since she and her husband had settled here before the war.

Gesturing toward the dining table, Sera invited us both to sit before she turned back to where a kettle steamed on the stove.

"You still take your tea with entirely too much sugar?" she asked as she swiveled around and placed two mugs on the table before us.

I said nothing, but immediately reached for the small sugar bowl in the center. As I heaped a few spoonfuls into mine, my sister laughed heartily. She dropped her hands onto the back of the empty chair across the table from me, watching as I swirled my spoon around and around to dissolve the sugar crystals.

Sighing loudly, my sister asked, "What do you need, Matthias? It's not like you to come by unexpectedly. Especially with company."

Gently, I set the spoon down and clasped my hands together on the table. "A human traveling through."

"A rebel?" she asked quietly.

"Former one—hopefully."

"When?"

"Last couple weeks, give or take."

The chair scraped loudly against the wooden floor as she pulled it out, and it creaked when she sat down. She opened her mouth to speak, but then a small voice came from behind me.

"Uncle Matthias!"

I turned to find my niece running at me at full speed. She launched herself into my arms, and I grunted loudly. Ignoring Tanner's curious expression, I focused on the young girl in my lap. While she resembled a human of about eight years old with her rounded ears and smaller stature, she and her brother had been born near the end of the war nearly twenty-five years ago. A momentary sting pricked my heart at how much she now resembled her father. The way her mouth twisted into a sarcastic grin and her blue eyes lit up like she was about to play a practical joke on me like her father often had.

But remembering my lost friend was not on the agenda for today, and I focused on the girl before me, scrunching my face as if I were confused.

"Who are you?" I asked.

She slapped both hands on my cheeks and shot me an exasperated look. "It's me! Lorynne!"

Closing my eyes, I shook my head vehemently. "No. Can't be. Lorynne is much smaller."

"I grew!"

I squinted at her for a moment, and then leaned in close, whispering. "My Lorynne is cuter too."

Showing no offense, Lorynne threw her arms around my neck and squeezed me tightly, as if I hadn't just visited a couple months ago. Nestling into my neck, she whispered, "I missed you."

"Missed you too, Ladybug," I said before planting a kiss onto her head. "But I can't stay this time, I'm afraid."

At this, she straightened and eyed me suspiciously for a moment before slumping her shoulders in disappointment. Before she could voice any complaint, though, my sister was speaking to her.

"Lory, I told you not to leave your brother outside." Lorynne started to protest, but her mother stopped her with a quick lift of her hand. "Go. You can come say goodbye when he leaves."

"Fine," she muttered, leaning toward my ear and whispering. "She's no fun anymore."

Sending my sister a sidelong glance, I whispered back, "That's what happens when you get to be that old."

Lorynne rolled her eyes as she climbed off my lap. "She's not that much older than you, silly."

"That's why we're both so serious," I said, pinching my face into the sternest expression I could manage.

"Speaking of serious," Sera interjected, "go on, Lorynne. Your uncle and I need to finish our talk."

Begrudgingly, my niece rushed off across the room and out the back door. I caught Sera's gaze.

"She looks like Gabriel," I said, struggling to ignore how his name tasted of ash on my tongue.

Sera bit down on her lower lip and nodded. "Indeed. Has more and more of his humor now too."

Tanner eyed me curiously. "Didn't know you were so good with kids."

I angled my head at him. "I'm good with everyone."

"Except the humans, apparently," my sister said, pulling my attention back to her and the matter at hand.

"Apparently," I agreed. "So have you seen her? Heard anything?"

She shook her head slowly. "I haven't seen anyone, but when Lottie delivered my last order from the market, she mentioned a human had been spotted slipping over the wall into Kinham. Whether it was the one you're looking for, I'm not sure."

Whether it was Raven or someone else fleeing to Kinham, there was little I could do without causing more political turmoil. I was just about to stand when Sera spoke again.

"There is something else though—unrelated to the humans but more important, especially if it turns out to be true."

Leaning forward, I rested my forearms on the table. "And what's that?"

"It's about Prince Brennan. There are rumors going around about his death."

My blood chilled. All we'd heard from Arenysen was that he had died and their healers were still investigating. But I knew as well as anyone that news traveled faster outside of the official channels—not that it was always the most accurate.

When she didn't say more, I prompted her with a raised brow.

"Word is it was no accident," she said.

I frowned briefly. "We'd be foolish to assume it was."

"And what if it was the queen—his wife—who killed him?"

The door to my carriage creaked open, but I didn't move. My glazed stare remained forward. I didn't want to be here. Didn't want to see them or hear their condolences. Didn't want their judgment for my cold demeanor and lack of outward grief.

A hand reached in and I promptly took it, checking my hold on my shadows while Isa guided me out into the too-bright mid-morning sunshine. She leaned close to me, bearing some of my weight as I stepped down onto the gravel drive in front of the Emeryn palace. Releasing my hand, she rested hers on the pommel of the sword hanging at her waist, as if she were expecting trouble. This was what made Isa a good soldier—always alert and always prepared.

If only something could have prepared *me* for this.

"Just give me the signal—at any moment—and I'll help you," Isa said quietly.

Drawing in a deep breath, I forced myself to focus on the ornate front of the royal home—his home. No, I could do this. I had to do this. For Brennan. For his family.

Maybe even for me.

Turning back to my friend, I shook my head.

She pursed her lips and studied me for a moment but then finally dipped her chin. "Offer still stands. I'm here for you, Calla."

I opened my mouth to speak, noting how her eyes widened ever so slightly in anticipation of hearing my voice for the first time in over a week, but I was interrupted by someone calling my name.

I pivoted to find the future queen of Emeryn, Lieke Durand, bounding toward me with arms outstretched. Isa stepped back a pace, allowing my sister-in-law to wrap me in a warm embrace. Folding my arms around her waist I let my chin drop to her shoulder and closed my eyes. As much as I had dreaded this the entire journey here, I couldn't deny the comfort she brought me with a simple hug.

"I missed you," she whispered, squeezing me once before retreating. She folded her hands at her waist as she stepped back and caught my gaze, her dark blue eyes lined with tears. "I wish you were here under better circumstances."

My bottom lip began to tremble, but pressing my mouth into a tight line, I managed to steady it.

"Me too," I said, wincing at how foreign my voice sounded to my ears.

Lifting herself up on her toes, Lieke peered over my shoulder to the wagon sitting behind my carriage. She pressed her hand to her heart and sucked in a breath, a tear spilling over and trailing down her cheek. I turned away quickly and clamped my eyes shut as the sight of her grief pricked my heart.

What was wrong with me?

Shouldn't it be comforting to know others missed him?

Shouldn't I find some solace in knowing I wasn't alone in this?

Instead, Lieke's mourning exacerbated mine, amplified it so much I feared my sorrow would burst from me—in what form, I didn't know, and I could not risk exposing my dark powers. Especially not here.

Isa stepped closer once more and cleared her throat. "Why don't you go inside, Your Majesty, and get settled. I'll see to everything out here."

"Of course," Lieke rasped. "We didn't expect you to arrive quite so early, or Connor and the king would have been out here to greet you. They're inside making the final preparations with the staff."

All I could manage was a nod as I avoided Lieke's sympathetic stare and focused on the palace entrance straight ahead. I didn't want her pityI just wanted to bury my husband so I could go home.

❦

Like a ghost of my former self, I drifted behind Isa and Lieke as they led the way to my room. If only the numbness I displayed could penetrate my fractured heart and shield me from the painful memories that bombarded me with every step. I tried to force my vision to blur, but that only helped so much. Brennan's memory lived on in these halls, and it took so much energy to keep the tears at bay as my mind ruthlessly recalled his stories of mischief and mayhem.

When Lieke stopped and opened the door to Brennan's former suite, a fresh ache sparked in my chest. Isa, taking one look at my face, stepped forward to speak quietly to my sister-in-law, but I touched her on the shoulder.

"It's okay, Isa. I can stay here," I said, weakly, curling my fingers into my palms to keep my shadows contained.

Lieke's face paled, her eyes widening with embarrassment. "Oh, no. I should have asked first. I just thought of what I would want, and I forgot...I'm sorry..." Hurriedly—and ignoring my words—she closed the door. "I will have the staff move your things to one of the guest rooms. It will only take them a bit, but I'm sure you would like to relax after your long trip."

I could do nothing but stare blankly at her well-meaning smile, and Isa had to respond for me.

"Thank you, Your Highness. Is there a quiet place where Her Majesty could relax undisturbed?"

"Of course, I know just the place," Lieke said. "It was one of—"

She cut herself short, her complexion now reddening as she realized she'd been about to mention Brennan's name. Is this what my life was to be going forward? Everyone tiptoeing around me, afraid to even say his name?

While Isa went off with Lieke to work out the details for our visit and help with any final arrangements, I sat on a worn window cushion staring down at the grounds where I had once laughed and danced and even helped Lieke prepare for her wedding among the trees.

A knock penetrated the silence, the door opening before I could answer.

King Durand stepped in, no longer the formidable male who had once ruled over his sons with an iron fist and barbed words. He said nothing as he approached, his head bowed low and hands clasped tightly before him. While Lieke and Connor's marriage— and underlying mating bond—had transformed the former tyrant into the doting father he must have been back when his wife was still alive, Brennan's death had clearly taken a toll on the male. Gone was the jovial smile that had always greeted me, and when he finally lifted his face to look at me, the spark of humor and joy that had so reminded me of Brennan's was nowhere to be seen. As if it had died along with his son.

"I'm so sorry, Calla," the king said, the words tear-logged and broken.

I couldn't move.

I couldn't nod or frown or cry or even turn away.

All I could do was stare at this male who resembled my dead husband in the curve of his nose and the crisp line of his jaw and the sharp arc in one of his brows.

King Durand cleared his throat awkwardly, turning his gaze past me to peer out the window as he spoke. "Thank you for allowing us to lay him to rest beside his mother. I know how hard this is, and I hope you know we are all here for you—even if what you need from us is nothing but space."

This time I managed at least a small dip of my chin, and thankfully he didn't reach out for an embrace or anything like that, but rather simply turned and headed for the door. Pausing there, he looked back over his shoulder at me.

"You're more than welcome to join us for meals while here, but I understand if you would rather eat alone."

I should have thanked him, but I couldn't find my voice before he slipped out the door.

I sat at that window—unmoving, unthinking, unfeeling— until Isa came to retrieve me, insisting I needed to try to eat. Nodding, I pushed to my feet and paused when worry clouded her expression.

"Not speaking again?" she asked, her words reigniting my guilt, but even so I could only hide behind my blank exterior.

Unfortunately, the route to our rooms took us past Connor's office, its partially open door making it impossible not to overhear the conversation within. Isa tried to keep me moving, but I planted my feet.

"I don't know how to help her," Lieke said.

"I don't think there's anything any of us can really do, Sapphire," Connor said, the first time I'd heard his voice since I'd arrived—and my breath caught at how similar he sounded to his brother. "We can't force her to heal before she's ready."

"If only we knew what had happened. How he..." Lieke's voice trailed off.

Not wanting to hear Connor's speculation or his attempts to comfort his wife, I continued on down the hallway, gliding down the stairs as fast as I could.

§

The weather refused to match the solemn mood of those gathered for Brennan's burial. A blue, cloudless sky looked down on the entire staff gathered in the small, gated garden in the far corner of the palace lawn. Brilliant sunshine warmed our skin and forced many to shield their eyes with lifted hands, as if they were saluting Brennan.

Squinting against the brightness, I stood between Isa and Lieke, folding my hands tightly at my waist and begging my shadows to stay hidden. I heard none of King Durand's address, nor Connor's, too conscious of everyone's eyes on me especially Lieke's, who stole regular glances in my direction as if I wouldn't notice.

This isn't about me, though.

This is for Brennan.

Who cares if they look at me or feel sorry for me?

I should be able to listen to their words and honor my husband.

Shouldn't I?

Unfolding my hands, I moved to wrap my arms around myself to hold myself together, but my shadows shot to the surface of my palms, forcing me to clasp my hands together again. I couldn't let my shadows out, couldn't let any of them know who I was, what power I possessed.

They're family!

I should be able to trust them.

The thought immediately conjured a wave of guilt that stole my breath with a gasp, and I dropped my chin, hoping they'd write it off as normal grief, hoping they wouldn't realize how horrible a wife I had been to not trust my husband with my secret.

What in the stars is wrong with me?

I've lived through grief already. I can handle more. I can do this.

I can do this.

I can.

For Brennan.

Brennan. My husband. Dead. Gone.

Forever.

My shadows itched to be freed, yearning to hide me and comfort me amidst the scrutiny and the incessant torment of my heart, but I held them at bay with every wring of my fingers. Lieke, with all of her well-intentioned sweetness, reached for my hands, but I jerked them away from her. The pained look in her eyes shot another fiery dart of guilt into my gut.

I'm sorry, Lieke. I'm so sorry.

The words I couldn't utter echoed through my head. All around me, tear-stained faces stared at his grave, shoulders shaking with sobs, arms wrapped around one another. Wearing their grief for all to witness. While I stood here trying to conceal mine. Lieke glanced my way again, but I couldn't meet her eyes.

I could only stand there as everyone whispered their final farewells to Brennan, staring straight ahead as they approached to offer their sympathies. Beside me, Brennan's family expressed their gratitude over and over while I stood there trapped by my own selfish need to not break down. Why couldn't I let myself be vulnerable? Why couldn't I be like everyone else, and show my grief so easily?

No. Grief is different for everyone. It's personal and private.

Brennan would understand.

Brennan *had* understood. When my parents had died, he'd let me grieve as I needed to, not once questioning why I didn't cry openly or why I didn't look as sad as others. He knew me, accepted me, loved me.

My legs tingled, my feet antsy to flee. My shadows stirred, licking against my hidden palms.

I couldn't stay.

I couldn't handle all the empty well-wishes.

I couldn't bear another hug, another sad smile, another moment here.

Seeing Connor and Lieke together made his absence even more potent and painful.

No, I needed to leave.

Turning to Isa, I carefully gripped her elbow, shooting her a desperate look. As if she could read my mind, she dipped her chin slightly and turned to lead me away from the graveyard. I didn't look back as we walked briskly across the palace grounds toward my carriage—toward my escape. Someone followed though, and I couldn't bring myself to stop for them.

Isa whispered to me as she pointed ahead to the carriage, "You go and get in the carriage. I will handle this."

Nodding quickly, my heart caving under the weight of my grief, I slipped my hand away from her arm and picked up my pace. Behind me, Isa addressed our hosts, but I didn't listen to her words. Instead, I focused on the muted thump of my boots on the thick grass, counting my steps as I struggled to control my breathing.

In...two...three...four.

My husband is dead.

Hold...two...three...four.

Someone killed him, stole him from me.

And out...two...three...

But who? Who could have killed him? And why?

My carriage waited in the drive in front of the palace, but no horses stood harnessed and ready. I could get in. I could sit and wait, but when my hand touched the handle, I pulled back as if it had burned me.

No. Lieke wouldn't let me leave without a goodbye, but I had to go. I needed out, to get away.

Risking one more glance to Isa, who hurriedly ushered Lieke back toward the palace as she spoke hushed words I couldn't hear, I darted down the driveway with fists clutching the fabric of my dress. I couldn't bring Brennan back. I couldn't fix my pain or undo my grief.

But that didn't mean I couldn't do anything.

I could find answers. I could make whoever had killed him pay.

All I needed was a stars-damned mount and a head start.

I just hoped Isa would forgive me for taking her horse.

CHAPTER 7
CALLA

The door to the old cabin opened before I'd even dismounted, and an angelic voice drifted out from the dark opening.

"Come in, Your Majesty. I've been expecting you."

A chill slipped up my back, but I approached without hesitation. There was no point asking how the old woman knew who I was or that I was coming to see her, especially if she truly had the powers I hoped she did. I stepped over the threshold, somehow keeping my breathing steady when I found myself standing, not in a cold and dark hovel, but a warm and bright great room better suited for a noble's manor than a creepy cottage.

I briefly noted the room's furnishings—a cluttered worktable, several chairs, and candles everywhere—but quickly focused my attention on the frail frame of the old mage stooping in front of the hearth to retrieve a steaming kettle.

"Please, sit," she said through thin, wrinkled lips, lifting a spindly finger to one of the chairs at the table.

"I don't have much time."

"Sit," she commanded, her dark eyes catching mine as the chair closest to me slid back from the table, inviting me to settle upon it.

Perching on the edge of the seat, I repeated my words. "I don't have much time, Minerva."

"Ah, but magic takes time, love," she said, her lips curving up into an unnerving smile. "Especially the magic you're needing."

"Then let's hurry this up, shall we?" I asked. "Can you find out who is responsible for killing him or not?"

The old woman sat down across from me and folded her hands atop the table, studying me intensely. "Of course I can—"

"Name your price," I said, impatiently. The sooner she told me who was responsible, the sooner I could have my revenge on them, and the sooner I could move on from this sorrow.

"But that is not the magic you seek," she said, her eyes darkening.

I leaned over the table and glared at her. "Of course it is. What else could I—"

"Revenge," she hissed through a sinister smile.

"I don't need magic for that," I said.

"Perhaps for simple revenge, but they murdered your husband, Calla. Don't act as though merely killing them will satisfy your need for retribution."

I studied the old woman for a moment. "You suggest I curse them?"

"Not you, child. Me. For you. Just a simple curse I've devised to—"

I waved a hand dismissively and settled back in my chair. "As long as it works. You guarantee it will make them suffer?"

"There are no guarantees in life or in magic, but by their very nature, curses generally do cause great suffering."

"Fine," I muttered, crossing my arms and dropping my head at an angle. "And what's the price for *that* magic?"

Minerva lifted her bony shoulders in a shrug. "Nothing tangible, if that's what you're thinking."

"Stop stalling or—"

Her smile shifted into a sneer. "Or what, Your Majesty? You'll find another mage to curse your enemy for you? There are no others in this land or in this time with the power to do it, so either you learn some stars-damned patience, or you leave my house and forget this vendetta."

Gritting my teeth, I pushed my breath out slowly before finally saying, "Very well. What do you require?"

"Silence," she said, and I pressed my lips together. A trill of a laugh escaped her withered lips. "Not silence now, love. Silence forever."

Instinctively I lifted a hand to my throat, which earned me more laughter. I glowered at her as I dropped my hand back down to the table. "Stop being so cryptic."

"Then stop assuming things," she countered, not saying more until I offered a small nod of agreement. "I will tell you who is responsible for killing your husband and ensure they suffer in return, but you must be silent about it."

My brow tightened. "Who would I tell exactly?" Even as I asked, though, Isa's face flashed in my mind.

"You may be surprised, love."

Raising my hands out to the sides, I muttered my agreement. "Very well then. I will not tell anyone."

Minerva's eerie smile returned. "You won't have a choice. If I do this, and you try to speak of it, try to inform someone of Brennan's killer and what I've done for you, you won't be able to. Your voice will choke. Your pen will fail."

Impatiently, I bobbed my head in a string of quick nods. "Fine, yes, I understand. Please, let's get on with it."

She angled her wispy-haired head to one side, and I squirmed under her scrutiny. "Why so antsy to return to your empty bed, Your Majesty?"

I sucked in a deep breath and released it slowly. "I simply want to get back to ruling my kingdom."

"Fair enough, I suppose." With those words, she snapped her fingers and the clutter disappeared from the worktable. A sweep of her hand summoned a map of Sandurdam, the five nations neatly labeled. Emeryn, Arenysen, Kinham, Wrenwick with Dolobare sitting in the middle of the Laraburn Sea to the east.

I stared at the map for a long moment, but nothing happened. From beneath my lashes, I glared at the mage. "Well?"

"Well," she started, seemingly unperturbed by my rude tone. "We never discussed the price for their identity and location."

Huffing out a loud sigh, I rolled my eyes at her. "Which is?"

"Your shadows," she said plainly, and I nearly choked on my breath.

"My what?"

"You think I can't sense the power you're so keen on hiding? You're a Shadow Keeper," she said.

"I don't know what—" I started, but a growl rumbled deep in the woman's chest, stopping my words short.

"Stupidity doesn't suit you, Your Majesty," Minerva said icily, but her cold stare soon melted into a kind smile as she reached forward and took one of my hands in hers. "Don't fret, love. I don't need them all. Just a bit will do."

"Why?" I stammered, wincing at how fearful and weak my voice sounded.

She offered a single, breathy chuckle. "That is not part of this bargain. But don't worry. It won't hurt, and you won't even notice it's missing."

Slowly she turned my hand to reveal my palm, and I stiffened. My breath caught as the magic in my blood thrummed against my will, as if Minerva was calling it forward. Clenching my hand into a fist, I forced my power back and braced myself for the mage's reprimands.

None came.

Instead, her other weathered hand fell atop my closed fist and she caught my eyes with a sympathetic look. "This power is nothing to be ashamed of, nothing you need hide or deny."

I swallowed past the lump in my throat and whispered roughly, "I've never denied them."

Minerva smiled sweetly. "Did you tell Brennan about them? Did you show him what you can do?"

Guilt stabbed my chest like a branding iron pressed against my sternum. I had planned to tell him, but worry had stayed my tongue and now he'd died never truly knowing me.

Pathetically shaking my head, I whispered a "no."

Her hands squeezed mine gently. "Why do you fear the gift you've been given?"

I pulled out of her grasp and opened my hands. Over each palm, darkness gathered, swirling, churning, billowing clouds of black.

"It is simply a shadow."

"Simply a shadow?" I repeated, incredulously. "Simple shadows do not do this."

With those words I commanded the shadows to extend beyond my hands straight for Minerva's throat. Dark tendrils wound around her wrinkled neck, tightening and squeezing until her breath hitched sharply. Her dark eyes widened, and her lips quivered for a moment before finally turning up into one of her unnerving smiles.

Then with a twist of her hand, she summoned a burst of light that sent my shadows retreating back into my veins and cackled almost triumphantly.

"Whether it be shadows or light or air or water or land, your magic does your bidding. It cannot do anything that you do not will it to. The shadow is not bad in itself; how you wield it could be."

"But the price to wield it—"

"What price? Powers we are born with come from nature and require no balance to be maintained. But the magic we harness outside of ourselves? That, Your Majesty, demands something in return."

Impatience gnawed at my nerves. Isa would worry if she arrived home to find me not there. I needed to hurry and finish my business here. Pulling in a deep breath, I opened my hand once more and coaxed several wisps of darkness to surface and swirl over my palm. When I met the woman's gaze, I could have sworn a challenge brewed in her eyes.

"Take your payment, and let's be done," I said sternly, leaving no room for further discussion.

Minerva raised one bony shoulder high toward her ear before twisting her hand around in the air and producing a small vial. She removed the stopper and offered a slight nod. Without a second thought, I sent my shadows forward, filling the vial with my darkness, never taking my eyes off the mage, as if she might disappear as soon as she had this bit of my magic.

No sooner had she closed up the vial than it vanished, a small blade taking its place in her palm. Before I could react, Minerva snatched up my fingers and sliced the knife across my fingertip. The sudden pain forced my mouth open, but no sound came as I watched drops of my blood fall to the map on the table.

At first nothing happened; my blood simply sat upon the parchment in tiny dark pools. I was about to question the mage, when they finally shifted. Slowly the droplets of my blood crept across the map, all heading for the same location.

Wrenwick.

But they didn't converge on the map's label of the human kingdom to the south. They settled on the northern peninsula, shifting to form the crude shape of a crown and dagger—the royal crest sitting in the very spot of Wrenwick Castle, where King Olander ruled.

CHAPTER 8

MATTHIAS

The entire journey back to the palace, Tanner and I rode in silence, giving me plenty of time to fret over how to broach the topic of Calla being responsible for Brennan's death. While Connor would likely be open to accepting the possibility, Lieke would not. She and the queen had become close since they'd wed the Durand brothers, and that friendship would make this a less-than-desirable conversation, especially since I had likely also missed the burial.

The sun had just dipped below the treetops when we finally arrived at the palace, and before I'd even dismounted, my future queen appeared at the entrance to the stables. Her lips quirked up on one side in a knowing smirk as she shook her head slowly.

"Is he that mad?" I asked, halting Storm and stepping down into the dust. I pulled the reins over my mount's head and tossed them to Tanner, who was already leading his horse inside.

Lieke pushed away from the wall and strode toward me. "Well, he certainly isn't pleased."

Rolling my neck, I tried to work out the tension from the hours of riding. As much as I wanted to retire to my own apartment, I couldn't ignore my duty to my crowned prince and best friend. Lieke fell in line beside me as I led the way to the palace entrance, but now her mocking expression had fallen away to reveal one of quiet grief.

"You seem to be doing better," I said.

A single, empty laugh escaped her. "Some moments are easier than others. I assume you didn't find Raven?"

I shook my head. "Seems she likely passed through Holsham as that Marstens fellow said, though she may have slipped into Kinham."

"Still no sign of Marin either?"

"Nope, and few are willing to talk. For all I know it could have been her sneaking south instead of Raven. Enough about my failures, though. How was the burial?"

Her shallow shrug brushed against my shoulder. I slowed my pace and eyed her curiously as I waited for her answer.

"As hard as you'd expect." She paused, and her brow tightened. "Though Calla surprised me."

Instinctively my teeth clamped down as if biting back the rumor my sister had shared, though that made it vastly more difficult to respond verbally, so I forced my jaw to relax before asking, "How so? She wasn't dancing a merry jig or anything I hope."

"Only if that jig consists of suddenly sprinting away from the gravesite and taking off on one of her guard's horses."

My next step faltered, and I pivoted, dragging Lieke by the elbow until she faced me. "She did what?"

Lieke's shoulders lifted clumsily as genuine concern pulled at her features. "I mean, I guess it makes sense. If I lost Connor, I wouldn't want to be around anyone either. Grief isn't easily shared for some. I should have given her more space."

"Regardless of what you *should* have done, you can't go back and change it. All you can do is move forward."

We continued on in silence, giving me the opportunity to ponder her description of the queen's behavior. If Calla had no hand in her husband's death, then her fleeing fit with the remorse she'd inevitably suffer; however, guilt too could drive someone to run like that.

Stars-damned rumors. I needed to talk to Connor.

8

Lieke followed me into Connor's office, where he stood looking out of the window behind his desk. I stopped behind one of the chairs that sat in front of his desk while Lieke settled herself into the other. Connor didn't turn fully, but angled his chin over his shoulder.

"You're late."

Clearing my throat was apparently the wrong thing to do, because my friend spun on his heel to face me, his eyes wide in silent question.

Lieke laughed quietly. "Settle down, Wolfie. I'm sure he has a good reason for missing it."

Connor held my gaze intently as his wife leaned toward me and whispered, "You weren't delayed by Hailee and her bed again, were you?"

I shook my head, but Connor remained tense. "Hailee tried to protect the woman, refused to give us any information, but in denying—"

"She confirmed Raven had been there," Connor finished my thought for me, and I dipped my chin in response.

"May have slipped into Kinham."

Confusion clouded Connor's eyes briefly. "You said Hailee refused to say anything..." When I didn't respond except to press my lips together into a thin line, he hummed in recognition. "You saw Sera?"

As expected, Lieke perked up at the name, her head pivoting from me to Connor and back. "Sera? Who is that?"

Connor broke his stare finally and offered Lieke a soft smile. "His sister."

"And she's a secret," I added as I shot a pointed glare at Connor, though he didn't seem to notice, let alone care. "Or at least she's supposed to be."

Waving his hand in the air dismissively, Connor said, "My secrets are Lieke's now."

I laughed sharply. "Apparently mine are as well."

"Lieke won't tell anyone."

"Not a soul," Lieke said. "Not even an animal."

What in the stars was this woman talking about?

Connor must have understood, though, because he gave a short laugh. Stars-damned mates and their private little jokes.

"There's more," I said and walked around the chair to take my seat as I motioned for Connor to do the same.

He reluctantly complied, muttering, "Never good news when you tell me to sit."

I bit back my usual joke at my friend's expense—it was too easy to poke fun at his shifter ability whenever he mentioned common hound commands—but Connor must have expected it, because he jabbed a finger in my direction.

"Don't say it." Before I could even lift my hands in surrender, his accusatory glare swung to his wife. "You either."

Lieke once again leaned toward me. "He's such a sensitive pup, isn't he?"

I had to bite the inside of my lip to keep from laughing. Connor had never liked the power he'd been born with—had always hated shifting into his wolfhound form—though he had done it on more than a few occasions for Lieke's sake.

Connor ignored her and directed his attention back to me as he settled in his chair with a slow exhale. "What is it?"

"There have been rumors. Well, just one. I don't know how far it has spread, but if Sera heard it, it will soon be throughout Sandurdam if it isn't already." Connor prompted me to continue with a lift of his brows. "Some think Calla killed Brennan herself."

"No," Lieke uttered immediately, while Connor remained still and silent. "She couldn't have. You saw her, Connor. That wasn't the behavior of someone who had just murdered her husband. She loved him."

After a tense silence, Connor agreed. "It seems quite the stretch. You saw them together, Matthias. Do you think she could have done that?"

I lifted my shoulder, ignoring the scowl from Lieke. "To be fair, I wasn't often here when they visited, and when I was, they weren't high on my list of concerns. How do we know things hadn't turned sour over the past couple years? Regardless, it would be foolish not to consider—"

Lieke stood abruptly and crossed her arms obstinately. "This is absurd! She just lost her parents not too long ago. She wouldn't. I don't believe it. I refuse to believe it."

Connor offered her a sympathetic half-smile. "Matthias is right, though, Sapphire. Until we know for sure what happened to him, we can't rule anything out—no matter how unthinkable."

Shifting her hands to her hips, Lieke huffed out a breath. "By that logic, I could be a suspect." She spun toward me and held out her arms, her wrists touching as if she were bound. "Better take me in, general. I could have killed Brennan."

"I know it's hard, Sapphire," Connor started, but Lieke didn't allow him to finish before she stormed out of the office. Both of us flinched when the door slammed shut.

"She does that a lot doesn't she?" I asked, gesturing behind me with my hand.

Connor breathed out a quick sigh. "The burial wasn't easy for any of us, but Calla's unexpected departure hit Lieke particularly hard."

"Understandably so."

"Do you think there's any validity to this rumor?" Connor asked, leaning forward to rest his forearms on his desk.

"Honestly? No, I don't. We have nothing to support it, but..."

Connor dropped his chin to his chest. "We also have nothing to refute it either."

"Exactly. How do we expect the Assembly in Arenysen to handle this? Do you think they'll pursue her as a suspect?"

"I don't know. It may depend on whether Calla has their loyalty or not."

"We should be ready to investigate on our own if needed. If she really is his killer..."

"Let's hope it's not her," Connor said. Lifting his face, his eyes blazed with an unnervingly calm anger. "Family or not, whoever killed my brother will suffer. I'll make sure of that."

CHAPTER 9
CALLA

The Olanders killed Brennan. Which, I couldn't be sure, but one of the Wrenwick royals had stolen my husband from me. Why? Were they angry that I'd allied with Emeryn? No doubt, but why wait two years to strike? Why now? Why him?

Perhaps I was crazy to not want the details of Minerva's curse, but with my battered mess of a heart drowning in a sea of brutal sorrow and bitter spite, I couldn't bring myself to care *how* they suffered just as long as I knew they *did* suffer.

I should have known the human kingdoms couldn't be trusted. Lief Olander was little more than a scorned lover turned warmonger, and now his cousin, Nils, seemed bent on following in his footsteps.

Blinded by anger, I saw none of my surroundings the entire ride home despite the full moon shining overhead as I raced toward home, taking few breaks to rest. The sun—and Isa, along with two of our guards—greeted me as I approached the massive stone and iron gates.

No one smiled.

No one spoke.

I simply stared at my general, ignoring the screaming ache in my backside, as I brought my horse to a halt and dismounted. She gestured to one of the guards to take the reins from me and ushered them toward the stables. As the guard led the horse away, I waited for Isa's chiding words, but when she opened her mouth, no reprimand came. Only concern.

"Where have you been, Your Majesty?"

I should have been thankful for her worrying, but it grated on me like a rough stone dragged across my nerves. I had wallowed long enough, and as grateful as I was to her and Graham for caring so much, I had a kingdom to rule. I couldn't hide in my grief forever. I couldn't leave my kingdom to falter from my weakness.

Rubbing my weary hands along the sides of my neck, I strode past her without a word. She murmured something to the remaining guard before coming alongside me and matching my pace.

"Back to not talking, then?" she asked, sounding far more understanding than I honestly deserved.

My chest caved inward, as if my grief and my rage together wielded a massive vise around my heart. It pressed in from all sides as I walked up the cobbled stones that led to my home.

Our home.

Except there was no *our* anything any longer.

Only mine.

Tighter, my sorrow squeezed. How could I face the room I'd shared with him, and the balcony where I'd found his body? My shadows prickled in my palms as my mind flooded with the horrible memories—his hand reaching limply for me; the light fading from his hazel eyes; my name choked out on his last blood-soaked breath; my worthless screams that could not save him. My knees buckled, and my shadows slipped out of my palms to help me, but I recovered before I could collapse completely, pulling my magic back and waving aside Isa's outstretched arms as I kept walking.

"I'm fine," I whispered hoarsely, thankful she didn't make some snide remark about my broken silence.

"Louisa should have a hot bath ready for you in the guest room, and I'll let Chef know to send up a breakfast tray," she said, but I shook my head.

"I'll be moving back to our...*my* room," I said, silently telling myself this was what I needed to do. "Arenysen has waited long enough for me, and I can't move on if I keep running from the pain."

"It hasn't even been a month—stars—*half* a month," Isa said, patiently. "You don't have to move on so quickly, Calla."

I halted at the castle entrance and rounded on my friend, my jaw clenched so hard my temples ached. Balling the fabric of my skirt in my fists, I tried to calm my anger, but it continued its rampage through my veins. "And if I don't, who else is going to run this kingdom? You?"

Isa started to reach for my shoulder, but I angled away from her. She dropped her hand back to the pommel of her sword. "Grieving your husband doesn't prevent you from ruling. You learn to keep living even as you heal, because life continues on—whether you're ready or not. That doesn't mean you have to rush to feel better or to ignore your loss."

Her words should have soothed the burned edges of my heart, but something within me recoiled at the comfort, like I deserved to wallow in this pain and misery. Drawing in a deep breath, I lifted my chin and repeated, "I'll stay in my own room."

I pivoted away from her and stepped toward the castle door. It opened before I could even lift my hand, and my heart jolted at the sight of Graham. While he was a fae around my age—born just before the war—he looked a bit older than me. His dark hair was graying slightly at his temples, matching the flecks of light gray that dotted his dark-brown eyes.

We had known each other since we were quite young, when he and his mother lived near my family during the war. Unfortunately Graham's mother had died shortly after the treaty was signed and the nations split, and my father insisted on taking him in as one of our royal staff. Over the years his great prowess in politics and history earned him a place as one of my father's trusted advisors, and now mine.

Graham eyed me with the same warm and worried gaze he'd worn since my parents hadn't returned from Dolobare. His sympathy had only grown more tiresome with Brennan's death, but I tried to be grateful for his compassion and help. His and Isa's.

Isa now spoke from behind me. "She'll be sleeping in her own room after all."

"And a bath please," I requested flatly. Graham's eyes widened slightly, flicking to Isa briefly. "Yes, Graham, I've found my voice."

"Thank the stars for that," he said, but the lightness in his tone didn't ease his intense stare. "I hate to drop this on you right now, but in addition to the latest shipment orders needing your signature, the Assembly has been eagerly awaiting your return, and there are a number of citizens needing to speak to you today as well. I've already delayed both groups for as long as I'm comfortable doing."

A sigh fell to my feet, pulling my shoulders down with it. As much as I needed to get back to work, it could at least wait until I had washed off the road's grime and soothed my poor muscles. Silently, I pushed past Graham and made my way for the grand staircase. He and Isa followed close behind. Though I couldn't escape them or the demands of my station, I needed a moment to think, to soak my weary bones and decide on a path forward—especially with regard to the information Minerva had divulged. Refusing to focus on the portrait of Brennan and me from our wedding that hung at the top of the stairs, I flicked my hand toward it as I walked past. "Have this taken down, please."

At the door to my room, I paused and quickly spun to face my two friends, lifting my palms toward them as if placating obnoxiously needy children. "It's been a long, difficult few days—"

"We could send for Hilde?" Graham recommended, but I shook my head.

"No, thank you. I don't need anyone to fix my emotions," I insisted. "I'm going to sleep, take a bath, and maybe eat some breakfast before I speak to anyone else. Understood?"

They each nodded as I turned away and retreated inside.

Slumping back against the door, I closed my eyes and pulled my hands into fists. The silence in the room seemed to smother me with the reminder that, even though I still had Isa and Graham, I was alone—no husband, no family. Uncurling my aching fingers, I summoned my shadows and recalled the words of Minerva. My power itself wasn't evil; it couldn't darken my heart unless I allowed it to. There was no shame in using it, if I needed––and I needed it now.

Everything in this room held hints of Brennan. Some of his clothes still hung in the wardrobe. A pair of his boots still sat by the sofa. His scent—like smooth leather basking in the sun as it dried up the last of a spring rain—still filled the room. So often I had nuzzled against his neck, wishing I could stay wrapped in his comforting scent forever, and now I couldn't escape it as it enveloped me, threatening to pull me back under the waves of grief.

At least my shadows could help hide the physical signs that he'd lived here with me—just until I could have my handmaid, Louisa, clear them away. My shadows spiraled from my palms and swirled through the air, covering the pieces of Brennan that remained behind. Slowly I closed my fingers once more, testing to make sure the shadows held fast and exhaling quickly when they did. After scrawling a note for the handmaid and leaving it on the entry table, I kicked my shoes off and glided to our bedroom.

I could have slept on the sofa, but my sore body urged me toward the more comfortable bed. Tears pricked my eyes as I pulled back the blankets and climbed in, not bothering to undress.

CHAPTER 10

MATTHIAS

The autumn thunderstorms had wreaked havoc on the army's training ground, leaving it a muddy mess as it did every year. My boots squelched sickeningly in the sticky slop as I paced down the line of soldiers practicing their sword drills. Not that I hated mud, but having it squishing and slipping beneath my feet brought back difficult memories of the carnage we'd endured—and inflicted—during the War of Hearts. So many battles fought. And so many warriors fallen. On both sides.

The real cruelty was how easily our minds could forget the good bits of our past—a friend's laugh, a female's touch, a parent's embrace—while being tormented by all of the painful parts. Though some minds were better adept at handling this wicked dichotomy, others cracked under the weight of those memories, unable to escape the past and doomed to be haunted by their trauma. I had watched so many of our own walk away from service, and I had spent every year since the war ended trying to rebuild our numbers to their former glory.

We were finally—nearly—there.

"They're looking good, general," a deep voice rumbled behind me, and I wheeled around to find the last fae I expected to see here, standing in the muck twenty meters away—the king.

"Indeed, Your Majesty," I said, tipping my chin down slightly. The king closed the distance between us, not seeming at all bothered by how his riding boots sank into the mud with each step. I couldn't remember the last time he had ventured out here to visit his troops. Had it really been since the war ended?

"To what do we owe this honor?" I asked.

King Nevan didn't answer, just pivoted so that we stood shoulder-to-shoulder to face the soldiers who, to their credit, had continued sparring despite his arrival. Focusing my attention on the pair training directly in front of us, I clasped my hands behind my back and waited patiently for his response.

"It gets boring in the palace," he said.

I huffed out a laugh. "Retirement not suiting you, Your Majesty?"

The king waved away my words with a flick of his fingers. "Save that title for my son, Matthias."

"All due respect, Your Majesty, you're still the king."

A smirk crept across the older fae's lips. "Then do as I say and call me what I wish."

"And what is that? Your Highness? Sir? Mr. Durand?"

I laughed again when the king's nose wrinkled at that last suggestion.

"Sir will suffice," he said, rolling his shoulders as he studied the line of troops.

"Yes, sir," I obliged.

"You've done a great job rebuilding our force. How do you think..." he paused, lowering his gaze to the ground before starting again. "What are the chances our advantage from the Arenysen alliance has disappeared with..."

His words trailed off, and I wasn't about to supply the end of that thought. It had only been two weeks since Brennan's death. Between his grief over this loss and his guilt from the years of abuse he'd inflicted on his sons, it was understandable he'd have difficulty speaking about it. Both appeared to have taken a toll on the male. Though his health had already begun to decline with the death of his mate years ago, his eyes now seemed dimmer, as if his very spirit was fading away. Still, he was my king until he officially passed the title on to Connor, and my duties as his general required disclosing intelligence as I received it.

"My scouts have noted potential…difficulties on the horizon."

"From Wrenwick?" the king asked, his eyes alight with what appeared like hope, which I regrettably had to douse quickly with the truth.

"No. King Olander appears to be distracted with personal matters within his own borders. Unfortunately, my concern is Arenysen itself."

The king's face fell. "Poor Calla. She lost her parents, her husband, and now these rumors. How anyone could think she killed him…" His voice tapered off.

"I'm keeping an eye on it though, Your—" The king's brow shot up, and I corrected myself, saying, "Sir."

The king nodded brusquely. For a long moment he was silent as he continued to watch our soldiers spar, though his attention appeared to be elsewhere. It wasn't until Tanner, from the other side of the field, called out the end of training for the morning that the king seemed to snap back to the present.

"Will you be dining with us?" I asked, though as expected he shook his head, rubbing his hand behind his neck.

"I appreciate the invitation, but Connor and Lieke are expecting me."

"Ah, the lovebirds," I said as sweetly as I could. Not that I begrudged my friend finding his mate, but it was a lot of affection to handle as a bystander.

"Careful, general. Your cynicism is showing," he said with a hollow laugh. His amusement didn't reach his eyes.

I offered an apologetic smile. "I'll work harder to keep it under wraps."

The king studied me for an uncomfortably long time. "I fear we've asked too much of you, Matthias."

Confusion swept over me. "What do you mean?"

"You've spent most of your life fighting for this family—leading our armies, supporting my son. All of your focus has been on our needs and not your own."

I pulled my mouth into a frown. "I wouldn't say all of my focus."

"But you won't find love on the battlefield or at the end of a sword."

"I find plenty in taverns and—"

The king scoffed loudly behind a half-hearted smile. "I said *love*, not lust."

I shrugged a shoulder and looked off to where the palace lay beyond the trees. "It's enough for me, sir."

"It won't always be," he said, and I clenched my teeth hard to prevent myself from arguing further. Not all of us wanted romance. Not all of us cared to find our mate—if they even existed.

Instead I dipped my chin, saying, "You sound just like your son."

⋄

The sharp thwack of wooden blades echoed off the high ceiling as Lieke parried my strike and quickly countered it with one of her own. Even years later, I marveled at how she'd improved. Her mortality still slowed her movements, but being bonded to a fae—and thereby lengthening her life—had brought unexpected benefits, like heightened agility and speed.

"I miss these sessions of ours while you're gone," Lieke said, trying to hide how breathless she was becoming as she backed away from me, though still continuing to circle. I didn't bother pursuing her as I would if we were seriously training. Instead, I slowly pivoted around with her as she moved.

"Oh, is Wolfie not satisfying your needs?" I asked. My smirk slipped into a triumphant smile at the sight of pink rising in her face. "The fact that you still blush over these things amuses me."

"Not my fault that your inappropriate comments conjure certain memories that I probably shouldn't be reliving in the company of my husband's best friend."

"Fair, fair," I said. "We done for the afternoon? I'd hate to send you back to your husband too worn out to reenact those *certain memories.*"

"Oh, I can always find the energy for that," she said with a quiet giggle. "Still, I'm sorely out of practice—*sparring* practice—with how long you've been gone recently, so..."

"No shame in knowing your limits," I said, accepting her practice sword so I could return them to the table against the wall.

"Is that what you tell your soldiers? Seems limits would need to be pushed, in certain circumstances."

"Of course, but with training, it's all about balance, and knowing when to press on and when to rest."

Lieke poured two cups of water and handed me one, scrutinizing me over the rim of hers as she took a long gulp.

"What?" I asked. "I always get so nervous when you get that look in your eye. I never know whether to expect a lecture, a compliment, or some random question."

"Would you prefer I warn you first?"

I lifted a brow, curious.

"I have a random question," she said, mischief twinkling in her deep blue eyes—the source of Connor's nickname for her.

I released an exaggerated groan, throwing my eyes up toward the ceiling in mock annoyance. "What now?"

"Why is your sister—Sera?—a secret?"

With a casual frown to hide my flinch, I turned away from her and shrugged.

"Connor hasn't told you already?"

"Said it's your story to tell...if you're willing. I won't pressure you if not. I'm just curious."

I couldn't help but laugh. "When are you not curious?"

Lieke merely shrugged, but shot me a wide-eyed look of anticipation. I needed to sit down for this conversation, though. I didn't know how much of it I truly wanted to divulge. Sliding down the wooden wall—my ass hitting the dirt a bit harder than I'd intended—I tossed my head at the spot beside me, then laid it back against the wall as she joined me.

"She's actually my half-sister. My father—a fae—had married Sera's mother—a human—first, but she fell ill when Sera was still young, well before the war, and he married my mother—a fae. Sera didn't inherit our father's fae ears, which wasn't really an issue—"

"Until after the war," Lieke chimed in quietly. I nodded.

"She lives in the woods outside of Holsham with her two children, relying on fae friends to bring her supplies during the most tumultuous times between our kinds."

"What about her husband? Is he human?"

A faded memory of Gabriel and Sera—smiling over their newborn daughter—came to mind, making it hard to swallow as my throat constricted.

"He was fae," I explained. "Fought with Connor and me during the war. Died in battle. Connor ensures she and the kids are looked after, though she has repeatedly refused his invitations to come live at the palace where she could be protected. She just couldn't bear to leave the home she'd built with him."

"Oh, Matthias," Lieke whispered behind fingers splayed before her lips.

"It's okay," I said, shrugging. "It was a long time—"

"Don't," she commanded. Dropping her hand into her lap, she stared out at the training ring. "Time doesn't actually heal our wounds. It just covers them up with all of life's other shit, keeping us distracted until something randomly reveals them and catches us off guard, reminding us they're still gone and we're still hurt."

"You're right. But some of us heal faster than others," I explained, but I couldn't tell if she really believed me. She was quiet for several breaths, and I let my eyes close while I tried to lock the unearthed memories back up in my mind.

"Is Gabriel why you refuse to love?" Lieke asked gently, but having the topic of my love life brought up twice in one day made it irk me more than it probably should have.

"No," I said, perhaps a little too curtly. "And I'll have you know, I don't refuse to love. I simply don't see the use for it."

Lieke swung her head around, her eyes as wide as the practice shields hanging on the wall above our heads. "Don't see the use... what in the stars...seriously?"

Offering her a tight smile, I nodded. "Believe it or not, some of us are perfectly content without...all that." I waved my hand at her and then swung it back toward the palace––and my best friend.

"One of these days, Matthias..." she said, flashing me a sweet smile beneath raised brows—a look my sister used to don when she was confident she was right about something I disagreed with. "Someone's going to come along and shake up this *perfectly content* life of yours, and I hope I'm there—"

"To say you told me so?"

She shook her head. "To see you *truly happy*."

CHAPTER 11

CALLA

As fatigued as I was from the long ride, sleep still proved restless. I was haunted by images of blood spilling from Brennan's mouth, his lifeless eyes shifting into those of my parents as they sank down into their watery tomb. After only a few hours of fitful rest, I forced myself out of bed with a growl.

Sunshine streamed in through the window, warming the room. Padding across the floor, I was at least pleased to find the staff had done as I'd asked, and the few remaining items of Brennan's had been removed from sight. A platter of fresh fruit and pastries sat atop the table in my dining room, but my stomach—having become accustomed to foregoing food for the past couple weeks—had no appetite. Not just for the food here, but for anything. The thought of eating turned my mouth dry and soured my stomach. I'd need to, though, if only to appease Isa and save myself from her lectures.

Spreading butter across a flaky biscuit, I nibbled on it as I made my way to the bathing room where a bath had already been prepared and kept hot by Louisa's elemental magic. It was no coincidence that the female had been selected for the esteemed position of royal handmaid by my mother years ago.

Lowering myself into the water, I plopped the last bit of

pastry into my mouth and tried to gather my thoughts. Time marched on even after death, and I could do the same.

I had to.

Yet, it seemed my weak heart and troubled mind refused to cooperate. Turning my head, I gazed out the open door to our bedroom beyond, and I could picture Brennan—as clearly as ever—leaning against the door frame wearing nothing but that cocky grin I loved so much.

I slammed my eyes shut against quickly gathering tears, but they spilled over all the same. Feverishly, I wiped them away with the back of my hand. Still they came, as if the past week's worth of unshed agony was finally bubbling up. With a roar I threw my fists down into the bath over and over, splashing water onto my face to mask these damned tears.

Opening my eyes, I turned back to the doorway. Empty. My heart fractured a little deeper, pulling me under the water, but I had barely slipped below the surface when a rapid knocking echoed through the room, followed by Isa's familiar, but muffled, voice.

"Calla, are you ready yet?"

My chin bobbed up out of the water as I mumbled, "Nearly."

Isa's face appeared, hard and unamused, in the doorway. "Nearly, my ass. You barely touched your breakfast."

I stared blankly up at the ceiling, relishing in the soothing effects of the water on my sore joints and muscles. It was a shame it couldn't also cure the numbness in my heart.

"Not hungry," I whispered, bracing for her rebuke.

But all my general offered was a deep sigh before changing the subject. "I've scheduled the meeting with the Assembly for tomorrow morning, but unfortunately Graham refuses to delay the citizens' grievances any longer. You're expected in the Great Hall within the hour."

Tilting my chin up, I closed my eyes and slid lower into the bath until the water covered my ears.

"I'll be there," I said and lifted a hand to wave her away.

Her voice seemed so far away when she asked, "Should I wait for you? I can escort you down."

"Fine," I said, not wanting her to know how relieved I truly was to not have to walk into a crowded room alone. "Make yourself useful then?"

"And?"

I pointed toward the bedroom. "Clothes?"

Isa didn't answer, but I counted her faint footsteps as she left the room.

While she was gone, I finished washing and stepped begrudgingly out of the hot water, wrapping myself in a towel just as she returned, holding out a simple, dark purple dress with long sleeves and a high neckline. I would have preferred black, but I had been the one to suggest I stop mourning and move on. This seemed as good a first step as any.

The Great Hall was more crowded than I'd anticipated. Hadn't I only been gone for a few days? How had so many developed grievances in such a short time? But then I remembered that we had postponed these hearings after my parents' deaths, and again after Brennan's. No doubt my subjects had grown impatient over these long months.

Isa, who normally stood behind my seat on the dais, positioned herself directly to my left, presumably to block my view of the matching, now vacant, chair. I could have kissed her for that courtesy.

For the first two hours, I judged several disputes between neighbors, approved aid to one family whose home was destroyed in a recent fire, and listened to countless requests for tax deferment and increased protection on the roads. Isa took notes, provided the necessary written declarations to each citizen, and offered her recommendations—whispered in my ear, of course—when I stalled on a decision. All in all, the morning proceeded better than I expected, and my confidence swelled. Perhaps I would be able to find some sense of comfortable normality and routine quickly after all.

But when the next pair of citizens stepped slowly forward and tucked their fine hair behind rounded ears, I bristled.

No, worse than that.

I burned.

Rage flared in my chest, pulling my teeth together hard.

These were not the humans who had killed Brennan. The Olanders were to blame for that, not these two women.

All logic and reason vanished from my mind, drowned by the incessant images of Brennan's body on our balcony.

His hand reaching for me.

His lips trying to speak to me as he lay dying.

My hands started to shake in my lap as my pulse quickened. I clasped my fingers tighter together, desperate to quell the rising flood of anger.

They didn't kill him.

These women are not to blame.

I repeated these words, over and over with every step the women took toward me, but the closer they got, the hotter my wrath burned. No, their hands hadn't killed him, but I couldn't ignore their mortal appearance, couldn't shake the memories and the grief. I couldn't look at them without seeing Brennan's dying eyes staring back at me.

I couldn't do this.

How could I rule them—how could I help them—when the very sight of them twisted my thoughts and clouded my vision with vengeance?

They stopped directly in front of the dais and bowed their heads in unison.

"Your Majesty—"

"No," I growled, pushing to my feet. Isa's hand lighted on my shoulder, but I nudged it away as I fought to keep my shadows reined in. "That is all I can manage today," I said.

Time. Yes, all I needed was time.

Time for Minerva's curse to dole out its justice.

Time for my heart to heal.

Time for my rage to quell and for my mind to calm.

The humans—two young women, sisters perhaps—exchanged bewildered glances before they both looked to Isa for guidance. Isa turned to me.

"What's the matter?" she whispered. "Do you need a break?"

"Please, Your Majesty," one of the women begged, but her voice scraped against my patience, worn dangerously thin from my torment.

"No," I said again through gritted teeth. My magic surged, and I had to clasp my hands together behind my back to keep my shadows from breaking free. "Leave. Now."

"Pardon?" one of the women asked.

My hands began to shake. My shadows seemed to be bucking against my resolve. "Get out of my home. Out of my kingdom."

An eerie quiet hushed over the room as everyone seemed to hold a collective breath. Only Isa moved, approaching me gingerly, like I was a wounded animal in the wild.

"Your Majesty," she said before dropping her voice into a low whisper near my ear. "What are you doing, Calla? Why would you—"

My head snapped around to look at her. "Because..."

The humans killed him. Just say it! Four little words.

But no matter my efforts, my lips, my tongue, my breath would not cooperate.

Stars-damned witch.

Yes, I had wanted to know the truth, and I had understood the price of that knowledge.

But how could I make Isa—make everyone in my kingdom—understand why I needed the humans—all humans—to leave? I didn't want to kill them, but I could not rule them any longer, at least not fairly. As irrational as my anger was, I could not look at them, let alone care enough about them to be their queen.

Breathing deeply, I searched for words that I could utter, hoping Isa—and Graham and the Assembly—would accept and support my decision.

"I need all humans out of the kingdom," I said as calmly as I could manage, given the weakening hold I had on my powers. I needed my general to understand, willed her to with an intense, pleading look. "I can't do this. I can't be their queen."

Isa searched my eyes frantically for a few breaths, but I couldn't tell what she noticed. When she finally spoke, it wasn't to me.

"Ladies, I'm afraid the morning has been too taxing for Her Majesty. Could your concerns be addressed at a later date, perhaps?"

I glowered at my friend before whirling on the women still standing before my dais with confusion still playing across their features. One of them inched forward slightly before bowing her head again. She elbowed her sister sharply until she did the same. When they finally turned to leave, I relaxed my fingers—now throbbing at every joint—but I had moved too soon, trusted myself too much.

"She's gone mad." The woman's words—mere whispers breathed into her sister's ear—slammed into me as if she had screamed them for the entire castle to hear. "No doubt that's what drove her to kill the king."

My shadows unfurled before I could stop them, shooting out of my palms like water streaming from a broken dam. The inky black tendrils writhed like snakes as they coiled around the limbs of the women. My grief-stricken heart raged within me as I threw my hands wide, and I watched in dark delight as my shadows tore the women apart, spraying their blood across the gleaming floor. I pulled the darkness back, and two pairs of arms and legs fell with a delightfully sickening thud atop their collapsed bodies.

As my shadows snapped back into my palms, an eerie cackle filled the room, and it took me a moment to realize that the laughter was mine.

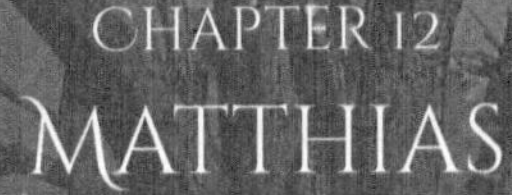

CHAPTER 12

MATTHIAS

hree weeks at home and I was already growing restless with the monotony of palace life.

Meetings. Meals. Training. More meetings.

Pointless meetings, about topics that could have been addressed in simple reports, but such was the life of a royal commander. At least my apartment—situated above the training ring—lay far enough away from the main house, allowing a bit of a respite from it all.

Of course, the distance didn't prevent Connor from occasionally coming here and drinking all of my brandy. Granted there had only been one time, over a year ago, when he had done so without invitation or permission, draining nearly my entire bottle of Vranić's—a rare Dolobare brandy—and showing up at Lieke's door, drunk off his royal ass.

I laughed quietly at the memory as I crossed my room to the wardrobe. It had taken me months to acquire a replacement for the one he had pinched, and out of an abundance of caution, I'd taken to hiding it among my undergarments. Pulling the drawer out, I reached to the back and pulled out the latest bottle. I held it up, tilting it slightly to verify Connor hadn't somehow found its hiding spot. Satisfied, I returned to the sitting area where glasses sat beside my inferior varieties of liquor and poured myself a healthy portion—or a bit more than what was considered healthy.

Settling into my favorite armchair, I swirled the dark liquid in my glass as I reached for the small stack of reports that had continued to grow since I'd returned. My scouts, scattered about Emeryn and beyond its borders in the three other kingdoms, sent word via falcon or rider twice a month, whether they had something to report or not. It helped me to know what was going on around the country, if anything.

Taking a sip of my brandy, I opened the first report from across the mountains in Fairden. My scout there was a female fae who owned the local market.

No news.

While not altogether helpful in my efforts to track down the humans, this was decidedly better than hearing word of violence or growing tensions.

The next report was from Holsham where a miller kept a close eye on the main road into Kinham. I was about to open it when someone knocked at my door, startling me. My brandy sloshed in the glass spilling out over my fingers and dripping onto the paper.

"Fuck," I muttered as I set the glass back down on the side table. Tossing the reports aside, I licked the spilled brandy off my fingers but remained seated. "Come in!" I called.

The door flew open, nearly hitting the wall before the young guard could catch it. Standing in the doorway, the male's wide eyes darted to mine.

"Mr. Orelian," he said, dipping his chin. I studied him for a quick moment, noting how he kept shifting his weight and tapping his fingers against the handle of the sword hanging from his belt.

"What is it?"

"Apologies for disturbing you, sir, especially at this late hour."

I pulled my watch from my pocket. It was barely after dusk. "You have an odd definition of late."

His lips thinned, and he bobbed his head again. "Yes, sir. You're needed at the gate."

At once I was on my feet, frowning at my unfinished brandy before retrieving my boots from beside my wardrobe and following the guard out the door. Hopefully I wouldn't regret not taking the time to hide my Vranić's before leaving, but the guard's uneasy demeanor pushed me to not delay. Grabbing my sword on the way out the door, I secured it around my waist as we bounded down the stairs and headed for the path.

"Anything I should know before we get there?" I asked, ducking under branches. "Is there a threat or—"

"No, no threat," the guard said, clearing his throat before explaining further. "But a...a development of a sensitive nature..."

My mind whirred with speculation as we pressed on. Could it be Raven? One of the rebels? Marin even? It couldn't be someone from Wrenwick if the guard insisted there was no threat, but perhaps someone from Arenysen?

While it was standard procedure for me to investigate situations before the royal family was notified, I hadn't been fetched like this in over a year when the rebel attacks ceased. Part of me was grateful for the change in routine, but another couldn't shake the sense of foreboding that deepened with each step toward the gate.

It wasn't long before I caught the warm glow of the lanterns hanging on the stone wall on either side of the wooden gate. The gate had been locked, as it was every evening at dusk, but the smaller doorway—just large enough for someone to pass through—was propped open with a guard leaning lazily against his spear. He straightened as we approached and turned quickly on his heel, lifting his hand in a salute when he saw me.

I nodded in acknowledgment, glad when he didn't bother with small talk but immediately ushered us through the doorway. Stepping outside the wall, I slowed as an unexpected scent assaulted me.

Blood.

Humans.

Another guard waited fifty meters away with his back to us, his head hanging low as he spoke gentle words to someone I couldn't see. With a quick glance over his shoulder, he said another few words to the surprise guests before pivoting around and approaching me.

I fought back the urge to peek over the male's shoulder or around his burly frame, deciding it best to respect his position and hear his assessment first.

"What happened? Who are they?" I asked as casually as I could, quieting the questions that screamed in my head.

"Children, from Arenysen," he said, sighing heavily.

"Humans," I said, not phrasing it as a question, but expecting confirmation all the same. He nodded rapidly.

"It's not good, sir," he said.

"Do we know why they came here?" As much as Connor wanted the humans to return to Emeryn, most mortals didn't consider our kingdom amenable to them, and last we knew humans were living peacefully in Arenysen. Occasionally they moved between the kingdoms, but we hadn't seen the same exodus of mortals from Arenysen as we had from Emeryn.

The guard rubbed his hand behind his neck and gazed off into the dark trees. A throaty sigh fell from him before he finally met my eyes again. "They're pretty shaken up, sir. The youngest seems to still be in shock."

What in the stars could have happened to them?

"How many?"

"Two."

"And they haven't said anything?" I scratched my hand along my jaw.

"Not much. They're asking to see the king."

Slapping my hand on the guard's shoulder, I said, "Thanks. I'll take it from here."

He offered me a sympathetic smile and stepped aside, granting me my first view of the pair. My breath hitched, my eyes quickly skirting back to the guard who nodded as if to say, *"I told you it wasn't good."*

The younger of the two—a girl of about maybe ten years—was perched on an old tree stump staring blankly ahead. Her hands twisted and rolled the blood-drenched fabric of her skirt between her fingers nervously. The older, an adolescent boy, had his arm draped over her shoulders as he slowly rocked her back and forth. When his eyes met mine, the too-familiar look in them gave me pause, my mind pulling forward inconvenient memories.

Desperate battle.

Terrifying shadows.

Fear-filled eyes that dimmed as life slipped from them.

Shaking my head, I forced my mind to clear and made quick work of removing my sword and handing it to the waiting guard. Cautiously, I approached them, sure to keep my hands raised innocently in front of me where they could see I meant no harm. As I grew closer, the stench of stale blood threatened to make me dizzy, reminding me of the gruesome scenes I'd witnessed during the height of the rebel attacks.

Blood—dried and cracked—coated their arms from fingertips to elbows and soaked their clothes in large swaths over their knees and torsos.

"I'm General Orelian, head of the Emeryn army and advisor to the king," I said, gently. "But you can call me Matthias."

They didn't say anything. The girl didn't even seem to notice my presence, but the boy lifted his chin slightly. I took that as progress.

"What's your name?" I asked.

"Teron," he said. "She's Tilly."

"Are you injured at all?" I couldn't see any visible wounds, and my gut said this blood was neither of theirs, but it had to be asked.

The boy shook his head. "No," he whispered. "Our mother..."

"Where is she?" I asked, dropping my head to the side.

"Dead," he said flatly. "She and our aunt."

Drawing in a deep breath, I took a moment to choose my questions carefully. "And you came from Arenysen?"

He nodded once.

"Did this happen there or in—"

"There. At the castle," he said, his voice cracking slightly.

My gaze fell to the blood coating their clothing. My gut tightened, my mind whirled, and my sister's words echoed in my head: *"What if it was the queen who killed him?"*

The rumors surrounding Calla's possible guilt had only gathered strength over the last few weeks, and now this. Maybe she was responsible, or perhaps someone was trying to implicate her, to oust her from the throne. Either way, more deaths—and brutal ones, by the looks of these kids' clothing—at the castle could not be ignored by Emeryn, especially when we were still trying to glean what had happened to Brennan.

"Do you know what happened? Did you...see...it happen?" I asked, meeting his eyes and realizing a bit late that my second question might not be the best to ask them in their current state.

The boy's eyes glazed over for a moment. Blinking, he peered up into the dark branches overhead. "We were there." He paused, swallowing hard. "She just ripped them apart in front of everyone...for no reason. They had no chance, no time to even scream before she... The blood. So much blood." He tucked his sister closer against him as his voice trailed off.

"Who? Who did this?"

Please don't say Calla. Please don't say the queen.

"Queen Vael."

Shit.

Roughing my fingers back through my hair, I drew in another slow breath. This didn't mean she'd killed Brennan. Stars, this didn't even mean she'd actually killed these women. The boy was clearly distressed. I'd need to confer with my scouts, find out what they knew, but before that, I had one final question.

"You said she *ripped* them apart," I said, hating how the girl flinched at my words and pulled her eyes closed. "How did she do that? Did she use—"

"Shadows," he blurted out, his head snapping up and his eyes burning into mine with such conviction as he repeated the word. "Shadows."

My blood iced over, seeming to freeze my heart and hold my breath hostage.

If this boy was telling the truth, then we had a much bigger problem in Arenysen: Their queen was a Shadow Keeper.

CHAPTER 13

CALLA

I heard them before they entered and sensed their apprehension before their cautious, fake smiles came into view. Isa and Graham approached my dais slowly. My shadows surfaced at my hands in anticipation, but I held my magic close, not allowing it to do more than dance in the creases of my palms. Straightening in my seat, I crossed my legs slowly as I opened one of my hands and watched my magic swirl.

"Your Majesty," Graham greeted me, and I shifted my eyes to glance at my two friends. Isa didn't speak, but her sharp gaze scrutinized me, as if searching for the madness I'd unleashed in this room weeks before.

"Are they leaving?" I asked, my tone rigid and cold like the icy heart that beat in my chest.

Isa's shoulders stiffened. "Most are."

I ground my teeth and stiffened my lips to keep from sneering. That wouldn't fix anything.

"And those who refuse?" I asked. Graham shifted uncomfortably, but Isa ignored him as she answered.

"Awaiting their trial, Your Majesty," she said. "All set to begin next—"

I lifted a hand to stop her, granting enough slack to my

powers so they could weave among my fingers, but Graham inter-jected before I could speak.

"It is what's right, Your—" He stopped short when I pressed a finger to my lips, instructing him to quiet.

"Did I not instruct all humans to leave Arenysen?"

Isa and Graham answered in unison. "You did."

I waved my hand lazily in the air, my shadows dancing along with it. "And did I not explain the consequences for ignoring this command?"

Isa—smart female that she was—immediately clamped her mouth shut. Graham, however, chose to answer me. "You did, but—"

This time he stopped himself from saying more, but I wasn't about to let his insolence slide.

"But what?" I asked. "What were you going to say?"

"But trials have always been—"

"Not anymore!" I hissed through my teeth. "Death. Death was the consequence for staying. I was quite clear about that, and I gave them ample time to leave. They *chose* to ignore it, and there-fore *chose* the consequence. There is no need for a trial. There is no reason—no excuse—they can give that would save them from the judgment they *knew* would happen."

For a long, tense moment, my general and advisor simply stood there, watching me cautiously like prey waiting to be pounced upon. Neither of them seemed apt to break the silence. Slumping in my chair, I rested my elbow on the armrest and dropped my head into my hand, where my shadows massaged away the tension at my temples.

Without looking up, I lowered my voice to a calmer tone and said, "It's for their own safety. Yes, I know the absurdity of that statement, but they need a ruler who can protect them and serve them. It can't be me."

For the past two weeks they had asked why I suddenly had some vendetta against the humans, why I could no longer rule them. I couldn't explain it. Stars, I couldn't even explain why I wasn't able to tell them; Minerva's magic seemed insistent on no one knowing I'd even made the bargain with her.

But this wasn't the question Isa asked. Not that I had an adequate answer to this either.

"Why kill them? If you want to protect them, let us escort them to safety."

Safety.

My nerves went taut, sending a million pinpricks over my skin as the word drowned me in images of Brennan choking on his own blood. What about his safety? Why hadn't anyone protected him? Why should the humans be granted what he had been denied?

"No!" I boomed, and Isa and Graham both flinched.

Slamming my hands down on the armrests, I stood. They didn't retreat even as I stepped down from the dais, coming to stand an arm's reach away from them. My shadows spilled from my palms and pooled around our feet like a dense, black fog.

"Those who defy the crown will face the consequences. I will not suffer such disrespect. These deaths will serve as a warning to any who remain."

Graham remained still, except for his eyes, which surveyed the room and my shadows that encircled our legs. Isa, however, didn't seem nervous at all. She held my gaze confidently, not in defiance, but as one whose loyalty came first above all else.

"Very well," Isa said, and Graham's head snapped around to look at her, his eyes wide with disbelief. He opened his mouth, but Isa spoke first. "I will issue your orders to the warden and have the executions carried out as soon as possible."

"No," I said calmly, and worry clouded Isa's expression. Inhaling slowly, I drew my shadows back in—hoping that would put my friends more at ease—and explained. "I will come with you. I need to see this through personally."

"Your Majesty," Graham started. "Isa and I have served the crown for most of our lives. You can trust us to handle it. You should—"

"Do not tell me to rest, Graham," I said, but the words came out sharper than I intended, and I had to take another calming breath. He recoiled when I reached out, but I rested my hand lightly on his forearm anyway. "I do trust you, but I need to do this. Just this once."

Graham and Isa shared a long glance, as if having a silent discussion, before turning back to me. "Just this once," Isa repeated. I nodded, but somewhere deep in my veins my magic lit with excitement.

It was a lie.

These wouldn't be the last lives I ended.

CHAPTER 14

CALLA

I wished I could end these blasted Assembly meetings—end the Assembly itself, actually—but my parents had insisted on structuring our kingdom differently from Emeryn. When the War of Hearts split Sandurdam's original two kingdoms into four over two decades ago, they had the opportunity to design a new process for governing. The chance to create a kingdom built on laws and rules that would hopefully prevent another war of such magnitude.

The Assembly—typically all fae, though humans had served in the past—was elected every ten years from the six regions of Arenysen and was little more than a group of advisors overseen by Graham. In extreme circumstances they could overrule and retract any of the crown's edicts, but they had never exercised that power. I'd always found their existence rather pointless, but my father had insisted that they kept a ruler's heart in check, providing sound reason and wisdom.

They were far from offering anything resembling either, though, as they sat here at my table with zero answers for all of my inquiries.

"So, we have no idea who killed my husband? Or how they

killed him? Still?" I asked for what felt like the hundredth time since Brennan's death.

The six advisors looked awkwardly at one another, avoiding my eyes at all costs. I failed to suppress my growl, though thankfully my shadows remained dormant for now.

"I know of the stars-damned rumors, but I did not kill him. I loved him! Why would I—"

A hand rested gently upon my shoulder, and I turned to peer up at Isa, who gave me a silent warning to calm myself. I offered a small nod. Appeased for the time being, she stepped back a pace, allowing me to resume speaking. Closing my eyes, I sought the comfort of my shadows flowing through me, ensuring the tether I had on them remained firmly in place. Assured I had control of my power, I met the eyes of each fae seated before me, steadied my breath, and spoke again.

"We will not give up on the search for his killer. I know the healers believe it to be an accident, but after all that happened in his home country years ago, we cannot assume a foreign poison wasn't used."

Fern, a mousy female from one of the southern regions, responded quietly. "We will do our best, Your Majesty. Perhaps a village from each region could spare a healer for a brief time to assist with the investigation here at the castle?"

"Can any of our villages truly spare someone though?" asked a newly elected male from the north whose name I couldn't recall.

"To be fair, Warren," an older male answered, and I mentally noted the new member's name. "With the banishment of the humans, our villages are now less fragile, less in need of healing."

I tensed and held my breath. They seemed reluctant to broach the topic of my decision to exile the humans. Each of them, including Graham, who sat to my right, seemed to have bristled at its mention. Even the male who had uttered the words stiffened, apprehension pinching his expression.

Graham cleared his throat and leaned forward to rest his forearms on the table. "Yuri brings up a valid point. We would not need more than one or two additional at any given time—"

"But why aren't we discussing the banishment itself?" asked a rigid female with harsh, bitter features who looked as though she were perpetually sucking on a lemon. "Her Majesty has killed a considerable number of humans who refused to leave––and rather gruesomely, I might add."

Fisting my hands around my shadows, I gritted my teeth. I shifted my feet and fidgeted in my chair, fighting the urge to leap up and scream at her. Graham slid his hand gently over my forearm and squeezed reassuringly. He rose to his feet and stared down at the icy female.

"Ursula, you will not speak of our queen as if she were not sitting before you. You will respect the crown and this Assembly, or you will be removed and replaced. Do you understand?"

Ursula pursed her lips and held Graham's gaze as she nodded. To my surprise, Graham didn't return to his seat as he continued speaking.

"We should commend our queen for knowing herself and her own limitations when it comes to ruling the humans. While we may not understand her reasons, we should respect them."

Ursula straightened in her seat. "I cannot respect the ruthless killing of those—"

Isa stepped forward, her hand falling to the pommel of her sword. "You mean the killing of outlaws? Of those who know the price of not complying, yet do it anyway?"

Warren threw up a hand. "Then they should get trials! As is customary! You cannot possibly believe these deaths to be ethical, general!"

Isa lifted her chin and stared down her nose at him. "I believe the queen to be worthy of our loyalty, sir."

Placing her clasped hands on the table, Ursula looked around the room as if she wore the crown instead of me. "She may not be the queen for much longer."

I froze, though inside a spark of panic ignited in my chest. Graham lowered to his seat, but sat rigidly on its edge, seeming to place most of his weight on the table than his chair as he glowered at the female.

"What do you mean?" he asked, a slight growl rumbling at the edge of his voice.

"Don't play stupid, Graham. As head advisor, you should recall all of Arenysen law."

Graham's head swiveled in my direction, but he peered over my head at Isa with a desperate question in his eyes.

"Would you care to help us remember, Ursula?" my general asked.

Ursula's gaze settled on me. My shadows itched to slap the smirk off her face, but I maintained my hold on them even as she answered Isa. "When King Brennan died, the assembly met to review the law, as this was the first time our kingdom has ever found itself with only one ruler. It appears your parents, with the aid of the inaugural assembly, intended for Arenysen to always be ruled by both a king and queen."

"But she is widowed," Graham protested. "Surely they allowed for an exemption for such a case."

Warren responded in Ursula's stead. "In a way, they did. The law grants the widower a mourning period before they must remarry."

Remarry?

The word sucked the air from my lungs and my chest caved inward. My hands trembled under the table. My palms tingled as my shadows threatened to emerge. My whole body began to shake as tension coursed through me. I attempted to breathe through the panic, but I couldn't ignore the weight that settled on my sternum.

"How much time?" Isa asked, dropping her hand to my shoulder again.

"One season," Ursula said curtly.

One season.

"But that is mere months," Isa argued. "Surely the assembly could consider an extension given the circumstances."

"To what circumstances are you referring?" I didn't see who asked the question. My vision blurred as my mind focused on restraining my magic.

"The loss of both her parents and her husband in a mere six months!" Isa said sharply. "Surely, she has been through too much —lost too much—to be forced to open her heart to another so soon."

Ursula scoffed. "The heart is inconsequential here. She need not *love* the male to rule with him and produce an heir."

"I'll never love again." The words floated away from my lips on a shaky exhale. Isa squeezed my shoulder.

The advisors, by contrast, continued to discuss the matter as if I wasn't there.

"At least give her an extra season," Graham said. "That's more than reasonable."

"We will, on one condition," Ursula said. "She must cease her attacks on the humans."

My growl filled the room, and I slammed my palms onto the table as I stood, my chair scraping against the wooden floor. "I will stop punishing them when they learn to obey!"

Most of the Assembly members recoiled slightly, but Ursula remained focused on me.

"Then you have a single season, Your Majesty. A single season to choose a new king, or *you* will be removed and replaced."

Isa inched closer to me, angling herself so her back was to the Assembly as she whispered in my ear. "You need more time, Calla. Agree to the deal."

Warren spoke up, clarifying. "Remember, it is one season from the death, giving her only eight weeks."

I caught Isa's eye and quietly said, "I cannot let the humans go unpunished." Before she could argue, I turned back to the Assembly and nodded. "Eight weeks."

CHAPTER 15
CALLA

For the second time in my life, I needed to choose a husband.

Last time, I only had three suitors to choose from—one from each of the other kingdoms on Sandurdam, and it had been a relatively easy choice. While I wasn't opposed to the idea of fae and humans marrying, the men from Kinham and Wrenwick had little to offer compared to Brennan. Brennan, despite his licentious reputation, had stolen my heart from the moment we met on my first visit to Emeryn. Of course, I had heard rumors that he'd been in love with some human on his palace staff, but Lieke later told me the entire story of how she and Connor had found themselves bound by fate.

The mating bond had not been in the stars for Brennan and me, though it had never bothered me before. I had known plenty of happily married couples who were tied by their vows alone, such as my parents.

Stars, I missed them.

My mother and father would have helped me navigate this. But then, if they were still here, I wouldn't be in this predicament at all.

Graham, thankfully, had cut the meeting short after Ursula's declaration, and both he and Isa had left me alone to think things through. Now my feet ached from the hours of pacing my study after the assembly meeting, and I dropped into one of the armchairs, debating whether to pour myself a drink.

"Stars-damned death," I ground out bitterly. "Death ruins everything."

"Indeed." Graham's silky voice filled the room, and from the corner of my eye, I watched him settle into the other chair beside me. He leaned forward, his forearms resting on his knees as he studied me for a moment before finally asking, "How are you feeling?"

I slowly pivoted my head toward him, my outrage over this stars-damned marriage nonsense pulling my mouth into a grim line. "Angry," I admitted.

A humorless laugh fell from my advisor, and he shook his head. "Understandably so. I do apologize that I had forgotten the law. You deserved to hear it from Isa or me, not the Assembly." He paused, dropping his gaze to the floor. "What do you think you'll do?"

"I'm not giving up my kingdom, if that's what you're asking," I growled, immediately regretting it. He wasn't at fault here. He didn't deserve my ire. I cleared my throat quickly. "I'm sorry, Graham. I shouldn't have—"

Graham waved away my apology. "You have every right to be on edge, Your Majesty. You've suffered a lot of grief in a short time, and while I know you were determined to start moving on and getting back to some new normal, I understand, too, that this isn't how you wanted to do that."

"I don't want to marry again. I shouldn't have to." I winced at how sad and pathetic I sounded. A queen shouldn't whine about her lot; a queen should stand tall and tackle whatever challenges came her way. If I was to rule my kingdom, to retain my family's claim to the throne, I needed to push past my fear and face this.

"You shouldn't have to," Graham agreed.

"But I do," I said, resolutely. "My heart may be shattered, but as Ursula noted, my heart doesn't need to be involved. I cannot risk loving again, but I don't need to love to remarry."

Graham shifted to the edge of his chair and clasped his hands together. "If I may, Your Majesty."

I nodded, but he didn't say anything more as he avoided meeting my eyes. My stomach writhed like snakes as I pondered what he might be hesitating to say. "What is it, Graham?"

"I'll do it," he said, quietly.

The imaginary snakes tied themselves into knots within my gut. "You'll do what?"

"I'll marry you, so you don't have to choose someone new, someone you don't know. So you don't have to risk another heartbreak."

I recoiled and then froze, watching my advisor's features shift quickly from hopeful to hurt before he released an awkward laugh.

"It's alright. I didn't expect you to accept," he said, though a hint of embarrassment tinged his words, and his cheeks reddened slightly.

"I do appreciate it, Graham. I do," I said. "But who could I find to replace you as my advisor? Ursula? Warren? No."

"I shouldn't have offered, Your Majesty," he said, pushing to his feet and walking away.

I opened my palm and released my shadows, sending them toward him. They lithely circled his body, forcing him to turn back to face me, but his eyes were on my shadows instead of me. His lip seemed to curl in a sneer, though it was hard to tell with his chin tucked. He finally looked up at me, his eyes alight with something I couldn't quite place. It wasn't quite bitterness or anger, nor was it the sheepish awkwardness he'd shown earlier.

"Please let me go," he said firmly, his tone colder than I'd ever heard from him.

"I didn't mean to..." I let my words trail off as his eyes darkened. As soon as I pulled my shadows back, freeing him, he turned and rushed out.

No sooner had Graham left than Isa entered.

"Turned him down?" she asked.

I wrinkled my nose at her. "You knew he was going to do that?"

Isa merely shrugged. "I didn't tell him to, but I didn't dissuade him either. It seemed a reasonable enough solution, no?"

"I can't believe this," I muttered, shaking my head.

Isa strode over, but instead of sitting as Graham had, she planted herself in front of me and leaned back against the edge of my desk, her arms crossed in front of her.

"So, what will you do instead?"

"I don't know," I admitted.

"You could always see if Kinham or Wrenwick would—"

"No," I snapped. I stared at my friend. How could she—given everything that had happened this past month—suggest I consider marrying a human?

Isa sighed knowingly. "Ah, of course. No humans. I forgot."

"It has to be a fae."

"There aren't any royal fae left on the continent, and I don't recommend reaching out to Dolobare."

"No, I wouldn't do that, not after..." My throat constricted as my parents' faces appeared in my mind's eye. Whether the Dolobareans had any hand in their deaths or not, I was as interested in that prospect as I was in considering a human. I swallowed hard and continued. "I will have to find someone in Arenysen."

"Why not Emeryn?" Isa asked, almost apologetically, but still the word shot a barb into my heart.

Could I choose a new husband from Brennan's home? Merely thinking about it caused my lungs to compress. Isa lowered her head to one side, and had she been anyone else, I would have resented the pity in her eyes.

"You will be sorely limited if you don't."

I waved her away. "How am I even supposed to choose again, Isa?"

She shrugged. "There's always Gra—" As I groaned, her words gave way to laughter. "Why not consider him?"

Wearily, I nodded. "He's Graham."

"You say his name like he's got some sort of disease," she said, stifling more laughter.

"I do not. He's just—he was my parents' advisor, and practically my brother. I couldn't."

For several minutes we were both silent, until Isa finally said, "What about a tournament? Like the old monarchs used to hold."

I leaned back in my chair and mulled over her suggestion. Little was known about the old trials our ancestors had been fond of. All I remembered from my schooling was they typically involved females being paraded before their rulers and judged on everything from their appearance and poise to their ancestry and breeding potential. The contests had grown out of fashion well before my parents were born, and no one had held one since.

Shooting a curious glance at my friend, I asked, "You want me to host games?"

She shrugged. "Why not?"

I grimaced. "They were little more than beauty pageants. Humiliating and—"

"Who said you had to model it after the original tradition? You don't want to pick someone, right?" My throat clenched, closing off my air, so all I could do was shake my head. "Then make them compete."

"What would they have to do?"

"I'm sure I can come up with a few ideas. I've been training our soldiers for years, after all. It can't be that much harder to devise obstacles to help select a new king. We could call on some friends to help. Asher and his brothers are always eager to earn extra coin."

"Mercenaries usually are," I muttered, and my shadows seemed to churn inside me as I mentally picked apart this plan. "This could work, on one condition."

"What's that? Don't want Graham to be eligible?" she asked, a hint of a laugh playing in her eyes.

I scoffed. "Let him compete if he wants to, but I want to be involved. I may not want to choose someone, but I'm not about to forfeit control over the process."

"Not even to me?" Isa smiled knowingly.

"Not even you, my friend."

CHAPTER 16

MATTHIAS

Onnor lunged, thrusting his sword at me. I easily parried his attack, finding the familiar sound of steel on steel oddly comforting. I stepped to the side and delivered a counter stroke, slicing through the space between us in a backhanded swing. Connor shifted out of reach as he brought his weapon up to meet mine, and in one swift motion, he twisted his blade around, forcing my wrist into such an unnatural angle I had to release my grip.

He began to laugh triumphantly, but cut it short when I summoned a quick burst of power to catch the hilt of my sword before it could hit the dirt floor of the training ring. Before he could move to parry or dodge, I jabbed the blade toward his gut, stopping before it could do more than nick a hole in his shirt.

A half-hearted groan rumbled from my friend as he jammed his sword home into its sheath.

"Done already?" I asked around my frown.

Connor looked at me quizzically. "It's been two hours. Lieke's expecting us soon."

Glancing outside, I noted how the trees' shadows had shifted since we'd started sparring this morning. "So it has," I said, and tossed my sword to my other hand before slipping it back into place at my waist. I moved toward the waiting water pitcher on the table against the wall, but Connor cleared his throat, stopping me mid-step.

"Got anything stronger?" he asked, his eyes flicking up to the ceiling.

"Not for you, I don't," I said, grinning.

Connor recoiled in offense. "That's some way to treat your future king."

I bowed my head reverently. "Simply watching out for your health, Your Highness."

"And protecting your precious brandy."

"We all remember what happened the last time."

"You're never going to let me live that down, are you?"

I smirked as I shook my head. "Not a chance."

"I could order you to share it."

"But you won't."

"How do you know?"

"Because Lieke would be disappointed with you if you did."

Connor stared at me blankly for a moment before finally letting his shoulders slump in defeat. "You're right. And even if she pretended not to be—"

"You'd still feel it yourself," I said. I scrunched my nose at him. "Makes me more and more glad I have no desire—or chance —of ever getting trapped in such a bond."

Connor gave a short laugh. "You can barely handle your own feelings. I can't imagine you having to deal with anyone else's."

I stiffened. Handle my own feelings? I managed them better than most—better than him, especially. I scoffed. "I don't know. I've handled your mood swings just fine for years."

Pivoting on my heel, I headed for the door. As soon as I stepped onto the grass, he was beside me, his hands buried in his pockets. "Seems like only yesterday you were lecturing me about needing to be open and honest."

Apparently, he wasn't going to let me escape this conversation easily—or at all.

I eyed him sharply as we walked. "With the woman you loved, Your Highness. Bit different."

Connor pursed his lips and nodded. "True, though I had to first be honest with myself about how I felt. You can't run away from—"

Gritting my teeth, I stopped short and pinned him with a glare. "Run away from what? The fucking past?" I narrowed my eyes, but Connor didn't react at all. "I realize this may be hard for you to understand, Connor, but not all of us need decades to process things. We lost a friend. It was fucking war! And yes, recent shit has brought those memories back, but my choosing to focus on the good rather than fixate on life's fuckery doesn't make me broken; it simply makes me different."

Tense silence stretched between us for a long moment before he finally shifted his gaze away from mine and offered a thin smile.

"Lot of emotion in that little speech."

"Fuck off," I growled under my breath as I turned away to continue trudging up the hill. He fell into step with me once again, but I said nothing.

"Sorry," he offered, but all I could manage was an annoyed grunt in response. We continued on in silence, and with each breath, my irritation eased a little more. It wasn't his fault that he struggled to understand. Stars, it had taken me decades to accept that he needed time to brood and mope and stew over things while I didn't.

When he finally spoke again, thankfully it was to change the subject though to an equally difficult one.

"You think Sera will be able to help those kids?"

The image of the pair with their clothes stained from their family's blood invaded my thoughts. Pulling in a long breath, I tried to picture them playing with my niece and nephew, helping my sister in the garden and around the house. "I wouldn't have sent them there if I didn't."

"I can't believe she's a Shadow Keeper," Connor said, and I

nearly wished we could go back to our previous discussion. Nearly.

"My scouts' reports from Arenysen corroborate the kids' recount. Word of it has spread quickly, and more and more humans are fleeing into Kinham and Wrenwick."

Connor hummed. "I can understand why she'd hide her power, especially with how misunderstood it is. But how did she conceal it from everyone? Do you think Brennan knew?"

Shrugging, I frowned at him. "I wouldn't be surprised if he didn't. It's amazing what someone can hide from others when needed. Shame? Fear? Either would be powerful motives to keep such magic a secret."

"I wonder if she's like the last Shadow Keeper we met," Connor asked, a hint of worry in his tone. If he was trying to force me to face our past to acknowledge some deep-seated, repressed emotions, this was a shitty way to do it.

I bit back my curse as the memory surged forward like a tidal wave summoned by Connor's stars-damned words.

In my head, black eyes stared back at me—empty abysses of malice threatening to swallow me whole. Long-forgotten screams pierced my consciousness as I relived the scene of Gabriel rushing at the Shadow Keeper on that distant battlefield. Then shadows flooded the image, and my nerves pulled taut as I once again watched the darkness smother him, silencing his screams. I wiped the image from my mind only to have it replaced by those blood-covered kids stumbling out of the trees.

Peering back at Connor, I whispered, "I sure as fuck hope not."

⁂

By the time we reached the gravel of the palace driveway, my stomach was grumbling, begging me to move faster to discover what Mrs. Bishop had prepared for lunch. Disappointment sank like a stone in the pit of my gut, though, when I noticed the official courier standing beside his horse, watching us approach.

I slowed my pace to allow Connor to greet the messenger, noting the Arenysen seal—a fox draped in ivy—fixed to his jacket and to his horse's blanket. I stopped a respectful distance away but angled my head so I could still listen to their exchange.

"Official word from Her Majesty, Queen of Arenysen," the courier said, dipping his sharp chin shrewdly as he handed a thick envelope to Connor.

"And the nature of this message?" Connor asked, eyeing the envelope he now held in his hand.

"Not my place to say, Your Highness. I'm to deliver these to the lords of each of your villages."

Connor swept an arm toward the stables. "Could your horse use a rest? We are happy to offer you and your mount whatever you need before you continue on."

"Much thanks, Your Highness, but I mustn't delay. Matter of urgency, I'm afraid," he said before quickly turning his horse around and galloping away.

❦

"A tournament?" Lieke balked at the letter she held, reading it over again as she paced in front of the cold fireplace. She stopped and glanced up over the paper at me and then to Connor. "I can't believe they're forcing her to remarry so soon, but what is she thinking?"

"If I were to venture a guess, I'd say she's wanting to avoid having to actually choose someone," I said from my seat on the sofa.

Connor, sitting in his usual armchair, met his wife's stare. "I agree. Assuming she chose Brennan out of love—"

"We know she did," Lieke asserted, and Connor offered a sympathetic smile before continuing.

"She's likely trying to protect her heart from being hurt again."

I leaned forward and cleared my throat. "Regardless of why she's doing this, we're sending someone to compete, yes?"

Connor nodded slowly. "One male from each village is to compete."

"But do the palace grounds count as one of the villages?" Lieke asked. "Would she even want us to send someone from the palace? Surely that will be too painful for her."

Scratching my jaw, I shrugged slowly. "It doesn't specifically prohibit us from sending someone, but we could always send someone from our ranks as representative for their hometown."

Connor reached for the envelope lying on the small table in the middle of the living space. Silently he pulled out a smaller sheet of paper before dropping the envelope back down. "Unfortunately, Sapphire, we do still need to consider the possibility that Calla isn't innocent here. It seems he may have been murdered after all, and with the same poison we've been battling."

Lieke's expression tightened, like she had just bit into a lemon, but she accepted the paper when Connor offered it to her. Her face shifted slowly as she scanned the writing, and I waited for her anger to appear as it usually did when we discussed Calla's hypothetical guilt. This time, though, she let her arms fall weakly at her sides, the paper still gripped in her hand. Tears surfaced, clinging to her lower lashes, but they refused to spill over.

Lieke began to shake her head. "But they said—"

"*Officially,* we were told they didn't know. This note was tucked in with the official tournament announcement. Someone at the castle didn't want us to suspect foul play."

"How do we know we can trust this"—she waved the paper in the air—"over the official report though? We don't even know who sent this!"

Connor shrugged. "We can't, but we must consider both possibilities. Someone doesn't want us to know the truth.

Whether that's Calla or someone working against her, I don't know."

I shifted in my seat and added, "Consider, also, that the poison appears to be coming from Dolobare, who does business primarily with Arenysen."

"Primarily, sure," Lieke said. "But not solely. That poison could be coming through Wrenwick."

Connor cocked his head to the side. "Anything's possible, but I think this tournament"—he paused to flick a finger toward the paper in Lieke's other hand—"is our best opportunity to try and learn the truth."

"How exactly?" Lieke asked, but she seemed to quickly determine the answer on her own, because she shook her head and looked to the ceiling as she said, "Compete to get close to her."

"And discover the truth," Connor added.

Lieke pierced her husband with a stern glare. "And if she did it? Then what? Vengeance?"

Connor's jaw pulsed under his clenched teeth. He balled his hands into fists that shook in his lap, but his anger was gone as quickly as it had come on. Stretching his fingers wide, he dropped them to push himself up from his chair. He closed the distance between them and took the paper from Lieke's grasp, passing it off to me without so much as a glance in my direction. With Lieke's hands now clutched in his own, Connor released a long sigh.

"I know it won't bring him back, but if Calla did this—if Calla killed him—she needs to pay the consequences."

The shimmer of fresh tears returned to Lieke's eyes, and I squirmed uncomfortably in my seat. This seemed too personal an exchange for me to be sitting here watching, but if I were to get up and retreat, it would prevent my friends from having the conversation they needed to.

"Why do *we* need to dole out those consequences though? Can't we leave it to her own kingdom to do so?"

"I don't know how loyal they are to her," Connor explained. "I don't trust them to do what's necessary."

"So who *do* you trust?" No sooner had Lieke asked the question than they were both staring at me.

"What now?" I asked, pretending I hadn't followed their conversation. They didn't seem to buy it.

"You willing?" Connor asked.

"Do I have a choice?"

"Of course. I know you've been busy chasing the rebels, so I would understand if you don't want to abandon that effort."

"Do we know how dangerous this is going to be?" Lieke asked.

Connor rubbed the back of his neck slowly. "They claim to be tailoring these after the historic games, which consisted of frivolous trials. Regardless, Matthias has faced his share of danger. He can take care of himself."

Lifting a hand to my chin, I tapped a finger against my lips as I considered the decision before me, though there was little need to deliberate. "I could use a change of scenery and a little adventure. When do I leave?"

CHAPTER 17
CALLA

If the Assembly disapproved of the tournament, they hid it well. In fact, a couple of them seemed practically giddy over the prospect of having some entertainment to break up their mundane lives, and I expected them to start placing bets on the males as they arrived. Others' reactions bordered on apathy. Ursula and Warren, unsurprisingly, had maintained their bitterness toward me, even going so far as to call me a bloodthirsty witch intent on watching males kill each other for my hand.

Their comments I could ignore. Their scathing looks proved harder to disregard, especially while gathered in a small room listening to Isa explain the games—how the trials were designed, how points would be awarded, and how a victor would be determined.

"How many males have been invited?" Fern asked sweetly, as if we were hosting a masquerade ball instead of a deadly competition.

"One from each village in our kingdom and Emeryn," Isa answered. "So, twelve total."

"Thirteen, actually." Every head turned. Graham stood in the doorway, a tense mess of hand-wringing and weight-shifting.

"Excuse me?" Isa asked, though there was no hint of surprise in her tone.

Graham dropped his hands and cleared his throat. "I would like to enter the competition."

Isa swung her gaze over to me, and a knowing smile played at the corners of her mouth. I couldn't be bothered to be annoyed by his decision. I'd expected him to do this, even while I hoped he wouldn't. The thought of marrying him was almost as difficult as the thought of remarrying at all.

Almost.

"Very well," Isa said, turning back to Fern. "Thirteen. They should begin to arrive over the next day or two and will have until the end of this week to show up lest their spot be forfeited."

"And will replacements be assigned in those cases?" Fern asked.

Isa shook her head. "No. With the queen's deadline fast approaching, we simply do not have time to wait beyond the end of the week. Calling and approving any replacements would take too long."

Ursula's harsh voice cut through the stale air. "And who is to act as the royal advisor if Graham competes? Whether he perishes or wins, he will need to be replaced."

Isa opened her mouth to speak but closed it when I stood.

Glowering down my nose, I addressed the vile female. "Ursula, those are not the only two outcomes. This tournament —as Isa has plainly explained ad nauseam—is not a 'last male standing' affair. Will some die? Possibly. Probably, even. But we do not expect, nor desire, for all but the future king to survive. Hence the use of a point system, which would be moot if we were just planning to kill everyone off."

Ursula's eyes narrowed and her lips twitched as her jaw tensed, but I continued unfazed.

"As to how to replace Graham: The crown can afford to rule without an advisor for the short duration of this tournament. We are not currently at war. The position can remain vacant until the victor is crowned. Should the need arise to replace Graham for whatever reason, that will be a decision for my new king and me."

The last words rent my heart as they spilled from my lips. My sorrow swarmed me—fresh and heavy, compressing my chest and stealing my breath so that my vision blurred and my head turned light. Giving a sharp nod, I pivoted on my heel and retreated as fast as possible before I collapsed.

CHAPTER 18

MATTHIAS

Storm nuzzled my hand as I ran the brush over her shoulder and back.

"I'm sorry I can't take you with me," I said. The mare nipped at my fingers in response, and I couldn't help but laugh. "I know, I know. You don't need to make this harder than it already is. But it's safer for you here."

She huffed out a breath and shook her head as if to express her disagreement. Gliding the brush down her legs, I stroked her neck and sighed. Storm had been with me since she was a young mare. Her mother, who had been my mount during the war, had grown too old to continue joining me on adventures.

"I don't know what I'll face—"

Swinging her head toward me, her big brown eyes locked on mine in a derisive stare.

"Fine, you're right," I said. "I do know what awaits me. At least partly. Can you blame me for not wanting you to face a Shadow Keeper though? Not that I like putting Sorel in that position either, but I can't risk the queen recognizing you and ruining my cover."

"Do all soldiers talk to their horses?" Lieke's voice pulled my head around to find her leaning against the doorway of the stable.

I shrugged. "The good ones do."

Lieke pushed away from the wall and approached Storm, holding her palm out for the mare to sniff in search of treats. Finding none, Storm blew out a snotty exhale into Lieke's hand, and Lieke laughed as she reached into her pocket and produced a carrot.

"You don't think I'd come empty-handed, do you girl?" she asked. Storm answered her by snatching up the food without hesitation. Lieke reached up to scratch behind her ears while Storm chomped away happily. "I'll look after her while you're gone, Matthias."

"You'd better," I said. "She's irreplaceable."

"So are you," Lieke said firmly, and I lifted my eyes to hers, surprised to find such sternness there. "You'd better come back."

"Yes, Mother." I tried to make it a joke, but the serious expression on Lieke's face had me on edge.

"I mean it." She folded her arms in front of her and looked more like Mrs. Bishop giving me a lecture than my friend's wife bidding me farewell. Storm, now finished with her snack, began to sniff around Lieke's pockets for more food. Lieke ignored her, though, holding my gaze.

Turning to face her, I mirrored her stance with my arms crossed. "I am slightly offended by your apparent lack of confidence in me."

Lieke was shaking her head before I was done speaking. "You don't know who—or what—you'll face in these games, and I can't watch Connor lose someone else."

"You may not have a choice, Your Highness," I said, and Lieke flinched. "The king's health will only continue to decline, and someday, Connor will have to let him go. We have little control over when death takes us or those we love."

"But you do have some control over whether you do stupid shit to get yourself killed," she chided, and I pressed my lips together to stifle my laughter, but I couldn't hide my amusement completely. She squared her jaw. "I mean it, Matthias. Don't do anything stupid in these games."

"I'll try, but I can't vouch for any of the other competitors. They might be complete imbeciles."

"And what if you win?"

This time I did laugh but cut it short when she pinned me with another glare. "I won't let it get that far."

"I'm not joking."

"I thought you wanted me to find love," I said.

"Not like this." She breathed deeply and released a long sigh, shaking her head once more. "Just do your best."

I cocked my head at her. "I always do."

Lieke opened her mouth, but Connor entered the stable then, drawing her attention away from me. He quickly placed a kiss to his wife's temple before lifting his chin to me.

"You ready?"

Lifting my arms, I glanced down at the wrinkled shirt and mud-strewn pants I wore and peered up at my friend from beneath my brow. "Yes, this is how I plan to look when I arrive at the royal tournament."

He looked me up and down and frowned. "You're already running late. I told you I could manage handing off your duties to Tanner for you. Won't do us any good if you don't arrive in time," he said, tossing a tightly bound bundle of cloth to me.

"And a lecture is sure to improve my timeliness," I joked. Unwrapping the bundle, I stared down at the wooden-handled dagger. "Good thing your healers thought to keep this. And it's still as potent as before?"

Connor nodded. "So they claim, though no one has risked touching it."

Holding the blade, it was hard not to ponder for the millionth time all that had happened since Lieke had returned to the palace with two poisoned blades from her rebel family. How different things would be had she not been sent away, had she not slain that fae piece of shit, and had she not subsequently ended up engaged to my best friend. Even with all the trouble the rebels had caused —and the months I'd spent searching for them since—and with the difficult task set before me now, I couldn't help but smile to myself as I wrapped the dagger back up, careful not to touch its still-poisoned blade. Moving across the stable, I tucked it into my saddlebag lying on the straw-covered floor.

"I don't like it," Lieke murmured.

"None of us do, Sapphire," Connor reassured her as he wrapped his arm around her and pulled her close. "But Matthias is our best shot at learning the truth—"

"So he can kill our friend," she said icily.

"If she killed my brother, she was never a friend," he explained as warmly as he could.

"Don't worry, Lieke," I said, shrugging. "If she's guilty, I promise to kill her quickly."

Connor groaned. Lieke scowled.

"Would you rather I make it hurt?" I asked with wide eyes. "It doesn't seem necessary to me, but if it's your—"

"Stop." Lieke ground out the word, and I sobered my expression but didn't retreat from Lieke's storming eyes.

"Trust me to handle this, Lieke," I said. "I will go, compete, determine who killed him, and ensure whoever is responsible suffers for it."

Lieke's features tightened. "You just said you'd make it quick."

I shrugged casually, frowning. "So I did. You know what I mean, though."

"And you don't plan to see Minerva on the way?" Connor asked.

Regarding him curiously, I asked, "Weren't you just rebuking me for being late as it is? There's no time to stop to see the mage, even if I wanted to."

"You should still consider it," Lieke argued.

I pivoted away from them and returned to brushing Storm. "One of her glamors would help me avoid Calla's objections—"

"She'll protest as soon as she sees you," Lieke interjected. Storm whinnied as if agreeing with her.

"Probably, but I have a better chance of being accepted into the games if I attend as myself. Her general can sense magic—both the innate and the acquired. She'll recognize the glamor the moment I arrive, which could get me banned from the tournament—or worse. And if I go see Minerva and she delays me even more, I could be disqualified before I ever arrive."

Lieke was silent for a moment before finally asking, "What about a more conventional disguise?"

"Perhaps, but that could be difficult to maintain depending on the type of trials they have planned. I'd hate to be skipping through a maze and have my fake mustache fall off."

Lieke wrinkled her nose.

"What?" I asked and ran my thumb and finger over my upper lip. "A mustache wouldn't look that bad."

"No," she said, biting her lip, but her giggle refused to be suppressed so easily. "I'm trying to imagine you skipping."

I nodded. I certainly couldn't imagine that either. Tossing the horse brush into the bin against the wall, I gave Storm a final stroke and leaned close to her ear.

"Watch after them for me while I'm gone," I whispered.

"What was that?" Lieke said.

I straightened and snatched my saddlebags from the ground, slinging them over my shoulder. "I told her to bite you if you try to feed her too many apples."

That earned me an exaggerated eye roll as Lieke turned on her heel and began to drag Connor back to the palace. But the prince stood fast, motioning for Lieke to wait a moment. He lowered his head and his voice as he leaned toward me slightly.

"Be careful, and try to stay alive. I can't watch her lose another friend," he said.

I studied both of them, marveling at how well they fit together.

"I had no idea I was so loved," I said, but Connor only walked away wordlessly with his wife, leaving me to my final preparations.

CHAPTER 19

CALLA

For four days I watched as male after male arrived. With each new contestant, my dread grew more intense. Isa insisted I remain set apart from the competitors, at least until she could process and register them officially once they all arrived. She cited some nonsense about needing to protect me from potential threats and would-be assassins, as if I couldn't adequately defend myself.

So I spent most of my time perched on the second-floor landing that overlooked the inner courtyard of the castle, watching as each of them marched through the glass doors from the grand foyer into the brilliant sunshine pouring in through the glass ceiling suspended high above. Each had, immediately upon arriving, stared up at me with one of two expressions: morbid curiosity or muted fear, yet always with the same unmistakable hint of pity. They tried to hide their emotions, of course, as they attempted to smile, but I'd received enough of these looks from my own staff and the Assembly to recognize them easily.

Part of me wanted to answer those looks with my shadows— to let them see what I was capable of, but again, Isa had given me strict instructions not to interfere with the games. I would be involved, but I would—under no circumstances—do anything to sway favor toward or away from any of them.

By the end of the week, two males—one from a village in the north and one from Emeryn—had yet to arrive, and I secretly hoped they wouldn't, if only to make this whole ordeal end that much sooner. If there were fewer to compete, then there were fewer who needed to die or fail before a victor could be named and a new king crowned.

I spent much of that last day pacing my study, avoiding my unwanted guests, waiting and hoping for the two stragglers not to turn up. I'd tried to read, to sit, to nap, but my limbs and mind were restless.

I needed out of the castle.

To breathe.

To think.

To escape the staff's incessant chatter about their favorite contenders.

If I had to hear one more whispered exchange about one male's strong brow or another's tight ass, I wouldn't be able to contain my irritation. Or my shadows.

Silently I slipped through the back corridors of the castle, careful to avoid any of the males. A side door led to the royal stables, and, once I was satisfied the way was clear, I glided across the narrow open space to where my mare, Luna, waited. When she neighed in greeting, I lifted a finger to my lips to shush her. I decided against taking the additional time to saddle and halter her and instead guided her over to the wooden steps I used to mount when I was younger.

Once on her back, I situated the bulky fabric of my dress evenly on either side of her, gripped her mane, and leaned over her neck to whisper, "Let's run, Luna."

Needing no further signal from me, she calmly exited the stables and shook her head as a warrior might stretch their neck before training. She bolted off toward the front of the castle, seemingly as happy as I was to be free from the stuffy walls. The forest loomed on my right, beckoning me, but Luna ran as close to the castle wall as she could. I had never taken her, or any of our horses, into the forest. My father had hired Minerva to enchant those woods to welcome only members of our bloodline, and while that did not affect animals, they naturally avoided it all the same.

As we swung past the castle entrance and onto the main road that provided the only safe path to the castle, I saw him—a male riding a buckskin horse. He was still a considerable distance away, so I couldn't make out any features beyond his confident stature. Sitting tall in his saddle, he appeared at home on his horse, as if he had been riding since before he could walk. His head cocked to one side as he continued to approach, keeping his horse at a gentle walk while I still had Luna running hard toward him.

My heart jolted into my throat as panic sent my pulse racing as fast as the creature I rode.

I couldn't meet this male. Not now. Not here.

Not ever, if I had my way.

Gripping Luna's mane in my fists, I yanked hard to the right, pressing into her belly with my thigh, and yelled at her to turn. I didn't care if this male thought I was insane. I didn't care how I must have sounded. I needed to get away from him.

Luna obliged, only seeming to realize we had entered the forest when we were within its darkness. Without warning, she locked her front legs and stopped, sending me careening over her neck in an ungraceful somersault. My shoulder slammed into the rotting leaves of the forest floor as all air was thrust from my lungs. I didn't need to turn to know my horse had already abandoned me, but then the sound of hooves grew louder. Maybe she hadn't left me after all.

Pushing myself up, I turned my chin over my shoulder to see, not my horse, but the male's, now riderless. Confusion pinched my brows together. Maybe he had fallen off too.

No such luck.

Stepping from behind his horse's neck, he loomed over me.

He smirked—too handsomely for his own good—like he was trying to suppress a laugh. I couldn't completely fault him for that; no doubt I looked ridiculous sprawled in the mud and leaves like a wounded animal.

He extended his hand toward me. "It's not often I have females flee in terror at the sight of me."

I merely stared back at him. My skin prickled.

I knew him somehow, but how?

He wore no insignia on his cloak, no signet upon his finger—though he did have a handsome gold band on the middle finger of his left hand. A ring of green stone that matched his eyes was inlaid in the center of it.

"Well?" he asked, and I blinked rapidly as if he'd woken me from some daydream.

"What?"

He raised his brow in obvious amusement as he moved his hand closer to me, and I peered at it, my insides warring over whether to accept it or not.

"I won't bite," he said, though something flashed in his eyes that seemed to contradict the statement. Movement drew my gaze to the ground, where a thorned vine slowly slithered toward his leg like a snake inching toward its lunch. I kept my eye on the advancing threat even as I warned him.

"You might not want to stand still for too long," I said, pointing down at where the vine had now slipped between his legs and started to wind its way up over his foot.

"What in the—" he cried, leaping out of the plant's reach. His hand began to draw his sword from its scabbard, but he stopped when I clicked my tongue at him.

"I wouldn't do that if I were you." I pushed myself up to my feet, brushing the wet leaves from my dress and the dirt from my hands. "The forest doesn't like intruders, but it especially hates those who pose a threat."

Slowly he let the sword fall back into its sheath as his eyes darted all along the forest floor around him, watching for any new adversaries that might be approaching. "An enchanted forest. Interesting," he said, seemingly to himself.

"So you're from Emeryn, then?" I asked, trying to ignore how my breath hitched upon uttering Brennan's home kingdom's name. Was this why this male seemed so familiar? Perhaps I had met him during my tour of their country. My insides writhed uncomfortably, and my head began to ache from the mental acrobatics of trying to place him in my foggy memories.

Stars. Why do I care who he is?

I didn't. Not really. All I truly cared about was being away from him, away from everyone. Stars knew I wouldn't have much time to myself once the tournament began. My instinct urged me to simply leave and travel further into the forest. Unfortunately, though, this male seemed the type to insist on accompanying me, and if he truly didn't know the dangers of these woods and followed me, I'd have to explain his premature death to Isa and the Assembly.

"Yes, Your Majesty. I grew up near Holsham." His voice cut into my deliberations, pulling my attention back to where he was dancing from foot to foot to avoid the still-creeping vine. The comical display dashed away any need to remember this male's face, and I had to put all my effort into hiding my amusement. I might have been able to, had his horse not begun to mimic his movements with its hooves. Angling my head down, I lifted the back of my hand to my lips to cover my smile.

A breath later, I cleared my throat and gestured quickly to the driveway behind him. "You should probably turn back."

Without hesitation, the male grabbed his horse's reins, though he didn't turn to leave.

"And what about you?"

I had already begun to pivot away from him, but I hesitated as Isa's warnings about potential assassins rang through my mind again. My general would certainly frown upon my turning my back on a stranger, whether I was in the safety of the forest or not.

"I'm safe here," I said. "Unlike you."

"Is that a threat?" he said with that same tinge of humor, even as he surveyed the trees around him suspiciously.

I widened my eyes at him and shrugged. "Not from me. While safe from the forest's magic, I don't control it. Plus, you're nearly out of time to register for the tournament, assuming that is why you were riding toward my castle."

At this he dipped his chin and moved alongside his horse. Once mounted, he started to turn back toward the path, but paused briefly to meet my gaze.

A fire burned in his eyes that I hadn't witnessed in anyone since...

Brennan.

My heart seemed to cease and race at the same time. The forest closed in on me, the trees spinning around me as my panic ignited in my chest. I shook my head, trying to rid myself of his name. I'd forgotten his eyes, his smile, his scent, everything.

I had started to heal—or at least I thought I had. But this male. This fucking male and his stars-damned eyes gleaming with a mischievous passion I'd only ever witnessed in my husband. My *dead* husband. Grief slammed into me like a wave throwing me against the rocky shores of Dolobare, and my shadows burst free as if they could save me from myself and my resurrected pain. Everything vanished, my world darkening as my shadows enveloped me in blissful emptiness void of strangers and memories and tournaments and pain.

CHAPTER 20

MATTHIAS

Shadows swirled around the queen like a dark tempest. Grim memories tightened my chest, but unlike the last Shadow Keeper I had encountered, the queen seemed to be at the mercy of her power. Her brown eyes, wide but unfocused, started to roll back as her knees buckled and her shadows closed in around her.

Shit.

The darkness had nearly concealed her completely by the time I slipped from my saddle. I ignored the fast-approaching vines and the growing dread in my heart, thrusting myself into the shadows, catching the queen before she hit the ground. Blinded by her shadows, I scooped her up into my arms and tried to escape the darkness, but her shadows persisted. I backed up and barely managed to stay upright as my heel caught on something. Stumbling, I spun around, but quickly stopped. I could easily wander deeper into the forest without realizing it and, assuming she had told the truth about the forest's dangers, that would mean failing this mission before I'd truly started it.

Except...

Holding my breath, I planted my feet and waited, listened, focused all of my attention on my feet.

Nothing.

I nudged a toe forward. No vine.

I swung my foot in an arch out to the side. Nothing.

Were her shadows protecting me?

Interesting.

Contrary to my words earlier, I did, in fact, know about the forest's enchantment, though the details had never been divulged by my scouts—or the royal family. We knew the Vaels had called on Minerva—as everyone in our world seemed to—to protect the castle. The price they had paid for such magic remained a secret, as did the fact that the spell didn't affect their bloodline.

As fascinating as it was that her shadows extended that protection to me, I couldn't trust them to guard me for much longer. But which way was I facing?

"Sorel," I called, hoping the beast hadn't darted off when I'd dismounted.

Thankfully, a soft nicker answered me over my left shoulder. I turned and walked toward him, following the sound of his footfalls as he backed away from the shadows that hid me. After a few tense minutes of wondering if my horse wasn't stupidly leading us in the wrong direction, the soft grass under my feet gave way to the crunch of gravel.

My shoulders slumped under my relief to be out of those woods, but there was still the trouble of escaping the queen's magic. I could have Sorel guide me all the way back to the castle, if necessary.

I let out a long sigh and muttered, "If only these shadows would clear out on their own."

I'd barely taken my next inhale when the darkness started to dissipate. Little by little I could see the outlines of trees and my horse, and I held my breath, as if it might cause the shadows to rush back into place. Now thin wisps of gray, they swirled around me as they disappeared into the queen's palms—one resting on her torso, the other dangling at her side. Assuming she had to have called the shadows back, I looked down, expecting to find her conscious, but her eyes remained closed, her face appearing almost peaceful with all trace of her earlier pained confusion now vanished.

I frowned down at her.

She hadn't recognized me.

While it weighed decidedly in my favor with respect to the tournament, for some reason it still stung—if only a bit.

Sorel nudged my shoulder with his muzzle, snorting at me.

"Right, right," I said. Unfortunately, there was no way to mount my horse while holding the queen, and tossing her unconscious body across the saddle, while effective, seemed less than ideal for my first impression at this tournament. With no better options, I trudged down the long driveway toward the castle.

Why they called it a castle was beyond me. It was more like the Emeryn Palace than the utilitarian castles once used long before my time, though I'd heard the humans had chosen to build the more historical, practical strongholds for their kingdoms in the south. Even so, the Arenysen Castle differed greatly from the palace where I served the Durands. Where their home was warm and inviting—and somehow remained so, even after the death of the queen—the castle I approached now was not.

The dark gray stone of the building loomed cold and ominous. Despite being in the dead of autumn, when the leaves should have been changing to deep oranges and reds, everything surrounding the castle was lush and green, as if the land here was as enchanted as the forest that surrounded it, caught in a perpetual summer. Vacant, depressing windows peeked out from behind a shroud of deep green—nearly black—ivy that reached up from the ground like massive hands seeking to drag the home into the bowels of the earth. I shuddered, reminded of the forest's vines inching toward me. Would they have sought to swallow me whole, like this web of foliage seemed to be doing to the castle?

Even the bright sunlight streaming down onto the castle couldn't seem to penetrate the gloom that surrounded it, like the castle itself consumed all light and life that came near it.

Well, that's a little melodramatic. I'm starting to sound as opti-mistic as Connor.

I laughed softly at myself. It was just a building, nothing more.

And yet.

I glanced back down at the sleeping queen in my arms, remembering how her eyes had darkened when her shadows had flowed from her palms. The castle itself may have been harmless, but that didn't mean the queen was. As serene as she seemed now, she may have killed my king's son, and I could not afford to forget that.

&

We were nearly to the front stairs when the grand doors to the castle opened and a serious-looking female stormed out toward us. I'd never met General Isa Marlowe face-to-face, but it wasn't difficult to recognize her. Even behind the deep concern on her face, she exuded pure confidence. The raised chin, crisp gait, and commanding gleam in her eye all testified to her authority.

She barely looked at me as she approached, keeping her attention firmly on the queen.

"What happened?" she asked, not accusingly. She glanced briefly up at me before she lifted a hand to brush a strand of hair from the queen's forehead.

"I was riding up the road when Her Majesty rounded the front of the castle. She noticed me and bolted into the forest," I explained, pausing to chuckle lightly. "Can't say it bolstered my confidence for this tournament."

Isa didn't seem at all perturbed by any of this, her expression softening as she asked, "How did she come to be in this state? As you're here to compete for her hand, I assume you didn't do this."

"I wish I could claim some heroics, but alas, I simply followed her into the forest to make sure she was okay. Turned out her horse had spooked and thrown her. She didn't appear hurt, but as we were parting ways, something...changed."

"What do you mean changed?"

"It was like she remembered something, like she saw something that frightened her? And then..." I hesitated.

"Then what?" the general prodded gently.

"Her shadows appeared, and she collapsed."

The general stiffened but recovered quickly and extended her arms toward me. "Let me take her."

"Of course," I said, handing the queen off like she was a sack of flour instead of a murder suspect.

Before Isa turned back for the castle, she tossed her chin toward the right. "The stables are around that way, and one of the grooms will tend to your horse so you can join us in the Great Hall. Registration will begin within the hour."

CHAPTER 21

MATTHIAS

Back in Emeryn I was used to keeping to the background, staying behind the royal family, always quietly observant. I only stood out and spoke up when needed, but this tournament demanded a different approach.

What that approach exactly was, though, I hadn't yet decided. Whatever strategy I devised depended greatly on my competition, all eleven of whom stood scattered about the large room I now entered.

A trio of males—one notably larger and more confident than his companions—gathered near one of the windows, giving me little more than a cursory glance as I walked in. While I didn't recognize the obvious leader or the scrawny male beside him, I instantly identified the third—a dark-haired male of average height—as Korben from Linley. He was a close friend of the late Griffin Ford, the fae noble who had inadvertently brought Connor and Lieke together by attacking the woman—multiple times—and dying at her hand.

In the middle of the large space, five other males of varying statures halted their conversation to gawk at me, or rather to glare straight down their noses at me. By their air of superiority and the silver ivy design embroidered at the hem of their sleeves, I surmised they were all from Arenysen, and likely felt that garnered them some favor in these games. Knowing their general, though, I doubted that to be the case.

The remaining three contenders stood alone, speaking to no one and watching everyone, including me. In the corner with slick-backed hair and an equally oily grin was Seb, former mayor of Engle, looking as self-important as the Arenysen males. Against the wall by the window nearest to me leaned a member of the Holsham garrison, Oryn Lain, his blond hair and downturned blue eyes giving him a youthful, but sad, appearance. While he had completed his initial training under me—as all garrison members did—I didn't know him too well. The last, a lanky male with graying dark brown hair and a suspicious look in his eyes, was situated near the dais where two thrones sat empty, a solemn reminder of why I was here. He had his arms crossed smugly in front of him, as if he had already claimed the throne and needed to guard it from the rest of us.

The invitation to these games had made it clear this competition would not be like the frivolous "beauty" contests of old, but the challenges we would face had not been disclosed. Regardless, alliances could make or break my chances at succeeding—or at least remaining long enough to learn more about the queen. The already formed groups would be nearly impossible to weasel my way into, which left the three loners. I could choose one as a partner or attempt to bring them together. It was too soon to determine which would be the best move, so I resorted to approaching the one nearest me—Oryn.

The male stiffened as I approached, lifting himself off the wall. His eyes widened, his throat bobbing as he swallowed hard, but he held my gaze as he spoke in an even tone. "If I knew I'd be competing against you, I would have stayed home." He extended a hand toward me. "Oryn Lain, from Holsham. I trained under you years ago."

Shaking his offered hand, I offered him an easy smile. "I remember. Call me Matthias."

Oryn's brows shot toward his hairline, and I half-expected his mouth to fall open. "Of course, s—I mean—Matthias." He uttered my name like he wasn't sure I truly wanted him to use it.

I cast a look around the room. "Weren't there to be thirteen of us?"

"Last never showed," he answered with a shrug. "One less to beat."

"Indeed."

"At least you made it in time."

He looked at me expectantly, as if I owed him some explanation for my late arrival. I didn't offer one. "Do you know any of these guys?"

"I only knew Seb and Rhett"—he gestured toward the big fae standing with Korben by the window—"before arriving. Not well, though they're both from Emeryn. I've gotten acquainted with the others over the last few days."

I swore under my breath. I had arrived later than I thought.

Oryn laughed dryly. "At least you weren't late like number thirteen."

"Have you all met our potential bride yet?" I asked, wondering how much of a disadvantage my delay had earned me.

"Not formally, no. That general of hers is mitigating risks, it seems."

I lifted a brow at him. "What kind of risks exactly?"

He smirked around a scoff. "Maybe they worry one of us has come to kill her."

"What?" I asked sharply and pulled my mouth into a grimacing frown. "Why would they suspect that?"

Another laugh answered me before he added, "Stars if I know." He paused to study me for a brief moment before aiming a finger hesitantly at my chest. "Wait, didn't you meet her on your way in?"

I nodded, still frowning.

He leaned in closer and lowered his voice. "What was she like? Is she as intimidating as she seems?"

I became acutely aware of the others' silent stares as they all awaited my response. Oryn hadn't been as discreet as he'd intended, it seemed. Rubbing my jaw, I weighed my possible answers. I could make her sound terrifying to scare the weak-hearted, but I didn't want to lie about her—at least not when I had other options. There was always the brush-off tactic of down-playing the power she wielded and the confidence she—mostly—displayed, even after having her ass dropped into the dirt and leaves. This would perhaps help boost my own image, but acting as if her reputation was unwarranted seemed wrong too.

That left me with the truth—most of it, anyway.

"I wouldn't say intimidating, but she certainly embodies her royal title," I finally said.

"Is it true you carried her to the castle though?" This question came from behind me, and I turned to see the shorter male had moved away from Rhett and Korben toward me.

"And you are?" I asked politely.

"Beck Dixon," he chirped, and then rushed to add more. "From Shoerda."

Nodding, I answered his earlier question. "I did, yes."

"Why?" another male asked, one of the Arenysen five.

I didn't bother to ask his name before answering. "It was the right thing to do."

A bark of a laugh came from the window. Korben's stare intensified. He shoved his hands into his pockets and lifted his chin. "Right or not, what happened to warrant such an act?"

Whispers filled the room as the others insisted on knowing the answer to that too.

I recounted the situation just as I had to the general, and when I finished, some of the males shrugged and turned away. I guess my story wasn't as deliciously scandalous as they had hoped.

"You're lucky," one of the Arenysen five said, shaking his head of blond curls, his baby blue eyes wide.

"What do you mean?" I asked, though I had a decent guess.

One of his companions—a tall, slim male with a hooked nose

like a hawk—spoke first. "You know what her shadows are capable of, right?"

Slowly, I nodded, looking around the room at the males who still studied me. "So?" I asked, but even as I uttered the word, that damned image snapped into my head of Gabriel being cut down on that old battlefield by a different Shadow Keeper's magic.

Silence answered my question, and I angled my head quizzically at the gathered males. "If you're all so afraid of her shadows, why enter this tournament?"

I certainly didn't expect honest responses from them all—stars, I couldn't give a truthful reason myself—but I wasn't prepared for what each male said.

The five from Arenysen shared a quick glance before answering in unison, "The Assembly made us."

Seb and Rhett, on the other hand, both viewed this as an opportunity they couldn't pass up, while Beck entered to save his family who struggled to make enough to live on. Winning the Arenysen crown would keep them fed for the rest of their lives.

Oryn merely shrugged, as if he'd entered out of boredom.

Korben snorted out a laugh—he seemed to do that a lot—before sharing how he'd been selected by his hometown as punishment for all the trouble he'd caused. Something in the back of my mind clicked as I recalled the mayor of Linley requesting royal aid to keep some uncouth rascal from pursuing his daughter.

Only one male remained unmoved from his original spot by the dais, silently staring at the rest of us as if we were muck he had just wiped from his boot. He seemed less a warrior than even the small-framed Beck, and from the paleness of his skin, I imagined he rarely stepped foot outside. I couldn't fathom how he expected to fare well in the upcoming trials; though again, I had no idea what they had in store for us. The hint of cockiness in this male's slight smile piqued my curiosity. He was obviously from Arenysen, as he too had silver ivy leaves adorning his sleeves, and he was quite comfortable assuming a position so close to the royal thrones. Whoever he was, he acted as though he held an advantage over the rest of us.

I lifted my chin as I eyed him. "And what of you? What's your name? Where are you from?"

The male blinked slowly like my questions exhausted him, but his dark, steely eyes remained fixed on me. His suspicion was almost palpable, but when he finally spoke, his voice was cordial, sweet even.

I didn't like it.

"Graham Harrison, advisor to the royal family of Arenysen."

Seb angled himself around Rhett and asked, "So are you here as an advisor or—" He stopped short when Graham shook his head.

"No, I will be competing, same as you," he answered, his lips curling up into a half-yet-genuine-enough smile.

"How is that fair?" Korben asked bitterly. Several around me nodded along as they watched Graham.

But it wasn't Graham who answered. Instead a confident voice—light yet commanding—pulled our attention to the door behind me where General Isa now stood, her hand resting lightly on her sword's pommel.

"I assure you all that Mr. Harrison will be receiving no preferential treatment in these games." She paused to land her stern glare on the advisor-turned-suitor, as if she were silently scolding him. "As you may have noticed, our thirteenth entrant has not arrived by the deadline, leaving us with you dozen. If there are no further questions, we are ready to complete the official registration. Follow me."

Korben moved first and the others all fell into line behind him. Graham and I brought up the rear, and I gestured graciously for him to go ahead of me, but he stopped short and angled his head.

"I don't trust you," he said quietly, his tone uncomfortably casual for his words.

I shrugged. "It would be odd if you did."

He dropped a heavy hand to my shoulder, and I frowned down at it.

When I glanced back at him, he hissed through his sneer, "I don't know what game you're playing at—"

I blinked in confusion and pulled my lips lower. "This is the tournament for the queen's hand, is it not? Would be so embarrassing if I showed up to the wrong games."

He scoffed. "That tongue of yours will get you in trouble." Before I could offer another witty retort, he pivoted on his heel and darted off after the others.

CHAPTER 22

MATTHIAS

General Isa led us into a smaller, windowless chamber on the other side of the castle's foyer, lit only by a handful of oil lamps on the walls and one on a desk at the far end. The general stood behind the desk, her hands resting on the back of a massive armchair as she watched us all file in. Once I clicked the door shut behind me, she cleared her throat.

"While the games have not officially begun, you might consider this your first trial. A pre-trial, perhaps, for all must complete today's task in order to compete. Those who cannot—for whatever reason—will be escorted promptly off the premises by one of the royal guards, and taken back to their homes. Yes, the guard will accompany you the entire way. This is to ensure not only your safety, but also the sanctity of what you have witnessed here thus far. It is imperative that this entire process remain confidential. You will not speak of it with others, not even once the tournament concludes."

From my position at the back by the door, I studied my competition, watching to see how each reacted to the general's rules. Seb, Korben, Oryn, and most of the Arenysen males stood confidently, seemingly unperturbed, while Beck, Rhett, and Graham seemed agitated. I expected as much from Beck, who seemed intent on snapping off some of his fingers with how hard he was wringing them. Rhett, despite his cocky demeanor in the other room, now danced on his feet as though he were standing on hot coals and might bolt at any moment. Unlike them, though, Graham didn't seem nervous so much as antsy to get moving, his heel tapping rapidly against the floor while his fingers drummed against his arms crossed tightly in front of him.

Stepping to the side of the chair, Isa studied each of us in turn as she continued to explain.

"These are volatile times, as you know, so per the direction of the Assembly—and with the approval of Her Majesty—each competitor must swear a blood oath." At this a couple of the Arenysens looked nervously at each other, but it was Korben who stepped forward and lifted his chin, a silent request to speak.

Isa gestured for him to proceed.

"Are we expected to basically confess our marriage vows preemptively then? And is this a lifelong oath or—"

I rolled my eyes. No doubt the general was planning to answer these questions regardless. The corner of the general's eye twitched, yet her response came out gracious as ever.

"I understand any qualms and concerns you might have, but no, these are not the standard marriage vows, nor do we possess the power to force you to keep this oath for your entire life. In order to compete, you must pledge fealty to the queen and promise to serve all of Arenysen beside her should you be crowned the champion of this tournament. For those who survive but do not win, this oath will be deemed void at that time. You are, of course, expected to honor and respect the outcome of these games."

"Did you say *survive*?" Beck asked, his voice cracking.

Isa nodded solemnly. "Indeed, I did. These are not the games of old with menial tasks and superficial contests. You will be tested, challenged, pushed to your limits, and yes, some of you may lose more than just your pride."

Well, that answers Lieke's question about danger.

"Why wasn't the danger noted in the invitation?" Korben asked.

"Did you truly think we would choose our next king based on how well he could prance around in a suit of armor?" She paused to glance around the room. "Should any of you not be willing to risk your life for this kingdom and its throne, now is your time to bow out."

No one moved, though a handful of the males shifted their weight nervously.

"What is to hold us to this vow? Some sort of magic?" Seb asked as he stretched his neck out to peer around Korben's bulky frame.

Isa chuckled softly and shook her head. "No. No magic or anything like that. Simply tradition, honor, and the consequence of death should you break it."

"Oh," someone muttered, though I couldn't determine who.

Smiling kindly, she produced a small vial and held it up for all to see. "This oath is not one-sided though. A drop of the queen's blood will be combined with a drop of yours to seal this oath for both parties. You vow to compete honorably and swear your unfailing loyalty to her, and she vows to accept you as a competitor and swear her own unfailing loyalty to the victor."

"How does she do that when she's not here? How do we know that's her blood, and not a muskrat's or something?" This time it was Oryn who asked, but most of the other males nodded along with his questions.

"You will simply have to go on faith and trust my word as General of the Arenysen army that she provided this blood for this purpose and granted me the right to vow by proxy." Isa's expression had been almost sweet this entire time, but now it darkened in challenge. "If you cannot accept or believe this, you are free to leave. Now."

With that final word she swept her arm out in the direction of the door.

Silence, tense and suffocating, filled the room, as we all waited to see who—if anyone—would accept this offer to leave. Beck fidgeted in place, looking at the exit and then back to Isa. Everyone seemed to hold their breath until he moved.

But he didn't leave.

He pushed past the other males, heading straight for the desk, where he stopped directly in front of the general.

"I'll be first," Beck said.

"Very well, Mr. Dixon," Isa said in her easy manner, but she didn't move to do anything except stare at him.

"What do you need me to do?"

Isa pursed her lips and cocked her head to the side as she surveyed him for an uncomfortably long moment. She hummed as she thought, of what I couldn't fathom. What was she waiting for? Why was she hesitating?

"There is one more thing I forgot to mention, and it will most definitely affect you, Mr. Dixon." The wait for her explanation was agonizing, but the tension didn't dissipate when she finally spoke. "Your oath includes an agreement—a promise—that you will not use any magic, including any powers beyond those all our kind possess."

"Wh—what—powers?" Beck stammered out, shrinking slightly away from the desk.

The general's eyes darkened further as she pressed her fingertips into the desk and leaned closer to the male before her. "We do not take kindly to cheats, Mr. Dixon, and to liars even less so." She straightened back up and announced to the rest of us: "It is fruitless to try to hide. I, myself, was born with the gift of sensing power—whether it runs in someone's veins or is wielded from outside of them. All will be granted the opportunity to demonstrate said abilities without fear of dismissal before swearing the oath, but failure to disclose now will be considered a breaking of the oath, and as such, consequences will follow."

Her attention returned to Beck, whose back stiffened. He shook his head jerkily. "Does it have to be demonstrated? Is the promise alone not sufficient?"

"If you are too ashamed to share what you can do, then I would strongly encourage you reconsider continuing on. The Arenysen throne has no place for cowardice," Isa explained, flatly.

"Just show us what you can do, Beck," someone said, and more encouragement poured from those assembled.

Beck sighed heavily before he held his right hand out to his side and opened his palm. At first nothing happened. Everyone inched forward, necks craned to see around each other. Then there, something emerged from the middle of his palm, uncurling as it rose toward the ceiling. In the dim light, it was hard to tell what it was until leaves began to sprout from it. The plant reached a height of half a meter when it finally stopped stretching, and I almost laughed when a few of the males gasped as the tip opened to reveal a bright purple bloom.

With his other hand, Beck plucked the flower and offered it to the general who took it, her lips pulling back into a thin smile as she laid it gently onto the desktop.

"Thank you," she said. "Now for the blood."

It took nearly an hour to process every entrant. As expected—given the rarity of fae being born with extra abilities—most swore the blood oath without any additional performances or promises necessary. Only two others, both from Arenysen, were instructed to demonstrate their power.

Fox, a wiry-framed male with a pointed nose and untidy hair the color of mud, had the ability to move far faster than any fae I had met—or any other creature, for that matter. One minute he was standing before the desk, the next he was casually leaning against the back of Isa's chair.

Phillip, who embodied the definition of plain, at least had a skill to counter his otherwise ordinary appearance. At first, he simply stood there, staring at Isa, and I wondered if perhaps he had a power we couldn't observe—like telepathy or empathic manipulation—but out of nowhere a whirlwind tore through the room sounding like a roaring dragon in my ears. It circled around us, sending hair and clothes waving and swaying erratically, and nearly knocking over a couple of the smaller males.

"Thank you, Mr. Cannon," Isa said, and immediately the wind ceased. "Is it only the air you can control?"

When Phillip nodded once, Isa beckoned him forward to perform the oath, leaving Graham and me as the last remaining.

Graham tried to decline my invitation for him to go ahead of me, but General Isa called for him. He sneered, but checked it quickly before Isa could reprimand him, and approached the desk with me close behind. It didn't take him long to deposit his drop of blood onto the paper the general held out for him, repeating the same words the others had. From the vial, a drop of the queen's blood fell to the paper beside his as Isa recited the queen's vow.

The general placed the paper into the flame of the lamp, and the former advisor stepped aside.

"And last but not least," Isa started, lifting her eyes to meet mine. "I apologize I do not know your name, as you arrived so late."

"Apologies for that, general. I am Matthias. Matthias—"

"Orelian?" Isa's brow lifted slightly, a brief sign of surprise as she noted my last name.

"The same," I said, bowing my head toward her. Behind me someone scoffed. Probably Graham.

"You are the representative from Engle?"

"I am."

"I wasn't aware you were from there," she said as she bent over her paper to jot something down.

"I'm not." Her head snapped up, eyes wide in question. I quickly explained. "I'm originally from Holsham. Unfortunately, no one from Engle wanted to compete, and rather than force someone to do so against their will, I agreed to go in their stead."

"Won't the royal family miss you at the palace though?"

"I do nothing without my king's blessing, general," I said simply.

She studied me for several breaths. My stomach knotted and icy dread crept up my spine, though I took care to keep my expression relaxed. Oryn's mention of mitigating risks flashed to mind. Would she suspect me as an assassin, sent to avenge Brennan's death? Would she deny me entrance to the competition? If that happened, I would need to find another way to learn the truth, but there was no point in worrying about that until I had to.

The general propped her elbows on the desk and rested her chin on her interlaced fingers.

"And your king is willing to lose his best warrior. Why?"

I shrugged as I donned a nonchalant frown. "His Majesty thinks I work too much." One of the other competitors let out a dry huff of a laugh. "He thinks I need to find love."

General Isa tilted her head and eyed me curiously. "And do you agree? That you need to find love?"

Scratching at the scruff along my jaw, I pushed back the memories of my talk with the king.

"Why does it matter?" I asked. "I don't recall you asking the others about their reasons."

"With all due respect, General Orelian, the others don't hold such close ties to the dead king you are vying to replace."

"Fair," I said, chuckling lightly. "In that case, no, I don't agree that I *need* to find love. I am quite content with my life as it is; however, I am open to new adventures, and falling in love is one I've yet to tackle."

"And you are ready to denounce your loyalty to the Durand family should you win?"

"I would have walked out already if I wasn't," I said, holding her firm gaze.

Again, her dark eyes searched mine as if she would find the truth there. I forced myself to breathe through the long silence, refusing to let her see my slowly fraying nerves.

"Very well, then," she said finally. She held out her open hand,

and without hesitation I placed my hand, face up, in hers. In her other hand she held a simple dagger and brought its sharp tip to hover over my palm. "When you're ready," she prompted, and I repeated the words the others had recited earlier.

"Today I, Matthias Orelian, vow to compete honorably for the hand of Calla Vael, queen of Arenysen. Should I prevail in these trials, I pledge my undying loyalty to the queen and all of Arenysen, foregoing allegiances to all others. I understand and acknowledge that this vow and my duty here remains until a victor is named or my heart ceases to beat, whichever may come first."

As I spoke, Isa pushed the blade's sharp edge into my hand and sliced it across my calloused palm.

Squeezing my hand closed, I held it over the paper Isa now held out between us. Crimson blood seeped from my fist. I watched the thick drops fall onto the paper as I finished the oath: "With my blood, I bind myself to this tournament, to compete and to serve."

Isa followed suit, letting two dark beads of blood fall from the vial as she recited the queen's oath. "With her blood, Her Majesty, Calla Vael, Queen of Arenysen, binds herself to this tournament, to accept your entry and to be loyal to the victor."

With the vows completed, Isa took the paper—as she had eleven times already—and eased it into the flame.

CHAPTER 23

CALLA

My shadows clung to me so tightly I could almost imagine being cradled by strong arms rather than collapsed on the enchanted forest's leafy floor. The comforting scent of the woods filled the fresh cracks in my resolve, but there was something more wafting on the air, penetrating my magic's dark void.

Warm brandy.

Oiled leather.

Sweet hay and apples that reminded me of horses.

Immediately those stars-damned hazel eyes appeared in my mind's eye.

Unlike Brennan's, which had been a dull brownish-green like the color of the forest on a cloudy day, these were bright with orange and gold swirling in a pool of deep green. Even in the dim light of my family's forest, his eyes had shone with an irritating optimism—a carefree mirth I couldn't help but envy.

Without warning, a forest rushed into focus, but it wasn't the enchanted trees and vines of my home that surrounded me.

The wet, earthy scent of mud flooded my senses, and I looked up to find feathery boughs lined with lanterns. Faint, familiar voices echoed somewhere in the distance. Something warm slipped into my hand, and I didn't need to look to know whose hand grasped mine, the contours of his hand and the squeeze of his fingers around mine pulling me back to memories I had tried to lock away.

Tears crowded my eyes, but I could not shut them no matter how hard I tried, as if the very stars demanded I remember this moment. Air refused to fill my lungs. My heart rattled behind my sternum. And then a finger guided my chin around, forcing me to face the male I'd loved and lost.

But Brennan wasn't there.

My hand turned cold, empty.

My chest caved, as if my heart itself were collapsing.

My body became heavy, weighed down by the intense loneliness of grief.

I wasn't alone, though.

Before me stood my friends, Lieke and Connor, their hands clasped between them as they peered lovingly at each other.

Don't make me witness this!

I can't bear to see their bliss when my own has ended!

My mind refused to listen to my cries, denied me the solace I sought.

Someone stepped into view, and I stopped short.

The male from the forest today.

My mouth went dry. My fingers began to tremble. My battered and broken heart climbed into my throat.

Of course. This is where I had seen him before—Lieke and Connor's wedding.

It had been an intimate affair with only close friends and family in attendance. So he knew the Durands intimately. My mind throbbed as I scrambled aimlessly for any details of that day that might help. The memory became clearer, the dark fog along the edge of my vision clearing, as I watched the male drop a hand onto the prince's shoulder. He pulled the bride into a one-armed embrace. They were close. They were good friends.

He turned to face me, the floating lantern light deepening the orange in his eyes, and then I caught his name on the prince's lips.

Matthias.

General Matthias.

My eyes flashed open.

My shadows were gone.

The comforting scent and soothing warmth vanished with them.

It took me a moment to recognize the rich wood beams of the ceiling above my bed. Sweat pooled under my legs, hot and restless. Thrusting the coverlet off, I leaped up. My vision blurred, spots and stars dancing in front of me as my head reacted to the sudden change in position, but I ignored it and stomped across my room and out into the hallway.

I needed to find Isa, tell her who this competitor was, warn her that he couldn't be allowed into the games.

Wait. I froze mid-step on the stairs.

How had I ended up back in my bed?

Had he carried me home?

He couldn't have. He wouldn't have.

Even as I wished that to be the case, I knew—somehow I knew—he never would have been able to leave me there, deadly forest or no.

I groaned softly to myself and pressed my fingertips to my temple. This would make it more difficult to disqualify him. I would be seen as ungrateful, unkind. I'd already been seen as worse, though. If tarnishing my reputation further could protect me from this male and the past life I wanted to forget, then so be it. I would endure the sideways glances and whispered rumors.

Isa would understand.

She would help me, as she always did.

Flying down the stairs—as fast as I could without falling—I rushed toward the courtyard, carried forward by sheer hope I would catch her before the registration and oaths. I stepped out into the square courtyard, welcoming the biting cold of the stone walkway against the soles of my feet. The door across the space opened, and Isa appeared, her face lighting up at the sight of me.

"Your Majesty," she said around a gentle smile. "How are you feeling?"

Males streamed out of the room behind her, and my stomach tightened at the thought of seeing Matthias again.

"He can't compete." The words rushed from my lips before I could stop them, louder than I intended.

Isa's brows lifted slightly, but otherwise she showed no surprise at my words. Her calmness—normally welcome and appreciated—now grated on me as she responded. "He can, and he will."

I stalked forward until I was nearly in her face and lowered my voice. "Do you even know who I mean?"

"It doesn't matter who you mean. All have been registered. All have taken their oaths."

"Undo it," I hissed.

Sympathy filled my friend's eyes. "You know I can't."

"Why would you let him enter?"

At this Isa glanced over her shoulder and lifted her chin, addressing the males standing awkwardly nearby. "Please return to your rooms. Dinner will be served at sunset."

Everyone started to move, and I fisted my hands. "No!" I barked, and they all halted in place, their apprehensive gazes locked on Isa and me.

She reached for my elbow, but I yanked it away from her. "He is close to..."

I couldn't say their names. All of this healing I'd thought I'd done, and I couldn't even utter his family name.

Isa lighted a touch on my forearm and said, softly, "I know, Calla."

Her words punched hard, sending me backwards half a step as if she'd actually hit me. "What? You knew and you still—"

"I had to." I opened my mouth to protest, but she raised a hand between us, stopping me from speaking. Leaning in close, her breath warmed my ear as she explained. "Perception is everything, especially right now. If we were to allow the other males of Emeryn but bar the general, simply because of his connections to the royal family, that would bolster the rumors that you are behind Brennan's death. By letting him compete—as painful as it is—you strengthen your claim of innocence by showing there is no ill will between your families and no fear of retaliation."

I stiffened at that last word, the blood in my veins chilling.

Could the Durands actually believe the absurd rumors? Would they truly seek to avenge Brennan's death?

I was family. *We* were family. Surely they knew I would never do such a thing.

Clasping my trembling hands in front of me, I fought to maintain some semblance of composure, but it was a battle I was losing quickly. Admittedly I hadn't behaved well at the burial, but they couldn't actually see that as anything but intense grief.

Did they hate me?

Did they blame me?

The questions swirled around my mind like a brewing storm, but the more I pondered them, the more my fear and regret shifted into a bitter anger. I kept my hands clamped together now, not to steady their trembling, but to prevent myself from doing anything reckless and regrettable.

Isa eyed me carefully, quietly assessing me as she had done so many times since Brennan's death. Securing my hands in hers, she offered a reassuring smile.

"I am not saying that is what I suspect, Calla."

"But it's a possibility." My words came out a growled whisper, not from caution, but rage. Her chin lowered slightly in affirmation. If his family could believe—or even just entertain the idea—that I had a hand in killing my husband, did that mean... I glared suspiciously at my friend who still wrapped her hands protectively around mine.

She didn't flinch under my silent accusation, and she held my gaze steadily. "I know you did not do it," she whispered softly. "I know how much you loved him, and how much he loved you in return."

Fresh tears stung the edges of my eyes, and I pressed my lips together as hard as I could to still them.

Isa lifted a hand to my shoulder, gently consoling me with easy strokes of her thumb. "I do not believe they would turn on you so quickly, even in their time of grief, but it would be unwise to ignore the potential risk." She leaned closer, once more whispering into my ear. "Better to keep him close where we can watch him."

I winced at the reminder that the dozen males remained with us in the courtyard, all their eyes watching us—watching me. Peering around Isa, I studied them. Some appeared nervous, their attention darting jerkily around the space as if they didn't know where to look. Others looked amused, sneaking glances at each other with irritating smirks on their faces. Graham, his face twisted with concern, restlessly stood there as if fighting back the urge to run to my aid as he would have as advisor.

And then there was the last. Matthias.

I couldn't read his expression. He seemed disinterested—bored, even—and the only indication that his mind hadn't wandered off to some daydream was the confidence with which his eyes found mine. Here in the courtyard light, their hazel hues outshone the others, but there was none of the earlier humor and passion in them now. Had I imagined it back in the forest? My insides squirmed uncomfortably, and I wrenched my gaze away.

"I'd best get some more rest before the dinner tonight," I said to Isa, knowing full well that no amount of rest could prepare me for any of this. Before she could respond, I pivoted away from her and headed back to my room.

CHAPTER 24

MATTHIAS

As soon as the door closed behind the queen, I released an anxious breath. We all did, it seemed. Except for General Isa, whose calm demeanor might have been off-putting had it not been for her glowing reputation. She offered no apology for the queen's behavior, and honestly, I might have thought less of her if she had. Her quiet confidence as she addressed us once again displayed the fearsome loyalty she held toward the crown and the one who wore it.

"As I said, dinner will be served in the ballroom promptly at sundown. Please do not be late," she said, sliding her hard gaze at me as if I might have a habit of arriving at the last minute. But then she gestured me forward with a flick of her hand before waving over a stout-looking male dressed in a simple but elegant uniform. "Mr. Orelian, your valet will be happy to escort you to your suite. If you need anything, do let him know. Otherwise, I will see you all tonight."

I should have probably paid close attention to my whispering competition, to gauge their reactions to the queen's behavior, but my valet—who had an unexpectedly long gait for his slight stature—was already walking away without me.

I caught up with him as he exited into the front hallway.

"How was your journey, sir?" he asked with cold formality.

"Uneventful," I offered, following him toward the castle's main staircase and surveying the castle's interior as best I could without seeming suspicious.

His brow lowered over small, wary eyes, and I could have sworn he laughed—just once—though it could have been a cough.

"If you consider carrying our unconscious queen back to the castle uneventful," he said, his tone as icy as his sidelong gaze. It must have been a cough then; it was impossible to imagine this strange little male finding anything amusing.

Shrugging, I pursed my lips as we started up another flight. "Technically that was at the end of my journey."

"The end is still part of the journey, sir," he said and ushered me down a dimly lit corridor.

The oil lamps lining the walls all burned low, barely surviving on their last droplets of fuel and threatening to go out at any moment. Our footsteps echoed off the unadorned stone walls, and the further we traveled, the more my skin prickled with unease.

I forced as casual a laugh as I could muster. "I suppose you're right. By the way, what's your name? I'd hate to have to call you *valet* through this whole tournament."

"A confident fellow, aren't you," he said, more an observation than question.

Pulling the corners of my mouth down, I nodded a few times. "Usually, yes."

He harrumphed. "Giles, sir. Though don't bother to learn it. I doubt you'll last the week."

I started to say something more, but he stopped short at the end of the corridor and pivoted sharply on his heels. Had he not then swept his arm out in front of him, I might have missed the door tucked into the shadows. Reaching into his pocket, he brandished a small key on a black ribbon and held it out for me.

"Your room, sir," he said, tucking his chin toward his chest.

Slipping the key from his open palm, I slapped him on the back with just enough force to cause him to teeter slightly, but not so much that he actually stumbled. To his credit he kept his head bowed, though even in the darkness I could see his jaw tighten.

"Thank you, Giles. Sure you won't come in?"

"No."

I had to press my lips together to keep from laughing at the male's curtness, but part of me pitied the poor valet. How miserable life must be, to warrant such a cold and dry demeanor.

Giles finally lifted his chin when I unlocked the door and moved to step inside.

"You will find your wardrobe stocked with varied attire for the games. If you need anything altered, our tailor can help, though your late arrival gives you little time before tonight's event."

"I'm sure I'll manage," I said.

"Yes, yes. Such confidence." He dipped his chin in a single sharp nod before asking, "Would you like me to fetch you for dinner?"

"No, that won't be necessary. I can find my way."

"Very well, sir. Try not to be late."

Somehow my suite—which was quite a bit smaller than those back in the Emeryn palace—was just as cold and uninviting as the hallway, despite the fire blazing in the small hearth. Beside it sat a lavish four-poster bed of rich wood and luxurious linens—perhaps a bit too elegant for the otherwise modest room. At its foot my bag rested on top of a tufted leather bench. It was there I moved first, lifting the flap of the bag and pulling items out. Holding my breath, tension roiling through my shoulders, I searched the bottom of the pack until I found the hidden pocket and pulled out the bundle of cloth, but I didn't relax until I had verified the blade was still there.

Quickly, I moved around the bed. Lifting the quilts and linens out of the way, I pulled my personal knife from my belt and—with a swift glance at the door—sliced a gash into the mattress just big enough to hide the poisoned weapon. It wouldn't fit while bundled, unfortunately, so once I had it wedged inside, I folded the cloth—careful to avoid the part that had touched the blade—and tucked it back into my pack.

For the first time since I'd arrived, I could breathe easily.

Well, easier, at least.

I probably wouldn't truly relax until this ordeal was over and behind me.

Stretching out my shoulders and back, I straightened up and appraised the rest of my suite. Across from the door a single window, reaching nearly to the ceiling and framed with heavy green curtains, divided the wall in half with a gilded mirror on one side and a large clock on the other. I half-laughed, wondering if all the rooms had such time pieces, or if they had purposely placed that here just for me. Sucking in a deep breath, I slowly sighed and shook my head. It would take more than that to offend me, but still, I hadn't actually been late. Nearly, perhaps, but not truly.

Nearly won't cut it here, though.

Nearly is the difference between success and death.

Below the clock sat a modest desk complete with a small bottle of ink, pen, and paper—not that I would use those much, as Connor and I agreed it best not to risk corresponding. Opposite the fireplace, the wall had been cut back to create an alcove with a clawfoot tub placed in the center and an enclosed privy to one side. An ornate tapestry depicting the signing of the War of Hearts Treaty adorned the back wall of the bathing space, reaching from floor to ceiling and spanning most of the width.

A quick perusal of the garments inside the wardrobe beside the door revealed a variety of items from formal suits to riding gear to combat leathers. By some small miracle they all seemed close enough to my size, so I wouldn't need to bother the tailor. At least that allowed me the next few hours to rest before I needed to make my way downstairs to the ballroom, but first I needed to wash away the grime from traveling.

In my effort to not be the last one to dinner, I ended up arriving first to find the staff still buzzing about the massive ballroom, setting up for the meal. Several individuals flitted about the long buffet table that lay against one wall. Once a dozen or more covered silver platters had been crowded onto it, other staff needled their way up to squeeze ornately carved fruit and fresh flowers between each elegant dome. At one end of the table two others arranged an assortment of chocolate tortes, cream puffs, and various pastries I didn't recognize onto a silver and gold tower.

My stomach rumbled just as a young female passed by with a small stack of plates in her hands. She smiled sheepishly at me as she headed toward the table. At least she hadn't been carrying a platter of food, or I might have snatched up a bite. While Isa and the queen hadn't arrived yet, I couldn't be sure they weren't somehow monitoring my actions. With Her Majesty already wanting me gone, it would be foolish to risk her wrath for a small morsel to tide me over.

As if in protest, my stomach growled again.

I had gone longer without food in the past. I could do so again. Even with a feast taunting me.

Ignoring the hearty aroma that enveloped me and the sharp pang in my gut, I forced my attention to the peculiar layout of the room. Unlike most royal dinners I had attended where a table of honor was set apart, distanced from the guest tables and often raised on a dais of sorts, here a single round table—large enough to host double the number of competitors—had been prepared on one end of the space. The other remained empty and open, and my heart sank into my gut as a door opened in the far corner and four fae filed in, each carrying a stringed instrument.

As long as dancing wasn't one of the trials and didn't factor into our final scores, I'd be fine. It wasn't that I didn't know how to dance—my mother had insisted I learn when I was much younger, claiming the rhythm and control necessary on the dance floor would only aid my fighting abilities. But even if my sword skills were improved by twirling and swirling and dipping and prancing in time to some melody, I detested the practice. If I was going to work up a sweat with a female in my arms, I preferred to be much closer, with fewer clothes on, and without an audience.

The musicians noisily settled into their seats and began plucking at their strings, making small adjustments to the instruments. While not a melody in itself, the collective sound as they tuned whisked me back to a simpler time of seasonal parties at the Emeryn palace, where I wasn't expected to dance but could seek out entertainment of my own choosing, usually with one or two of the female guests.

Behind me someone groaned irritably, and I glanced over my shoulder to see Oryn entering.

"I thought this was merely dinner," he muttered, coming up beside me.

"Not a dancer?" I asked.

"Only when forced, which thankfully isn't often." He briefly scanned the room before leaning toward me. "I heard the entire Assembly is to attend tonight."

"That would explain the extra chairs around the table," I noted. "What role will they have in these games, do you know?"

"The others suspect they're here to observe only, but..."

"When have you ever known politicians to not meddle?"

Oryn chuckled quietly. "Exactly."

A hum of quiet voices began to buzz in the room. The others had arrived. All of them, in fact.

Or nearly all.

Nowhere in the throng of new arrivals could I find the queen's dark hair or her intense brown eyes. None of the other competitors greeted me as they swarmed in, though only one—Graham—went out of his way to scowl as he brushed past me. He was definitely one to keep an eye on, especially since he seemed to have singled me out, not giving any of our fellow contenders the same treatment.

"I see you've made a friend," a pinched voice said. It belonged to a rail-thin female whose nose was as narrow as her hips—and likely her mind, too, by the disdain simmering in her gray eyes. She extended a delicate hand, which looked like it might disintegrate if I wasn't careful. Accepting it, I barely squeezed as she offered her name.

"I'm Ursula."

"Matthias," I said in turn.

"Ah, the famed general from Emeryn who saved our beloved queen from the forest," she said, lifting her sharp chin even higher. I bit down on the inside of my lip to keep from scoffing at her claim. She had all but hissed the word *beloved*, making it plain she held Calla in as much esteem as Graham held me. Yet it was her mention of the queen's rescue that gave me pause. Either the Assembly member did not know of the forest's protection of the royal bloodline, or she was baiting me into revealing what I knew about those enchanted woods.

Meddling politicians, indeed.

Shrugging, I swiveled my attention to a server passing by and plucked two long-stemmed glasses from their tray. The Assembly member accepted the drink I proffered, and tipped it slightly toward me in a silent salute before taking a shallow sip. I might have downed mine in one gulp had the female not been staring at me so hawkishly, but instead I simply held it in my hand, swirling it so it caught and reflected the light from the hundreds of candles hovering above in the chandelier.

"So, is the Assembly making any wagers?" I asked, casually, and finally lifted the glass to my lips as I awaited her response.

I half-expected her to balk at the insinuation, but instead the female laughed, or more accurately, cackled.

"Why do you ask, general?" she asked, her lip curling into a sinister smile.

"Just making conversation," I said.

"Of course," she breathed, and then, dipping her chin, she tapped her not-yet-empty glass against mine. "Do excuse me, general, I have other competitors to meet. Good luck in the games. And don't worry about Graham. The boy is merely jealous."

I watched Ursula retreat, mulling over that bit of information briefly before tucking it into the back of my mind for future use. Free from her scrutiny, I lifted my glass to my lips again and started to tip my head back to finish off the remaining wine, when a door at the far end of the room opened.

The queen—dressed in a blood-red gown that accentuated her soft curves and paid homage to her deadly reputation—stepped into the room and froze. Her eyes found mine at once, her disapproval undeniable from where I stood, and for the briefest of moments, for the first time in ages, my confidence wavered.

CHAPTER 25

CALLA

Of the dozens of faces staring at me, why was his the one to catch my attention first? My heart—its bruised, broken pieces held together by sheer will alone—plummeted. With each step into the ballroom, I felt myself trampling it, stomping on it, bruising it and battering it further.

All the while, I held Matthias's stare, refusing to be the first to look away and reveal my discomfort—to him, and to everyone gathered. Drawing in a long, steadying breath, I forced my features to relax and pushed the tension down into my chest where it was easier to conceal, though more painful to bear.

Behind me, Isa followed with her gentle, reassuring hand resting on the middle of my back, grounding me.

"Are you okay?" she whispered, and I offered the tiniest of nods, her words helping to snap my attention away from the Emerynian general.

To my left, musicians were settled in their seats, their instruments resting in their laps. Slowing my gait, I shifted my chin over my shoulder, and Isa stepped up beside me.

"I thought this was just dinner. Who invited the musicians?" I asked.

"It was the Assembly's idea," Isa explained. "A last-minute suggestion from this morning."

"Who specifically?"

"Warren and Ursula," she said, and I had to purse my lips to keep from sneering. Had it been any other member, I might not have minded, but these two had been a thorn in my backside since my parents' deaths. Nothing they did was without an agenda. Nothing they did was innocent.

"You should have asked me," I said. In the corner, a few of the Assembly huddled together. One, Fern, lifted her glass toward me in greeting. I nodded slowly and tried to smile, sure I was not fooling anyone here.

"Apologies, Calla. Can I get you a glass of wine before we eat?"

"Not yet," I muttered and stopped abruptly. I was now in the middle of the open space, on display for a dozen would-be-kings and half as many politicians who didn't want me as their queen.

Lifting my chin, I counted my breath silently to myself to steady my nerves. My palms itched at my sides as my shadows stirred, and I had to fist the fabric of my dress to quiet them.

"Welcome, all of you," I said, well aware that my icy tone was at odds with my words not that anyone here expected warm hospitality from me, the shadow queen who killed her own people without warning. "General Marlowe will be briefing you all on the games, the rules, and the first trial, but first, let's eat."

Nobody moved.

Nobody even coughed.

Everyone simply stared at me as if I'd just been speaking in some foreign tongue, like there wasn't a feast waiting to be devoured.

I was about to open my mouth to say something—though I wasn't quite sure what exactly—when finally, someone shifted. Heavy, confident footsteps reverberated through the room and all heads turned toward the sound, continuing to swivel as they followed the individual's movements. I couldn't see who it was, nor was I about to crane my neck and stand on my toes to see over the others. Rather, I pivoted on my toe and made my own way toward the buffet table, set on enjoying my cook's food and ignoring my guests and their reason for being here. Focused solely on the stack of plates at the end of the table, I ignored the movement in my periphery despite the spark of curiosity that begged me to at least steal a peek at who had moved first.

We arrived at the table at the same time, but my resolve held fast, and I kept my attention firmly on the decadent spread my staff had prepared instead of worrying about the audience behind me or the male to my left. To his credit, he didn't try to make conversation as he followed my lead and began stacking food on his plate. My stomach grumbled, rumbling loudly through the quiet room. The male next to me chuckled, and the scent of wood and leather hit me, as if it rode his laughter.

Shit. Matthias. Of course.

Why weren't the musicians playing? Why be here if they weren't going to do their job?

As if they could hear my thoughts, the musicians immediately slipped into a soft, soothing melody that filled the awkward void, while remaining quiet enough to allow guests to converse. With my plate topped with a small portion of each dish—all my favorites, thanks to Isa—I made my way to the table and chose a seat at random.

"Let me get that for you," a friendly, familiar voice said. Graham was already gliding the chair out. Relief loosened the tension in my body, and my once-racing pulse eased a bit. He offered a sweet smile as he gestured for me to sit.

"Thank you, Graham," I said and added a quick command to "go eat" before I settled myself at the table.

Keeping my eyes down, fixed on my meal, I listened to the shuffle of feet as everyone finally followed suit and meandered toward the buffet.

Matthias, thankfully, did not come sit beside me, but instead selected a seat several chairs away.

So he doesn't have to look at you all night.

Not that I wanted to stare at him either, but some small, idiotic part of me was stung by this mild rejection.

Could I blame him, though? I had called for his disbarment. Even if he wanted to leave the games, he couldn't. Not while under the blood oath. He was here until someone won...or he died.

The meal was an altogether uncomfortable affair as the Assembly bombarded the contestants with questions, as if they had come here for a simple interview rather than a deadly competition. None of the males said much in answer, though, which brought a smirk to my lips that only deepened with each failed interrogation. Isa tried, on several occasions, to engage the Assembly in other conversation and give our guests a break, but she eventually gave up and resorted to speaking with me instead.

"This roast lamb may be Xavier's best yet," she said, plopping a tender piece into her mouth.

I nodded. "It's got nothing on his mashed potatoes, though. Have you tasted them?"

"I've already had two helpings," she admitted, and speared a piece of beetroot.

My staff hustled around the table, refilling wine goblets and replenishing water glasses, carrying away empty plates and bringing back second helpings upon request. As much as I wished to relax and simply chat about potatoes, my frayed nerves had me on edge, my shadows churning in my veins and tensing every muscle in my body. Keeping my head lowered, I stole a glance at each male who had sworn to compete for my hand. One of them would win. Some would likely die. I knew I should feel remorse over that fact, but no one had forced them to enter—unlike me, who would be forced to accept one of them. They had been warned of the risks, and still they had come. Whoever among them was to rule with me needed to prove himself, but I couldn't shake this sense of foreboding that had burrowed into my bones.

Twisting my neck around to hide my lips from the others, I whispered to Isa as quietly as I could. "Are we sure Asher will be here?"

Isa nodded discretely, lifting her glass as if to take a sip, but answering me quickly before doing so. "He arrived last night and is camping on the southeastern edge of the forest."

"And you're sure he—"

"Yes," she said, not bothering to lower her voice this time as she faced me. "He knows what to do. Now, can I fetch you some dessert? A tart or a macaron? Maybe a cream puff or two?"

I looked down at my plate and the meal that appeared barely touched. The unease in my stomach had sabotaged my enjoyment of the food, but I wouldn't turn down my chef's confections.

Once Isa rose from the table to raid the desserts, others opted to do the same, and the collective scraping of chairs against the stone floor nearly drowned out the quartet's music. I remained seated along with two Assembly members so deep in their quiet discussion they hadn't seemed to notice everyone had left. Awkwardly, I turned to watch the musicians, swaying lightly to their music so as to pretend I cared about or even heard what they were playing.

"No dessert for our shadow queen?"

I snapped my head around and winced as the sudden movement strained my neck. My eyes widened against my will at the sight of the male standing there.

Matthias.

His name on my thoughts drove my teeth together, and I tried to swallow, but my throat had closed up.

Why is he even here? Why did they send him?

He leaned forward and rested his forearms on the back of the chair beside mine, holding a small plate of pastries in his hands.

What is taking Isa so long?

I couldn't see her through Matthias, and I started to crane my neck to peer around him, but the strain I'd caused earlier whined in protest.

"Would you like one?" Matthias asked.

Shit, I had forgotten to answer his first question, though he didn't seem to notice or care either way. Glancing from his plate to his face and back, I shook my head reluctantly.

My voice came out uneven as I explained, "No, General Marlowe is fetching me some."

Matthias didn't fully stand as he twisted his neck to look at the buffet table. Turning back to me, he half-smiled.

"So she is," he said, but he didn't leave even when Isa marched past him to set my dessert in front of me.

She didn't stay, despite the irritated look I shot her, giving me a patronizing smile as she quietly warned me to "be nice."

"Which one is your favorite?" Matthias asked, and I looked up at him, thoroughly confused by his casual demeanor. Most of the other entrants could barely look at me, let alone find the nerve to talk to me, and Matthias had been the last I'd expected after my outburst earlier in the courtyard.

Plucking a chocolate macaron from his plate, he held it up as if studying its construction. "I'm rather fond of these, personally. I've never had them before. Are they unique to Arenysen?"

My confusion deepened.

I was basically ignoring the male, yet he didn't seem perturbed in the slightest, even carrying on with the conversation by himself.

"They're called macarons," I said, glad the angst had disappeared from my tone. "Our chef's recipe. The strawberry cream ones are even better than the chocolate." I watched as the general placed the whole confection in his mouth and ate it in one bite.

Swallowing, he licked his lips, and I tried not to let my gaze drift to his mouth.

"Would pair perfectly with a brandy," he said.

I stilled.

Brennan had always teased me for preferring the woody-sweet liquor—said it was a drink for bachelors and crotchety old warriors. Frustration built in my chest, growing into a low growl that I barely suppressed. If Matthias noticed my poor reaction, he hid it well.

I didn't want to get to know these males, and I certainly didn't want to have anything in common with them. This tournament and the resulting union were nothing more than a formal arrangement for the sole purpose of keeping the crown. This wasn't about affection; this was politics.

It's not like he's asking you to dance or offering you a glass of brandy, Calla.

He's just talking to you.

And that was precisely the problem.

I couldn't stay here and make small talk with him.

Or with anyone.

The music. The conversations. The lit chandeliers and the elaborate feast.

It was too much, too familiar.

"Excuse me," I said, pushing my chair back from the table and standing. I didn't know where I was going or what I was doing, but I spun around and forced my feet to carry me across the ballroom.

Each step, though, seemed to lead me back into my grief, deeper and deeper as I tried to retreat.

My breathing shallowed, my chest tightened, and the room spun out of focus.

This might not have been a lavish affair like that night, but it was the first time we had entertained any guests since...

I slammed my eyes closed against the damned memory, but the scene played out in my head regardless.

Brennan, collapsed on the balcony. Me, screaming for help. His final gasp, and his body going still.

Brennan had been an unexpected blessing. He had brought laughter and joy into my once lonely life, and he had steadied me after my parents' death. But who would help me now that he was gone? Isa tried to, but she had a kingdom to protect. She couldn't spend all of her time soothing my pain. And the thought of having a new husband—one of these males—attempt to fill the hole Brennan's death had left behind...

I can't.

You have to.

Or you lose the throne, your home.

My shadows licked at my palms, trailing to my fingertips as I ambled blindly through the room. I couldn't release my magic here, couldn't cause a scene and give the Assembly reason to act against me, but my magic was feeding off my panic, preparing to wrap me in a protective shield. I fisted my hands into the fabric of my dress, but it didn't help. Even through my foggy vision, I could see wisps of my dark magic dancing over the red chiffon.

No, they would see, they would talk, and I couldn't deal with any more rumors.

Clasping my hands together in front of me, I silently begged my magic to stop, as if it was an entity unto itself and not knit into my very being. Some part of me—some small, but terrified part of me—was calling my shadows out, and I didn't know how to stop it. I needed to breathe, to calm, to figure out some way to gain control.

Somewhere in the distance Isa called my name, calm and soothing even through the muddled haze of my panic. Music swelled around me, blocking out her voice as I spun around to find her. But someone else caught me. A hand pressed against my lower back, guiding me around. Their other hand cradled mine, and that sweet scent of leather and wood caressed my senses.

"Easy there, Killer. I've got you."

Matthias's voice, a thick whisper that warmed my ear, coaxed me out of the darkness, bringing the world back into focus. My shadows retreated into my palms—one wrapped in his, the other resting on his arm—and I closed my eyes, hating myself for allowing him to hold me, but more so for not wanting to let go.

CHAPTER 26

MATTHIAS

hat in the stars-damned fuck am I doing?

One moment I was having a conversation with the queen—or trying to—and the next I was dancing with her in front of the entire Assembly and all of my competition. What else was I to do though, when she had suddenly spooked for the second time today, that same look of horrified shock flashing in her eyes? At least this time I'd been able to catch her before her shadows could expand fully.

I was now all-too-aware of our audience as I guided Calla in slow circles around the ballroom to the musicians' romantic melody. She kept her face tucked close to my chin, and while she said nothing, her pulse slowed against my chest, her breaths deepening with each step. Letting everything in my periphery disappear, I tried to ignore the way her hair smelled of the sweet berries Mrs. Bishop used in her tarts and the violets my sister grew in her garden, but the scents summoned memories against my will. Instinctively I pulled her closer still, as if I needed to wrap myself in that comforting warmth of home.

No sooner had I done that, though, than Calla stiffened in my arms, effectively snapping me back to the present and to the task at hand.

It's just a game.
I'm just playing a role, doing my job.
Nothing more.

Stopping abruptly, I pulled away and released her. Our eyes met, and for a couple breaths I studied her expression that seemed an odd mix of shock and confusion and...was that guilt?

I'd seen that same look of self-loathing in Connor's face enough times to recognize it now in Calla. Not that this proved anything, of course. Grief was a bitch in that regard, causing us to carry responsibility whether it was warranted or not. Bowing slightly toward her, I lifted her hand to my lips and brushed a kiss across her knuckles. A hint of a gasp lifted her chest, and normally I would have smirked with pride for having such an effect on someone, but this was no ordinary female.

I caught her eye once more and offered a thin smile, which—as expected—she did not return.

"Thanks for the dance, Killer," I whispered before pivoting and passing a rather flustered Graham as I walked away.

The nickname had been a risk the first time I'd used it, but to utter it again...what the fuck was I thinking?

Running my hand across the back of my neck, I stalked over to the buffet table, grabbed two of those macaron things, and popped one in my mouth. I turned to head back to my seat, and ran straight into General Isa.

"Excuse—"

"Thank you," she said quietly, gesturing discreetly for me to follow her back to the desserts. Keeping her head low, she proceeded to place a few confections on a plate as she spoke. "You didn't have to do that."

"All due respect, general, yes, I did," I said, taking this opportunity to select another macaron.

She didn't argue, merely shrugged. "Either way, you'll have a target on your back now."

I laughed once. "As if I didn't already?"

"A larger one then," she said, not even a crack of a smile on her lips.

"Why are you warning me?" I asked, stealing a glance around the room and to where Graham now led Calla away to the far wall.

"Call it a courtesy from one general to another. But it's the only one you'll get."

Isa excused herself with a single nod and marched over to the musicians, who quickly ended their song and rested their instruments in their laps. Everyone in the room returned to their seats, except for Calla, who remained by the wall as if she could sink into the shadows and disappear. Moving to the middle of the open space, Isa clasped her hands behind her back and addressed the room.

"There will be more time to dance if anyone wishes to, but I do need to ensure you all know what to expect going forward in this tournament. Some of you have traveled a great distance to be here, and for that we are most grateful. This is not an easy time for our kingdom, especially for our queen. Losing a spouse is a hardship no one should have to bear. Having to replace them so quickly is...well..."

Her voice trailed off as she looked toward the queen for a full breath before returning her gaze to us.

"It is what it is, unfortunately. Her Majesty, Queen Vael, has tasked me with planning and overseeing the trials, of which there will be four, testing the qualities necessary for our future king: courage, strength, wisdom, and grace."

Around the table, each male exchanged looks, as if silently surmising what the trials might be.

"In each trial, contestants will earn points based on criteria set forth at the beginning of each. Quite simply, the male with the most points—who is still alive—at the end of trial four, will be crowned king."

The Assembly members nodded grimly along with Isa's every

word, some donning wicked smiles as if already imagining what bloody entertainment was to come.

Isa continued, shifting her weight and folding her hands in front of her now.

"Your first trial begins tomorrow at sunrise. We will convene outside the castle's entrance before dawn, at which time you will be given further instruction. I do recommend you try to enjoy yourselves tonight. Our staff will attend to you for as long as is needed, so feast and drink, dance and laugh. Tonight very well may be your last."

Isa bowed her head silently and strode over to the queen, whom she promptly whisked out of the room. As soon as the door closed behind them, the conversations started, excited and nervous voices all filling the ballroom and drowning out the tune the musicians had dived into at the general's exit.

"What do you think it is?" Oryn angled his head toward me as he asked.

I shrugged. "Assuming they're testing the qualities she listed in order—which they might not—we'll be facing the courage trial first."

Korben appeared behind Oryn, leaning forward on the table to look at me. "Think they'll just stick us in a room with Her Majesty and her shadows?"

I nearly laughed at how some of the males appeared genuinely afraid of that prospect. Not that I didn't think Calla was dangerous; she was a Shadow Keeper, after all. But knowing Isa's reputation for cunning, and having witnessed her impressive loyalty to her queen, I highly doubted she'd devise a trial so simple while having Calla directly involved.

Shaking my head, I weighed whether to voice my speculations or not. I could use them to my advantage—assuming my theory proved right—by being the only one prepared.

"Know something we don't, Matthias?" Rhett asked bitterly.

Before I could answer, others were chiming in with their own questions.

"Did the queen say something to you?"

"What did you learn from her?"

"What did her shadows feel like?"

That last one pulled a sharp bark of laughter from me, but I'd barely started to respond when Graham sniggered.

"He doesn't know anything, and Her Majesty certainly didn't say anything to him."

All heads—including the Assembly members'—swiveled in his direction and then back to me.

"Graham's right," I said. "Her Majesty didn't say anything—nothing of consequence anyway. I simply have my theories about the trial."

Silence fell among us, and I casually took a sip from my water glass. A half dozen or more heads leaned closer in anticipation of my next words. When I remained silent, one of the Arenysenians—Aric, perhaps, or maybe his name was Fritz, I couldn't be sure—scoffed loudly.

"He's as clueless as the rest of us."

I shrugged a single shoulder. "Perhaps. And I know nothing for certain, but if I was the betting type, I expect them to send us into the one place in Arenysen that all fear."

"The forest?" several of them asked in unison, but one of the Assembly members—a timid-looking female—looked apprehensively around at her colleagues.

"They wouldn't," she said, unconvinced of her own words. Her eyes landed on mine. "It's too dangerous."

So the Assembly didn't even know what the trials were.

I chuckled quietly to myself, holding the poor female's gaze.

"What's a deadly competition without a little danger?"

CHAPTER 27
CALLA

"What happened in there?" Isa hissed at me as soon as we were alone in the hallway.

I lifted my hands between us, palms toward the ceiling. Shaking my head, I stared down at them, surprised to find them steady.

"I don't know," I said. Isa didn't buy it.

"I think you do," she said, her glare stern but still somehow kind. "If we're going to get through this without a stars-damned incident, Calla, I need you to get a hold of it. The Assembly—"

"I know," I interrupted as irritation began to burn in my chest. "They're looking for any excuse to be rid of me."

Grabbing my hands in hers, Isa squeezed my fingers reassuringly, and her eyes softened. "Twice now you've lost control of them. And both times, it was around him. If he did something—"

"No," I blurted out. Isa's eyes widened as she jutted her chin forward, waiting for my explanation.

But only a string of curses rattled through my mind.

He called me Killer! What if he believes the rumors? Allowing him to stay is a risk.

Here was a chance to get him removed from the tournament and sent home, assuming that was the only punishment he'd face.

As much as I didn't want him here—as much as I worried about his motives, I didn't want him to be executed either.

Drawing in a deep breath, I slipped my hands from hers and fisted them at my sides as if I could harness my magic's power that way and find the courage to explain this.

She's your best friend.

You can tell her.

"He reminds me of..." I started, but my voice gave out before I could finish.

"Emeryn?"

I shook my head. "Brennan."

His name was a choked whisper, the first time I'd uttered it since that night. Isa flinched but said nothing for a long moment.

"How?" she finally asked, expression twisted in confusion.

"I don't know. One moment I'm fine—relatively speaking—but then he has a look or he says something, and it's like I'm drowning again. The shadows...my shadows...they just appear, like they're responding to my distress and trying to protect me or something. It sounds ridiculous."

"It sounds anything but ridiculous, Calla. We all respond to trauma differently, and sometimes subconsciously."

"How do I control it though?"

"You hid it for years. How did you do it then?"

"I was happy, Isa. It's like my heart didn't need their help then. My parents' death roused the shadows a bit. I could feel them stirring, but I don't know. Maybe it's because I had Brennan steadying me. I didn't need the darkness. And then...he..."

Thankfully Isa didn't finish the thought for me but bobbed her head slowly, her eyes peering up to the ceiling as she contemplated all I'd said. A few shaky breaths later, she caught my gaze again, and her face lit up with hope.

Gripping my shoulders with both hands, she said, "I'll talk to the healers tonight. I'm sure they'll have something to help with the panic when it hits. If we can quell that, it should keep your powers from reacting."

"But what if I need them?"

"The hope is not to suppress the shadows completely but to calm the emotions that are calling them out. You should be able to harness them as needed. We need to keep you in control of them, not the other way around."

"Are you sure the healers can help?"

"If such a tonic exists, they will know of it, and I will get it for you. Once the first trial starts, I will bring it to you."

Ice shot up my spine at the mention of the trial. My mind flooded with images of what the forest would do to the males who entered tomorrow. While I'd never witnessed it myself, I had heard the screams of the unlucky souls who had traipsed through it the first time. I had seen the bones left to decompose on the forest floor.

"Are you sure this first trial is wise? Is it too cruel?"

Isa's brow tightened, lowering over her eyes. "It was your idea, Calla, and it was a good one. You don't have a lot of time. The faster we cull the lot, the closer we get to securing your crown." She paused, a hint of suspicion clouding her gaze. "Are you concerned for a particular male's safety?"

"Of course not," I balked. "Don't be absurd. I don't want any of them to die, but that's not the same as worrying over their safety."

"So why the hesitation now, after weeks of preparation?"

I searched my mind for a reason, for any hint of the cause for the unease building in my gut.

Isa continued to speak through my silence. "They all knew what they were facing in these games. We made the danger clear. We need our next king to—"

"You're right," I said quickly, but her words had already stung my heart.

Next king.

Was this to be my life from now on—constantly, continuously having my soul's wounds ripped open by mere words and glances from strangers?

"You're right," I repeated. "But do you think it was wrong to hire—"

"Stop. No more second-guessing yourself. You know we don't have the numbers to guard the entire forest; we need his help. Trust yourself. Trust me."

Biting down on my lip, I repeated her words in my head.

Stop second-guessing yourself.

We had spent countless hours devising these trials, ensuring they tested the males for the qualities that would best serve our kingdom. I had known this plan would mean some would die, and even suffer greatly as they did. If I couldn't escape the torturous fate of having to marry again, then why did I want to spare them pain as they fought for my hand?

No, if I hurt, then so would they. If they wanted to one day share my bed, they were going to have to earn it.

CHAPTER 28

MATTHIAS

From the haggard looks of everyone gathered outside the castle, it was plain that no one had gotten any rest since the dinner last night. Even the queen's general appeared less put-together than usual, her body rigid and muscles tense despite her casual stance. She didn't bother with any pleasantries but dove right into her instructions, lightly kicking a wooden crate sitting beside her.

"Once the sun peeks up over the horizon, you will enter Vael Forest at your assigned positions."

Everyone stiffened at the mention of the enchanted woods. Reaching into her pocket, she produced a circular gold pendant barely larger than her palm, dangling at the end of a black cord. She held it out in front of her and pivoted so we could all see—as best we could in the pre-dawn light—the fox and ivy leaf design carved into it.

"Twelve medallions bearing the Vael family crest have been distributed throughout the forest. Your objective is two-fold. First, survive. Second, retrieve one of these medallions. Return to these steps once the skies fade with the setting sun, and not a moment before. Each survivor who arrives on time with a medallion in hand will qualify for the next round and earn forty points.

For every quarter hour you are late, though, ten points will be deducted. Lose all forty points by arriving late, and you will be disqualified. Should you survive with no medallion in hand, you will be disqualified and remain at the castle until the tournament's conclusion. You can collect multiple medallions, but you will only receive points for one of them; any extras retrieved will earn you nothing."

She tucked the medallion into her pocket and pulled out another, this one a black vial attached to a gold chain.

"A dozen pendants similar to this one have also been hidden somewhere in the woods. While these are worth no points, they provide immunity from the forest's dangers, but not from one another."

A couple of the Arenysen males—Aric and Fritz, I believed— turned to sneer at me over their shoulders. Apparently Isa had been right about my being a target. I winked, and as expected, they looked at each other, bewilderment plain on their faces. I returned my attention to Isa.

"You must remain in the forest until sundown. And yes, we do have guards stationed around the perimeter to enforce this rule; anyone who steps out of the wood's bounds—including to arrive back here early—will be deemed in violation of their oath and promptly executed."

Beside me, young Beck gulped loudly, and had I not shared his apprehension, I might have laughed.

"To keep things as fair as possible, you will each be supplied with a pair of daggers and a compass. Any personal weapons you have on you must be turned in. These will be returned to you upon completion of the trial. The sun will be rising shortly. Please step forward to receive your weapons and entry point assignment."

At this, a valet from the castle staff stepped forward from behind the general and lifted the crate in his arms so the general could select the weapons as each of us approached. My stomach flipped and twisted like a fish struggling to return to water. Isa hadn't described the specific dangers the forest itself posed. Did everyone here know of its enchantment? Did they know what to expect? Did any of us?

Not my problem.

Get in. Get the medallion. Get out.

That's all you need to do.

Positioned at various locations along the castle's entry road, we all stared into the forest's darkness, periodically checking the horizon opposite the castle's entrance for the first sign of the sun. The Arenysen general, mounted on a black horse, paced up and down the line, ready to give the call to begin at any moment. Standing halfway down on the north side of the road, I waited between Oryn and Graham, who stood fifty yards on either side of me, to my right and left, respectively.

Remembering Calla's warning, I had sheathed both of my daggers at my belt. Graham appeared to be the only other one to have done the same, which was to be expected, I supposed. As advisor to the crown, he would certainly know the ins and outs of this forest and its enchantment. I anxiously tapped the handle of one of mine, waving my other hand discretely to catch Oryn's attention. Gesturing to my stowed weapon, I hoped he'd understand my advice, but his face twisted in confusion. He was still holding one of his weapons in his hand when the first slice of sunlight kissed the horizon.

"It begins!" Isa bellowed, easing her horse into a trot as she passed down the line of competitors.

I held my breath as I stepped forward, as if that might keep the woods from noticing my intrusion. The dense tree limbs immediately blocked out what little sunlight there was, blanketing me in an eerie darkness that tugged at the hairs on my neck and trailed icy whispers up my spine. As I moved deeper into the forest, I could hear the vines begin to crawl along the earth, following me.

A scream rent the still air, startling me, but it was somewhere in the distance, on the other side of the forest. I winced when it was abruptly cut short, not letting myself wonder who had just died. Watching both the ground for obstacles—and murderous plant life—and the branches for signs of the pendants, I made my way painfully slowly through the trees, but at least I kept moving. At this time of year, we would have a good thirteen hours before we could return to the castle. I tried not to think about how difficult it would be to stay in motion for that long—and even then, there was no guarantee that strategy would work the whole time.

Still, it was the best plan I had until I could find one of those vials.

The thick foliage made it nearly impossible to hear anything beyond my own heartbeat. No insects chirped. No birds cried out. There was nothing but the soft thud of my boots against the leaves and dirt.

A flash of movement to my right yanked my attention around, and my hand flew instinctively to my weapon, but I didn't draw it.

I stalked forward, my eyes surveying my surroundings, watching for another sign of whatever prowled nearby.

Lengthening my breaths to quiet them, I listened.

There. Something to my right. A low growl rumbled.

Tightening my grip around my dagger's handle, I ducked under low branches and crept slowly toward the sound.

A dull thumping sound hit my ears, and I froze for the briefest of moments to listen closer.

That wasn't some beast growling, but someone groaning, struggling.

Shoving aside the fronds of a large fern, I darted around a large tree and stopped short.

A pair of feet hovered half a meter above the ground, heels hitting a massive tree's trunk as the male struggled to free himself, but his movements were slowing. Glancing higher, I caught Oryn's frantic gaze and blanched face. Thorned vines, twisted together like the strands of a barbed rope, wound around his neck and squeezed tighter with each attempt he made to free himself. His bloodied hands—now empty—clawed at the vines as he grunted from the exertion, but he was quickly losing the strength to keep his arms lifted.

I pulled my dagger and with a flick of my wrist sent it flying toward the vine. The blade sliced through a couple of the strands, leaving only one. His body fell a few centimeters, but he never reached the ground, as three more vines shot down from the branches above to take the place of those I'd severed.

I needed to get up there and cut him free.

"Stay awake," I ordered, but Oryn's eyes were already fluttering closed, his movements growing weaker and weaker.

A thick branch jutted out from the tree directly above Oryn, and I darted forward, retrieving my dagger from where it had fallen into the leaves on my way. Placing my blade carefully between my teeth, I scrambled up the tree as fast as I could, cursing with every slip of my foot and every piece of bark that broke away under my grip.

As I crawled onto the branch, inching along on my belly, I noted the vines appearing behind me, slithering straight for my feet like two blind snakes.

What the fuck had I gotten myself into?

Connor was going to owe me multiple bottles of that damned brandy when I made it home.

I managed to reach the vines that held Oryn hostage—pulled taut under the weight of his now-still body—and with one quick movement sliced through all of them. Waiting only long enough to ensure no new vines caught him, I swung my legs over the side of the branch just as the vines reached my heels. I smirked as if they could see me and dropped to the ground beside Oryn.

My friend's coloring was slowly returning to normal, his lips no longer that ghostly blue. His eyelids fluttered but didn't open as I shouted his name. "Oryn! Oryn, you need to wake up. We need to keep moving." I slapped him on the cheek in an effort to rouse him.

Without warning something clamped down on my ankle and pulled.

"Fuck," I barked as one of the stars-damned vines started to drag me away. Twisting around onto my back, I hauled myself up to sitting and slashed through the vine with my dagger. At least General Isa had supplied us with good weapons. That did little good for me here, though, because no sooner had I freed myself from that one, than another latched onto my wrist. It yanked me toward the tree, spinning me around on my backside so that I now faced Oryn, who still appeared only semi-conscious. The forest appeared to be leaving him alone—for now, at least.

But I was on my own.

The vine squeezed my arm until I dropped my weapon, though I managed to draw my second dagger from my belt even as the possessed plant continued to pull me along the ground. Grimacing from the vine's grip, I twisted my wrist until my hand could grab the vine, and then, with one burst of energy, I hauled myself up closer to it so my other hand could cut me free.

Immediately I tucked the blade back into my belt.

"There!" I shouted at the forest around labored breaths. "I'm unarmed. Not a threat. You can leave me the fuck alone now."

Surprisingly, it seemed to work—well enough, anyway—even when I reached down to retrieve my other dagger I'd dropped. The vines still crept toward me from multiple directions, but they kept their distance as I rose to my feet and backed away to check on Oryn. His eyes were fully open now, but he didn't seem at all aware of where he was.

"You okay?" I asked, though he was obviously not.

He slowly looked my way, his features relaxing when reality dawned on him.

"What in the fuck is wrong with these woods?" He choked out the question in a hoarse whisper.

"Impressive, isn't it?" I asked, surveying the surrounding woods and noting how the vines and branches and ferns—every living piece of this forest—all seemed to be watching us, waiting for us to make a wrong move.

Oryn scoffed, and his voice came out a strained croak. "If you find possessed flora intriguing, I suppose."

Offering my outstretched hand to help him up, I laughed. "We can discuss its merits once we survive this, but if we're going to do that, we need to keep moving. Think you can walk?"

He nodded as he slowly pushed himself to stand, stumbling a bit and muttering his gratitude when I steadied him.

"I dropped my blades somewhere around here when that demon plant grabbed me," he said, searching the ground.

I joined him in his hunt for the blade, all the while keeping my eye on the encroaching forest.

"Aha, here's one at least," he finally said a few minutes later, pulling a blade out of the leaves and wiping the dirt off on his pants.

"Make sure you keep it sheathed unless you absolutely need it. This forest doesn't seem fond of weapons."

"It doesn't seem fond of anything." He slipped his dagger into his belt and gave it a couple taps with his hand. "So where to now?"

"Wander aimlessly until sunset?" I suggested.

"And hope we come across two medallions?"

I pulled my mouth into a casual frown as I bobbed my head in affirmation. "Would have been nice if they'd given us some clue as to where to find them. Even hidden in plain sight, it could take us forever to find one of the twelve, let alone two of them."

"Should we split up?" Oryn asked, stepping over a fallen log and eying it suspiciously as if expecting it to try and eat his foot. "We could cover more ground that way."

"Perhaps," I said, continuing to trudge on. "But what if you get in a mess again?"

"What if *you* get in a mess? They're after you just as much as they are me," he argued, and I couldn't help but laugh.

"Exactly my point. It's up to you though. You're welcome to take on all the demon plants by yourself if you want."

He jerked his head around one way and then the other, almost stumbling over his own feet as he went. "Nah. I'll stick with you, I guess. But let's hurry up and find our medallions."

"And then try to stay alive long enough to get them back to the castle," I added, barely hiding my laugh when his face fell.

We walked on, and I had to admit, having an extra pair of eyes did help, allowing us to move faster through the ferns and around the trees. He watched the ground while I scanned the trees, hunting for any sign of gold anywhere.

"What in the..." Oryn mumbled. I pivoted around. He was staring down at the base of an old tree with gnarled roots that jutted out of the ground in various places. He pointed a shaky hand at the tree. "Do you see this?"

I leaned closer, periodically looking about to ensure the forest wasn't about to ambush us. "We can't stand still for too—"

My mouth went dry, hanging open, unable to say the final word of my warning. Tucked in among the tree's roots, a skull stared up at us with gaping holes where eyes had once been, its jaw hung open at a grotesque angle, as if silently screaming. Not far away, a hand—well, what was left of it anyway—twisted up from between two other roots that had grown close together.

"It's as if..." Oryn started.

"The tree ate them," I finished his thought for him.

Slowly he turned to face me. "Don't let me get eaten."

"I'll try," I said, shrugging off the tingle that rose up my back, but the sensation didn't go away. As if suddenly remembering where I was, I spun around and swung my arm straight into one of the thickest vines I'd seen, so large my strike didn't budge it at all. It continued to track its way over my shoulder ,moving slowly, like it thought I wouldn't notice.

Dumb plant.

Dropping into a crouch, I escaped the exploring vine only to find more slinking toward me along the forest floor.

"We need to get out of here," I said, but as I tried to scramble away, my hand slipped off the root, right onto the dead guy's bony face. Hastily I jerked back, but my sleeve had caught on one of the teeth, ripping the lower jaw away. Tearing it loose, I went to return it back to its resting place when I noticed something lodged in his mouth.

Grimacing, I slipped my hand inside, my fingers fumbling around until they wrapped around something cold and delicate. Lifting it up, I stared at the black vial now dangling from my fingers. I could have kissed that poor dead face, because while it might not be the medallion we needed to win, this would certainly help.

I scrambled over the roots and nearly tripped as I rounded the tree. Oryn, bent over, worked to catch his breath. Slipping the gold chain over my head, I was about to hold the vial out for him to see when I stopped, rethought that plan, and tucked it into my collar. He might be an ally, but he was still my competition. I had no problem keeping him alive—and would do it again as often as I could—but I had no idea if he'd show me the same courtesy.

Guilt soured my gut, twisting my insides uncomfortably with my selfishness. I couldn't share the vial with him, and I couldn't afford to fail this trial. I'd just need to do my best to keep the male alive by any other means.

Grabbing his arm, I gently pulled him upright.

"We can't stand still for too long, and we certainly can't sit or lie down to rest at all. Unless we want to end up their breakfast." I dragged him away from the tree and urged him forward.

As we marched on, deeper into the forest, I noticed that for the first time since I'd entered, the woods didn't pay any attention to me. Vines still crept slowly toward Oryn as he passed them by, but on my side the forest appeared to be like any other boring wood.

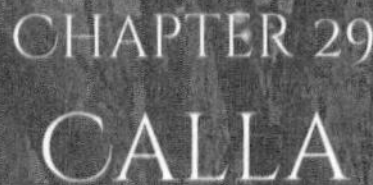

*E*asy there, Killer."
"*Thanks for the dance, Killer.*"
Killer.

Killer.
Killer.

All night Matthias's words haunted my sleep, echoing over and over as my mind replayed the same images: Brennan taking his last breath, the humans whispering that I'd killed him, and my shadows—no, me—ripping them apart, strangling the life from all who had defied my laws—laws intended to protect them.

And now I was sending a dozen males into a forest designed to kill them.

I had killed, yes, and I would kill again before death claimed me. The Olanders would pay for taking Brennan from me.

But why had Matthias called me *killer*?

It could have been an innocuous nickname, innocent and playful.

Or...

Ever since he'd arrived, the troubling questions had plagued me, and his nickname only made them louder, more incessant. Did the Durands believe the rumors? Did they actually think me capable of killing Brennan? Did they send their general here to avenge him?

Lying in bed, I stared at the ceiling and watched the darkness slowly fade into dawn's pastel hues. My limbs, my gut, my chest, every part of me tensed, desperate to move, unable to relax, as if a million tiny snakes wriggled under my skin. At my palms, though, my magic swirled—the only part of me that felt at ease. Lifting my hands above me, I beckoned my shadows out. They trailed down my arms, soothing the anxious tension as they wrapped around them.

Assuming Isa had gotten to the healers last night as planned—and assuming they could help—I'd soon be able to control my shadows. While I knew it was for the best, the thought of taking any kind of tonic had me nervous. How would it work? Would I still be me? Would I be able to use my shadows when needed, as Isa claimed?

The moment the knock sounded at the door, I reeled my shadows back in and sat up. Isa strode in, not waiting for an invitation. Shoulders back, chin high, she looked every bit the intimidating commander she was. Her stern expression softened when she saw me, but her body remained tense.

"Good, you're up!" She stopped at the foot of my bed and crossed her arms.

Rising from the bed, I plodded over to the wardrobe and pulled out the first dress my fingers touched.

As I dressed, I asked, "Did everything go okay this morning?"

She drew in a slow breath and swung her gaze toward the window, where bright sunshine streamed inside.

"As well as we could hope for. Did you not hear anything from up here?"

My bedroom was located near the front of the castle on the northeast corner; from my balcony I could see the driveway if I leaned far enough over the edge.

"I vaguely recall hearing you announce the start, but other than that, nothing. Why?"

Isa rubbed a hand at the back of her neck and pulled her lips down into a grimace. "You could say the forest is doing its job. Rather efficiently, too."

"I'd worry if it wasn't, honestly," I said, slipping my arms into the sleeves and motioning for Isa to help fasten the buttons at my back. "How many lost already?"

"At least two, but that's only an estimate."

"An estimate based on what?" I asked. Isa fastened the last button and cleared her throat, but said nothing. I slowly turned to face her and found her avoiding my gaze. "Spit it out, Isa."

Her brown eyes flashed to mine. "Their screams."

"Was that really that hard to say?" I asked, shaking my head as I sat down on the bench beside the wardrobe. I bent over to put my boots on. "Have you forgotten I grew up with these woods and the screams they elicit?"

"To be fair, we haven't had anyone enter the forest in many years," she said.

"Haven't had anyone caught entering, you mean." Isa stilled, and the muscles in her jaw twitched, as if she were literally chewing on my words. I smacked her arm with the back of my hand to pull her out of her head, asking, "Any luck with the healers?"

She blinked rapidly as she buried her hand in her pocket. "Right, yes. They gave me this."

I expected a vial or bottle like the many that lined Minerva's shelves, but instead she held out a small canvas bag, tied with a black ribbon. Taking it in my hand, I was surprised to find it light, as if it were completely empty.

"What is it?" I asked, moving to untie the ribbon. Inside lay a mix of dried flowers and plants with such a pungent fragrance I coughed as I closed it up again.

"An herbal concoction, much like a tea. Said to steep it in boiling water for several minutes and drink one cup in the morning and another before bed."

My nose wrinkled at the thought of drinking something that

smelled that ghastly—like stale dirt and dying flowers dipped in sugar. "How did they prepare this so quickly?"

"They used to make it for your mother, apparently. She suffered bouts of agitation much like yours. Healers said it's a malady that can run in bloodlines, unfortunately. Your mother never told you?"

I shook my head as I tried to recall memories of my mother, hunting through them for any evidence that she had suffered as I did. How long had she needed this remedy? What had triggered her episodes? Tears pricked the corners of my eyes, and my arms ached to hold—and be held by—my mother. These attacks had never happened to me until their deaths, and even then they'd been mild, quelled by Brennan's peace and love.

My inability to control my emotions and my shadows was a shame I'd carried for weeks now, but somehow knowing my mother had suffered similarly and also needed help made me feel a little less broken, less alone.

"Thanks, Isa, and please give the healers my gratitude as well."

"Of course," she said, smiling kindly. "I've also informed the kitchen to ensure you have a kettle of water brought up twice a day. They should be bringing it with your breakfast this morning."

I was about to thank her again when a shrill shriek in the distance pierced my senses. Both of us turned to stare out the window.

"What are your plans for the day?"

"I thought I might go for a walk."

Her sharp gaze burned into mine. "Promise me you won't go in the forest, Calla."

I stayed quiet, though, unable to make such a promise. Before she could rattle off her lecture, another scream pulled our attention back to the window.

CHAPTER 30

MATTHIAS

We should be nearing the edge of the forest by now," I muttered, mostly to myself as I double-checked the compass, but Oryn grunted like a bored adolescent behind me.

"How long have we been in here, do you know?" he asked, throwing his head back to look up at the canopy. "I can't see the sun to tell."

"Good thing I have this." I dug into my pants pocket and pulled out my old watch, a gift from my sister. Now it was my turn to groan. "Two hours. Barely."

Oryn sighed loudly in defeat. "Two hours and nothing? No medallions, no sign of anyone else. How is that—"

Something buzzed past my ear so fast, I couldn't see what it was until it struck Oryn in the shoulder.

His hand flew up on instinct, and he stumbled backward, barely staying on his feet. I ran over to him, my hand already drawing my dagger from my belt to dig out whatever dart or spike the forest had spit at him.

I skidded to a stop, a growled "fuck" flying from my lips.

It was nothing from the forest; it was a fucking dagger, identical to the ones we'd been issued.

Whirling around, I shoved my weapon back into my belt and scanned the forest for the attacker, focusing my hearing for any hint of a heartbeat or breath or footstep.

There.

One pulse—no, two—thumped faintly in front of me.

Oryn groaned behind me. Looking back over my shoulder, I barked out an order as if he were one of my soldiers instead of my competition.

"Pull the blade out! Before you begin to heal."

I couldn't wait to confirm he'd listened to me, because our attackers' heartbeats grew louder in my ears.

I spun back around in time to watch another dagger fly past and land somewhere in the grass behind me.

"You missed!" I called out.

Silence.

Someone darted behind a tree.

My hand hovered over my own dagger, not from fear of the forest's wrath since the pendant protected me, but I sure as fuck was keeping my newfound immunity a secret for as long as I could.

"You really are a piss-poor shot," I taunted, easing my way forward.

A male stepped out from behind a tree to the right with an ugly sneer plastered to his face.

"And you really are a conceited little shit, aren't you? Always assuming it's about you," he said. The toughness in his voice hung on as shakily as the left hand dangling at his side. The vines tracked his movement.

I shrugged lightly and added a smirk for good measure.

"It usually is about me. The assumption saves time," I said. "Though usually I'm facing opponents with at least some skill. I mean, that blade you tossed was off by a whole meter. Aric, is it?"

He didn't answer, just continued to sneer at me as though I hadn't said anything.

Someone moved off to my left, their footsteps quiet, but still quite noticeable. I kept my focus firmly on Aric. Or Fritz. Whoever he was didn't appear to have any weapons on him, an assumption further confirmed by the way the forest kept its distance from him—ready to strike, but waiting, watching.

"So what now?" I asked. "You gave up your only weapons. Were you planning to sort this out with our bare hands? Like civilized fae?"

The attack rudely came before I'd even finished my question, but I still managed to draw my blade in time to meet the steel of the other male's dagger as he lunged for me. He snarled, yanking his arm back and dodging a vine that rushed at his arm. Having missed its target, the plant brushed past my shoulder and quickly swung around, but instead of going after my attacker, it shot off behind me.

I risked a look over my shoulder to see the vine already coiled around Oryn's legs, pinning them together at the ankles and pulling his feet out from under him. He groaned in pain when his back slammed into the dirt, but with a sharp crack his head thwacked hard against a tree root, silencing him.

The vine started to drag him away, but I leaped toward it, drawing my dagger in the process, and sliced through the plant. Oryn lay still. One hand rested lifelessly on his chest while the other was slowly being pulled under the leaves carpeting the ground, as if the forest was truly trying to consume him.

"Get him, Fritz!" The unarmed man—that would be Aric, then—shouted as he continued to move among the trees to keep the forest from latching on to him.

Fritz bobbed and weaved around me, looking more like a desperate male bird during mating season than a fearsome adversary. I remained still and angled my head as I watched him, pivoting as he circled. Even the forest seemed to be watching him with amusement rather than attacking him, as if even these enchanted trees no longer viewed him as a threat.

I craned my neck to look around his dancing form and caught Aric's attention.

"Seriously?"

With a growl rivaling that of a baby bear, Fritz charged, slashing at me with one hand. I dodged that strike easily--his second, though, nicked my arm just above the elbow. Fritz kept up his dance, narrowly avoiding the forest's efforts to subdue him. I dove away from the next swipe of his blade, drawing one of my own daggers as I dropped to the ground and rolled myself into his path. The swift slash of my weapon only caught the back of one ankle, but severing that single tendon was enough to halt him long enough for the vines to seize him.

Two of them immediately caught his arms at the wrists and hauled them in opposite directions so that his body formed a *T*. He howled in pain as the plants slowly pulled his limbs, but a third vine dropped from the forest's canopy and looped around his neck several times, silencing him as it squeezed.

I'd seen a lot of death during the war, and witnessed a couple gruesome scenes when the humans had started attacking the fae on our roads in Emeryn, but even I had to look away, bile rushing to my throat, when the vines ripped Fritz apart. I cringed with each heavy thud as pieces of him fell to the forest floor.

"What the fuck," Aric muttered over and over to himself. He had stopped moving, his hands resting on his knees as he leaned over, seemingly trying not to retch. He didn't seem to notice the forest closing in on him.

"Aric," I said, slowly rising to my feet and moving toward him. "You need to keep moving."

He didn't seem to hear me, his eyes fixed on the chunks of his friend strewn about.

"Move, Aric," I warned, louder this time. His eyes slid to mine slowly, but still the encroaching danger didn't register on his face. "Move!"

This final shout finally snapped him out of his stupor, but he acted too late. He'd barely straightened up, his foot in mid-stride, when a vine plunged into his back, its end—armed with multiple sharp thorns—shooting out of his chest. His gaze locked on mine before the light in his eyes dimmed. His head lolled to one side before falling forward. When the vine retreated, Aric crumpled to his knees before his lifeless body fell forward, his head making a sickening thunk as it hit the ground.

Fuck.

I pressed my hand to my chest where the black vial lay hidden and thanked the stars I had found it when I did. How did the queen and her general expect any of us to survive this wicked place? I had to admit, though, this was an efficient way to diminish the pool of suitors.

Maybe too efficient, I thought, eying the two dead males lying in front of me.

Shit, Oryn!

Remembering my friend, I whirled around. His arm was now mostly buried by mud and leaves and small tendrils from the deadly vines. I dropped beside him, relieved when I caught the faint, but thready, sound of his pulse. My knuckles scraped against the sharp grooves of the root he'd struck as I reached behind his head, but I barely registered the discomfort as my hand slipped into the thick and sticky mess of blood coating his hair.

"Better to just leave him," said a voice, flat and emotionless, from somewhere to my right.

Gritting my teeth, I cleared my throat as I met the cold eyes of Graham. "He's not dead."

"Not yet, but he will be soon." He stalked around me, clicking his tongue and shaking his head when he looked past me to the fallen males. "Looks like you've had some excitement here."

"Sorry you missed it," I quipped.

He let out a single, dry laugh, continuing to circle Oryn and me. The vines didn't seem to pay him any attention, and my scowl pulled at my lips before I could think better of it.

Another laugh erupted from him, this time longer, louder. "You're not the only one to find one of the vials, *friend.*"

Oryn groaned then, a weak and pitiful sound that sent guilt rippling through me. I should have shared the vial with him somehow. Should have protected him. As much as I hated to admit it, Graham was right. He wasn't going to last much longer unless he got help. Reaching across his body, I pushed aside the undergrowth to free his arm and shifted his other off his chest. Well aware of Graham's scrutinizing stare, I lifted one of Oryn's legs, threaded my arm underneath it, and rolled my back onto his chest, bringing his leg onto my shoulder as I moved. Using the momentum of the roll, I hauled him up so that his body lay across my back, an arm over one of my shoulders and a leg over the other. Pushing to my feet, I shifted his limbs so they draped comfortably.

"You can't be serious," Graham protested, his tone more bitter than incredulous.

I raised my brow innocently at him. "You may be a heartless prick, but lucky for Oryn here, I'm not."

Something shifted in Graham's expression, like he almost felt bad for being such a dick. His voice softened, only a hint of bitterness remaining, when he asked, "Where do you plan to take him?"

"They have the forest guarded, right? Surely one of them will take him to the healers." Careful not to let Oryn fall, I reached into my pocket to retrieve my compass.

"You're planning to carry him the whole way?"

If I didn't know any better, I'd think he sounded impressed, but from what little I knew of Graham, I was probably imagining it.

"We should be nearing the forest's outer edge," I said, pivoting with my compass until I found the heading I wanted. Slipping it back into my pocket, I adjusted Oryn higher onto my back and set off.

"They'll have to carry him around the forest back to the castle, though," Graham protested.

I called back to him but didn't stop. "Better than trying to keep him alive in a forest trying to kill him."

"Wait," Graham said, and this time I did pause. He strode past me and knelt beside Aric's body. I was about to ask what in the stars he was doing, when he suddenly produced the medallion. He barely even glanced at it before tossing it at me, and I nearly missed reaching out in time to catch it.

"Why would—"

"Maybe this prick isn't as heartless as you think," he said, standing and brushing dirt from his knees. "Plus, I already have my own."

"Thank you," I said, shoving the large medallion into my pocket. "Will you be coming with me? Or is this where we part?"

"Don't misinterpret my actions as actually liking you, Matthias," he said, but the disdain in his eyes seemed less potent now, and I couldn't help but chuckle to myself as I walked away.

I had only walked a hundred meters when I got the uneasy sensation that I was being watched. Stopping, I turned slightly to look behind me. Maybe Graham had changed his mind and was trailing after me. But no one was there. Something moved to my right, but again, I found nothing—nothing but darkness among the trees, except this darkness was thicker, heavier, as if nightfall had already reached that part of the forest.

These woods might not kill me now, but they seemed starsbent on toying with my mind.

Shaking my head, I drew in a deep breath to clear my mind. But when I looked that way again, the darkness seemed to move, like a shadow dancing with the shifting of the light.

Shadows.

I stiffened and stared deeper into the lingering darkness.

It couldn't be. Could it?

Though spying on her contestants did seem like something the shadow queen might do. I listened intently for a heartbeat, but could hear nothing beyond mine and Oryn's, growing slower and weaker still.

"Is that you, Killer?" I threw the question at the shadow, which seemed to still for a moment, drawing a smirk from my lips, before slowly retreating deeper into the woods.

A string of curses screamed inside my mind as I scrambled backwards, nearly falling over a tree root.

He had looked right at me.

It had only been for a moment, and, while it was clear he hadn't actually seen me, the fact that his eyes had seemed to latch onto mine at all had my heart racing and me desperately trying to chase it out of the woods.

I'd never been able to do that with my shadows before now—to peek out from within them while remaining hidden to others. I didn't know if it was some change from the healers' tonic or from the simple act of being more in control of my powers, but I'd been thrilled by the prospect.

Spinning around, I pushed myself to put distance between Matthias and me. He obviously had one of the protective pendants—black vials filled with my blood to protect anyone who held them—and as unnerving as I found him and his nickname for me, I couldn't help but feel a slight twinge of relief that he still lived. Maybe it was because he'd been the only one besides Graham to show me any kindness. Not that I wanted kindness from any of these males, but it had been surprisingly nice to be treated like an actual fae and not the monster many saw.

After a few hundred meters I stopped and bent at the hips to rest my hands on my knees to catch my breath. Using my shadows in this way—maintaining my sight while remaining concealed—apparently took more energy than usual. I wouldn't be able to hold them in place if I didn't slow down and pace myself.

"Your Majesty?"

I knew that voice all too well. Graham.

Could he see me? I peered up through my lashes to see my shadows still held in place.

I didn't answer, didn't move.

"I know it's you, Calla," he said, sweetly. "You shouldn't be here."

I gritted my teeth, my hands balling into fists at my knees. He wasn't my advisor anymore. He'd lost that privilege when he'd insisted on entering this ridiculous tournament. Slowly I angled my head, spotting him over my shoulder. The trees and vines paid him no attention. Of course, he'd found a vial. I was glad he wasn't dead, but I was in no mood to speak to him now, especially when he had the gall to try to tell me what to do.

Sucking in one last, long breath, I prepared to pull my shadows back and remind him of the choice he'd made.

"Is that—is that the queen?" a new voice asked from behind Graham. I only caught a brief glimpse of him before Graham spun around, drew his blade, and threw it into the male's gut in one swift motion.

My mouth fell open; my breath caught somewhere between shock and apprehension. I'd only ever witnessed his wielding of words––never a weapon.

He didn't hesitate to walk over and retrieve his dagger, pulling a haunting groan from the dying fae. Bending low, Graham yanked the medallion from the dying fae's neck. Whether Graham had killed the male to win the tournament or to protect me, I didn't know, and at this moment, I didn't much care. I just needed to get out of here before anyone else could spot me and potentially give the Assembly reason to accuse me of meddling.

Pulling in one last deep breath, I straightened and took off once more.

I pushed myself harder, ignoring the beads of sweat sliding down my temples, but the effort was too much. My shadows were fading quickly. If Graham had followed me, he'd be able to see me soon. Ahead, though, I could see the first slivers of light through the trees. I was almost there. No one could follow me beyond the edge without risking their place in the competition. My shadows grew weaker and weaker with each pounding footstep until they disappeared completely, and I squinted against the too-bright light, only realizing I'd exited the forest when someone stepped in front of me, his arms outstretched.

Unable to stop myself in time, I slammed into his muscled chest with a yelp.

I pulled back, panting as my hand flew to my chest, and stared up at him.

The man—unnervingly tall and broad-shouldered—towered over me, the afternoon sun accentuating the lightness of his blond hair, cut short and neatly styled around his rounded ears. His stone-like arms dropped slowly to his sides as he stepped back, flashing me a cocky smirk beneath his amber eyes.

"Asher," I said, more breathlessly still than I would have liked.

His expression darkened, his smirk shifting into a frown as his eyes flicked to the forest and back again.

"Your Majesty." His voice was thick honey on a knife's edge. "Someone chasing you?"

"No," I said, "nothing like that."

"What are you doing in the forest, anyway?"

"Being stupid, apparently," I muttered to myself.

"What was that?" he asked.

I dropped my head to the side and squinted up at him. "Is your shifter hearing failing in your old age?"

His frown deepened into a scowl only to turn up into a wide toothy grin as he belted out a hearty laugh. "Hardly, just as I'm hardly old."

"Older than me."

"Not hard to do, princess." He flinched, and bowed his head. "Apologies, queen. Old habits die hard."

I lifted my hand to his forearm and started to assure him I didn't mind, but then footsteps—heavy and quick—approached us from inside the forest.

Asher stepped around me, gently nudging me behind him. I tried to resist, but I was too tired—and he was too strong. He swiveled around, bending his face low so his bronze eyes pierced mine.

"You hired me for a reason, Your Majesty. Let me do what I do best."

Thinning my lips, I nodded. He wasn't wrong.

But when Matthias appeared at the edge of the trees, still carrying the injured male on his back, and Asher stepped forward with a deep growl, I wondered if maybe I hadn't made a mistake hiring the shifter mercenary after all.

CHAPTER 32

MATTHIAS

Oryn's quickly fading pulse spurred me on. Reaching one of the guards was his only hope at surviving, so I pushed through the strain in my lungs and the aches in my muscles toward the light up ahead. The sound of voices sparked new hope. Maybe he'd stand a chance.

Or maybe they'll execute me on sight.

I shoved that thought aside. It was a possibility, sure, but focusing on fear wouldn't help me save my friend.

Three steps from the clearing, I spotted Calla. Her dark hair was plaited down her back, but loose strands framed her face, some stuck to her forehead and temple with perspiration. An intimidating male ushered her behind him, except this was no fae. He had rounded ears—a human—yet, Calla seemed more than comfortable with him. She trusted him.

Keeping my feet firmly planted in the shade of the trees, I locked eyes with Calla, who watched me from behind the man's massive arm.

"Hey, Killer," I said, half-smiling.

I should have known better, of course, but the nickname had grown on me. The man took a step forward, hostility blazing in a pair of eyes that reminded me of Connor's—in shade and intensity.

"That's no way to speak to your queen," he said.

I raised my chin as best I could with Oryn still draped across my neck. "To be fair, she's not my queen."

Calla's gaze swung up to the man, and I could have sworn that was concern written across her face; though whether it was for me or for him, I didn't know. Not that it mattered.

"Yet," he clarified. "Did you forget you're not allowed to leave the forest?"

"I don't intend to," I said. Balancing Oryn, I reached a hand up to my collar and pulled the black vial from beneath my shirt. "I know the secrets of the forest. I can live here quite happily...for the next ten hours."

"Then why are you here?"

"My friend here was gravely injured. He needs a healer, now."

"Unfortunately for your friend there, I'm to kill any contestant who leaves before sundown," the man explained.

My eyes narrowed at him, and I dropped the pendant back to my chest so I could readjust Oryn. "So I carried him all this way for you to just...kill him anyway?"

"Appears so."

Sighing loudly, I knelt down and eased Oryn off my back and onto the ground. Stretching out my back and shoulders, I rolled my neck to ease its aches as I rose to my sore-as-fuck feet. Calla watched me, brows lowered over her dark eyes. I slowly wet my lips, chuckling when the queen's gaze lowered to my mouth.

"You know, Killer—" The man growled in warning, and I raised my hands in a placating gesture, dipping my head in reverence toward Calla. "Your Majesty. A little mercy shown here could go a long way in fighting the rumors."

She didn't move, though her expression shifted ever so slightly.

Jutting my chin toward the male, I shrugged casually. "I'm

sure your guard dog here could handle getting him to a healer, no?"

As I'd hoped, the man snarled, his shoulders tensing as if he actually had hackles to raise.

"Nice doggy," I said, patting the air with my hand.

"Easy, Asher," Calla said, lifting her fingers to his arm, though she kept her attention firmly on me. "It's not wise to taunt him."

"Maybe you should put a leash on him," I said, knowing the queen wouldn't warn me without cause, but I was having too much fun to quit now. Asher's lip curled, revealing impressively sharp teeth—and oddly enough a small dimple in his cheek, though I refrained from commenting on how it ruined the terrifying vibe he was going for.

"Do you put a leash on that mutt prince of yours?" Asher asked, obviously trying to wriggle under my skin.

Not that it would work.

Offering a congenial smile, I widened my eyes in satisfaction. "So you know who I am. Seems best to keep the barbs between us. You don't see me offending your queen."

"She's not my queen either," he noted.

Interesting.

I stilled. His name rolled around in my mind, familiar yet difficult to place. Not from my scouts' reports, no. No one had mentioned an Asher or a human with close ties to Arenysen.

Asher's bronze eyes studied me, unnerving and...

Oh, shit. I know those eyes.

At the signing of the treaty—the one depicted in the tapestry in my room—this man had been there, standing with the queen and princess of Arenysen as their king penned his name on that parchment. He and his brothers had notoriously fought for both sides during the war, working for whichever side offered the best financial return. Why so many still trusted them enough to hire them—as Calla had evidently done here—was a true testament to how efficient and effective they were.

"Asher? As in the dragon mercenary Asher?" I asked and pulled my mouth into an impressed frown.

Calla nodded, eyes closed. Asher stood even taller, which I hadn't thought possible.

I swung my arm toward him and then gestured to Oryn. "Then he should have no trouble taking Oryn to your healers. Unless—wait—you take passengers, right? Can't say I know much about dragons."

He growled again, deeper and longer this time before addressing Calla. "There's another guard a few hundred meters away. Get him to come retrieve the wounded."

Calla's forehead creased with concern. "Why? What are you going to do?"

"Nothing, as long as this bastard keeps his mouth shut, but I don't trust him not to break the rules and leave the forest if I go."

"No. It'll be faster if you take him. I can handle Matthias," Calla insisted, her eyes flashing my way.

A smirk pulled at my lips before I could think better of it. "I bet you could, Killer."

The words were barely out of my mouth before Asher gently shoved Calla away from him. Now, I'd seen Connor shift enough times that the process had lost all its novelty. Asher's was different. While Connor's transformation seemed to roll over him, like he was stripping off his fae form to reveal the wolfhound beneath, Asher's was explosive.

Not literally. He didn't actually explode, but it was as though the dragon within burst through his human exterior. His arms swung out wildly as scale-covered muscles and glassy-black claws erupted into place. With a deafening roar—which I barely tolerated without covering my ears—he gave his head a violent shake until the blond hair and dimpled cheek changed into a massive horned head. Snarling, his jaws chomped at me as his clawed feet tore at the ground beneath an impressive body of gold and bronze scales with a silvery-white belly and immense golden wings.

"There he is," I crooned, holding my ground. He stared me

down with those same bronze eyes, now ablaze with fury that reminded me so much of Connor's when his temper got the better of him.

"Stop it, general," Calla said, though it was hard to hear her over Asher's loud attempts to intimidate me.

"I had no idea dragons had a chivalrous side, did you?"

"Just go," Calla commanded. "I'll get your friend to the healers, but only if you return to the forest. Now."

"Alright, alright. I'm going," I said and started to back away slowly, hands up once again in surrender. "But next time you want to ogle me, you don't need to hide in your shadows to do it. You may not be my queen yet, but I'm yours to handle whenever you need a little release."

Her lips parted slightly, and I managed to send her a single wink before Asher bellowed with such force the trees themselves seemed to cower away from him. Then, digging his claws into the dirt and tucking his wings in tightly against his back, he charged me. I turned and ran, dashing around trees and ducking under low branches, not daring to look back at the beast now crashing through the forest behind me.

Adrenaline—and maybe a bit of fear—forced an almost hysterical laugh from my lungs as a plan began to form in my mind. A risky one, sure, but in certain cases—like being chased down by a gigantic, winged creature—there was nothing but risk.

Barreling through another large fern, I abruptly changed course, darting to my left and circling back around on him. I had underestimated his reflexes—and his sight—because he didn't slow down remotely as he spun around after me, his clawed feet skidding in the dirt. His tail swept through trees, smashing them like they were made of paper. He was so close, a blast of hot air—moist and earthy—hit my face when I risked a glance behind me.

My foot snagged on a root, sending me careening toward the ground, but I twisted my body so that I rolled instead. Unfortunately, even with my quick reaction, my mishap gave Asher enough of an advantage to swipe at me. A sharp flash of pain hit as one of his claws met the back of my neck, snagging on my shirt briefly before slicing right through the fabric.

I couldn't outrun him forever—stars, how I had outrun him this long was surprising. Then again, dragons weren't forest-dwellers, and the densely packed trees inevitably slowed the beast down. Up ahead, a large tree to the left had some limbs and vines hanging low. I'd get one chance at this, and I wasn't as spry as I was when I was younger. Not that I'd admit that to anyone.

Closer.

Closer.

Here goes nothing.

I launched myself at the tree and bounded up from one limb to another. Asher's horned head lifted, his fierce eyes tracking me as I jumped into the air and caught one of the vines in both hands. My palms slipped, the coarse plant biting into them and stripping away my skin. I squeezed tighter, wincing through the searing pain at my hands, until I finally stopped.

As I'd hoped, Asher slowed enough for me to drop onto his back near his neck, but unlike the vine, his scales were smooth. My feet and hands scrambled for purchase. Asher slid to a stop, slamming my face into him so hard my nose cracked to one side and my teeth sliced open the inside of my lip, filling my mouth with blood. Wrenching my head to the side, I spat out the blood at the same moment that Asher whipped his head around to snap at me with his large jaws. My blood landed squarely on his snout. With a huffy snort, he shook his head and reared up onto his hind legs.

I could have sworn the damn beast was laughing now as I slid helplessly down his back. Reaching down to my belt, I drew my dagger and stabbed it hard at his shoulders. The blade's tip snapped off and came flying past my face.

Fuck. I should have known that wouldn't work.

I let go of the useless weapon and flung both hands out to my sides, curling my fingers against his scales until they caught the top edge of his wings. The sudden stop pulled hard on my shoulders, and I hissed in pain.

Asher gnashed his teeth at me again, but he couldn't quite reach. When he dropped back onto all fours, I lost my grip on his wings and began to slide forward. Despite his low growl filling my ears, another sound—familiar and formerly terrifying—caught my attention.

I twisted my head around, and sure enough, the vines were creeping up on my reluctant mount. Scrambling to get to my feet, I turned and ran toward his tail, ducking as it swatted at me. I dropped to the ground, hitting it harder than I intended. Nearby, thick tree trunks protruded out of the earth, twisting over each other to create small alcoves—perfect places for me to hide and let the forest do its job with the shifter.

Asher rounded on me, and I ducked under one of the tree roots just as a vine caught his back legs. Another one latched onto his tail, but both snapped as he wrenched himself free. More vines came, and I started to smile, until I realized one was coming straight toward me.

Something tightened against my feet, and the wood around me started to creak.

The damned roots were closing in on me. Confused panic settled in my chest.

I had the pendant.

I had immunity.

Yanking my feet free from the encroaching roots, I rolled out from under them and reached up to my neck.

Nothing.

I swept my hand around and around but found nothing except a sticky gash where Asher had nicked me.

And tore off the chain in the process, apparently.

Where had it dropped? Spinning in a circle, I looked back at the path of destruction Asher had left. The pendant would be too small to see from here. I pushed forward to begin my hunt for it, but a large fern smacked into my face and stayed there, like it was trying to smother me in its fronds.

That's exactly what it's doing.

Thrusting my hands up, I tore the plant away from me and

managed one sharp inhale before vines lashed out, quickly tying my legs together as another tied my wrists and lifted them up above my head. I counted it a small mercy that they didn't pull me off the ground, but even so, my shoulders were still tender from my dragon ride and resting in this position only exacerbated the pain. I refrained from struggling, letting the forest know I was surrendering. Without a weapon on me, it should have realized I wasn't a threat, yet here I was, tied up like a stag waiting to be dressed.

A deep rumble like distant thunder filled the forest from where Asher was held fast by vines, latched around each of his four legs, his tail, and even his neck. Though his head hung low in defeat, his eyes—glowing like hot embers—stared straight at me. His lips curled up over impressive teeth as he continued to growl, and that same dimple peeked through on his scaled cheek.

"Looks like that temper of yours has gotten us into a bit of a pickle," I said, flatly, unable to fake amusement in this situation.

And my mouth, for that matter.

At least I had my medallion.

I just needed to get free somehow, find where I'd dropped the pendant, and make it back to the castle before dusk.

Asher shifted his head to the side, angling his ear upward as if listening for something. I did the same, and felt ridiculous for it. All I heard was our two heartbeats, ragged breaths, and the creepy shifting of the vines as they held us.

"Do you hear something or are you just stretching?" I asked. He ignored me. "This whole conversation thing would be easier if you weren't...you know...still a dragon."

At that moment, two fae came barreling through a stand of ferns. Beck and Korben took one look at the captured dragon and stopped short.

"Fancy seeing you two here," I called, and they shifted their gaze to me for half a breath before looking back to Asher. I sighed heavily. "It's not polite to gawk, you know."

"It's a..." Korben mumbled.

"Dragon." Beck whispered the word. "I thought they were a myth."

Bobbing my head from side to side, I introduced them. "Asher, this is Korben and Beck. Guys, this is Asher. Dragon-shifter extraordinaire."

"Doesn't seem too impressive all tied up like this, does he?" Korben said, nudging Beck with his elbow before sidling up to Asher, who didn't seem to notice, aside from a slight twitch of his eyes. Korben pulled out his dagger. "My brother won't believe it when I tell him. Perhaps a souvenir is in order."

"Don't—" Beck and I both started to warn him, but stopped short when Korben sliced his blade through one of Asher's clawed toes. The dragon didn't bellow or roar, but a low, menacing snarl started, like he was brewing up a plan for revenge on this asshole of a fae.

Korben's face twisted with brutal delight as he picked up the toe and examined it before finally pocketing it and once more stepping toward the restrained beast.

"Although, it'd be even more impressive if I bring back his head," he mused.

Asher bared his teeth and snarled fiercely, but Korben merely laughed.

I scoffed, and he swung toward me.

"How exactly do you plan to do that with a mere dagger?" I asked. "It will take you all evening with such a small blade. And are you expecting Beck here to help you carry it all the way back?"

I nodded toward the smaller fae, who stood off to the side, wringing his hands at his waist.

"Fine," Korben muttered, but then turned to Beck. "Won't get another chance like this, B. Imagine how much someone would pay to have this mounted on their wall. Your family would be set."

"I don't know." Beck shifted his weight back and forth as if he were about to flee.

"At least until Asher's brothers find out what happened," I

said, and Beck's eyes widened. "I imagine they won't be too merciful to those responsible."

"He's right, Korben," Beck said. "And we still need to find our medallions."

I balked at this. "Wait. You guys don't have those yet? I mean, a dragon's head—while impressive—won't win you the tournament."

"Who needs to win that bitch's hand when you can score a prize like this?"

"Ah, yes," I said. "A dragon's dismembered head is far greater a prize than the throne of an entire kingdom. I do wonder, though, how the general and Her Majesty will take to you killing their friend."

"Friend?" Beck asked. I nodded solemnly. "Korben, let's just go."

Korben hesitated, lifting his dagger in the air until it was level with Asher's eye. "Maybe just one more trophy. His eye perhaps."

I groaned in exasperation. "Leave the poor bastard alone. The forest is going to finish us both off anyway." As if to prove my point, the vines twisted tighter around both Asher and me, squeezing another pained moan from both of us. I strained to get my next words out. "In my right pocket, I have a medallion. It's yours if you just leave."

Korben studied me with narrowed eyes. Shrugging, he strolled over to me.

"Alright. Matthias, is it? Deal."

Instead of reaching a hand into my pocket, though, he slashed his dagger across my upper thigh, cutting through the heavy fabric so the medallion fell out into his outstretched hand.

"Seriously? These are my good pants," I complained, only to realize a breath later that his blade had sliced a decent-sized gash in my leg, from which blood was already seeping. He had just missed the artery but had still cut deeply enough I might not have been able to heal fast enough while strung up like this. My vision blurred at the edges.

"Don't worry. As you mentioned, the forest will kill you soon enough," Korben said, backing away into the trees and motioning for Beck to follow. The smaller fae offered a sympathetic look as he too ran off.

CHAPTER 34

MATTHIAS

I must have dozed off or passed out, because when I finally opened my eyes the forest had grown quite dim. The gash in my leg still throbbed, but it didn't seem to be bleeding quite as profusely. Unfortunately my hands had gone numb, and my wrists and shoulders throbbed from the vines holding my arms upright for so many hours. At least I assumed it had been hours.

"How long—" I started to ask Asher, but the dragon was gone.

The vines in front of me now hung limply, uncoiled and empty. Others lay motionless on the ground, their ends still looped as if their captive had simply vanished. I blinked a few times and tried to turn my head to scan the area, but a vine had coiled itself around my neck. My attempts to move only earned me a tighter noose. Keeping my head still, I resorted to shifting my eyes to the left and to the right.

Still nothing.

No dragon.

No shadows.

No fae.

I dropped my head forward, closing my eyes. I couldn't give in to defeat yet. I simply needed time to figure out a plan—except I didn't have much time, if any. I shouldn't have provoked the mercenary. Then I could have been on my way back to the castle, on to the next trial, and on my way to discovering the truth and completing this disaster of a mission.

"Rise and shine, general." A too-cheery voice drew my eyes open. Asher stooped in front of me, looking up with his dimpled, smirking face—no longer in dragon form.

"How'd you get free? And how are you *still* free? Why am I still strung up?" My questions tumbled out of my mouth in a barely coherent mess, and Asher chuckled darkly.

"My limbs are quite a bit bigger as a dragon. Once I shifted back, I pulled free. Being unarmed kept them at bay long enough for me to find this." He pulled the vial—my vial, I assumed—out from his collar.

"And you stayed to gloat, did you?" I asked, lifting a brow at him.

He didn't answer my question but dropped the vial against his chest and stepped back, his head falling to one side as he tapped a finger to his chin.

"Why did you stop that fae from taking my head?"

I shot him a confused look. "Why wouldn't I?"

"Most—especially those I had just tried to kill—would have cheered him on."

Lifting my brows, I feigned shock. "Wait, you were trying to kill me earlier?"

"You can drop the act, general."

"What act would that be?"

He eyed me for a moment, and then his features relaxed in understanding. "I had a brother like you."

"Handsome and charming?"

"Always quick to mask pain with a joke," he corrected.

I frowned at him. "Oh, I'm not trying to hide my pain. I'll describe it to you if you want. My shoulders hurt. I can't feel my fingers. My head is pounding like crazy. And I have an itch between my shoulders that I can't scratch."

He didn't seem at all amused. "You know what I mean."

"You got me," I said, shaking my head. I let my bottom lip tremble a bit. "It's easier to make a quip than to acknowledge the deep-seated angst within"—I sniffed loudly—"but it's just hard not having anyone to really confide in when life is tough. Everyone claims to care, but no one is truly willing to listen. You know?"

His face was cold stone, unmoving and emotionless.

"Would you listen, Asher?" I asked in as pathetic a tone as I could muster.

Looking up into the trees, he sighed loudly. "Are you ever serious?"

"I think so. Only when necessary, though. Life is too short to waste time lamenting shit we can't change."

Asher simply stared at me for several breaths, his expression unreadable. He drew in a long breath and scratched the edge of his jaw before finally speaking again.

"I don't particularly like you, but that doesn't mean I don't respect you. You carried your competition through a deadly forest to ensure he survived. That's admirable."

"I didn't do it to impress you," I said, but he brushed aside my interjection with a wave of his hand.

"More importantly, though, you saved my neck—literally—when you didn't need to. For that, I'll help you out."

I twisted my body as best I could given my restraints. "You mean you'll get that itch for me?"

His lip curled in disgust. "No. You can take care of that on your own once I get you loose."

"Going to give me back my pendant?"

Asher shook his head slowly.

"Then how am I—"

"We'll share it."

"Not sure how that will work, unless you're offering to carry me or something."

He stepped forward, laughing silently as he lifted the chain up over his head. "You don't know what it is, do you?"

"Am I supposed to?"

He shrugged. "I just thought you were supposed to be some wise warrior or something."

"Battle strategies and political maneuvers I can manage, but guessing how a magical bottle works to curb a bloodthirsty forest is beyond my expertise."

"You talk too much."

"So I've been told. Are you going to explain it, or do you really want me to guess?"

Asher carefully removed the stopper from the vial, placed his finger over the opening, and tipped the bottle slightly. When he lifted his finger, he revealed a spot of dark red that slowly began to trail down his skin.

"Blood?" I asked, and the pieces clicked into place. "Of course. Calla's—"

"The queen's, you mean," Asher chided.

I ignored his correction. "Do you happen to have another vial, or some other container, on you?"

He shook his head. "I figured we'd just"—he waved his hand in the air, palm toward me, like he was washing a window—"smear some on you."

"Why not on you?"

Asher regarded me, looked down to the vial in his hand, and then peered up to where the vines still held my wrists.

"Because you're the desperate one here. Not me."

I started to protest that *desperate* was a bit of an exaggeration, but then, he wasn't actually wrong. Without his help, making it back to the castle on time—let alone surviving the forest at all—would be nearly impossible. I didn't have the luxury of failure here, not when Connor and Lieke were relying on me.

"Fine," I said, sighing. "Smear away."

I winced as the blood painfully rushed back into my arms and hands, and even shaking and stretching them out, it took longer than expected for the feeling to fully return. The first step I took brought a fresh burst of pain down my leg and through my hip, and I hissed through my teeth as I reached down to the wound and found it bleeding again.

"Shit," I muttered, and Asher—who had already started to walk off—stopped mid-step and looked back over his shoulder.

"Need something?" he asked.

I started to shake my head no, but his gaze dropped to my bloody hand and he turned fully, making his way back to me.

"You're not going to make it far on that leg," he said.

"I don't need to make it far. I just need to make it to the castle—"

"Which is far considering your condition," he noted.

Another wave of pain stabbed my hip, pulling my expression tight and straining my voice as I added, "And find a gold medallion on the way, of course. No point rushing back if I don't snag one of those first."

Asher appeared to be waging some internal battle as his jaw pulsed with tension. His shoulders slumped in seeming defeat, as he said—with an almost regretful-sounding tone—"I might be able to help with that."

"Oh?" I asked, ignoring how my face twitched again from the worsening pain. "Can you sniff out gold or something?"

Pressing his lips together in a thin line, he hesitated before finally admitting quietly, "Actually, yes."

"So you really are like a—"

His expression darkened, lips curling as if he were about to snarl. "Don't say it."

"Fine, fine. But how do we find it? And quickly?"

A sorrowful sigh fell from him, his hand falling forward as he shook his head, as if he were arguing with himself again.

"I'll carry you," he said.

I could barely keep the amusement from creeping onto my face, and I started to ask him to repeat what he'd said just for fun, but thought better of it.

"Are you sure? I don't want to be a burden."

"Too late for that," he said. "But you saved my life, and you seem to be somewhat decent. Compared to the rest of the remaining suitors, I'd much rather have you win the hand of my friend than have her shackled to a heartless prick who chops off toes for fun."

"How is the hand, by the way? Or was it your foot?"

He held up his left hand and wiggled his fingers. Where his index finger should have been, a single bony nub remained.

"He didn't take the whole toe?"

"Oh, he did," Asher said, smiling as if he had a secret. "We heal fast. Should be good as new in a few days."

"Wait, are you saying you regrow limbs?"

"Depends on the limb, but yes. Legs and arms don't regenerate quite as thoroughly, but appendages like fingers and toes—"

"And...other important appendages?" I asked hesitantly, cursing my curiosity as I swayed precariously on my feet.

Asher laughed heartily. "Never tested that, honestly. Never want to, either. But I thought fae were supposed to heal quickly too." He pointed toward my injured leg. "Why are you still bleeding?"

I looked down at my leg and nearly toppled over, the world spinning around me. "Ah, shit. The poison?" Pressing my fingers to my neck, I checked for a pulse and found it still strong. If it had been poison, it wasn't the potent, fatal kind at least, but how had Korben gotten a hold of it? And why didn't it affect Asher?

"What poison?" Asher asked.

Jerking my head up, I tried to blink away the dizziness, but it only got worse. I opened my mouth to answer, but before I could utter a word, I was falling into darkness.

I hadn't visited the healers since Brennan's death. The dark, cold rooms, tucked away on the first level below ground in a corner opposite the kitchens, had never bothered me before that night. While I rarely needed to see the royal healers, I had always found them to be friendly enough and always eager to help no matter the ailment, whether it was a splitting headache I couldn't shake or a pesky burn in need of a soothing salve.

I could have simply let the guard take Oryn's injured body back to the castle on his own, but a pang of guilt pushed me to personally see he made it to my healers. If Matthias could carry him for a few kilometers through the forest, then I could accompany him and ensure his healing.

Assuming he would heal at all.

The wound on the back of his head had only started to heal, as all fae's injuries did, but not as fast as usual due to the location of the injury. I didn't exactly know how our healing abilities worked, only that head injuries—injuries that harmed the brain specifically—slowed the process significantly, making it almost impossible to recover without a healer's help.

"Will he be okay, Ami?" I whispered from the foot of the bed where I stood, watching our senior healer dress his wound.

Silently waving her sister, Brit, over to help her, she didn't look at me as she answered. "I wish I could say definitively one way or the other. Had he arrived sooner, I could possibly give a more confident estimation, but... At least that general did what he could and got him to you when he did. He could have left him there to die, after all."

I pushed aside the image of Matthias's cocky grin, biting back my frustration that Asher had let his goading get to him. Whatever happened between those two, they damn well deserved it after acting so immaturely.

I nodded crisply to Ami. "Thank you, truly. Anything you need—anything he needs—it's yours."

Allowing myself one quick look at Oryn's sleeping face, I pivoted away and headed toward the exit.

"I will keep you informed of his condition should it change, Your Majesty," Ami said.

I didn't look back as I called over my shoulder, "Any updates should go through General Marlowe."

I had nearly made it to the door when our third healer, Jocelyn, stepped in front of me. Her big brown eyes searched mine with such an intense concern, I couldn't help but look away, focusing instead on the shelves beside the door, stocked with all manners of herbs, oils, mortars, and bottles, somehow seeming less creepy than the stash at Minerva's cottage.

"Is the tea helping?" she asked quietly, though I couldn't fathom why.

I nodded, still averting my eyes. "Yes, thank you. It has been such a blessing."

"And you're still able to use your powers, yes?"

Slowly I met her gaze, silently debating how much to divulge to her. "I am."

"No noticeable differences?" she asked, her brows twitching as if they couldn't decide whether to raise or lower.

I shrugged casually. "Seem easier to control, which is nice."

"Good, good," she muttered, wringing her hands in front of

her. "I'm glad it's helping. If you need anything else, or if it stops being effective, do let me know, yes?"

"I will, of course," I said, lightly dropping my hand to her clasped ones. "Perhaps you could use some of that tea yourself, Jocelyn?"

"I'm fine, Your Majesty. Just nervous about this tournament, is all. I doubt this will be the last injured male we see before this is over."

"They knew the risks," I said, hoping to reassure her somehow, but my voice sounded as empty as the fake smile I wore.

"Of course, I know that," she said, nodding several times before sliding out of my way.

"I will have the general come check on Oryn later tonight after this trial ends." My eyes widened, as if suddenly realizing the time of day, and I swung my glance over to the clock on the wall. The sun would be setting soon, if it hadn't already.

"Go," Jocelyn urged, gently nudging me out the door.

By the time I stepped out through the castle doors, the sun had already retreated below the horizon. Isa, standing alone on the stairs, offered a wan smile when our eyes met.

"No sign of anyone?" I asked.

She shook her head. "Not yet, but it only just set. They have a bit of time."

It was another ten minutes before someone stepped out of the forest onto the main road and began jogging toward us. Graham. Even from here I could see his triumphant smile beaming.

I dug my elbow into Isa's arm and whispered out of the corner of my mouth, "He does know there are no bonus points for arriving first, right?"

Isa chuckled lightly. "I'm sure he assumes he's the only one to finish at all."

The thought hadn't occurred to me, and I began scanning the edges of the forest for any sign of more survivors. I was still searching when Graham bounded up the steps, barely out of breath, and handed a gold medallion to Isa.

"Forty points," Isa said, marking the amount next to his name on her roster. "Five more minutes and it would have been less. Good job, Graham."

He started to walk toward me, but Isa stopped him with a hand on her chest and a slight shake of her head.

"Not tonight. Competitors will get to speak to Her Majesty tomorrow."

"But—" he started to protest, swinging his gaze to me, though I avoided it, still staring at the forest.

"Those are the rules for tonight," Isa said, sternly. She pointed to a crate beside her feet. "Return your daggers and stand aside, please." Graham immediately obliged, pulling two blades from his belt and dropping them noisily into the bin.

I caught Isa's attention and mouthed my gratitude. If I hadn't had such a friend, I didn't know how I would survive any of this.

Graham's disappointed groan floated up to us. Two more fae —one notably larger than the other—were racing toward the castle. Isa checked her pocket watch as they reached the bottom stairs, both doubling over and panting.

"Korben. Beck," Isa said. "Thirty points to each of you. Daggers in the bin, please."

The smaller one—Beck—started to protest, but Korben elbowed him hard in the ribs before Isa could even lift a hand to stop him.

He looked down at his companion. "We're late, it's fine. We at least beat the general. He's probably dead by now anyway."

My stomach hollowed out, and I stepped up alongside Isa, already blurting out my question. "What do you mean? What happened to him?"

Isa rounded on me, her eyes wide and silently screaming at me to shut up and let her handle this.

Shit.

I retreated, refusing to look at any of the males gawking at me. Any attempt to explain my reaction would go ignored, no doubt. They would see it—no matter how truthful it was—as nothing but a poor excuse for my obvious favor for the stars-damned general.

"No daggers, Korben?" Isa asked, scratching away at her paper.

"Lost 'em," he said, his eyes roving over me as he answered, sending a shudder of pinpricks up my back.

Looking back to the tree line, I pretended to be searching for more survivors, but in truth I was frantically considering what possibly could have happened to Matthias and Asher in there. Had they killed each other? I swallowed hard when I remembered Asher hadn't been wearing a pendant. He had declined, insisting he didn't need one as he was staying out of the trees. Had the forest caught him? How would I explain to his brothers if anything happened to him?

Vaguely I noticed the arrival of two more fae, Isa's voice sounding muffled and far away as she noted their names: Seb and Phillip. Time passed, the skies fading into a deeper and deeper blue as we continued to wait. It was Graham's voice that finally snapped me back to the present.

"Fifteen more minutes and he'll have zero points, general," he said. Isa didn't respond. "Longer than that and he's disqualified."

Isa shifted her eyes to him. "Yes, I'm aware."

The five males swiveled their heads toward the main road again, but it was empty. I swallowed hard, cursing the damned Emeryn general in my head. If he hadn't been such a prick, he wouldn't have had Asher trying to kill him...and seemingly succeeding.

I couldn't wait and watch any longer. Dropping my hand to Isa's shoulder, I gestured toward the door and she nodded in understanding. My presence here had no bearing on the outcome of the trial, and I didn't want to deal with the inevitable gloating from the other males when Matthias failed.

As soon as my fingers touched the door's handle, though, a loud gasp brought my head spinning back around. Two of the males were pointing, but I couldn't see around everyone. Isa lifted her hand to her mouth. Quickly I came up beside her.

"What is it?"

"Asher," she whispered, lifting one finger away from her lips to point toward our friend.

Stepping forward, I pushed past the others—ignoring Graham's feeble attempt to reach out and stop me. Asher, still in dragon form, lumbered up to me. His eyes were glassy from exhaustion as they shifted up toward his back. Lowering his body to the ground, he dropped the wing closest to me to reveal Matthias lying there, motionless. Even in the dim light, I could see the pulse at his neck, but it seemed much too slow and weak.

Somewhere behind me Isa called for guards to come quickly and take the general to the healers.

"What happened?" I asked, though I knew neither of them could answer me in their current states.

Asher let out a slight rumbling sound as he nudged my hands with his front foot. Lifting it higher, he held it over my hands, and it took me a moment to realize he was trying to hand me something. I opened my palms and nearly choked when from his grasp fell a heavy gold medallion.

CHAPTER 36

CALLA

I slumped in the large armchair in my sitting room, staring into the fire, when the door creaked open and someone poked their head in.

"May I come in, Your Majesty?" Asher asked.

Keeping my gaze on the flames, I nodded. "Of course, and you can drop the title."

He groaned as he settled onto the sofa and stretched out his back. "He will be fine, if you're wondering," he finally said.

I slowly turned my head to face him. "Who will?"

Asher let out a single breathy laugh. "You don't need to play dumb with me, Calla."

"I don't know what you're talking about," I said, shrugging as I looked away.

"The fuck you don't," he said, his smile evident in every syllable.

"What happened in there anyway?"

"I chased him, managed to almost snag him—losing his bloody pendant in the process—and then your forest did its job and roped us both up. Two of your suitors came by, took my finger"—I gasped as he lifted his hand to show the new finger that was already growing—"stole Prince Charming's medallion—"

"He's no prince," I muttered, but he ignored my interruption.

"Then they stabbed him. He seemed fine at first, but when he lost consciousness soon after, I knew something was amiss. I shifted back, got out of the bonds, found your blood, and got him loose. Unfortunately, despite waking up, he was in piss-poor shape by then and fading quickly. Before he passed out again, he said something about poison."

Poison.

How had one of them gotten poison?

It hadn't killed him—yet anyway—so it didn't seem to be like the rebel's poison Emeryn had faced years ago. But then again, Brennan had mentioned something about the rebels creating different versions of it to have varying potencies. Is that what had been used on Matthias?

Asher's voice was low and solemn when he said, "Should speak to Isa about it. I don't know if all the daggers were poisoned or just the one, but either way, someone's fucking with your tournament."

I could only nod, my mind a whirl of questions that had no obvious answers. Asher leaned forward, propping his elbows on his knees, and cleared his throat as if he wanted to say something, but he remained silent.

"You're leaving," I said, not bothering to form it as a question.

Regret twisted my friend's features. "Unfortunately, yes."

"It's fine," I said, waving a hand in the air as I sat up. "I know how your line of work goes. But before you go, there is one thing I'm curious about."

He hummed quietly, an invitation to continue.

"Why did you help Matthias? He pissed you off enough to get you to shift and chase him into my forest with no protection. You could have just left him there."

Asher laughed lightly and shook his head. Settling back into his seat, he scratched his jaw as if buying himself time to formulate his answer. Finally, he shrugged and flashed an amused smirk.

"He's a right pain in the ass, sure, but he's got a good heart," he said.

"And you're an excellent judge of character."

"I think I am."

"Isa wonders about the possibility he was sent by..." My throat tightened as I tried to say Brennan's name. Why couldn't I get over this already? I was stronger than this, wasn't I? Why did it still hurt so fucking much?

"Brennan's family?" Asher asked, and I pressed my tongue hard to the roof of my mouth to hide my reaction. "You think they believe the rumors?"

"Fucking rumors," I muttered, and grief's grip on my throat shifted, falling into my chest where it ignited into rage. I gritted my teeth, as if actual flames might burst out of me if I opened my mouth.

"No offense, Calla," he said, smirking. "But you look like you want to burn a whole kingdom down."

"Not the whole kingdom," I seethed. "Just those forcing me into this mess. They all think I killed him. I can see it on their pathetic faces."

Asher shrugged and leaned forward onto his legs one more time. "Well, did you?"

I opened my mouth to deny it, but no sound came out.

My tongue grew heavy, my mouth going dry.

My breath stalled. My chest splintered under the weight of the words I couldn't utter.

Tears stung my eyes. I dropped my face to hide them, staring down at my empty hands.

I was about to summon my shadows—which had at least remained leashed despite the emotional surge—but Asher was now kneeling in front of me, his hands closing around mine.

"If anyone understands this guilt, Calla, it's me."

I shook my head. We may have shared this grief of losing someone, but his circumstance was different. He *had* been responsible for his loss, and he beat himself up over it—guarded himself because of it—despite it being an honest accident. But I couldn't explain any of this to him.

I never should have made that deal with Minerva. What good was knowing who had killed Brennan, when I couldn't do anything about it? Sure, I'd paid the mage to curse them, but how could I trust that she had done it adequately?

"Calla," Asher said, squeezing my hand once more. "Whatever you need, you can always call on me. Want me to burn the Assembly to a crisp?"

This time when I shook my head, I at least managed a slight chuckle.

"Tempting," I said.

"I mean it."

"I know you do, but you've got your next job."

"True. And it may be a long one from the sound of it, but if this all goes to shit—more than it already has—send the word."

"I wish I didn't have to do this," I whispered.

Asher scratched his chin again and stared into the fire. "Understandable. But it's not completely hopeless. Matthias could be a good choice. If he can survive without my help, that is."

"And assuming he's not here to kill me," I said, smiling weakly.

"Just a small detail," he said. "Let's hope that's not the case."

CHAPTER 37

MATTHIAS

Being poisoned wasn't all that bad—like a bad hangover without the initial enjoyment.

At first it was like being rocked to sleep, rhythmic swaying as I sank deeper and deeper into peaceful darkness.

And then it ceased.

How long ago, I didn't know. Unlike my room in the castle, my subconscious had no giant clock available. But the rocking had stopped long enough for me to find a new comfort in the stillness.

Here in the warm darkness, there were no enchanted plants trying to strangle me, no asshole fae trying to kill me, no dragon shifters trying to eat me.

But it wasn't completely peaceful, as my thoughts spiraled into a chaotic mess.

Had Asher gotten me out of the forest?

Had he found a medallion for me?

How did Korben get the poison?

Were all the daggers poisoned?

What happened to Graham?

And Oryn? Had he made it back to the castle?

Was I still in the tournament?

As if in answer to my multitude of questions, a voice slipped in among my thoughts, faint and almost inaudible, as if it were tucked somewhere in the shadows of my mind.

"You're lucky, it seems," she said.

Calla? The queen? Why was she here in my head?

I tried to pry my eyes open, but they wouldn't budge. Attempted to lift a finger, but nothing.

Maybe this was just a byproduct of the poison, though Connor had never mentioned hallucinations. Shared dreams, sure, but that was from his bond with Lieke, not from the poisoning.

Maybe I'm talking to myself.

In Calla's voice? Unlikely.

Hearing what you want to hear?

Of all the voices my mind could use to process shit, why not hers?

"How you won Asher over, I don't know," she continued. "But you're still in the tournament because of him. Never thought I'd see the day when he befriended anyone new."

Silence settled around me again, long enough for me to wonder if she'd gone—and to be disappointed by that prospect.

I scoffed to myself.

It's just a bit lonely here.

Not like I want her specifically.

When she finally spoke again, my heart perked up at first—delighted that she hadn't left—until her words sank in, like a barb pushed slowly into my chest.

"I don't want you here."

Why did that simple statement hurt so much?

"I don't need a king to rule beside me, yet here I am." She paused to release a huffy growl. "No choices. No options. No freedom. A queen should be able to rule as she wants; not have to bend to the will of an Assembly of peasants. I should have just killed them all in that meeting. Killed them all and been done with it."

Killed them all.

As much as I wanted that to be an admittance of guilt so I could finish my work here and go home, I couldn't trust anything I heard in this condition. For all I knew, this was my own consciousness putting words into her imaginary mouth.

But then a weight settled on my hand and squeezed my fingers. Her breath tickled my ear, and I swore I caught the unmistakable sound of a tongue wetting lips. I almost chided myself for letting my imagination run amok, but then she whispered.

"You might be the only good one left, so please don't die on me."

Everything vanished. The weight. The breath. The voice.

And I was alone again with a new tangle of questions.

❧

Eventually the world faded back into my consciousness. I didn't open my eyes immediately, but the first thing I noticed was the pungent scent of smoldering herbs. Second was my pants were missing, followed shortly by the realization that someone was fondling my thigh.

Slitting my eyes open just enough to verify someone was actually there and I wasn't dreaming it, I pulled my chapped lips apart. My mouth had gone uncomfortably dry, but I managed to croak out my words.

"I prefer to be awake when a female's touching me."

She didn't pull away as I expected—didn't even seem surprised to hear me speak, as she continued to rub something warm on my wound.

"You needed your rest, general," she said, her voice an odd combination of sweet and sharp. It reminded me of Mrs. Bishop's actually, where in the same tone she could both commend and reprimand quite effectively.

I pried my eyes open more, thankful for the dim light, though my head pounded all the same. Dark stone surrounded me—on the walls, the ceiling, and presumably the floor as well. My lips curved downward when I realized the female beside me wasn't the queen, but some fae I didn't recognize. Maybe it had just been my imagination.

Or maybe you've been out so long she left, because she had better things to do than sit around and wait for your sorry ass to wake up.

Either way, for whatever reason, it wasn't her dressing my wounds now.

"And you're a healer? I hope?" I asked, resting my head back and staring at the ceiling.

"One of the three here in Arenysen, yes. Along with my sister. I'm Brit," she said.

"How long have I been here?"

She hummed for a moment, as if calculating the time that had passed. Had it really been that long?

"Five days. While the antidote to the poison took effect rather quickly, it took quite a while for your body to recover from the damage done. Thankfully, Jocelyn is quite adept at dealing with toxins. Without her..."

"I'd still be out," I finished her thought, but in my periphery I noticed she shook her head.

"You'd be dead," she said matter-of-factly.

I breathed out an empty laugh. "Is she here? I should probably thank her."

"No, she's busy elsewhere." A heavy sigh fell from the healer. "She could use it, honestly. She's beaten herself up pretty badly for not being able to help more with the other male."

Oryn?

Jerkily I propped myself up on my elbows, a wince pulling my face tight as fresh pain shot through my hip. I ignored it—and ignored Brit's hand flying to my chest as she attempted to force me to lie back down. I glanced around the room, turning my head this way and that but finding nothing but a handful of empty beds and cluttered work tables covered with bottles and bandages at the far end.

"Mr. Lain is not here."

"But he was? What happened? Did he—"

"He's been taken to his room upstairs. We felt it better to have him in a more comfortable environment for his last days."

"His last days?" I asked. "I need to see him." I shifted toward the edge of the stiff cot. Again, the healer tried to stop me, her hand pressing firmly against my shoulder.

"You need more rest," Brit said, though not as forcefully as I expected.

I slid my legs over the side. "I'd prefer to rest in my room, like him."

Brit slumped in defeat, her hands falling to her sides as she shrugged. "Fine. I'll let Her Majesty and the general know your decision."

Planting my feet firmly on the ground, I offered the healer a half-smile. "You give in too easily."

She shrugged again. "I have better uses of my energy, and you're a grown male, supposedly."

Her eyes flashed down quickly to my waist before lifting again, this time to the ceiling rather than meeting my gaze. I twisted my lips into a smirk. "Quite grown."

"Mr. Orelian," a harsher voice called from the doorway. There stood another fae, who looked strikingly similar to the one still blushing beside me, except this one had a dourer way about her that reminded me of my sister when she was lecturing me.

"You must be the sister," I said.

"Ami." She nodded crisply, her lips sliding into a stern smile that matched her grim stare. "Glad to see you're awake." By her tone and her rigid form, this female didn't seem to know what the word *glad* meant at all.

"Thank you." I pushed myself up off the cot slowly, keeping my hands on it until I could trust my legs to support me. "I was just leaving though."

"I'd be more comfortable if you waited until we cleared this with General Marlowe and Her Majesty first."

"And I'd be more comfortable if I had my pants."

"Of course. Apologies," Ami noted before gesturing to Brit who quickly slipped around to the end of the cot and retrieved my clothing from where they'd stashed them. Brit smiled sheepishly as she silently ducked out of the room, leaving me alone with her sibling who seemed wholly disinterested as she watched me dress.

"Speaking of Her Majesty," I started, straightening my collar before smoothing out the fabric of my shirt. Ami lifted a brow in question. "Did she happen to visit me here?"

Ami's expression remained as unenthusiastic as ever. She pursed her lips as she breathed deeply. "Not that I'm aware of. She doesn't—"

I waved my fingers in the air to cut her off. "No worries. Must have just..." I let my words peter off. This healer would probably force me to remain here longer if I admitted to dreaming of the queen or hearing voices.

Ami eyed me curiously, as if trying to deduce what information I had withheld, but she must have deemed it unimportant, because soon enough she gave an almost kind smile. "If you're set on leaving, at least go speak with General Marlowe first."

"I will do just that," I said and dipped my chin in gratitude. "Before I do, though, can I ask something?"

She said nothing but gave the slightest of nods.

"The poison. Had you seen it before?" I asked as casually as I could.

Frowning, she said, "Only in the samples your healers sent us to study. As you know, we didn't encounter the same attacks here as you did in Emeryn."

"Did you ever encounter it outside of what we sent?" I asked.

Suspicion clouded her eyes. "Why do you ask?"

"Merely curious how you acquired an antidote," I noted, remembering how Minerva had saved Connor by magically stripping the poison from his blood. As far as I knew, she was the only one in this world who possessed the power to do anything like that.

"Jocelyn—our other healer—has a natural talent with concocting remedies, and she spent the last year studying that dagger your kingdom sent us. She worked to extract the poison from the blade and manipulate it to create a counteragent. Of course, it had gone untested until you showed up."

I narrowed my eyes at her. "What about with Brennan? Was he poisoned with something different altogether?"

Ami stiffened, standing taller with her chin lifted, but her expression remained blank, her hands relaxed and casually folded in front of her. Her tone, however, held a tinge of defensiveness. "Who said he was poisoned?"

My thoughts churned uneasily, and I had to act quickly before she grew even more suspicious. "Oh, no one," I lied. If she didn't know the Durands had been notified of suspected poisoning, I certainly wasn't going to be the one who warned her. "Coming from Emeryn and years of battling poison-wielding rebels, and it's hard not to simply assume."

"Assumptions are dangerous, general," she said.

"Well, if it wasn't poison, how did he die?" I asked, leaning toward her slightly.

This time the healer's knuckles whitened as she squeezed her hands together, and somehow her tone became even less hospitable. "I don't think it prudent that I divulge such information to a competitor. I've already said too much as it is. You should go."

Raising my palms to her I bowed my head once more before moving for the door. Her expression remained stoic even as I stumbled slightly with my first steps. It wasn't until I was out in the hallway that I realized I had no idea where I was within the castle and no clue how to find Isa from here. If this castle was at all like the Durands', then the healers' quarters were likely on a lower floor near the kitchen. I sniffed the air, noting the faint aroma of roasting vegetables. Yes, the kitchen was close. Now if I could just find some stairs...

No sooner had I rounded the next corner than something—or someone—shoved me hard into the stone wall. My head smacked against it with a gut-turning crack. Instinctively, my eyes clamped shut, and I barely opened them in time to see a fist—albeit blurry with my distorted vision—careening toward me. I attempted to duck, but my movements were sluggish. The attack grazed off my cheekbone so the knuckles slammed into my ear.

Growling, I spun away from my attacker, but his other fist swung low, landing square on my leg wound. My knee buckled, dropping me to the floor in a groaning, pathetic heap. The male reared his leg back to kick me, and gritting my teeth against the pain, I grabbed his other leg with both hands and jerked it out from under him.

"Fuck!" he growled as he crashed to the ground, but he pivoted on his backside and sent a foot straight into my face. My hands flew up to cradle my nose, which was already gushing blood all over the floor.

Maybe I should have stayed with the healers after all.

The other male scrambled to his feet and landed another kick to my gut, forcing me to curl up to protect myself. I tried to look up to see who it was, but my face was quickly swelling, obscuring my vision even more. Then the familiar sound of a blade clearing its sheath hit my ears, and every muscle tensed as I tried to find any way out of this fucking mess. The rustling of fabric and creaking of joints told me whoever he was had kneeled beside me.

"You were supposed to die in the forest," he said, and my mind fought to connect the voice to its owner. "But apparently a dragon, a haunted forest, and even a poisoned fucking blade can't kill you."

Korben.

Of course he'd try to finish the job in between trials.

I cleared my throat, shifting it into a weak laugh. "What can I say? I'm a stubborn ass."

"Stubborn or not, another dose of poison and you won't be walking away this time."

I pulled the corner of my mouth back into what was meant to be a half-smile. "Offering to carry me? How kind of you."

A roar burst out of his chest, and I looked up to see him lifting the blade up by his ear, preparing to drive it into me. Time seemed to slow. The flames from the wall sconces reflected on his dagger's edge, and then vanished as the candles were snuffed out and the corridor filled with an unnatural darkness I'd experienced once before––back in the forest when I'd first arrived.

Except this time, they weren't a soft blanket called to soothe and comfort. These shadows were cold and hard, like icy daggers pressing in from all sides, churning bitterly.

Before Korben could stab blindly at me, I rolled away from him, hissing as the floor dug into my injury.

"What's hap—" Korben's voice snapped off like a twig beneath a boot, and a second later came the dull sound of his body falling to the floor.

Almost immediately, the shadows cleared, and I opened my mouth to greet her with a *Hi Killer* or something equally charming, but the hallway was empty.

CALLA

I was halfway up the stairs when I called my shadows to retreat, but when they snapped back into my palms, my foot slipped. My shin struck the edge of the step hard. Biting back a curse, I pushed myself to keep going. Two more flights of stairs and I would be safe in my room. No one needed to know where I'd been or what I'd done.

At least I hadn't killed the asshole. That would be a much bigger mess to clean up, and this was already going to be a pain and a half to keep quiet; Matthias would undoubtedly tell someone.

I groaned, realizing just how stupid I had been. What the fuck had I been thinking? Attacking one of the competitors? And with my shadows, no less!

But no one would believe the general, right? He'd been poisoned, injured, unconscious for nearly a week. No one would believe him. It was my word against his.

Except...

What good was my word now?

No one seemed to believe my innocence.

Stars, even Asher believed I killed my husband.

Asher. One of my oldest friends.

At least he didn't judge me, though. I guess.

I should have probably found comfort in that fact—that my friend still supported me even when I'd all but admitted to being the killer.

Killer.

I'd fled the hallway before Matthias could utter that blasted nickname, but shit, I was going to need to fix this. I couldn't rely on others not believing him. I needed to keep him quiet.

Good luck with that. That male never shuts up.

A smile threatened to creep up, but I fought it, biting down hard on my lower lip as I slipped into my room. I just needed a moment to think and come up with a plan. Maybe a bath could help. Maybe—

"What did you do?" Isa asked, slipping into her disappointed, parental tone, accentuated by the severe gleam in her eye. She leaned against the doorway to my bedroom, her hand falling to her hip.

I clicked the door shut and drew in a deep breath before turning to face her. Widening my eyes a bit, I donned my best air of innocence.

"I took a walk. Why?"

Isa's already weary expression now darkened knowingly. "I know you, Calla. Your heart is racing erratically, almost as fast as you ran down that hallway. Add in you wringing your hands in your dress, and I assume this has something to do with your shadows."

I shrugged. "It's nothing."

"That shake in your voice—that one you think no one hears? —says otherwise. Now what happened?"

"The asshole had it coming," I said, rolling my eyes as I strolled over to the sofa and plopped down, kicking my boots off and pulling my feet up under me.

Isa calmly joined me before the cold fireplace. She didn't seem at all shocked by my answer as she sat and draped her arm casually over the back of the sofa.

"Which asshole was that?"

"I think his name was Korben."

"Was?" Fear sparked in her eyes, but vanished when I clarified.

"Is. He's still alive."

"You're sure?"

I nodded.

"And? What did he have coming exactly?"

"I might have strangled him. Just a bit. Enough to knock him unconscious."

Isa leaned forward slightly, fresh concern washing over her face. "Did he try to hurt you?"

"Not me."

"Then who—" Understanding shifted her question into a whispered *oh*. "Matthias?"

I pulled my lips into a thin, pathetic smile, but said nothing.

"Is he okay? What about the healers? Where were they? And how did Korben even get down there?"

"I assume he's fine, but I didn't stick around long enough to find out. I thought it best if he didn't see me."

"But your shadows..."

"Yes, obviously he knows it was me, but I couldn't deal with him and his whole *killer* thing."

Confusion twisted my general's brow. "What *killer* thing?"

Rolling my eyes again, I gave small shakes of my head. "It's just a dumb nickname he's given me."

Isa lifted a hand to her mouth, whispering, "Interesting."

"You don't think it means something, do you?" She merely leaned her ear toward one shoulder in a silent gesture of uncertainty. "Either way," I continued. "They were in the hallway, not in the infirmary."

After a few moments of quiet, Isa peered up at me from beneath her thick lashes. "What were you doing down there? Did you run out of the tea? Jocelyn said she'd deliver more so you wouldn't have to venture down there."

Shit. I didn't have an excuse ready. I sat there looking at her like an idiot, and by the time I thought to lie—to say I'd simply had a question for Jocelyn—I'd been silent for so long, she'd never believe it. I prepared myself for another displeased glare and the accompanying rebuke.

The corners of her eyes and lips twitched slightly as she worked through her thoughts, but when her expression finally settled, I found what looked like an unnerving mix of worry and... hope.

"What?" I asked.

"What do you mean, what?"

"You're looking at me strangely," I said, cocking my brow suspiciously.

Isa angled her head at me and pursed her lips for a moment before finally saying, "I'm merely waiting for you to answer my question, which you still haven't done."

"You look like you're expecting me to answer a certain way," I noted.

"Were you checking on a certain foreign general?" Isa eyed me almost eagerly, like she was hoping that was exactly what I had been doing. If only I could answer her honestly without giving her the satisfaction of being right.

"What if I was? It doesn't mean anything."

"Of course it doesn't," Isa said through a slowly widening grin.

"Why?" I asked, not caring how childishly defensive I sounded. "Why does it matter?"

Isa shrugged smugly. "No reason. But"—her gaze darkened with a tinge of worry again—"I want to see you happy again, friend. I know you say you can't love again, but maybe, with the right match, you could. And that's all I want for you. Another chance at love."

"Oh, is that all?" A hollow laugh tumbled from me, and I offered her a weak smile. "That's what best friends are for, right? Believing in us when we can no longer do it ourselves? I can't get hurt again, Isa."

She reached forward and rested her hand on mine. "But you can, Calla. As long as you draw breath, pain is possible—perhaps even inevitable—but life isn't about avoiding hardship; it's about being the good in someone else's life, so they don't have to endure any of this shit alone. You cannot avoid heartache, but you're not alone in it either."

My eyes misted against my will, and I swiped my free hand across them.

"Fucking stars, Isa. Why do you have to do that?"

"Do what?" she asked, her voice cracking under her own emotional weight as she wiped away her own tears.

"Make me feel. You know I'd rather just be numb."

"Numb or angry, you mean?" She laughed when I shrugged in agreement.

"That was a bit of a stretch, though," I said, and she shifted her gaze to the ceiling as if backtracking through our conversation in her head. "Since when does checking on an injured guest indicate *chance at love*?" I emphasized the last three words with a wiggle of my fingers in the air between us.

Isa rubbed the back of her neck slowly as she studied me. "I suppose it doesn't."

"Thank—"

"Or it wouldn't," she interrupted me. "Had you not ridden in on your shadowy horse and saved him."

I had to fight to keep my mouth from falling open. What would she have had me do back there? Let him die?

I was about to ask her just that when she noted, "You're different with him."

Groaning, I rolled my eyes. "I've barely been around him."

"But you *have* been around him," she said, arching one brow. "That's more than can be said for any of the other competitors."

"Except Graham," I said, but she was already shaking her head before I finished saying his name.

"Even Graham. You may have spent time with him before these games, but have you since?"

"At that first dinner he talked to me in the corner," I said, a tad too triumphantly.

"You mean, after the general rushed over to protect you from a shadowy disaster by dancing with you?"

"I also saw Graham in the forest." I realized my mistake too late.

All amusement vanished from Isa's face, hidden under a shroud of disappointment. "So you did go in there during the trial."

I said nothing. Her hard stare made me want to sink into the sofa's cushions until I reminded myself that I was still her queen, mistakes and poor decisions be damned. A queen didn't cower.

"I thought you knew," I lied, shifting my gaze away from her to inspect my fingernails.

"You're a shit liar, Calla. How would I have known?"

"Figured that brilliant mind of yours would have deduced as much when I escorted the other injured male back from the forest." I lifted my eyes to her again, forcing the muscles in my face to relax despite the apprehension this whole confrontation had brewed.

"Flattery? That's what you're going with?"

"To be fair, I never promised not to go. You only asked me to promise."

"Silly me to think you might actually listen to me for once. I told you to buy yourself more time to choose a new king, but this strange vendetta you seem to have against the humans kept you from listening to reason. And now we're here, with only five weeks left. What do you think the Assembly will do if they find out you interfered with a trial?"

"But I didn't—"

"You know the truth doesn't matter, Calla. Perception matters when you're the fucking queen! Especially when you're a queen suspected of murdering her husband!"

Her words shot straight through my chest, igniting fresh rage. Of course I knew all of this. I didn't need her throwing it in my face, constantly reminding me of the stars-damned rumors. Balling my fists, I pressed my hands down onto my lap as hard as I could. My arms shook with tremors, which only got worse the harder I tried to subdue them by pulling them tightly against my ribs.

Just as quickly as she'd gone cross with me, Isa softened, reaching for my hand once more and giving it a squeeze.

"You know I don't think you did it, right?"

I swallowed hard. My body was still tense but now from fear instead of anger. I wanted to ask her how she knew, but I couldn't. I'd already walked into that awkward conversation with Asher, and he had taken my silence to his question—the question Isa would surely have as well—as proof of my guilt.

Instead I only nodded, dropping my eyes to my lap where I slowly uncurled my fingers.

Isa stood and stretched out her back. "As much as I've loved getting to talk with you, there is a little bit of a mess downstairs I need to figure out how to clean up. Do you think Korben knows it was you who attacked him?"

I blinked up at her and lifted a shoulder. "I honestly don't know."

"Well, knowing the general, he probably delivered Korben to Ami. If I can get down there before he wakes up, maybe we can spin this in your favor. In the meantime, I need you to prepare."

My throat tightened again, and my words came out weaker than I intended. "Prepare for what?"

"The Assembly insists you meet with each of the survivors from the first trial."

"And you agreed?"

She lifted her chin slightly. "Yes. I know you don't plan to choose one yourself, and while this isn't one of the official trials, I do think it would be good."

"You're the one who told me not to take any unnecessary risks. How is it not risky having me alone in a room with males who could be here to assassinate me?"

"This was deemed necessary."

"Why? How is this at all necessary? I've already vowed—with my blood even—to accept and marry whoever wins! How could this possibly help me?"

"It's not for you," she said. "Yes, you'll gain some insight into the males seeking your hand, but this is to help us avoid any of them complaining about favoritism."

I started to scoff, but Isa halted any argument with a stern look. Shaking her head, she explained, "Matthias cannot be the only competitor you ever speak to, Calla."

CHAPTER 39

MATTHIAS

I should have left the bastard lying in the hallway, but if he woke up and told anyone what had happened to him, it could create problems for the queen and jeopardize this tournament and my chances of learning the truth about Brennan's death. So, here I was, with Korben's blade tucked safely back in its sheath and hidden in my boot, dragging the good-for-nothing male back to the healers while my weary body protested every movement.

By the time we reached the closed door of the infirmary, the ache in my feet had traveled up my legs until they were shaking with fatigue. My shoulders throbbed from the heavy load, and my fingers—their tips severely chafed from gripping him by the rough leather he wore—finally gave up, dropping him to the floor with a dull thud. It took every bit of energy I had left not to crumple to the ground beside him.

Resisting the urge to kick him, I rounded on the door and knocked.

I leaned forward, straining to hear any trace of a footstep, but there was nothing but silence. Hadn't I just been here? Had Ami left? And if so, had she not witnessed Korben's attack?

Pushing out a pained sigh, I let my shoulders fall heavily with the realization that I'd have to keep moving him by myself. I flexed my hands a few times and rubbed my fingertips against my thumbs, trying to soothe away the discomfort before I had to lift him again.

I had just gotten his shoulders and head off the ground when a pair of footsteps pulled my attention around behind me. Ami and another female rounded the corner. Their eyes flashed from Korben to me as they approached, though no sign of alarm showed on their faces.

"What happened here, general?" Ami asked.

Her words, while not terribly loud, bounced painfully around my head, forcing me to clench my eyes shut as I turned back to Korben and let him fall at my feet. Touching my fingers to my temple, I worked to massage away the throbbing headache as I moved to speak with the healers.

I gestured to my still-swollen face. "Korben happened."

The females exchanged a quick glance. The younger one—her cheeks dotted by warm freckles and framed by a cascade of dark red hair—eyed me curiously.

"And what happened to him?" she asked.

"He attacked the wrong male," I said, frowning casually.

"You did this?" Ami asked. "In your condition?"

"Never underestimate what someone can do when their life is threatened," I explained, lifting a shoulder in a painful shrug.

"Let's get him inside," Ami said. "General, could you get the door for us?"

I started to protest and offer to help carry him, but the pain in my ribs flared up as if my body begged me not to do more until I was healed. Sliding the door open, I watched in a bit of amazement at how easily the two females lifted the male and carried him inside to a cot opposite the one that had been mine.

"Don't look so impressed," Ami said, winking as she passed by me. "It's a bit easier when you have someone else helping."

"Or when you're not recently injured—or poisoned," chimed in the other.

"And you are Jocelyn, I presume?"

She nodded, smiling sweetly, though not going pink as Brit had.

After they settled him onto the cot, Ami looked over his face and neck, shifting his head from side to side. She didn't look up at me when she asked, "And you did this?"

"He was about to stab me," I said, nodding.

She peered up at me from where she was still hunched over Korben. "That's not an answer."

Smirking, I narrowed my eyes at her. "You miss nothing, do you?" She gave no response, not even a slight lift of a brow or tiny twitch of the mouth, so I dipped my chin. "Yes, I did."

Her gaze slid over to Jocelyn, who stood on the other side of the cot, checking Korben's pulse.

"We will take it from here," Ami said. "You still need to find General Marlowe, no?"

"Indeed. Will he be okay though?"

This time it was Jocelyn who answered. "He should be fine. Not the first time we've seen—"

"He'll be fine," Ami interrupted, shooting a glare Jocelyn's way.

I pretended not to notice the silent reprimand. "Good. I'd hate for him to miss out on the next trial."

Jocelyn smiled, ignoring the way Ami still glowered at her disapprovingly. "Well, they've postponed it several days for you already. No doubt they'll do the same for Mr. Hoff here as well."

Nodding, I started to turn for the door but stopped. "You don't happen to have anything to help with this pounding headache, do you?"

"Of course," Ami said, but she directed Jocelyn to go and fetch it for me. "You may find you don't heal quite as quickly as usual."

"You mean the poison's still lingering?" I asked, genuinely curious how it worked.

"Not really, no. More like the poison damaged your body's ability to heal."

"Permanently?" I asked. This was certainly going to make the remaining trials—let alone the rest of my military life—more dangerous.

Ami pursed her lips as if she wasn't sure she wanted to answer, but finally said, "We aren't sure, to be honest."

"Well, can't expect you to have all the answers, I suppose. What should I tell the general about..." I waved my hand in Korben's direction.

"The truth usually works nicely," Ami said just as Jocelyn returned holding out a small leather pouch.

"Dissolve this in water and take as needed for the pain," she explained. "Also maybe see about getting some ice for that nose of yours. It's not broken, but you won't be pretty again until that swelling goes down."

Angling my head toward my shoulder, I grimaced as if I'd just tasted something bitter. "Are you saying I'm not pretty anymore, Jocelyn?"

She lifted a hand to my cheek and patted it tenderly. "You've had better days."

The healer hadn't been lying about the delayed healing. With the wound on my leg burning, my head throbbing, and my face and ear aching—not to mention my body being utterly exhausted from my ordeal with Korben—it took me an embarrassingly long time just to reach the second floor of the castle. Why did Isa's office have to be on the fourth?

My lungs screamed at me to stop and rest, so I turned the corner to lean against the wall, trying to look casual as I gave my body time before continuing the rest of the way. Thankfully none of my other five competitors came by, and the few staff members I met averted their eyes and scurried past me without a word.

I'm the fucking leader of the Emeryn army, and I'm here holding up the wall.

What the hell is this competition doing to me?

Fuck this. I can rest once I get to my room. Find Isa, then go lie down.

Pushing away from the wall, I pivoted back around the corner, only to collide with someone who had just ran up the stairs. She backed away immediately, nearly falling down them, but I caught her by the shoulders.

"Watch where you're go—" she barked out, stopping herself when her brown eyes met mine. The fiery irritation in her features vanished. "Oh, General Orelian. I didn't see you there."

"I hope not, or it might make things awkward when I win this tournament," I said, giving a half-hearted smirk.

She angled her head slightly. "Awkward how?"

"You throwing yourself at me like that could make Her Majesty jealous."

Isa scoffed. "She'd have to witness it to be jealous."

I pressed my hand to my chest. "But my conscience would not allow me to keep such a secret from my bride."

That last word tasted wrong on my tongue, but it was worth it for how perturbed the general became, gazing up at the ceiling and sighing.

"I really should be going," she said, attempting to skirt around me. But I moved out of her way at the same moment, inadvertently stepping into her path.

I bowed my head in apology and shifted away from her. She rushed past me, seemingly careful to give me a wide berth. She was halfway up the next flight of stairs when I suddenly remembered I'd actually been looking for her. Maybe that poison messed with more than just my healing abilities.

Or maybe I'm just tired.

Either way, I needed to stop the general before she got further away and forced me to climb more stairs.

"General!" I called out, doing my best to hide my limp as I hobbled over to the center of the staircase and looked up at her.

She glanced over her shoulder at me, but didn't fully turn as she raised a brow. "Yes?"

"Your healer, Ami, told me to check in with you. I was actually on my way to find you when you accosted me."

"I didn't…" Her protest faded into a long exhale, and she reluctantly turned and came back down, stopping a step or two higher than the landing so that her eyes easily met mine. "What's her message?"

"Oh"—I frowned—"no message from her really. Just wanted me to inform you that I was awake, well, and planning to stay in my own room rather than in the infirmary."

Isa's features pinched as she studied my face. "You're well, are you?"

"Well enough," I said. "It's nothing really."

"You were poisoned though. That's not nothing," she said.

Shrugging, I smirked. "I've had worse."

"I'm sure you have. I don't recall you having these injuries when you exited the forest though. Did our healers rough you up a bit?"

I watched her for a moment. Something in her tone and the little curve at the corner of her mouth indicated she knew more than she was letting on. Of course she knew. No doubt the queen had gone to her at once. Isa was testing me, baiting me to divulge what I knew or suspected.

I could have played dumb, but Isa's previous words to Beck during our registration echoed in my mind. Lying would not go over well with this general. Better to use this moment to my advantage.

Pointing to my face, I chuckled lightly. "Oh, this was a get well present from Korben. Along with this," I said, pulling the male's blade from my boot.

She feigned surprise, almost too convincingly. Perhaps she was more shocked that I'd actually told the truth.

Taking the blade from me, she slipped it carefully into her belt and said, "Well, I assure you, General Orelian, we will see that he is rightly punished for attacking you outside of the trials. But, I am curious. How did you get away? Ami said your injury along with the poison would weaken you quite a bit even after you awoke."

I rubbed my still-sore fingers along my stubbled jaw and looked to the ceiling as if contemplating my next words. "I think you know, general."

Isa's expression remained still, but she shifted her weight slightly—enough of a confirmation for me.

I leaned in slightly and lowered my voice to a whisper. "No need to fret, though. I deposited him back at the infirmary and informed the healers of what happened."

"Which was?"

"He attacked me, and I subdued him."

"You? In your condition? And our healers believed you?"

I flashed a wink that was probably more grotesque than charming given the state of my face. "I can be quite convincing, I promise."

"We'll see. I plan to go speak with them later this morning. Will you be visiting Oryn? I know you two had a bit of a connection."

"Actually, I intended to after I found you, but I'm a little worse for wear than I anticipated. I may need to rest first."

"Very well. I'm also more than willing to postpone your time with the queen for tomorrow if you prefer."

I recoiled slightly but hopefully recovered quickly enough with a half-smile. "What time with the queen? Is this the second trial?"

Isa waved a hand between us. "No, not a trial. Just a casual meeting with Her Majesty."

My huffed laugh brought her brow low over her eyes. "Sorry, sounds rather funny to use the words *casual* and *majesty* in the same sentence."

The general mulled that over for a bit. "I suppose you're right. Still, this is more a chance for Calla to get to know each of you a little better."

I frowned. "That doesn't sound like it was her idea."

Shaking her head, Isa blew out a tired breath. "No, it wasn't, but it's necessary all the same. Would you like to postpone—"

"No," I said, a little too quickly. "I'm happy to see her this evening. Just let me know when and where."

"Very good," Isa said, lifting her chin. "I'll get the information to your valet as soon as I have it settled."

❧

A heavy thumping of boots woke me from my dreamless—yet still restless—sleep, and I clutched my head as I rolled over to find my valet stomping across the room to open the drapes and let in streams of deep gold afternoon sunlight. When the final curtain slid open, throwing bright light across my face, I winced with a low groan and tried to roll over, but that only stoked pain elsewhere in my body.

Was this how humans felt when they got hurt?

No wonder humans were such a miserable lot.

"Mr. Orelian," Giles said, tapping his heels loudly together. I peeked back over my shoulder but kept my eyes squinted against the brightness as I hummed in recognition. He let out a weary breath, as if talking to me was the last thing he wanted to be doing. "General Marlowe expects you to present yourself in one hour to Her Majesty in the solar on the uppermost floor."

I groaned again at the thought of climbing more stairs.

"And she said this wasn't a trial," I muttered to myself.

Giles responded all the same. "It is not a trial, and I am to offer my assistance should you require it."

"No need for that," I said, sitting up and dropping my feet to the floor. Though my back was to the valet, his relief was evident in his next words.

"Very good, sir. I have taken the liberty of drawing a bath for you."

"Thank you." I pushed myself to stand. "And don't worry, I don't need any assistance with that either."

Giles nodded and promptly fled the room, as if my injuries were contagious.

I bathed as quickly as I could—and as well as I could—with my body still protesting every movement. Selecting a plain black button-down shirt and dark gray trousers, I dressed and afforded one brief glance in the mirror. At least the swelling had subsided enough that I looked somewhat like myself again. My first step toward the door sent a jolt of pain shooting down my leg, and I grimaced and hissed through each subsequent step I took back to my bedroom, where the healers' pouch and a glass of water sat on the bedside table. Thankfully, the herbs—as nasty as they were—took effect almost immediately, and by the time I reached the door, my pain was barely noticeable at all.

Oryn's room was at least close by, making my visit an easy detour before I needed to meet Calla. I knocked on the door and a stout little female whose round smiling face greeted me in stark contrast to my valet's.

"Yes, sir? How can I help you?" the female asked, her pleasant voice washing over me like a warm blanket on a crisp day.

I intended to ask after Oryn, but a different question came out when I opened my mouth. "Why couldn't I have gotten you as my valet?"

Her laugh, hearty yet still somehow quiet, put me at ease, though I couldn't understand why.

"Ah, sir, I'm the one they call on when someone is in need of comfort."

"Ahh," I said, realization dawning on me. "So this warm fuzzy feeling is thanks to you."

She smiled kindly. "You're welcome. Name's Hilde."

"Not sure I like it, to be honest," I said. Even with the

comfort she manipulated within me, it was unnerving to know someone else was mucking with my emotions.

She didn't seem at all offended by my candor, nodding with that same smile on her lips. "It's not for everyone, but I am at least able to shield others from pain when there are no other alternatives." She waved a hand loosely in the air. "Never mind all of that. Are you here to see Oryn?"

"If I may. I can't stay long, unfortunately."

Without a word, she beckoned me inside and across the living space to where Oryn was tucked soundly into bed. His chest rose and fell evenly, and apart from the bandage wrapped around his head, he showed no sign of being injured. In fact, he looked so at peace, I half-expected him to open his eyes at any moment.

"He doesn't have long, I'm afraid," Hilde whispered beside me.

"Is there no way he can be sent back to his family?" I asked.

She shook her head and shrugged. "Not my decision. That's up to Her Majesty and her general."

I peered down at her and smirked. "Guess I'll just have to speak to the queen then."

Her smile vanished instantly, and something akin to fear filled her eyes. "It's not worth the risk," she whispered, her gaze shifting around the room as if Calla herself might be lurking nearby, listening.

"There's no risk. Her Majesty and I have...a bit of a rapport."

Eyes widening, recognition lit across her face. "You're the Emeryn general everyone's going on about. You carried her to the castle. Danced with her at the dinner. You of all people should know better."

"Know better about what?"

Hilde lighted a hand on my forearm. "How dangerous and volatile she is. After what she's done to the Emeryn royal family—"

"What do you mean?" I asked, lowering my face toward hers slightly.

Lifting herself onto her toes, she hid her mouth behind her hand—as if needing to ward against any eavesdroppers—and whispered, "She killed her husband."

I released a long, slow breath, dropping my shoulders wearily. "Yes, I've heard the rumors."

"It's more than mere rumor; it's the truth."

"How do you know?" I asked, not wholly convinced this female was a reliable source regarding the queen's possible guilt.

"I can soothe others' emotions, general, but in order to do that I have to—"

"To feel their emotions yourself." I completed her sentence for her as she nodded along. "And you sensed the queen's."

"I did. When she first returned home from the burial, I was there in the entryway. The guilt she carried—and carries even now —is more than that of one who simply wishes they could have prevented a death."

"Emotions can be difficult to interpret, even when we are the ones experiencing them firsthand, let alone sensing them as a bystander. That's quite the accusation to make based on only that."

Grabbing my arm, she turned me to face her, her brows reaching for her hairline. Her eyes searched mine frantically as if desperate to make me believe her.

"You didn't see the delight she took in ripping those poor women apart," she said, horror dripping from every syllable. "I could feel it, as clearly as if it were from my own heart. And she laughed, such bone-chilling laughter I'd never heard before. I'll never forget it either."

Memories of those children covered in their mother's blood snapped into focus in my mind, and the bottom fell from my gut. How had I forgotten them?

Yet even now, reliving their deadened stares and silent tears, I couldn't reconcile that horror with the queen I'd encountered both here and before Brennan's death. Was she the monster Hilde believed her to be, or was someone spreading the rumors to oust her from power?

It could be both.

Hilde whispered something else, but I was too lost in my own thoughts to catch it.

"Excuse me?"

"No poison," she said. I pinched my face, not quite following what she meant, and she clarified. "The king. There was no poison in his system. No marks on his body."

"How do you know this?"

"When you have talents like mine, you work rather closely with the healers. I wasn't there when they examined him, but I heard them discussing the peculiarities of his death."

"Do you know how he died?" I asked cautiously, expecting her to withhold information as Ami had.

"Suffocated," she said. "Like something choked him without touching him."

CHAPTER 40

CALLA

I was going to kill someone, and I didn't even care who at this point.

A whole afternoon spent meeting with the competitors —my suitors—and I was ready to snap any one of their necks. Even Graham's.

Especially his, perhaps.

I had expected the fearful meekness of Beck, the smallest male among the lot. Phillip wasn't much better than him—unforgettable at best. Seb had been as pompous as ever during his time with me, describing his harrowing tales of surviving the forest, as if these might impress me in the slightest. Those were easy enough engagements, albeit dull and pointless. I'd learned nothing from those three males other than how miserable marriage to them would be.

Graham now sat on the very edge of the armchair across from me. Leaning forward, his forearms resting on his legs, he inched his hands ever closer to my legs, and I had to fight the urge to scoot my chair away from him. I stiffened when his fingertips lightly grazed over my knee in a gesture I assumed he intended to be comforting. Instead, it conjured a million pinpricks down my arms.

"You should have just accepted my offer, Calla," he said softly.

I pressed my tongue hard against the roof of my mouth so as to hide my irritation that made me want to gnash my teeth together. Drawing in a slow, calming breath—that failed to soothe anything—I pulled my lips into a relaxed smile.

"Perhaps, but then we'd miss all the fun of these games."

He laughed dryly. "Yes, you seem to be having loads of fun."

Stiffening, I pinned him with a glare. "Don't mock me."

His face fell, and he slid his hand away from me, shifting back in his chair. "Apologies, Calla. I only wish to spare you this—"

"I don't need you to save me, Graham."

"Oh, that's right," he said, his eyes darkening before he looked away. He slowly crossed his ankle over his other knee and dropped his arms to the armrests. "That's Matthias's job, not mine."

Heat gathered in my chest, and though my shadows stirred just beneath the surface of my palms, they remained contained. That remedy Jocelyn had created for me worked better than I could have imagined. I didn't even need to fist my hands now to keep my magic subdued. Too bad it didn't temper my anger though.

"What the fuck is that supposed to mean?" I asked, trying to keep my tone as even as possible.

Graham's dark, speckled eyes snapped to mine, but I couldn't quite read his expression. Anger, pain, rejection, disgust. His features seemed to display all of these at once. When he answered me, though, his words dripped with jealousy.

"You know exactly what I mean. You claim you can't open your heart to anyone else, but then the moment you need help, you let *him*—"

"I was fucking unconscious in the forest that day he arrived! I didn't *let* him do a stars-damned thing." My hands clenched tight, my fingernails biting into my palms.

"And the dance?"

"What was I supposed to do, Graham? I couldn't risk making a scene with the Assembly there."

"Convenient," he muttered, now crossing his arms at his chest.

"We're done here," I said and pushed to my feet.

Graham simply stared up at me, his lips sliding into a cocky grin. "My time's not up yet."

"I say it is."

He didn't make any effort to move but rather dropped his head to an angle. "The Assembly might be interested to find out you're playing favorites."

"Favorites? I'm beginning to detest you all equally."

Graham dropped his chin to his chest, closed his eyes, and shook his head slowly. "I'm sorry, Calla. I shouldn't let him get to me. It's just..." He didn't bother finishing his sentence as he looked to the large wooden clock standing in the corner. He released a weary breath. "I have just five more minutes. Then I will leave. I don't want to get you in trouble with the Assembly by leaving early."

My scoff came out more of a growl, and then I turned away from him.

"I need a fucking drink," I mumbled to myself and strode over to a small cart tucked between two bookcases.

I'd resisted pouring a glass of brandy during the previous suitors' visits, but as irritated as I was with Graham, I knew he wouldn't begrudge me this one comfort. I poured a small amount of my favorite brandy, Vranić's from Dolobare, into a crystal glass and lifted it to my lips, relishing its sharp scent.

I'd just tilted my head back for a sip when someone knocked at the door. I didn't move to answer it, and Graham grumbled as he rose and stomped across the room. Closing my eyes, I imagined myself far away from here, away from this room, this tournament, this entire situation.

"What the fuck are you doing here?" Graham grumbled, and I squeezed my eyes tighter, wishing the peaceful image in my head was real—a remote cottage tucked away in a mountain forest with no need for enchanted protection.

"I was told to be here."

That damned voice. I breathed deep, catching hints of his wood and leather scent.

Matthias.

"You're early," Graham said through gritted teeth.

"Am I?" Matthias asked, and I downed the remainder of my drink and turned in time to see Matthias stepping past Graham who stumbled back a half-step. His eyes caught mine immediately, and a dashing smile lit up his face, which somehow still looked handsome despite his slowly healing wounds, though in a more roguish way than before.

"Killer," he said, dipping his chin in greeting. My stomach squirmed and tightened in response. Was I actually starting to like the absurd nickname?

Graham straightened, squaring his shoulders. "Don't call her that," he commanded.

"It's alright, Graham," I said, which earned me a quirky look from Matthias that I did my best to ignore. "He doesn't mean any harm by it. It's just a joke."

"Not a very funny one," Graham said, tension still evident in his rigid stance as he tried to block Matthias from entering further into the room.

"Your time's up, Graham," I said. His head swiveled around, and he opened his mouth—probably to argue—but slammed it shut again. His eyes, however, remained furious. I bowed my head. "Thank you for coming to chat with me."

Graham stood there, gawking at me for a few painfully long breaths, until I mouthed the word *go*.

Fuming, he stormed out, ramming his shoulder into Matthias's as he left. Matthias grimaced and started to lift a hand to his stomach as if he was in pain, but then he stopped, shoving his hand into his pocket instead. The door slammed so hard the portrait frame on the wall beside it rattled precariously.

Matthias tossed his thumb toward the now-closed door.

"What's eating him?"

I waved my empty glass in the air dismissively. "He's just being Graham." I spun back around to the cart, still holding my glass up. "You like brandy, right?"

What am I doing?

I'm not here to fucking connect with any of them!

Especially not him.

It's just a drink though, and I could use another one.

"I do, in fact," Matthias said. "Are you offering?"

I peeked over my shoulder at him where he remained near the door. "Just this once."

His laugh filled the room, rough and low. He took slow steps toward me. I tensed, waiting for his warm scent to invade my senses, but he stopped sooner than expected. With a strained exhale, he dropped into one of the armchairs, and his voice came out weary when he finally spoke again.

"I don't like to share either, especially not the good stuff."

Turning on my heel, I slowly walked back to the sitting area and offered Matthias his glass. He breathed it in, and I nearly smiled when his eyes closed with an appreciative sigh.

"You've had this before?" I asked, pivoting around to settle into my chair across from him.

"Indeed," he said, lifting his drink toward me in a silent toast. "The Vranić family makes the best brandy I've tasted, and I've had my fair share." Carefully he drew the glass to his lips and tipped it up to let the dark mahogany liquid slide into his mouth. Another sigh escaped him as he pulled it away and stared at it longingly, whispering, "I've missed you, old friend."

I hid my laughter behind my glass, but when his eyes—alight with pure bliss—met mine, I sobered up, remembering why he was here and why I didn't want him to be. Tossing my drink down my throat, I set the empty glass on the table beside me. I started to pull my legs up into my chair, to tuck them under me as I usually did, but I quickly thought better of it. Dropping my feet to the floor, I stiffened in my seat.

Matthias chuckled again, but this time it was quiet and

subdued. "I thought a couple drinks were supposed to help you relax."

I bristled. "I am relaxed."

His eyes trailed down my rigid posture, past my tightly clasped hands in my lap, to my feet.

"Clearly," he muttered. "So am I the last for today?"

I dipped my chin. "One couldn't make it."

I immediately regretted bringing up Korben, even more so when understanding lit on Matthias's face.

"Ah, yes. Thanks for your help with that, by the way."

My pulsed picked up speed, and I lowered my brow slightly. "Help with what exactly?"

The corner of his eye twitched, and for a moment he seemed about to argue with me, to remind me that I'd attacked Korben. Instead, he offered a soft, conspiratorial smile along with a series of small nods. "Right, right. I forgot," he said, and then lifted his fingers to his mouth to turn an imaginary key, which he pretended to drop into his glass, his lips pressed firmly together.

His eyes narrowed as his lips lifted into a lopsided, mischievous grin. "I suppose I don't have to thank you for visiting me in the infirmary either then?"

Shit. He'd heard me speaking to him. I'd specifically gone when no one else was around, trusting the healers' assessments that the poison had rendered him unresponsive. Still, this was easy enough to refute.

I wrinkled my nose at him. "What makes you think I visited you?"

"I heard your voice, felt your touch—"

Scoffing, I rolled my eyes. "You were poisoned, general."

"So you didn't ask me not to die?" he asked, lifting a hand to his lips. I shook my head. "Well, this is embarrassing."

Pressing my lips into a thin smile, I lifted a shoulder. "Could happen to anyone in your state."

"Has to be pretty flattering to you, though," he said. "My dreaming of you, that is."

"Ah, yes, I do aim to be on the minds of every incapacitated male."

Matthias leaned forward, dropping his arms to rest on his legs. As he spoke, he stared down at the near-empty glass cradled in his hands.

"Speaking of incapacitated. My friend, Oryn."

"What about him?"

"First, thank you for getting him to the healers. Unfortunately, he's not going to make it," he said, his voice growing quiet yet still confident. "He should be sent back to his family so he can be surrounded by loved ones when he passes."

I stilled, recalling the words I'd spoken to Ami. *Anything he needs—it's yours.* Matthias wasn't wrong, but his request conjured the memory of me clutching Brennan, begging him not to leave me.

Dropping my chin into my hand, I fought back the threatening tears. I pulled in a deep breath, hoping Matthias saw it as my buying time to think rather than needing a moment to rein in my traitorous emotions. Finally, I cleared my throat—a test to ensure my voice was prepared to answer him.

"I will speak with Isa tonight about it. We should be able to spare one carriage and a guard detail to escort him home."

Matthias's face brightened as he sat upright. "You'll allow me to thank you for this, right? Or is this another secret I need to keep?"

Bitterness gripped my heart as I stared at this male. He didn't know the first thing about keeping a stars-damned secret, of having to stay silent about something to the point that it threatened to strip you of the last remaining good things in your life.

"Why are you here, general?" The question was on my tongue before I could reconsider it. He opened his mouth, that mischief returning to his eyes, but I lifted a finger. "And I don't mean here in this room right now. I mean here in my kingdom, competing in this tournament."

His mouth snapped shut with a dull pop. Spinning the gold

ring back and forth on his finger, he settled back in his chair and shifted his eyes to the wall of windows behind me. I followed his stare to the pristine view of the setting sun and didn't turn back to him even when he finally responded.

"As I told your general when I registered, with the approval of my king, I stepped in as Engle's representative."

Isa had indeed said as much, though Matthias now kindly omitted the little point that no one from Engle wanted to vie for my hand, as if I'd take some kind of offense to that.

"Out of the goodness of your heart," I said, slowly turning back to look at him and marveling at how different he seemed from the other competitors. Unlike Beck, he didn't seem at all wary of me. And unlike the others, he didn't act superior at all. He spoke to me as if I wasn't a queen suspected of murder, but a simple female in need of a friend. It should have been a welcome comfort, but that was the last thing I wanted from him or any of them. The Assembly—and even Isa to some extent—may have hoped these forced encounters would help the efforts to select a king, but they certainly didn't help me.

"Something like that," he muttered, falling silent for a few breaths before he asked the last question I expected. "Why are *you* here?"

He stared at me with such compassionate curiosity, as if he actually cared about my answer—cared about me—which seemed far more worrisome than if he were here to kill me.

"And don't say because the Assembly made you," he added, barely a hint of humor present in his tone.

"Arenysen must be ruled by both a king and queen," I said, trying to hide my bitterness over this law. "If I must find a king, why not make it fun?"

His eyes widened, genuine shock written plainly across his face. "You have an odd definition of the word *fun*."

"I thought warriors lived for danger and mayhem," I challenged. "Or are you getting soft in your old age?"

Matthias's laughter came out hollow and forced, then he lifted his glass and poured the last of his brandy into his mouth. "Mind if I get a refill?"

Of course I minded, but for some unknown reason, I waved my hand toward the bar in invitation. He nodded appreciatively before helping himself to my favorite brandy. Bastard was going to drink it all, and I didn't know when I'd be able to get more.

"Don't worry," he said, looking back over his shoulder. "I won't take it all."

"It's fine," I bit out, and this earned me a dark laugh.

"I see that. Would you like another?" He held up the half-empty bottle, but I shook my head.

I couldn't sit still anymore. Pushing to my feet, I walked over to the window and looked down at the forest's canopy bathed in gold. I lowered my head to one side as I continued to stare out at a world that had lost all its luster when Brennan died. Why did I fight so hard to keep this kingdom? Why did I bother trying to hold onto my throne? It would be so much easier to just give up and let the Assembly select a new pair to rule.

Maybe I should have accepted another drink after all.

Pivoting on my heel, I spun around, expecting to find Matthias still at the bar or back in his seat. But he was standing directly behind me, nearly an arm's length away. Startled, I retreated, my back hitting the window. My arms flew out to my sides to catch me, my palms smacking the glass hard.

I glowered at him. "You shouldn't sneak up on me like that."

A smirk pulled at one corner of his mouth. "Sure you don't want it? It is yours after all."

I gawked at him, realizing too late that he was referring to the brandy in his hand, the brandy he now lifted higher between us.

"No," I said, dismissing his offer with another shake of my head. Pushing past him, I returned to my seat and folded my hands in my lap. "You need it more than I do anyway."

He followed me to the sitting area, but remained standing. The corners of his mouth drooped down into a thoughtful frown and all amusement disappeared from his face as he peered down at me. "I beg to differ," he said, his tone dripping with pity that lit a new fire in my blood.

I shrugged, attempting to appear casual, though my movements were probably too stiff to be convincing. "I'm not the one who got myself stabbed, poisoned, and nearly killed."

A hint of laughter flashed briefly in his eyes.

"Known risks of your tournament, Killer," he joked, but his expression darkened again almost instantly. "You, on the other hand, didn't know you'd lose both your parents and your husband, and in such a short time too. That's a lot to handle, even for someone as formidable as you."

Why did he have to mention Brennan? Why remind me of all that I'd lost? Not that I could ever forget.

He lifted the glass toward me. "Take it," he whispered.

A tidal wave of grief crashed into my sternum, threatening to drown me as it had that first week, but I refused to cave to it as I had then. I wouldn't be bent to its will—not now, not with an audience.

Pulling my shoulders back and down, I lifted my chest as if to greet the pain. Tears started to gather in the corners of my eyes, and I silently cursed my stars-damned sentimental heart. I wanted to move on, not dwell on a future snuffed out by death.

Pressing my tongue high in my mouth, I slid my eyes closed. I would not cry in front of him. I dropped my chin to my shoulder, angling my face away from him and focusing on the steadiness of my breathing, counting my inhales and exhales until my thundering heart began to settle. My shadows licked at my palms, as if eager to help soothe me, but I urged them to rest, amazed when they listened and curled back into my veins. Jocelyn's remedy worked wondrously, but it was still unsettling to have my powers obey my will so easily.

I had almost calmed myself completely when a warm, rough hand slipped over mine. I froze, my breath snagging on my next inhale as that comforting woodsy scent swarmed my senses. Snapping my eyes open, I slowly turned to find Matthias crouched in front of me. His hazel eyes held mine, and I couldn't look away no matter how much I wanted to, like he had captured me in an invisible embrace. Slowly, his thumb brushed over the back of my hand, and as if coaxed out by the movement, my shadows appeared, washing over my skin and up over his hand. He didn't seem to notice as he still stared at me with a curious mix of regret and compassion.

"I'm sorry," he said. "I shouldn't have brought it up. It was—"

"Fine, it's fine," I choked out, my voice weak and broken. I waited for him to comment on how not fine I clearly appeared, but he didn't.

"No, it's not." He lifted his hand to my face, his fingers trailing along my jawline and sending ripples of prickly warmth through me.

I cleared my throat, trying to keep myself from leaning into his touch. "You weren't wrong, though. I've lost my entire family." My voice cracked embarrassingly, but I still couldn't pull my gaze away.

His thumb brushed over my cheek. "And now you're forced to replace them. Doesn't seem fair, does it?"

A dry laugh escaped me. "I don't know if you've ever heard, general, but life isn't fair."

"You don't deserve this, though," he said.

With a quiet sigh, he stroked my cheek again, and my resolve melted under his touch. Closing my eyes I nestled against his hand, letting myself relish in this moment of comfort, no matter how fleeting. Slowly, he shifted, moving his hand up to tuck a lock of my hair behind my ear. Then his fingers tenderly traced the length of my neck, blazing a trail of fire over my skin. Even after he pulled away, that heat remained, washing across my chest and plummeting lower to my stomach until it settled in my core.

No.

I can't want him.

I can't let this happen.

I pushed to my feet so forcefully Matthias toppled backward, barely catching himself with his hands before he could fall onto his backside. Finally breaking his stare, I retreated back to the windows. My shadows slowly followed me, pulling back into my palms almost reluctantly.

Standing there, I waited for the fire he'd ignited within me to fade.

It didn't, not when he walked away wordlessly, not when he left the room and shut the door.

It burned on, a desperate yearning that terrified me.

CHAPTER 41

MATTHIAS

At least Calla hadn't killed me when I touched her.

I'd known better, yet I'd done it anyway, driven by some bizarre need to comfort her. I was growing as soft as Connor. If I wasn't careful, I'd become a damned romantic before I knew what had happened.

Rising to my feet, I watched her standing at the window. She had her arms wrapped around her middle, her fingers clutching at the fabric at her waist as if she were trying to hold herself together. In the deathly silence, her heartbeat pounded feverishly, nearly as fast as my own.

In any other circumstance I might have been offended at a female fleeing my touch, but I'd been utterly relieved when she did. I couldn't want her, let alone care for her. I had a singular mission, and that wasn't to make her feel better. I simply needed to learn the truth, and now I was no closer to meeting that objective. This was as close as I could hope to get to her, and I'd fucked it up.

Without a word, I retreated from the room and closed the door as quietly as I could. In the hallway I slumped against the wall, leaning my head back on the hard stone, trying to recall everything I had gleaned in the short half hour I'd spent with her.

The queen had good taste with that brandy, not that that mattered so much with regards to Brennan's death, which she was clearly distraught over. She'd controlled her shadows, holding them at bay when she became visibly angry. She'd actually remained far calmer than I'd expected at the mention of her parents' and Brennan's deaths.

While nothing I'd witnessed supported Hilde's accusations, I couldn't ignore that someone had possibly lied to Connor about Brennan being poisoned. Of course, Hilde might be the one lying. Either way, something wasn't adding up, and I'd need more information before I could come to any definitive conclusion.

Unfortunately, I wasn't likely to get much more from Calla directly, especially now after I'd crossed the line. I needed to speak to someone closer to her. Isa was out, of course. She was too loyal and too smart to ever incriminate the queen, even unknowingly. I needed someone who had been with her before and after Brennan died, who knew her well, but who cared more for themselves than for her.

I needed Graham.

The next morning, I reported to the courtyard as directed by Giles and found the other survivors standing silently about the open space. Only Korben was missing, and I was confused for a moment until I remembered Isa's promise to punish him. Before I could approach Graham, a valet entered the courtyard and ushered us all out to the front steps of the castle, where four carriages waited, their doors held open by a guard. Without a word, the valet pointed to me and then to the second carriage in the line. I settled myself on the plush black leather of the seat and waited, my heart thumping with excitement and anticipation over whatever this next trial would be.

The carriage shifted as someone climbed the steps, and I nearly laughed at my good fortune that the valet had sent Graham to share a ride with me. Graham, of course, refused to acknowledge my presence as he lowered himself to the seat opposite me, even when I offered a friendly "good morning." He simply stared out the window in silence.

I wasn't one to give up easily, though. I'd charmed one of Calla's friends—and a dragon shifter, at that. How hard could it be to do so again, even with this jealous prick?

Resting against the tufted back wall of the carriage, I crossed my arms loosely in front of me and tried again.

"I never got the chance to thank you for helping me out in the forest," I said.

Graham's eyes flicked my way, but he refused to look at me directly, immediately shifting to watch the guard close the door and rap lightly on the roof. As the carriage lurched forward, Graham's lips twitched, like his voice was trying to break through his stubbornness. Swallowing hard, he finally slid his gaze sideways at me.

"You're welcome," he muttered, the muscle along his jaw pulsing.

I lifted my brows in feigned shock. "That sounded almost genuine, Graham."

"It is genuine. I don't say things I don't mean," he said, his expression as flat as his tone.

"Never?" I asked. "Not one lie? Not even when you were younger?"

"You don't get to be the royal advisor by being dishonest." He shrugged as if this answer was obvious.

"I thought dishonesty was a requirement in politics."

"Maybe that's how you do things in Emeryn, but not here."

I smiled politely and changed the subject. "I do want to apologize for yesterday though."

"For what?" Graham asked.

"For interrupting your time with Her Majesty. I shouldn't have barged in as I did, even if it was truly my time." Graham's features twisted with surprised confusion. Leaning forward, I extended my hand to him. "I'd like to put all this animosity behind us, if you're willing."

His dark eyes darted down to my hand, regarding it suspiciously. "I don't like you," he said.

I chuckled lightly and lifted a shoulder. "I'm not asking you to be my best friend or anything. Just think it's a waste of our energy hating each other like this."

For several breaths he simply stared at me, looking like he wanted to take all that hatred out on me right there in the carriage. Then he cocked his head to the side.

"You think I hate you?" he asked.

"A bit."

"You're right, just a bit. Are you saying you hate me?"

I frowned and rocked my hand back and forth in the air. "Just a bit, but I'm willing to set it aside. After all, when I win—"

His sharp glare cut off my words, forcing me to amend them.

"I mean, *if* I win, it would be nice to not have to replace the Vael's trusted advisor. And I don't know. If *you* win, maybe—"

"I'm not choosing you to replace me, general."

Lifting my palms to face him, I laughed. "Of course not."

When the carriages finally came to a stop, we stepped out to find Isa standing in front of a large lake. Korben stood beside her, cradling his bandaged left hand. His right eye was so swollen it couldn't open, and a laceration across his eyebrow had been sewn closed, but looked far from healed.

Isa gestured to him as she spoke. "Before we dive into the second trial, I need to make something quite clear to all of you. Korben, here, chose to attack one of the other competitors outside of the official trials, as well as injure a dear friend of Her Majesty. For that, he has been punished accordingly. A finger for a finger. A beating for a beating. And a small dose of poison to keep his wounds from healing immediately."

At this she caught my eye and dipped her chin crisply before continuing.

"He has not been stripped of any points earned in the first trial, but his punishment will put him at a significant disadvantage for the next one." She paused for a long moment, studying each of us in turn. "Let this be a warning to each of you. Whatever happens among you during the trials is fair; expected, even. Attacking one another outside of the trials will not be tolerated. Do you understand?"

Beck nodded silently. The rest of us voiced our assent, albeit mostly in whispers.

"Very well," Isa said, pulling her shoulders back as she clasped her hands behind her back. "Today's trial will test strength in *all* its forms. Behind me lies Lake Vestia. Two hundred fifty meters across. Three hundred meters wide. One hundred fifty meters deep. At the far end, it feeds the Veslane River. Your task is to swim out to the buoy in the middle, dive to the bottom, select a rock, and bring it back to me."

Korben scowled at his wounded hand. Beck laughed, albeit nervously. Seb shot Phillip a haughty glance, but the Arenysen native didn't share his cocky demeanor. Phillip's face drained of all color, a stark contrast to Graham's stern, calculating expression devoid of fear.

Isa didn't seem to notice anyone's reactions as she continued. "The points awarded for this trial are not as clear-cut as for the last one. Part of your score will be determined by your stone's weight. The one to retrieve and deliver the heaviest will earn fifty points. Next heaviest, forty points. Third, thirty points, and so on. Should you return empty-handed, you will receive no points for that portion. However, you can earn—or lose—points by how you demonstrate strength of mind and spirit as well. Those points are awarded at my discretion. You should know, these waters harbor many dangers, not the least of which is the possibility of merely drowning. Any questions?"

Beck lifted a tentative hand. "What are the other dangers?"

"They are for you to discover on your own," Isa said, smiling kindly. "Anything else?"

"What about weapons?" Korben asked, avoiding me as I smirked at his question.

Isa regarded him, her brows lifted high. "Thank you for the reminder." She paused to snap her fingers toward one of the carriage drivers, who hastened to retrieve a box from his seat. "As we did in the first trial, everyone must relinquish their personal weapons and choose one we provide. Everyone except you. You will be competing with no weapon today."

Korben's features twitched as he silently fumed. Before he could make the mistake of arguing with the general, Graham spoke up with his own question.

"Are we all going in at the same time or individually?"

"For the sake of time, you will all go in at once. While this is not a race and points are determined solely on the weight of your stone, we will not wait past sundown. If you are not back by then, we will assume you did not survive."

"So when do we start?" I asked, my nerves thrumming with the same excitement that hit before a battle.

Isa looked at each of us in turn, as if she were committing our faces to memory should we not survive, and then stepped aside as one of her guards stepped up beside her holding several daggers.

"You will be issued *one* sheathed blade and gauntlet. Once you've received yours, you're free to begin." She swung her gaze to Korben, a warning bite entering her tone. "The trial does not officially begin until you hit the water. Attack a fellow competitor before then, and you will be disqualified."

Seb was first to rush forward, request a weapon, and take off running ahead of us. Kicking off his boots and leaving them in the grass several meters from the lake's edge, he stripped down to his skivvies—his clothes discarded in a hapless pile—strapped the gauntlet to his wrist, and dove into the water before anyone else had even moved. All five of us watched as he swam out further.

When he was about a quarter of the way across, he turned and waved back to us.

Cupping his hands to his mouth he yelled something that sounded like "What are you waiting for?"

We all seemed to hold our collective breath, waiting to see if one of those mysterious dangers might claim him, but he was soon turning away from us, taking a deep breath, and diving below the surface. Korben nudged Beck with his elbow, nodding to the guard. Once the smaller male had received his dagger, they went on toward the lake. Graham followed close behind them. The three of them each left a pile of garments behind on the beach, and, with blades in place, dove into the water.

I stole a look at Phillip who was still as pale as before, his head shaking slowly from side to side. Reaching forward, I accepted my weapon from the guard and tossed my head in Phillip's direction. "I'll take his to him, if that's okay."

The guard looked to Isa, who offered a quick nod.

Tapping Phillip's arm with the sheathed blade, I tried—and failed—to get his attention. He didn't seem to notice me until I snapped my fingers in his face and held the dagger in his line of sight. Even then his stare remained blank.

"You okay?" I asked. "You can swim, right?"

Phillip blinked a few times, as if just now realizing where he was. "Huh? What? Oh, yeah. I can swim."

"Then what's got you so nervous?"

"The Vestiliaga."

"The what?" I asked, wondering how many secrets Arenysen had effectively kept from my scouts and me.

Phillip seemed to be choking on his own breaths, and then with wide eyes he whispered, "The monster."

I peered up at Isa, but she didn't appear to be listening, having fixed her gaze on the water where the other three swam away from the shore.

"What is it?" I asked, more curious than anything else. Most of these lake monsters were pure myth meant to con travelers out of coin, but Phillip had survived the forest, so seeing him so spooked was off-putting.

"They say it has a snake's body with the head of a dragon. And it's massive."

"You haven't seen it before?"

Shaking his head, he gawked at me. "Not personally, but my cousin used to live in a nearby village. He saw it."

I tapped a finger to my pursed lips before asking, "And how much had he had to drink?"

Phillip's face fell a bit. "Go ahead and make your jokes. No one ever believed him."

"Okay, okay. Well, you could always leave the competition," I said.

The male's vision glazed over again, his mouth forming the word "no" before he found his voice and explained. "The Assembly would kill me if I quit."

I froze, briefly remembering how the original five Arenysen competitors had all been forced to enter. At the time I had assumed it had been their villages as a whole who had made them step up. Had it really been the Assembly members?

"Well, then," I said and started to reach for his left arm. "Which is your knife hand?" I asked. When he lifted his right hand, I snatched his left and promptly bound the gauntlet above his wrist, sliding the blade out and back in to test it slid well enough. "You've got nothing to lose, right? So come on. I'll go with you."

Phillip's eyes locked on mine, focusing on me for the first time this morning. "Why would you do that? Why are you helping me?"

Shrugging, I pulled my mouth into a frown. "Maybe to make up for not believing you about the vestigli-whatever-it-is."

"Vestiliaga," he corrected.

"Right, that's what I said. We can watch each other's backs out there." As I fastened my own gauntlet into place, I shifted my attention back to the water to see Graham dive beneath the surface. Beck and Korben were nowhere to be seen.

"Alright," Phillip finally replied.

With our boots and outer garments discarded in the grass, we silently made our way into the water. Surprisingly enough, Phillip didn't hesitate, keeping stride with me all the way out to the buoy.

"Ready?" I asked Phillip, whose eyes constantly scanned the clear water below him and all around. He said nothing, but nodded shakily. "Remember. We dive, get a rock, then swim out."

Catching Phillip's eyes, I took a couple deep breaths before signaling to descend. Thankfully, I didn't have to hold his hand the whole way down; he stayed beside me as we dove toward the lake's rocky bottom. We didn't have many lakes back home, and the couple we did have were murky, not like the crystalline water here. Sunlight streamed in easily, and while it did get darker, the bottom was visible already. Off to the right I spotted Beck and Korben each hovering upside down, kicking their feet to stay low enough to choose a stone.

Phillip hit my arm a couple times and pointed off ahead of us to where Seb appeared to be swimming upwards, but in the entirely wrong direction, away from the shore where Isa waited with the carriages. I shrugged to Phillip and pointed back down to the stones, but his eyes went wide. I spun my head around in time to see Seb being whisked away, as if an invisible hand had snatched him up and dragged him off, leaving nothing but clear, open water where he had once been.

Before I could stop him, Phillip was madly kicking for the surface.

Stars-damned fool of a male.

I took off after him. I'd already let down Oryn by not sharing the vial in the first trial. I wasn't about to go back on my word to Phillip that we would do this trial together.

Perhaps I was the fool.

When I broke the surface, Phillip was gasping and wheezing for air, barely keeping his head above the water as his limbs fatigued. Reaching a hand out, I helped lift him up enough for him to catch his breath.

"What was that?" he asked, fresh panic in his eyes.

"A current, I imagine. Isn't that where the river starts?"

"A current in a fucking lake?" He sputtered out the question.

I wrinkled my nose. "Or it's an invisible vestiga."

"Vestiliaga," he whispered, as if the name of the supposed monster actually mattered in this moment. "And thanks for that. As if I needed more reasons to fear the beast."

"Use that fear then," I suggested. He lifted a brow, his expression twisting with confusion. "Let the fear spur you on, keep you moving, push you to finish. If we wait much longer, we're not going to have enough strength left to swim back to shore."

Nodding silently, Phillip took several steadying breaths before drawing in one big one and flipping himself back under. I lifted a hand to block the splashes of water from his feet, and then froze. On the surface about fifty meters away, a dark shape slithered. It wasn't coming toward me, but rather it was swimming off to my left where Graham had just surfaced, facing the opposite direction.

Cupping my hands to my mouth, I shouted, "Graham! Behind you!"

The male spun around quickly just as the darkness reached him, and with a jerk, he disappeared into the water.

CHAPTER 42

CALLA

The castle's silence grated my nerves as I walked along the paths among the trees in the courtyard. With the competitors off the grounds for the second trial, my staff had a much-needed day off from tending to our guests. Most seemed to be spending that time locked in their rooms. Maybe they preferred the quiet, but a large part of me suspected their fear of me drove them into hiding.

Not that I could blame them. I'd likely behave the same way in their shoes—serving a queen with a temper and the power to rip out throats without lifting a finger. My shadows stirred, as though awakened by my thoughts, and—after glancing around to ensure I was truly alone—I called them out.

They swirled around my palms, weaving through my fingers and spiraling up my arms. I was about to let them loose to dance over the stones at my feet when a voice, bold with a wary quake at its edges, rang out.

"Your Majesty, the carriage is here."

My shadows perked up. Like a snake spooked by an encroaching danger, they swept around me and reared back, pointing in the direction of the speaker.

Hilde tensed, her eyes locked on the dark wisps surrounding me.

I whispered to my power, "Easy." Slithering back to my hands, my shadows succumbed to my call to return, though I allowed them to continue to trail across the backs of my hands and around my wrists—a comfort in my loneliness and a reminder of my strength.

"For our guest?" I asked, and her brows twitched slightly as she nodded.

"Oryn, yes, Your Majesty."

Slowly I strode toward her, both relishing and loathing how she trembled in my wake. I craved her fear, but also her respect—though I recognized the inherent contradiction in that. This had become my new normal, this walking conundrum that was my heart—desiring solitude but also companionship, wanting power but also relief from my burdens. I could never have it all.

"Thank you, Hilde," I said, as I stopped in front of the female, sure to give her more than an arm's reach of space.

She recoiled, her eyes growing large. "You remember my name?"

I bristled. What kind of queen did she think I was? I may have been more temperamental of late, but did she—stars, did the entire staff—really think I didn't know them?

Tamping down my disappointment, I offered a half-smile. "Of course, I do."

Hilde said nothing, but her gaze flicked down once again to my restless shadows still playing around my hands and arms. I lifted my hands slightly, trying not to take it personally when she flinched as if I were about to strike her. Gradually, I pulled my shadows back into my palms and tucked my hands into the pockets hidden in the folds of my dress.

"Have a few of the staff help you move Oryn to the carriage," I instructed.

She dipped her chin crisply and muttered, "Yes, Your Majesty."

She'd turned halfway around to leave when she stopped and looked back at me. "Thank you for being willing to send him home. When General Matthias said he was going to ask you…" Her voice trailed away as she peered down at the ground.

"You thought he was mad?" I asked, fighting back a smile.

Hilde nodded. "You haven't been the most approachable since—"

"I know." I snapped out the words harsher than I meant to, but the pity in her eyes was enough to darken my spirits. I wasn't about to let her utter a word about my dead family. "Thank you for doing what you could to keep the male comfortable. I know it will give his family some much-needed peace."

That was a lie.

Death brought no peace. Only misery and pain.

I expected Hilde to leave, but instead she squared her shoulders to me. Bitterness brewed in her eyes and pulsed in her jaw, and on instinct, I tugged my shadows from my veins, my hands still buried deep in my pockets.

"And what about peace for the families of the fallen?" she asked, and I had to give her credit for such a display of courage, talking to me like that.

"General Marlowe is overseeing the logistics, but I assure you we are showing the competitors' families the respect they deserve."

"And your own subjects you've killed?"

I should have taken a breath.

I should have counted or some other calming nonsense the healers had recommended.

I should have remembered to take my tonic this morning.

But I did none of those.

My shadows were at Hilde's throat, squeezing her neck before I'd even pulled my hands free from my pockets. I lifted her slowly, until only the balls of her feet remained touching the ground. Walking toward her, I reveled in the renewed fear playing across her features.

"Hilde, Hilde, Hilde," I said, clicking my tongue. "As you yourself mentioned, I'm not approachable. So what made you think you could speak to me in such a way?"

"Can't breathe," she rasped out, her hands grasping feverishly at my shadows. With nothing tangible to grip, her nails found only her own flesh, clawing long gashes in her neck in desperation.

"If you would like to continue to live here, you will stay that tongue of yours," I said in a low, dark tone. "Continue this insolence, though, and you will be punished so harshly, so slowly, that you will beg me to kill you too."

She tried to nod despite my shadows' iron hold, and in a flash, I pulled my power back and watched her fall to the ground, her knees hitting the stone walkway with a heavy crunch. Looming over her, I peered down and nudged her with my toe until she lifted her chin to look at me.

"I appreciate your help with the injured and dying, Hilde. I do. But as long as I'm your queen, you will show some respect."

"Yes, Your Majesty," she whispered, lifting her hands to her injured neck. When she pulled her fingers away to find them streaked with blood, the fear in her eyes slowly shifted into the bitter defiance she'd shown earlier.

Guilt hollowed out my gut, and I pressed my palms together in a vain attempt to calm my nerves.

What the fuck had I done?

Isa was going to be furious.

The Assembly would hear of this and do all they could to drag me from the throne.

I needed a stars-damned drink.

CHAPTER 43

MATTHIAS

Without hesitation, I took off toward the spot I'd last seen Graham, diving beneath the surface to search for him. There, ahead of me, a beast just as Phillip had described—with a sleek, nearly forty-meter-long black body with a horned and spiked head—glided in a downward spiral. In its jaws it held Graham by the leg, blood trailing behind it as it swam lower and lower. Slipping my dagger from its sheath, I kicked furiously.

I might not have liked Graham, but he was my best chance at learning more about Calla.

I needed him alive, not drowned in this lake or eaten by this creature.

The beast moved lazily through the water, confident and unthreatened by any of us trespassers. But just as with fae and men, confidence could be a detriment. I caught up to its tail and swiped quickly at it with my blade, but it arced out of the way at the last moment. Swimming harder and ignoring the blood that tinted the water around me, I pushed myself forward until I was alongside the back part of its body, just ahead of the slithering tail.

This time I jabbed my blade at it, but the tip simply slid along the thick scales that protected the animal.

Pushing aside my initial frustration and disappointment, I reminded myself of the first lesson I'd learned as a warrior: every enemy has a weakness. I just needed to find and exploit it, hopefully before Graham bled out or drowned. Unfortunately for both of us, my lungs couldn't hold as long as usual—another gift of the poison, I supposed—and I had to return to the surface quickly to grab more air.

Lifting my face out of the water just enough to suck in another deep breath, I immediately descended to find the beast, still clutching a now-unconscious Graham in its vicious maw, swimming straight for me. At least I wouldn't have to hunt for it.

I dove straight down, hoping to get beneath its head, but it shifted effortlessly to cut off my descent, swinging its massive skull toward me. It struck me hard in my ribs, and I had to fight not to gasp for air from the blow. I adjusted my grip on the handle and watched the beast circle me.

My lungs ached, burning with the need for another breath, but I persisted, even when the edges of my vision started to fade into darkness. On the creature's third rotation around me, I threw myself toward it, thrusting my blade up under its jaw, slicing easily into the tender skin beneath its snout. Yanking its head away from me—and wrenching the weapon from my grasp—the beast opened its mouth in a roar of pain, deafening even when muffled under the water. Graham's body fell from its jaws, drifting slowly toward the lake floor.

Ignoring the agony blazing in my chest, I rushed down to catch him. As I kicked for the surface, I hauled Graham up with one arm locked under his shoulder, his body resting against my back. My vision darkened more with each passing second, and from somewhere far off, a voice called for me to stop and rest, promising me an end to all the pain and discomfort. I had to admit, it was tempting in the moment, and I might have succumbed had the shock of the cold breeze on my face not snapped me back to the present.

Cramps shot through my limbs, protesting the effort it took

to keep myself and Graham afloat. The edge of the lake was so far away, I'd never make it by myself, let alone while dragging dead weight. I tried to wave an arm to Isa, but as soon as I lifted my arm, I went under. Maybe it wasn't worth saving the bastard. For all I knew, he was already dead, but if I concentrated, I could still catch his heartbeat, though faint.

I'd need help getting him back to shore, so I spun in a circle, searching for anyone else, but the surface was clear.

Except for a dark shape swimming toward me.

Fuck.

I should have known I hadn't killed it.

I tried to propel myself backwards toward the lake's edge, keeping my eye on the approaching threat. My heart beat wildly against my sternum. My breaths rushed painfully in and out. My mind whirred around the few options I had left.

Releasing Graham seemed the best chance I had if I was going to survive at all. If I died here, we'd never learn the truth and Brennan's death would never be avenged. Loosening my grip on Graham, I was about to sacrifice him to the beast when Phillip surfaced behind me, heaving and gasping for air. He held up a stone that barely fit in his hand. It glistened in the sunlight, bits of gold shining through the slick green moss that coated it.

"Can you take him with you back to shore?" I asked through gritted teeth, fighting to ignore both the burning in my limbs and the beast that still swam toward us.

Phillip's eyes widened as he glanced over my shoulder to where the monster was closing in.

"I'll lure it away," I assured him. "You just get him to safety."

Phillip bobbed his head a few times, and as quickly as I could with arms shaking from the exertion, I transferred Graham onto Phillip's back and turned back in time to see the darkness stop a few meters away and vanish.

Quickly I ducked my head under the water.

The monster had shifted direction at the last moment and was now slowly swimming toward Korben and Beck, who were back in the middle of the lake hauling up their stones, each one the size of their heads. They didn't seem to notice the beast swimming toward them, their focus solely on the surface.

If I was smart, I'd grab the smallest stone I could find and swim back to shore—leave these two to fend for themselves. It was what Korben deserved after what he'd done to Asher—and to me —but Beck's only fault was choosing to follow the bastard. He shouldn't die for that.

Growling and cursing myself, I urged my tired muscles into action, swimming toward them.

Why did I have to fucking care so much? Was Connor's damned savior complex contagious?

Finally spotting the predator, Korben and Beck ceased kicking and seemed to freeze halfway to the surface. Korben shoved Beck out in front of him like a fucking coward. Beck still held onto his stone, tucking it precariously under one arm as he fumbled to pull his dagger free from his belt.

If only I could shout at Beck to drop the stone. Whether that would actually help or not, I didn't know; it was a wild guess based on what I knew of dragons and their affinity for gold.

But he didn't. He held it in the crook of his arm even when his dagger slipped through his fingers and drifted down to the lake's bottom. The monster was still taking its time, swimming leisurely and occasionally snapping its teeth, as if it enjoyed stoking its prey's fear.

Pushing myself to swim faster, I chased after the falling dagger, but Korben had the same thought, flipping himself over to dive for it. A muffled scream pulled my attention up to where the beast had finally lunged for Beck, clamping its rows of jagged teeth down on Beck's free arm. With a sudden jerk, the monster released the fae, blood streaming from where his arm had once been.

Bile rushed up my throat, but I swallowed it back down as I swam harder upwards to help Beck. He could still survive without an arm, but only if I got to him in time—and if I convinced him to give up the stars-damned stone. Being disqualified from the tournament was better than dying.

I had nearly reached Beck when something wrapped around my ankle and yanked me down.

Then searing pain shot through my calf.

Kicking my other foot backwards, I slammed my heel into Korben's face just as he yanked Beck's dagger free from my leg. The once-clear water was now twinged with blood, both mine and Beck's. As I moved to continue helping the smaller fae, a stone drifted past me, and I looked up to see Beck's body floating by. What was left of it anyway. The beast had bitten clean through his torso from hip to opposite shoulder.

The monstrous spiked head spun toward me, its nostrils flaring, but its gold eyes snapped to my left where Korben—still holding his stone in one arm and Beck's dagger in his good hand—swam away from me toward the surface and the beach. The monster's muscles twitched in its neck as it snarled, baring teeth that appeared to have bits of cloth and flesh stuck in them.

Before it could dart after Korben, though, I used what little energy I had left to launch myself at its head. When those gold eyes shifted back onto me, I braced myself for its attack, but it never came. It immediately returned its attention to the retreating Korben, and that's when I made my move. Angling myself under its jaw, I gripped the handle of my dagger still lodged in its chin with both hands and thrust it away from me, slicing through its throat and neck.

It bellowed, thrashing its head around. I yanked my blade free and, by sheer luck alone, in its flailing it drove its eye straight onto my dagger. Marveling at my good fortune, I didn't hesitate to pull the dagger free once more and swipe it along the underside of its jaw, slicing through its major artery that ran along its neck. The sea around me darkened with black-red blood and its jaw opened and closed as it fell away from me, the life slowly fading from its good eye.

My lungs started to cave in on themselves, as if they were

trying to use every last bit of air in them. I needed to get to the surface. I needed a breath. But my body had given the last of its energy in the final attack on the beast, and it refused to respond to my desperate efforts to pull myself to the surface. My vision darkened as it had before, and this time when the voice called for me to rest, I listened.

CHAPTER 44

MATTHIAS

I'd nearly surrendered completely to the sweet lull, when it shifted into a panicked growl urging me to breathe. My world remained dark, but my face warmed as if I were lying in the grass back in Emeryn instead of drowning in a lake far from home.

My chest ached as air filled my lungs, expanding them as far as they would go before rushing out again.

"Breathe!" The growl echoed in my head, reminding me a bit of King Durand when he was angry. Or Connor, for that matter. My friend's temper could rival his father's, under the right circumstances.

More air rushed into my lungs, more refreshing than painful this time.

"Breathe." The command came again, softer now, bordering on desperate even.

I must have been dead and imagining it. No one in a deadly tournament would go to the trouble of saving me; they weren't all fools like me, trying to help my competition when I should be trying to win the damned thing and finish the mission.

Air came again and with it came the sound of water lapping

against my ears and somewhere far off the calls of birds flying overhead. Then something hit me in the face, like the one time my sister had slapped my cheek for making a crude joke at her expense.

Water bubbled out between my lips, and my eyes flew open only to slam shut against the sudden brightness.

I received a couple more light taps on the cheek. "Wake up, general. It's over."

"What happened? What's over?" I whispered, trying again to open my eyes and see who had saved me—assuming I was indeed still alive. Phillip's face came into focus.

"You nearly died," he said.

"And you saved me, how? Why?"

As if in response, a gust of wind swirled by. A memory flashed through my mind of us registering at the castle and Phillip demonstrating his power.

Air.

"Got you breathing again. You helped me push past my fear; figured saving your ass was the least I could do. Though don't get used to it. We're still opponents."

"But you weren't supposed to—"

"Would be a dick move to report me to the general now," he said, his brow rising in challenge.

"Fair," I said around a quiet laugh that brought a stabbing pain to my side.

"Can you swim back to shore?" he asked, but before I could answer he shook his head. "Never mind. I'll get you out."

We remained silent as he hauled me back to the lake's edge, and when he dropped me with a thud onto the grass, I simply lay there for a long while, staring up at the sky, watching it fade to a cerulean blue as the sun sank lower. Then Isa's face slid into view, regarding me with a peculiar look that seemed a mix of relief and impatience, as if my nearly dying had caused me to return late.

"Welcome back, general. Whenever you're ready, we can award points," she said flatly.

I lay there for a few moments longer, slowly moving my muscles little by little to ensure they still worked. It wasn't until I bent one of my knees that pain shot up my leg. Oh, right. I'd been stabbed. Twisting my leg a bit, I noted the wound had just barely started to heal, still slowed by the earlier poison.

Damned Korben. Apparently the punishment he'd received hadn't been enough to deter him.

Hissing through my teeth, I inched my way up to sitting and then groaned as I pushed to stand. My injured leg buckled under my weight, and I would have toppled to the ground like a toddler learning to walk had Phillip not caught me by the arm. I nodded my thanks, glad that he released me just as quickly and simply walked attentively beside me the whole way back to the carriages.

Isa stood beside her carriage, a portable table setup beside her with a brass scale waiting. Near her, Graham sat in the grass, his long legs bent so he could rest his arms and forehead on them. Unlike my leg, his appeared to be healing nicely—at least from what I could see through the rip in his trousers. The bleeding had been staunched and the ragged edges of his flesh and skin had begun to reconnect. He'd have a pretty impressive scar from that one.

Phillip walked me over to my carriage, opened the door, and directed me to sit there. It groaned slightly under my weight, and I once again offered Phillip my silent gratitude as Isa cleared her throat.

"Congratulations on surviving the second trial," she said. "General"—I jerked my head up to acknowledge her—"the others have described the unfortunate fates of Seb and Beck, and my own guards have ventured under the water to verify. For this reason, I am not waiting until dark to close this event. Did you see anything under that water that would warrant waiting the entire allotted time?"

Blinking slowly, I flicked my gaze to Korben, who stood proudly opposite Isa, his foot resting on the large stone lying in front of him in the grass and a purpling bruise over his right eye where I'd kicked him. He leered at me, daring me to accuse him of attacking me––but doing so would have been a waste of precious air. It had happened during the trial; it was fair play.

Shaking my head, I closed my eyes. But the images of Seb being yanked into the darkness and Beck being killed instantly played against the dark backdrop of my eyelids. I opened them quickly to find Isa still staring at me, concerned confusion playing across her features.

"No," I said, my voice still hoarse. "There's no one to wait for."

She nodded once in acknowledgment. "As of this morning, Graham had fifty points, Korben had forty, Phillip had twenty, and Matthias had zero."

Of course, Korben sniggered at my pitiful performance. Graham raised his face wearily, his gaze landing on me, though I couldn't read his expression at all. Was he angry at me for saving him? Did he even know I had saved him? Phillip had been the one to carry him back to shore, after all. If he didn't know, then it would have been for nothing. Not that his life was worthless, but finishing last in two trials was not going to keep me in the running long enough to learn what I needed to.

"Graham, do you have a stone to present?" Isa asked, glancing down at him. He reached a hand into the pocket of his pants and produced a stone about the size of a chicken egg. Isa picked it up and then placed it on one of the scale's plates, which crashed to the table with a heavy clang.

"Phillip, you next." Isa gestured for him to step forward and place his palm-sized stone on the opposite plate. The scale gradually shifted until Phillip's side now rested on the bottom. Isa hummed and moved Graham's off to the side of the table.

"Korben?" she asked, but he was already on his way, heaving his stone onto the table which creaked under its weight. When he started to retreat, she flicked a hand at him. "On the scale, please."

Korben balked, rolling his eyes, but obeyed, though he seemed to drop it haplessly onto the scale so that a resounding clank rang out. Haughtily he walked back to where he'd been standing, glaring at me as he passed by.

"And Matthias? How about you?"

Patting my still-damp shirt and undershorts, I frowned. "Damn thing must have fallen out while I was busy doing other things."

Isa's gaze narrowed. "And what *things* were you doing?"

I pinched my lips together, but I was too exhausted to take this act as far as I normally did. Shrugging, I answered, "Stabbing the vestiliaga to save Graham, trying to save Beck but getting stabbed, and killing the beast so Phillip could get Graham safely back to shore."

Isa stared at me with unblinking eyes for a moment before swinging her attention to the others in turn. "Is this true?"

Korben, as expected, scoffed loudly. "Sounds like an elaborate excuse for not completing the trial."

Graham shrugged slowly and muttered, "It's possible. Last thing I remember was him calling my name at the surface and then seeing him swim toward me as that monster dragged me down by my leg."

Phillip glanced thoughtfully at me, and my gut hollowed out. Would he betray me now? Even after saving me?

But then his lip curved into a slight smile.

"While I didn't personally witness most of those claims, I have no doubt he's telling the truth. He could have left me to panic at the surface when the trial started, but he didn't."

Isa returned her attention to me and asked, "Why? This is a competition. Do you not care about winning?"

Korben started to laugh but stopped as soon as Isa glared at him. I didn't answer at first, taking the time to stretch out my stiff neck and roll my aching shoulders.

Finally, I cleared my throat and explained. "I absolutely care about winning, general, but winning isn't everything. The pursuit of it should never blind us from what truly matters: helping others—even our competition. I wasn't able to save some in the forest, and I regret that. Figured if there was something I could do here, I would."

"Give me a fucking break," Korben muttered, but everyone ignored him.

Isa rubbed a hand at the back of her neck and pressed her lips tightly together as she studied me, as if trying to decide if I was as full of shit as Korben seemed to think.

"And who stabbed you?" she asked, gesturing to my leg.

I shot her a half-smile. "I think you know. At least the blade wasn't poisoned this time."

She nodded several times, humming to herself. With another snap of her fingers, the guard brought her a small leather ledger where she presumably logged our points. Flipping open to a page marked with a black ribbon, she pulled an ink pen from her pocket and began to scribble something onto the page.

"We will start with the points for stones. Korben retrieved the heaviest, so he will receive fifty points for that. Phillip, forty. Graham, thirty, and Matthias, zero."

Korben let out a low laugh. I gritted my teeth together, trying to keep my disappointment from playing on my face, but stars. Even for all that talk of winning not being important, I sure despised losing.

"Now for the discretionary points. These are awarded using my own judgment, based on the information I've received from each of you and from what my guards can glean from what they found in the lake. These points are awarded—or lost—based on the strength of spirit displayed during this trial. Her Majesty and I value strength in all its forms. Arenysen needs a king who not only has the strength to defend his kingdom, but also the conscience to do what is right. Even if it means potentially sacrificing one's own desires."

Everyone seemed to lean in toward Isa as she explained this, and even her guards standing behind her appeared to shift closer to hear her decision.

"Graham, for this portion you receive zero points, as you unfortunately were rendered unconscious soon after the trial started. This leaves you at a total of seventy points."

I risked a sidelong look at the fae, but he was uncharacteristically calm, shrugging casually as if this outcome was expected.

"Phillip, you not only hauled Graham to safety, but also took the risk to swim back out to find and save Matthias, despite already having your stone. For that I am adding forty points, bringing you to one hundred."

Phillip smiled and dipped his chin graciously, obviously thrilled to have come out so well in this round.

"Korben," she said, letting out a low sigh before she continued. "You were issued no weapon at the start of this trial, yet you returned with someone else's. Each dagger had a number etched into the handle so we could know who was issued which blade. The one you had—the one that still had blood on it—had been Beck's. While I cannot know for sure what happened under the water, based on your past actions it's safe to assume you did whatever you could to win this trial, even at the expense of the others in that lake with you."

Korben scoffed loudly and lifted his eyes to the sky.

"For this, I am deducting thirty points."

He snapped his head down and glowered at the general, throwing his arms angrily out at his sides. "Thirty?! You don't even have any proof of—"

"Be glad it wasn't more," Isa said with impressive calmness. "Now, Ma—"

"This is bullshit!" Korben shouted, taking a step toward her, but he didn't make it very far before her guards had him restrained, his hands pulled tightly back behind him, and a sword point pressing against the base of his throat.

Isa strode slowly up beside her guard wielding the blade and stared confidently into the male's eyes. "Your mother should have taught you some manners. Speak to me—or anyone—like that again, and you won't just be disqualified from the tournament."

"You can't—" Korben started to protest.

"I can, and I will. Do *not* test me again," Isa said with such finality that Korben finally closed his mouth and remained silent, even when Isa called her guards away from him.

"Now, Matthias," she said, lifting her ledger once more. "I watched you at the start of the trial. The care you took to help your rival overcome his fear is commendable. As Phillip has attested, you saved Graham and ensured he was brought to safety. You also devoted your energy—to the point of nearly drowning—to defeating the beast that guards those stones, all so your competition could survive their swim back to shore. Some may think you foolish for caring more for the welfare of others than for your own success, but for the purposes of this trial, it was precisely what we were hoping to see. You not only demonstrated the impressive physical strength necessary to push your body to its ultimate limits and still defeat the vestiliaga, but you also displayed a prime example of a strong spirit. For this, I am awarding you one hundred points."

I froze, unable to speak—possibly for the first time in my entire life. No one spoke, in fact, as all four of our mouths fell open.

Isa didn't seem to notice as she concluded. "This leaves us with you and Phillip tied at the top and Graham and Korben trailing behind you. Now, let's return to the castle. I'm starving, as I'm sure you are as well."

As we all climbed into our carriages, I braced myself for some snide comment from Graham, undoubtedly upset that Phillip and I had each knocked him from the lead, but it never came. As he settled into his seat, the guard closed the door, giving a single tap on the side of the carriage to signal the driver.

After several minutes in tense silence, Graham finally whispered, "Thank you."

"It was nothing," I said.

"No, it wasn't."

I exhaled loudly. "I know. You're welcome. You would have—"

"No, I wouldn't," Graham admitted, his eyes wide in awe. "Who knew that you could end up winning by losing?"

CHAPTER 45

CALLA

The solar had grown considerably darker with the coming night as I lay on the sofa, nursing another glass of brandy. I'd spent the entire afternoon fretting over what was happening in Lake Vestia. We had agreed not to tell the competitors that the *stones* they were to retrieve were actually an ancient stash of gold sunk in the lake and guarded by a water dragon that had become little more than a myth for most in my kingdom.

Who would survive?

How many?

And why did I care?

I don't care. I can't.

I took another sip of brandy, or tried to. My damned glass was empty again.

What was I doing here, drinking alone in the dark like a common village drunkard?

"Time to stop, Calla," I said to myself, nodding as I slid my feet down to the floor and set the glass beside them.

Standing proved difficult—walking even more so—but I made it over to the small table where one of the kitchen staff had deposited my dinner not too long ago. Hopefully it was still hot, but even if not, I needed something in my stomach to combat the drink.

Poached fish, potato mash, roasted vegetables. They all smelled divine, and tasted even better. I wondered if Isa and the males had returned yet. From up here, I couldn't hear much of what happened outside. While the far wall was primarily windows, it was thicker than normal for security reasons, and blocked out most of the sound outside. Actually, the quiet was why this was one of my favorite spots in the castle.

Brennan used to sit up here with me for hours just reading whatever tome he pulled from the shelves while I sat and stared out of the windows. I had originally balked at the idea of holding my meetings with the competitors here, but when all was said and done, it hadn't tainted the space as I'd feared it would. It had actually helped to set me at ease—somewhat.

Letting myself think of Brennan was risky, though, and I should have known better than to allow it.

The lonely ache of loss settled in my bones until I couldn't even enjoy the last bites of my meal. It dulled my senses while pricking my shattered heart. I wanted to forget the pain, to forget all that had been taken from me, to forget that I was alone.

Before I could think better of it, I stood, grabbed one of the lanterns from beside the door, and left the room, thankful that Isa had agreed to not post a guard here. It had taken some persuasion, but in the end I'd convinced her the extra security wasn't needed with our guests off the premises for the day.

At the end of the hall, I found the tapestry—skillfully woven to depict the crowning of my father as King of Arenysen—and pushed it aside to reveal a crevice in the wall, just big enough for me to slide in sideways.

My father had had this castle built with a slew of hidden passageways connecting all the rooms—and some of the corridors —to a tunnel that led out to the forest—a precaution in case of siege.

Tonight, though, I didn't use it to escape.

This was quite possibly the stupidest idea I'd ever had, but the general's words—careless and flippant as they might have been during the first trial—would not leave my mind.

I'm yours to handle, whenever you need a little release.

Release was exactly what I needed tonight, and I was going to get it.

Assuming he'd made it out of that lake alive.

CHAPTER 46

MATTHIAS

Every part of me ached from today's trial. The healers had done their best to patch up the gash in my calf, but they could do little to help the fatigue that had settled into every other muscle. Thankfully, I walked into my room to discover dinner and a hot bath waiting for me. The queen and this tournament may have seemed bent on pushing us to our deaths, but at least we were provided some comfort until then.

Kicking my boots off, I pulled my shirt up over my head as I walked toward the tub set up in the alcove opposite the hearth where a fire crackled hungrily. I had just started to slide my pants down when something moved out of the corner of my eye. Deep shadows—darker than expected even with the moonlight streaming in—gathered on the far wall where the tapestry hung.

I stood still. Staring into the darkness, I had that same inkling I'd had back in the forest.

I was being watched.

The hair on my arms and neck rose. I couldn't see her, but I could sense her.

That scent of ripe fruit and violets was subtle yet intoxicating. It could have simply been a lingering trace of her on my clothes from the other day, but with those tossed in the laundry basket in the corner, that was unlikely.

No, the queen was here.

Watching.

Could this be part of the tournament? Was the queen spying on each of us? Testing to see how we'd react?

Pushing out a slow, exaggerated breath, I shrugged. In one quick motion, I shoved my pants to the ground and stepped out of them, grinning at the faint sound of a gasp. Perhaps it was my own ego making me imagine it––after all, it wouldn't have been the first time I had elicited such a reaction.

When I reached the tub, I dipped a hand into the water and swirled it around gently, but I didn't get in.

"Hey, Killer," I said quietly, keeping my eyes on the inviting water.

Silence answered me.

Except for a quietly quickening pulse, barely audible, but clear now that I was listening for it.

"I distinctly remember saying you don't need to use your shadows to ogle me," I said, giving a breathy laugh. I stepped a foot into the bath and slowly climbed in, sinking lower until all of my sore muscles were submerged in the steaming waters.

"You're welcome to join me if you like," I crooned as I lay my head back and closed my eyes. "Plenty of room for two."

For a while I simply lay there, letting my muscles relax in the heat, wondering how long it would take for her to find the nerve to step out of her shadows and speak to me. Rolling the kinks out of my neck, I waited, listening to her quiet heartbeat dancing along with mine.

I had nearly convinced myself that my mind was playing tricks on me and that she wasn't actually here, when her whisper sliced through the silence, much closer than I expected.

"You're filthy," she breathed, pulling my eyes open. Staring down at me, she seemed to be struggling to keep her gaze locked on my face.

I flashed her a smirk. "You have no idea, Killer."

At this her eyes indeed shifted lower, and I could have sworn she was fighting to hide a smile.

She cocked her hip out and rested a hand on it. "Did my staff not provide you any soap? Or do you just expect water alone to suffice?"

Lifting my arms out of the water, I rested them along the edges of the tub. "Oh, there's soap around here somewhere. Want to find it for me?"

"Don't be ridiculous. You can find it yourself."

"Where's the fun in that though?" I asked, reaching my fingers out until they just grazed the soft fabric of her dress. A little further, and I managed to pinch a bit of it and tug, urging her to move closer.

"I've already had a bath," she insisted, though by the look of her dry hair, that must have been hours ago.

"Is there some rule that you can only have one per day?"

"I have no need of a second one."

"They're not just for cleaning, you know," I said.

She pursed her lips and trailed her gaze down over my arms and chest before finding my eyes again. "Perhaps they should be, in your case."

I couldn't help but laugh softly, nodding. "Perhaps you're right."

Sitting up, I shifted in the tub and leaned over the side opposite from the queen. A small table had been situated there with all manner of soaps and oils and salts, all more complicated than any male needed, honestly. I selected one of each, and swiveled back to Calla, cradling the items in my hands.

Her face twisted with incredulity. "You said you lost the soap in the water."

"No, I didn't. I said it was around here somewhere, and so it was." I lifted my hands to her and shifted my expression into one of pleading innocence. "Any chance you can show me how to use these?"

"You don't know how to use soap?" Her eyes were wild with skepticism.

"Don't be silly. Of course I do, but what are these other things for?"

Slowly, Calla lowered herself to kneel beside the bath, taking a moment to move her dress out of her way before taking the two bottles from my hand. Reading the labels, she wrinkled her nose in disgust.

"These will never work together. What else did they leave you?"

Reaching back over to the table, I collected the remaining four bottles and offered them to her in my open palms. Gingerly she fingered the bottles' labels, humming sweetly to herself, and I couldn't help but watch her as she concentrated on something as frivolous as bathing scents. Her forehead crinkled in the middle, and the corners of her lips twitched. Finally, she plucked two of them from my hands and waved away the others.

She set one on the floor beside her, and then carefully removed the stopper on the other, slowly pouring a small amount of oil into the water. A warm, sensual fragrance surrounded me, slightly sweet and intoxicating. Replacing the stopper, she placed that bottle next to the first as she used her free hand to swirl the water, her fingers coming dangerously close to brushing my thigh.

"What is that one?" I asked, my voice not nearly as strong and controlled as it should have been.

"Amber," she said as she retrieved the other bottle filled with tiny grains. She proceeded to sprinkle the light green salt into the bath, once again swirling the water with her hand as she spoke. "Balsam salt. Ideally added with the water to allow it to dissolve before you get in, but it should still help you relax."

She started to pull her hand from the water, but I caught it with mine, not really sure what I was planning to do next and surprised that she didn't retreat from my touch.

"Thank you," I said. "Not just for this, but for what you did for Oryn, too. I heard he was sent home to his family today."

Calla only offered a slight smile as she bowed her head. She started to pull away, but I squeezed her hand in mine, holding her fast. I met her gaze, expecting to see the usual wary discomfort she displayed around the competitors, but there was no sign of it in her deep brown eyes now.

Maybe it was the flickering lamp light—maybe I was simply imagining it—but there was a longing there I had only witnessed once since we'd met. Like she wanted to surrender, to give in. Like she hungered for something more than the empty loneliness life had dealt her.

"Could you help me, Killer?" I asked, holding the soap toward her. "I can't reach my back with how broken that last trial left me."

"What happened?" she asked, slipping her hand from mine.

I lifted my leg out of the water to show her the gash in my calf. "Just a little love tap from a friend," I said, too tired now to feign any humor.

A low rumble pulled my attention. She scowled at my wound, and the muscle along her jaw pulsed fiercely.

"It's noth—" I started to assure her I was fine, but her gaze quickly snapped to mine.

"Who did this?" She growled out the words, sounding more like an agitated bear than a grieving queen.

I shrugged, trying to hide my wince as I lowered my leg back under the water. "Isa handled him already."

"A name, general," she demanded, her dark eyes burning into mine. "Some things demand...royal treatment."

"He's already had the pleasure of receiving such treatment, actually," I noted.

Understanding flashed across her face, and I half-expected her to immediately stand and rush out the door to find Korben. But she didn't, and instead she glanced down at her lap, her jaw still working steadily as she seemed to focus on her breathing. I was about to apologize—why, I wasn't sure—but she was soon lifting herself up onto her knees and reaching to take the soap from me.

My heartbeat quickened, and she hadn't even touched me yet. I chided myself for being so easily swayed by such a simple action, but when she dipped both hands with the soap into the water, her knuckles skimming along my hip, I had to remind myself how to fucking breathe.

"The ring you wear," she said. "Does it hold any significance?"

Lifting my hand so she could see it, I explained, "It was my father's. Passed down through the generations. Supposedly brings good luck, though I don't ascribe to that type of thinking."

"It's kept you alive this long," she said softly.

I shrugged. "I've kept myself alive. Well, with the help of Connor and our soldiers. And you."

An oddly comfortable silence fell between us, and then she released a light sigh that conjured a ripple of flutters across my bare skin. Her touch was light at first, fingertips trailing up my arm and over my shoulder, and I shifted sideways to allow her easier access to my back. Then the soap slipped across my upper back and over the other shoulder, and I couldn't contain the traitorous sigh that escaped me as I closed my eyes. She glided the soap along my skin in slow circles that became long strokes.

"What's this tattoo?" she asked.

I cleared my throat. "A laurel branch."

"For victory in the war?"

I shook my head slowly. "For my niece, Lorynne. So I'd remember what I was fighting for."

"And the letters?" She traced over them with her finger. "G.H. A lover's initials, perhaps?"

I might have chuckled more at the slight tinge of jealousy in her voice, but the memory of Gabriel dying on that battlefield flashed in my mind, dampening my spirits.

"For Lorynne's father, Gabriel Hawthorne. He was my sister's husband."

"Was," she echoed in a whisper, and I nodded.

"Killed during the war."

"Were you there?"

I nodded again, my throat tightening against my will. I hadn't lied when I told Connor that I'd dealt with this pain, that it had ceased to hurt, that I'd moved on. But, somehow, Calla's touch—and the reminder that she possessed the same powers that had killed him—seemed to split that wound open again.

Could I tell her how he'd died? How would she react?

"What happened?" she asked, tentatively. When I didn't answer right away, she added, "You don't have to talk about it. I shouldn't have—"

"A Shadow Keeper," I said, cutting off her apology. Her hands stilled on my back, but she didn't retreat. For a handful of breaths neither of us moved, until I dared to peer over my shoulder to see how she was faring.

Her expression was blank, similar to when she'd collapsed in the forest that first day, but different, more in control. Her shadows were contained this time, though she wore that same lost stare.

I turned around to face her, encouraging her to move her hands to the edge of the tub, the soap slipping from her fingers and sliding down into the water. I rested my hand on hers, brushing it with my thumb as I tried to search her eyes for any hint as to what she was thinking or feeling.

"It's okay, Killer. It was a long time ago."

"Don't call me that right now," she whispered, looking straight through me.

"Alright, Calla. What can I do?" I asked, not really sure what to expect from her.

"This was a mistake," she said, standing. She turned, not for the door, but for the tapestry on the back wall where I'd seen her shadows.

Without thinking, I rose and stepped out of the tub, ignoring how the air chilled my skin. All I knew was I couldn't let her leave. She stopped mid-stride but didn't turn to face me, instead dropping her chin to her chest, her hands clenching into fists at her sides.

I approached slowly, noting how the muscles in her shoulders tensed with each step I took. She didn't move, but her pulse raced, gradually growing quicker the closer I got. When my chest was nearly touching her back, her breath hitched, and she swallowed hard.

"You came here for a reason, Calla," I said, sending my words to warm her ear. She trembled, leaning slightly back against me before straightening away again. "Why?"

Being this close to her, her overwhelmingly sweet scent lit an unwanted fire in my core. When my body responded to the blaze, she shocked me by leaning back, pressing her backside into me. Slowly, she rolled her hips, and fucking stars, I couldn't stop my eyes from closing. Or my hands from finding her waist.

She slid her chin over her shoulder as she continued to shift and roll and press against me.

Her voice came out husky with lust, little more than a ragged breath. "You said you were mine to handle, when I need a release."

That had been a joke meant to rile her dragon guard, not an invitation, but now that she was here, no matter the logic that screamed a warning in my mind, my need—pulsing and growing within me—would not let me deny her.

"So I did," I said, brushing one hand over her stomach, daring to inch higher and higher, ever so slowly, expecting her to stop me at any moment. My fingers trailed over her breast and slipped inside her dress. She shuddered as I grazed over her pebbled peak, pinching it lightly. My lips caressed her ear, and I breathed out the question, "And does my Killer need a release now?"

I realized my use of the nickname too late, but she only rolled harder against me, her head falling back against my shoulder, offering the tender skin of her neck to me. Dropping my mouth lower, I nipped at her skin, dragging my teeth down to her bare shoulder. When I pulled back, I noted the hint of ink trailing across her shoulder blade and sliding underneath her dress. Trailing my finger along it, I opened my mouth to compliment the design—vines of thorned ivy—but she spoke first.

"I need a distraction, general," she whispered. She reached one hand up, tangling her fingers in my hair. "Can you give me that?"

The sweet scent of brandy coated her words, and I froze. "How much have you had to drink?"

She stilled, and for a moment I worried I'd offended her, but she finally whispered. "Enough for me to ignore every reason I shouldn't be here, but not so much you should feel guilty for giving me what I want."

"Well then, distraction is my specialty," I said, kissing her neck and shifting my hand to explore her other breast. She hummed, her chest thrumming against my hand, but then she stepped away from me.

I didn't resist, letting my hands slip away from her body and raising them in total and utter surrender. A brief warning flashed in my mind, wondering if she might be here to kill me as she possibly had her husband. But when she turned, her tear-soaked eyes finding mine, I saw no danger, no risk, only a desperate desire to escape.

I could be that escape for her.

She held my gaze as she undid the laces down to her waist, and her tongue peeked out to wet her lips as she slowly gathered her dress in her hands, lifting it ever higher until she slipped it off completely and dropped it to the floor. She wore no shift beneath, wore nothing at all, and simply seeing her standing there in all her bare confidence was a delight in itself.

When I met her gaze again, any trace of tears had vanished, and now she wore a sly smirk on her lips. Slowly she backed away until she hit the tapestry, beckoning me forward with a curve of her finger. As I complied, her shadows slipped loose, spilling from her palms. I waited for them to come for me, but instead the dark trail of shadows caressed her skin, over her torso, down her hips. When they slipped between her legs, she laid her head back against the wall, her mouth parting to let her ragged breath escape. She held my gaze as her shadows moved over her skin, pulling a moan from her chest. If I wasn't careful, she was going to undo me before I ever got to feel her.

"On your knees, general," she commanded as her shadows slipped down her thighs, lifting her leg out to one side to invite me to taste her glistening center.

I ignored my own throbbing need and knelt at the queen's feet. Her shadows shifted her leg up over my shoulder before slipping under my chin and gently nudging my head up. If I'd thought she was intoxicating before, it was nothing compared to being this close, breathing in her warmth. Trailing one hand along her raised thigh, I kissed the other, teasing her with my breath and tongue and teeth as I moved closer to her center.

With a sensuous, impatient growl, Calla slid down the wall, her shadows holding me against her—as if I had any desire to stop now. My own needy groan hummed past my lips as they found her bundle of nerves, relishing in the way her hips moved against my mouth. And when I finally let my tongue slip out to taste her, I lifted my eyes to see her head tilted up, one hand fisting her dark hair, her other holding her breast where her thumb worked heavenly circles.

I couldn't get enough of this female, who tasted sweeter than any other I'd enjoyed over the years. I was so engrossed in drawing out her whimpers, in savoring her, that I didn't notice her shadows—sensual and warm now, instead of the icy cold I'd experienced before—had moved down my chest and torso to where my body begged for release, their heat caressing every inch of me. Her darkness seemed to react to my need, moving with me as I pushed both of us toward that blissful end we both craved.

I worked my tongue and fingers faster against her, inside her, all the while her shadows kept pace along my length. Moving with her rolling hips, I fed off the sound of her pleasure filling my ears, my room, my world. I wanted nothing more in that moment than to give her everything she wanted, anything she needed, whatever she demanded. With our heartbeats racing together, our groans building off one another, we soared over that edge together, a perfect harmony of ecstasy. I gripped her thigh, still teasing her as her warmth tensed around me and my body trembled against her shadows, until we both stilled.

Slipping her leg off of my shoulder, I pulled away from her, my hands holding her waist, as I rose to my feet. Her shadows slowly retreated back into her palms, now pressed against the wall by her sides. When she finally opened her eyes to find me staring at her, a thin smile graced her perfect lips, but when I moved closer to claim those lips for myself, she stopped me with fingers pressed to my mouth.

She shook her head.

"That will do, general."

Stepping past me, she gathered up her dress and slipped it over her head. She looked back once, not at me, but at the tapestry-covered wall behind me. Huffing out an annoyed breath, she turned and walked out into the hallway without another word.

CHAPTER 47

CALLA

I stepped out of Matthias's room into the dark corridor, my shadows concealing me despite the dim light. Leaning back against the cold stone, I begged my pulse to steady. Closing my eyes, I relived every moment of our encounter—his chest against my back, his breath in my ear, his tongue working unexpected miracles—which did nothing to help slow my heartbeat.

Stars, though, that general knew what he was doing.

The thrill gradually faded with the realization that it could never happen again. The other contestants already believed I favored him, and I didn't trust the Assembly not to use any misstep to steal my throne.

No, it couldn't happen again.

I wish it could, though, because I'd never been worshipped so completely.

With that thought, a cloud of shame descended on me, not because of what I'd done or for enjoying myself, but for comparing Matthias to Brennan. The way Matthias had accepted my command without hesitation—yet somehow also knew precisely what I craved and how to deliver—was like nothing I'd ever had with Brennan, and just thinking about it again nearly made me storm back into his room and demand more.

I might have done just that had the handle on his door not started to turn, snapping me out of my lust-filled thoughts. Pushing away from the wall, I fled down the hallway and around the corner before he could find me. I didn't stop running until I was back in my room. Slamming the door behind me, I collapsed against it and dropped down to sit on the floor.

"Where have you been?" Isa's harsh tone startled me. She stood in the middle of my living area, arms crossed, eyes blazing with bitter worry.

Shrugging, I leaned my head back against the door, but all I could do was smile like an idiot.

"You were with Matthias," she said, as if she could read it on my face. My smile vanished. "Oh, don't act so shocked. I can smell him all over you, Calla. And if I can, everyone else will, too. What in the stars-damned fuck were you thinking?"

I knew how risky it had been. I didn't need a lecture. My gut writhed angrily, and I pushed to my feet. Stalking toward my friend, I crossed my arms at my chest and glowered at her, but before I could say anything, she was speaking again.

"I get it. I do. I know you're stressed, but—"

"I'm not *just* stressed, Isa. I'm angry. I'm tired. And I'm lonely. So yes, I needed one little distraction. One that won't be repeated."

She angled her head and eyed me suspiciously. "It better not. Though from the look on your face, he won't be easy to let go of."

I gave her a half-hearted smile. "It was just a bit of fun. Nothing serious."

"For now, perhaps, but what happens if you fall for him? Or he for you? Your vow to honor this tournament's outcome still holds. He may be tied for the lead right now, but there's no guarantee how he will score in the next trials."

"Isa, it will take more than a skillful tongue to win over my scarred heart."

She didn't seem to believe me, and if I was being honest, I was a bit skeptical myself. Something about that male had woken part of me I thought I'd lost forever, the part that felt capable and strong.

"Well, it's been a long day," Isa said, unfolding her arms and wrapping me in a hug. Pushing me back, she held me at arm's length and shot me a motherly look. "Now, go wash his scent off of you and get some rest."

She'd made it halfway to the door when she paused and pivoted around slightly.

"One more thing. Can we please be more careful about strangling the staff? Hilde went to the healers after you attacked her."

"I didn't attack her." Isa's brows lifted high. "I reprimanded her for her insolence."

"With your shadows."

I scoffed.

"Must I remind you that the rumor isn't just that you killed Brennan, but that you suffocated him with your shadows, just as you did to Korben and nearly did to Hilde. The Assembly will undoubtedly hear of it, and I can only protect you so much."

"Wasn't the tonic supposed to help—"

"It only helps calm your power's response to your emotions; it doesn't keep *you* from using them. You are still responsible for what you do, Calla, with or without that tonic."

Accepting that night as a singular encounter was easier said than done. As a precaution, I resorted to avoiding him for the next two days, but I couldn't escape the memories that flooded my dreams each night. Without fail, every time I lay down and closed my eyes, he was there, and every morning I woke up with fresh guilt.

Unfortunately, there was no avoiding him when the Assembly, in their infinite wisdom, requested another group meal so they could get better acquainted with the final four males. Unlike our welcome dinner, this was to be held in our smaller dining room where my family had taken our meals together. I tried not to think about it, but my stomach was in uneasy knots the entire day while I hid in my room. As I sipped on Jocelyn's tea, though, I found my confidence growing. I just needed to make it through one meal without anyone discovering what had happened between Matthias and me.

I waited until the last minute to head downstairs; the less time spent with him the better. Pausing outside the door, I closed my eyes and listened to the voices on the other side. Slowly I counted my breaths, willing my nerves to calm. I was so focused on my breathing and the sound of my own pulse, I didn't notice a second heartbeat approaching until it was too late.

"There's my Killer."

His voice caused heat to bloom in my core, and I stiffened, my mind immediately replaying the last time he had been behind me. A small part of me wanted to pretend that I hadn't heard him and just enter the dining room, but that would only let him believe he had some kind of power over me. I couldn't have that.

Turning slowly, I donned a casual expression and lifted my chin as I greeted him, ignoring how he'd called me his. "Late again, general?"

Matthias's lips curved down into that frown of his, and curiosity flashed in his hazel eyes. "Not yet. But if you'd like to make me late, I don't mind having my first course somewhere more private."

His gaze slid down my body suggestively, and I had to clasp my hands together behind my back to keep my shadows from slipping out, as if they, too, longed to feel him again. I dropped my chin, noticing how he was already growing hard, which flared my desire higher.

No, I couldn't have him again. But, my mind—my traitorous, whore of a mind—insisted on wondering how it would feel to have him inside me.

"We can't," I said in a less than convincing tone.

"You're the queen," he whispered. "You can do anything you want."

A smile tried to creep across my mouth at that, but I bit my bottom lip to hold it at bay. When I didn't say anything, he leaned closer, his lips brushing over my ear.

"You know where to find me, Killer."

With that, he slipped past me and headed into the room. I hesitated, sure it would look suspicious if we arrived together. Pacing the hallway, I tried to clear him from my mind, to think of things that were decidedly less attractive—pond scum, fat slugs, pickled fish. I'd nearly doused the flame he'd re-ignited when Isa came out and tapped me on the shoulder.

"You can come in now, Calla."

I glanced at her sidelong as I kept pacing. "I wasn't doing anything with him, I swear."

Isa was already nodding. "Great, but now you need to go in there and pretend nothing happened. Can you do that?"

"Okay," was all I could manage before she led the way into the dining room.

Twelve places had been set at the long table, with my seat at one end and Ursula at the other. Isa either had a sick sense of humor, or she had not taken the necessary precautions to keep us apart, because Matthias was standing behind the seat directly to my left. I couldn't request he be moved without raising suspicions, so with a nod and a wave of my hand, I invited everyone to sit, noting that the Assembly members were seated among the competitors.

At once, the servers entered and began pouring wine and water into our glasses. I hurriedly lifted my wineglass to my lips and downed as generous a sip as I could without raising any eyebrows. Something tapped my left knee, and from the corner of my eye, I noticed Matthias's eyes meet mine and then dart toward the opposite end of the table where Ursula sat gawking at me, her glass lifted as if she had been about to make a toast.

Matthias's earlier words echoed in my head. *You're the queen. You can do anything you want.*

Anything I want, my ass. I couldn't even drink my wine

without offending someone, but now was not the time to start a fight, especially with this witch on the Assembly.

"Apologies, Ursula." I said, offering a curt smile and lifting my glass toward her. Ten other glasses lifted in turn.

Ursula cleared her throat. "I simply wanted to congratulate the males here for surviving the first two trials, and wish them good luck in those to come."

All four contenders bowed their heads and lifted their glasses higher before we each took a sip. The servers returned with the first course, and to my right, Isa smiled reassuringly as she speared a tomato with her fork. At the far end of the table, Ursula and Opal—the youngest female member of the Assembly—were asking Graham how the tournament had gone for him so far. I didn't catch his answer, though, because something had brushed against my left ankle, slipping under my dress and up my leg.

I stole a glance at Matthias, who twirled the ring on his finger as he intently listened to Phillip's answer to some question I hadn't caught, but the corner of his mouth curled up mischievously. Then he hooked the toe of his boot behind my calf and pulled my foot toward him, spreading my legs wider than was proper with so many present—even if it was hidden under the damned table.

Determined to ignore him—and the way each stroke of his foot against my leg stoked the growing heat in my core—I looked past him to Yuri, sitting on his left.

"Yuri, how are things in the west? I know the tournament has forced us to delay our meetings with the citizens."

Matthias's foot continued to caress my leg as he turned to Yuri and asked, "Your province shares a border with Emeryn, doesn't it?"

Yuri nodded his balding head to Matthias. "Yes, it does. Up near Engle." He turned to me, then. "Things have been relatively quiet in my area. We are all eager to see which of these males will be our next king, though. There are some matters that have come up, but I have been able to work with the local officials to square those while you are occupied here."

Beside Yuri, Warren chimed in, his dark eyes fixed on me. "How are you feeling about the competition so far, Your Majesty? Any favorites among the four?"

My gut tightened, and I pressed my tongue hard to the roof of my mouth, even as I smiled as genuinely as I could manage with this swine of a male.

"Seems hardly proper for me to choose a favorite, and even if I did, I would not discuss it with anyone, especially with them present," I said, popping a slice of cucumber into my mouth.

"Of course, Your Majesty," he said, dipping his chin. "Though the seating arrangement seems rather convenient, given the rumors."

Before I could protest, Isa spoke up. "We have had quite enough of rumors, Warren. Even if there was any preference on Her Majesty's part, I assure you, it would have no bearing on the outcome of the tournament. The queen has vowed to honor the victor, whoever wins."

"Seems you have some fantastic options, Your Majesty," spoke Fern from beside Phillip near the middle of the table. "To have survived both the enchanted forest and Lake Vestia? Arenysen will surely have a strong king on the throne."

I promptly lifted my wineglass and said, "To the future king of Arenysen, whoever he may be." Without looking at any of the males, I emptied my glass and set it down on the table.

Warren leaned back in his seat as a server removed his barely-touched salad and locked eyes with Isa. Swirling the wine in his glass, he spoke in his usual high-and-mighty tone. "Speaking of delaying the citizens' hearings, the Assembly feels it unwise for the queen to shirk her duties simply because she needs a game to choose her next husband."

Matthias stiffened in his seat, his foot retreating from where it had been massaging my calf. He opened his mouth to speak, but I quickly jabbed my toe into his shin in warning. He stalled long enough for Isa to do what she did best—which was why I trusted her implicitly as my second.

"I assure you, *your queen* is shirking nothing. The tournament was historically used for kings to choose their brides, so I do not see how our using it to choose a king is any different. And unlike the historic *games*, we are testing character, strength, courage...not bust size. Or dick size. Though, if you would like us to hold more closely to historic tradition, I'm sure the males here wouldn't mind whipping their goods out so we can measure."

All the males froze in their seats, some with their glasses half-raised to their mouths. I half-expected Matthias to stand up and start to undo his belt. In fact, he was probably about to when Warren finally responded with a quiet, "That won't be necessary."

Isa relaxed back into her seat, just as Warren had, inspecting the wine in her glass as she continued. "I do agree, though, that perhaps it would behoove us in our selection of a new king to have them present—and perhaps even participate—in one of the citizens' assemblies."

I wanted to smack her with the back of my hand and promptly ask her what the fuck she was thinking, but it would not look good for me to refuse to meet with my subjects. Plus, if she was suggesting this, there was a good reason.

Slowly, I nodded at my friend and lied, "You're right. How soon can we have that arranged? Is there room in the tournament schedule?"

"I think so. We could delay trial three until next week, and schedule a forum with the citizens for later this week. Give them enough time to travel."

At the other end of the table, Ursula leaned forward. "Couldn't this be an official trial in itself? Letting the males aid Her Majesty in hearing grievances and handling disputes? It could help us all to see how well they work together—how they will potentially rule together."

A hand lighted upon my left knee and gave a gentle, reassuring stroke, and I peered sidelong at Matthias. He wasn't looking at me, but somehow I knew his easy smile and slight dip of his chin was meant for me—his silent way of letting me know I wasn't in this alone.

Through the next two courses, the Assembly made small talk with the contestants sitting among them. I heard none of it, though, as my mind was a jumble of worried thoughts over what would happen when I was to meet with my subjects again. While no more humans had been discovered since the tournament began, it was always a possibility. I had specifically not asked about the status of moving the humans out of the kingdom, as it was the last topic I wanted to discuss in mixed company, but I should have known one of the Assembly advisors would mention it for that very reason.

Ursula waited until all the plates had been cleared away before finally broaching the subject.

"Does anyone know where we stand on getting the humans out of the kingdom? I believe all have been evacuated from my province. How about you, Opal?" she asked the young advisor to her right, who nearly choked on her wine.

"Oh, yes, no, well..." she stammered. "For the most part we have helped them relocate to Wrenwick."

I tensed at the mention of the kingdom responsible for Brennan's death. I'd hired Minerva to appropriately punish them, but I knew none of the specifics of the curse she'd offered. I should have asked more questions, but knowing the mage, she would have refused to answer them anyway—not without requiring even more payment from me, that was. So that left me sitting here pondering how she might have cursed them and if they were suffering as I had.

Hopefully worse.

"Your Majesty?" Ursula's crisp tone pierced through my thoughts, and I blinked, looking up at eleven pairs of eyes all staring at me.

"Yes?" I asked as casually as I could, but Isa cleared her throat beside me and flicked her eyes down to the table, where my clasped hands were now obscured by my creeping shadows.

Shit.

I couldn't let them see my panic, though. I needed to demonstrate I was in control, despite my careless lack thereof that I'd just displayed, letting my shadows emerge as they had. Calling my power back into my veins, I opened my palms for all to witness them disappear, but I said nothing.

Warren smiled—though it appeared more like a friendly sneer, if there was such a thing. "It's nice to see you've gotten yourself under control now."

Slowly, I slipped my hands into my lap, maintaining my hold on my shadows despite the rage his words lit within me. The fucking prick had the nerve to deride me in front of guests. While I didn't want to be forced to marry any of them, I sure as fuck didn't want to be insulted in their presence either. But I couldn't make a scene, couldn't let my anger get the better of me.

Nodding, I donned a polite smile. "Thank you, Warren. I've been working on being more intentional with how I use my shadows."

Matthias coughed behind his hand, and my smile broadened as I tried not to laugh at just how intentional I'd been with him the other night.

"Though, I won't hesitate to use them when necessary," I added.

The table went silent, as if everyone was contemplating when my shadows might be necessary. The servers returned with small plates of macarons, and I tried to ignore the way Matthias's eyes lit up—just a bit—at the sight of my favorite dessert.

"When would such power be necessary?" This question came from Korben, who was leaning back in his seat, staring at his dessert as if I might have poisoned it.

"Oh, I don't know," I said, shrugging. Keeping one hand in my lap, I picked up a macaron with the other and turned it this way and that. As I did, I called my shadows out beneath the table, directing them to drift toward Matthias. "They come in quite handy when I can't sleep."

Matthias gulped down his macaron just as my shadows crept up his thigh, slipping beneath his waistband, and finding him already anticipating what was to come. Slowly, I guided my shadows along his rigid form, and smiled when I noticed him shift in his seat, giving my shadows better access.

"They also work surprisingly well to move items, to subdue attackers, or to punish criminals."

Putting another macaron in his mouth, Matthias leaned forward, letting his eyes drift closed as if he were simply savoring the decadent sweet and not getting secretly stroked and teased. I noticed Isa eyeing me with a warning glare, and I turned to her with a wide, innocent stare.

Warren's sharp gaze hit me. "Or attack your own staff?"

"When they need reminded of their places, yes. Am I not to use my powers to protect the kingdom?" I glanced around the table. "What good is it to have such abilities if I can't use them to help others?"

On those final words, I tightened my shadows' grip around Matthias's hard length, gave him a few more vigorous strokes for good measure, and then pulled the darkness back into my hand. Matthias stared down at the table for a second before lifting a hand to his temple, as if he were suddenly suffering from an intense headache. No one around us seemed to notice—except Isa, who still glowered at me disapprovingly.

Spreading my hands wide above the table, I clasped them together and bowed my head to my guests.

"Now, if you would please excuse me. It is getting late, and I could use a bath after such a long day."

I didn't wait for a response before pushing back my chair and turning to leave. No one moved. No one said anything. No one came after me. And I couldn't be bothered to give a shit what they said about me once I left.

As Matthias had reminded me, I was the stars-damned queen.
And I could do whatever I wanted.

CHAPTER 48

MATTHIAS

It was another half hour before I could even think about getting up from the table once Calla left, and there wasn't enough ice water in the room to cool me off. By then everyone had departed except Graham and Phillip, and the three of us walked back to our wing together in silence.

When we reached the stairs, though, Phillip cleared his throat quietly and noted, "I don't know why, but the thought of meeting the subjects with the queen is more stressful than the last two trials."

Graham shrugged. "It's not that bad. Usually they're just arguing over stolen property or need help after a difficult harvest season."

"But what about the humans?" Phillip asked, quickly looking back over his shoulder as if the queen herself might attack him for even mentioning them.

"They should have all left by now," Graham said, though by his tone it seemed he didn't believe that to be true.

I waited a few moments before asking my own question. "Did we ever learn why she banished them?"

Graham and Phillip shared a quick look before shaking their heads. It was Graham who elaborated. "After the king died, she seemed to blame the humans for his death, but she refuses to talk about it beyond repeating her edict that she can't serve them."

"Can't?" I asked. "Not won't?"

Graham nodded. "The most she ever said to me and General Marlowe is that she cannot be objective with them, cannot rule them as they deserve."

"So it's like sending away a lover before you can break their heart," I mused.

Phillip sighed. "Only to crush it for them when they refuse to go? It doesn't make any sense to me."

"Whether it makes sense or not, she's the queen," Graham said, as we turned the corner into our darkened hallway.

"Do you miss your old accommodations?" Phillip asked Graham.

"Not really. It's quieter in this wing, actually. Though, I'll be happy to move into the royal suite when I win."

Phillip scoffed lightly and stopped at a door, saying his good-nights before going inside and leaving Graham and me alone. The silence between us—broken only by the soft thuds of our boots on the stone floor—was less awkward than usual, but still far from comfortable.

I lifted a finger and pointed ahead of us. "I'm at the end of the hall."

He eyed me from the side. "Are you asking me to walk you home?"

"I mean, you're welcome to come in for a drink. Except, I don't actually have anything but water."

"I'll pass," Graham said flatly as he paused at a door halfway down the corridor. "Maybe another time."

"Can I ask you something?" I asked, taking a quick glance around us to ensure we were alone and no queen-hiding shadows lurked nearby.

"What is it?" Graham asked, doing a fairly decent job of hiding his annoyance.

"How did the king die?"

Graham quirked a brow. "Why does it matter?"

Frowning casually, I lifted a shoulder. "He was my best friend's brother. Would just help him find some closure if he knew for sure."

"Is that why you entered the tournament? To spy on Calla for your prince?" Graham asked in a low protective voice, though he didn't show the same hostility toward me that he would have a week ago.

"I entered because no one in Engle wanted to, and it was important to Connor and Lieke to honor the queen's call for contestants. If I don't win, I'd at least like to bring home some good news, you know?"

Graham was nodding along with my words. He took a moment to mull things over and then finally asked, "What have you heard?"

"Not much, honestly. The rumor, of course, that the queen killed him. But, you spend enough years chasing down human rebels who are armed with fae-killing poison, and well, you tend to get suspicious any time a fae winds up dead."

"Understandably so. I know as much as you do, I'm afraid. No wounds. No sign of struggle."

"So it could have been poison?" I pressed.

Graham pursed his lips. "Perhaps? Stranger things have happened."

"Like flesh-eating trees and a mythical gold-hoarding beast," I said. "Do you think Calla could have done it?"

He was silent for a couple breaths, his dark eyes searching mine as if testing to see if I could be trusted. He leaned closer in. "I've seen her rip limbs off women for merely mentioning that possibility."

"So you won't say either way." I didn't bother phrasing it as a question. He shook his head.

Slapping Graham on the shoulder, I gave a sharp nod, said good night, and turned for my own door.

I entered to find my room much like I did most nights—the bed turned down, the fire burning steadily, the drapes drawn closed. Just being in here conjured memories from that night, the feeling of her shadows gripping me––then, and today. My body eagerly responded to the images crossing my mind, and I growled in frustration.

Whether she'd killed Brennan or not, she certainly knew how to drive a male mad.

Kicking my boots off to the side, I stripped out of my clothes and walked to the window, leaving a line of crumpled clothes trailing behind me. I threw back the heavy curtains and dropped my hands to the handle of the window, preparing to fling it open and let the cool night air calm the heat coursing through me.

The familiar cold touch of darkness slid up my spine, and I was about to write it off as nothing but a typical stroke of unease except it circled back down, around my ribs, and lower, gripping me as it had under that stars-damned table.

"Hello, Killer," I said, my voice a raspy growl. In the window, Calla's reflection smiled wickedly back at me. "Come to finish what you started?" I asked, trying not to sound too eager.

Her reflection shrugged and then walked away, taking her shadows with her, leaving me even colder and once again begging for release. When I turned I found her sitting on the edge of my bed in a most-unladylike position, her legs spread wide and her dress hiked up to her knees. She leaned back onto her hands, giving a seductive arch to her back. The movement forced her breasts higher until they were nearly spilling over the top of her untied bodice.

It must have been a lie that she didn't favor anyone, because I certainly felt like the queen's pet with her displaying herself like this for me. Perhaps I should have been warier—especially since I still lacked any definitive proof of her innocence—but I'd been sent here to get close to her; I was merely doing as I had been instructed.

And having a little fun in the process.

Not that Connor would see it that way, but still. What was the point of life—of duty and service, even—if I didn't get to enjoy it a bit?

Wetting my lips, I swallowed hard at the sight of her and the thought of getting to feel more than just her shadows consuming me. I stepped toward her slowly and marveled at how confident and powerful she looked even as I towered over her. Her eyes never left mine, except for one brief moment when I caught her glance down at my full length, and I could have sworn she gasped as if she was seeing me for the first time. When she tucked her bottom lip between her teeth, I couldn't suppress the growl in my chest, couldn't stop my hand from reaching for her, clutching her neck as if she were mine to possess.

She didn't flinch, and a wicked fire burned in her brown eyes. Her breasts heaved as she sucked in a slow, deep breath. When she spoke, her voice was rougher than I expected. "Tell me, general, how would you use me if I let you?"

My mind swarmed with images—each one filthier than the one before it, but which could I admit to, and which did she want to hear?

"You don't want to know all the things I would do to you."

She pursed her lips. Despite my firm grasp, she shook her head and purred. "I wouldn't have asked if I didn't want to know."

Inhaling, I savored her sweet scent and brushed my thumb over her parted mouth. A hungry growl rumbled in my chest.

"I'd see if this mouth of yours feels as good as your shadows." She hummed appreciatively, as if she were imagining it already. "Thrust myself between these perfect lips."

Her gaze darkened a bit, the corner of her mouth twitching, barely holding back her wicked smile. With my thumb, I tugged at her bottom lip, and my chest heaved with want as her mouth fell open and her tongue slipped out to taste the rough skin.

"I'd watch you take all of me, as deep as you can, while you fill yourself with your shadows—as I know you like to." She squirmed, and heat pulsed through me. Leaning in closer to her, I lowered my voice. "I want to see you swallow every last drop I spill down your throat."

She hauled in a breath. Her tongue swirled around my thumb, and it took all the strength I had not to drag her mouth onto my ready length right now. But I was no fool. This was the queen—a queen who may have very well killed my best friend's brother, and while I'd say a lot of dirty things, I wasn't about to act on them until she gave the word.

"What else?" she whispered, her hips shifting ever so slightly on the bed. The scent of her arousal made it nearly impossible to think of anything beyond burying myself between her legs.

Somehow, I forced myself to focus, using my thumb to tilt her chin up even higher so she looked straight at me. My other hand trailed a line down her throat, hooking on the top of her bodice and tugging it down to reveal her breast—pebbled and inviting. I flicked my thumb over the hardened peak and relished in the way her breath hitched and her chest shuddered.

"I'd throw you back on this bed so I can memorize every inch of your breasts and pull those whimpers from your lips until you beg me to fuck you."

"You think I'd beg?" she asked on a quivering breath.

"I know you would, Killer."

Her eyes were pure challenge, a dark and delicious dare as her brow angled up, her lips pulling into a cocky smirk. "Prove it."

CALLA

Matthias had almost undone me with his words alone, but I refused to let him see how much I wanted him to act on them. By the way he consumed me with his eyes now, though, I could tell I'd failed. He knew what I craved. I expected him to move as soon as I voiced my challenge, to take action quickly and decisively––but instead he moved painfully, irritatingly slowly.

Brushing his thumb over my bottom lip as he had earlier, he studied me hungrily. He parted my lips, and his eyes drifted down to the slow dance of my tongue on him.

When he finally spoke, the words came out rough with wild desire. "You want to taste me, Killer?"

I nodded.

Gently, he slipped his hand along my jaw, cupped the back of my head, and pulled me to him. Locking my eyes on his, I let him guide me, relishing in how he took control, treating me as if I was the most precious thing in the world to him, yet not so fragile that he wouldn't wield me as he wanted.

Shifting his hips, he angled himself to meet my lips, forced me to open for him, and then pulled me onto him until I was filled so deeply I forgot how to breathe. Moving my tongue around him, I would have grinned at how his eyes threatened to roll back with pleasure, but it was impossible to smile with my mouth spread so wide. I swallowed hard, pulling him in deeper, hollowing my cheeks, as I lured him in as far as he could go, feeling him slide into the back of my throat.

Fuck, I was nearly to the edge and we had only begun. I tried to slow the pace, but he gripped my hair and pulled me to him over and over, finding a steady rhythm to match our rapid heart-beats and ragged breaths.

"Your shadows, Killer," he reminded me on a rough whisper, and I lifted my hand to where my mouth ended and he began, calling my shadows out. I only had to direct my power to the aching space between my legs, and then let it take over, just as I let Matthias.

A deep moan filled his chest, echoed by my own that hummed along his length pulsing past my lips. My shadows swirled around my bundle of nerves, slipping further between my legs and filling me with a refreshingly cold pressure.

Matthias's fingers curled in my hair, holding me steady as he thrust greedily into my mouth. I watched him, feeding off the rapture on his face as much as I did his body. We moved together —his hips, my shadows—faster and faster, building and swelling, until our frantic need sent us tumbling together into a euphoric sea where he filled me, drowning me with his delicious end.

When he relaxed his grip on my hair, trembling as he slipped from my lips, I wiped a finger at the corner of my mouth and mimicked his favorite casual frown and shrugged.

"Not bad, general."

His laugh—rough and booming—filled the room and warmed my world with a joy I'd thought impossible for me to ever experience again.

"Shadows away, Killer."

As I obliged, pulling my shadows back into my palm, Matthias caught me by my shoulders, lifted me gently, and tossed me backward onto his bed. A laugh escaped me, lighter and brighter than I had heard from myself in so long. He was hovering over me before I had finished giggling. Wagging his brows at me, he flashed me a devilish smirk as his face disappeared from view, lowering down to where my breasts lifted and fell with each heavy pant.

His tongue painted slow circles around one peak, pulling such a gasp from me that I had to cover my eyes with my hand. Biting down hard on my lip, I tried to ignore the agonizing ache that throbbed in my core, and to hold back the pleading words that already wanted to escape. I couldn't let him win so soon, but that stars-damned tongue of his was making it nearly impossible.

As he devoured one breast, he found the other with nimble fingers, rolling and flicking and pinching until the walls of my resolve threatened to crumble around me. His other hand slid up my thigh, falling between my legs, grazing over my slick center to tease every frayed nerve I had.

"That's not fair, general," I chided in an uneven, unconvincing tone.

"Oh, did I not mention what my hands would be doing?" he said against my skin.

I shook my head against the bed. "No."

His strokes—perfect in their pace and pressure—didn't let up even as he asked, "Do you want me to stop then?"

Yes, I thought, but my lips uttered a too-desperate, "Never."

Nipping my breast with his teeth, he laughed when I released one ragged breath after another.

"What's that, Killer? Is this too much? Have you had enough?"

Stars danced behind my eyelids, and I fisted the bedding with both hands.

"No. Not enough."

"What do you need?" he asked between the overwhelming sweeps of his tongue.

"You," I gasped.

"Where?"

"Here," I said, my eyes slamming shut as I grabbed his length and feverishly tried to pull him to where I ached most.

"Are you sure?" he asked, his husky voice teasing me in the worst ways.

"Fuck, general. Yes, I'm sure." I slid my fingers into his hair and curled them against his head, yanking his face up to look at me.

He lifted his brow in silent question, his hand not slowing its teasing between my legs.

I rolled my eyes and whimpered like a pathetic wench. "Fine. You win."

"What? I didn't hear you," he said, his voice irritatingly taunting.

"Please, general."

"Please... what?"

Sighing, I lifted my head off the bed until my breath tickled his ear.

"Fuck me...please," I whispered.

No sooner had I said the words than he was there, his hand replaced by the edge of him. He lifted my hand away from where I still gripped him.

"Lift your hips for me, Killer," he commanded.

I obeyed, nearly falling into that bliss again when he gave inch after inch to me. Filling me over and over, thrusting and pulsing, giving me all of him so readily, so completely—so tenderly, even— that it brought tears to my eyes. I wiped them away with my hand, trying to savor the way our bodies moved together, perfectly in tune with each other.

I nearly froze beneath him.

What was happening here?

This was just supposed to be a fun distraction.

It wasn't that he was better than Brennan—they were equally skilled in these matters—but I'd never felt this strong of a connection before. What did that mean?

Why did it need to mean anything?

Just enjoy yourself, Calla!

I growled as I pushed my thoughts past the inconvenient, absurd feelings.

This was only physical. Just a release. Nothing more.

But the closer we edged toward our shared bliss, the more our bodies melded into one, and the more my doubt grew.

This was more. This was everything. This was *impossible*.

This couldn't happen.

I didn't want connection.

I didn't want *love*.

I wanted distraction.

Just this one last time.

This had to be the last time.

I opened my eyes to find him watching me intently, as if he were trying to hear the thoughts roaring in my head. He slowed his movements, his eyes searching mine.

"Should I stop?" he asked, brushing my hair away from my forehead.

Yes. No. Fuck, I don't know.

I shook my head and gripped his hips to pull him closer, determined to not let him see me break down. As he picked up the pace once more, his eyes dropped to my mouth. He drew closer, bringing his lips dangerously close to mine, and I panicked, turning my head away so that his kiss landed on my jaw. If he noticed my objection to being kissed, he didn't show it—pressing his lips under my ear in a feverish trail down my neck.

Biting down on Matthias's shoulder, I channeled all my fear and worry into my hips as they rolled madly beneath him, torn between wanting to finish so I could run away and never wanting it to end. When we finally collapsed into a heap of satisfied breaths and trembling bodies, I pushed him off me and sat up.

What had I done? What was I to do now?

I couldn't risk my heart to another, and I'd been a stars-damned fool to think this wouldn't have consequences.

Matthias lifted himself onto his elbow, his hazel eyes following me as I pushed to my feet, lacing up my bodice and smoothing down my dress as I turned to leave.

"Leaving so soon?" he asked.

Peering back over my shoulder at him—hating how he looked at me as if he'd risk the whole world to please me, and hating my fractured heart more for delighting in it—I narrowed my eyes.

"I didn't peg you as the cuddling type," I said. I resumed my retreat, but I wasn't fast enough.

My hand barely touched the door handle when he spoke again.

"Calla."

I stilled at his use of my name, but I refused to turn.

"What?" I asked, the word more clipped than I intended.

I could feel his gaze burning into my back as I waited for him to say something, hoping he wouldn't chase after me as he had the other night. For a long moment, the only sound in the room was our heartbeats—mine still quickened, his slowing steadily. Irritated by his silence, I called my shadows out to conceal me as I turned the handle. Only when I pulled the door open did he finally offer a hollow "goodnight."

I sat there for an embarrassingly long time, staring at my door, picking apart what had just happened. The confident strength Calla had initially shown, even when she yielded control to me, had gradually faded, and I couldn't figure out why.

It had been good—no—it had been stars-damned perfect.

Maybe that was the problem.

Calla needed a distraction, something empty and frivolous. Whatever this was between us may have started out as that, but somewhere in the midst of it all, something had shifted. I'd seen it in her eyes. I'd felt it in my own veins. This wasn't some casual fuck with some pub owner. This was... fuck, I didn't know what it was. All I knew was this was going to complicate everything.

The mission remained, though.

Regardless of what may or may not have been happening between the queen and me, even with the blood vow I'd made, my duty—my loyalty—was to the Durands first and foremost. I would do what needed to be done for the good of my kingdom and for the peace of my friend, even if it meant killing this female.

I just needed to keep myself focused on the reason I was here.

And it was not to fuck the queen.

Having fun was fine, unless it put the mission at risk--and whatever had changed between us tonight was an undeniable risk.

❧

They postponed the next trial until after the citizens' forum, which left me with altogether too much time with my own thoughts—traitorous, mutinous thoughts that insisted on returning to the queen no matter how hard I tried to stop them. What the fuck had she done to me? Never before had I felt such a loathsome emptiness after bedding someone.

Growling, I pushed to my feet for the hundredth time that morning and began pacing. I needed to do something, anything, aside from sitting here wallowing. I was no closer to knowing if she'd killed Brennan or not, but who could I speak to? Where could I look?

What did I already know?

First, Connor had received word from the healers that Brennan had been poisoned.

But Hilde worked closely with the healers and claimed they had ruled out poison, pointing instead to suffocation.

The healers refused to speak on the matter, understandably so, and Graham had been little help except to confirm there were no visible wounds, which could indicate poison—or not. He was obviously too afraid—even as Calla's former advisor—to say anything to implicate her and wouldn't be of any more help.

Maybe I could try the healers again, or find something helpful in the infirmary. They must have kept records or files on Brennan's death. But how could I get in there without them seeing me?

It's too bad I don't have shadows to hide in.

That thought snapped my eyes to the far wall where I'd first noticed Calla hiding in my room. How had she gotten in here? She probably had a master key to every room in her castle, but something nagged at me. That night, she'd looked back at this wall, as if contemplating something. Hastily, I rushed across the room and examined the tapestry, running my hands gingerly over its soft surface and curling my fingers around its edge. The palace in Emeryn had its own secret gates and passages, so I wouldn't be surprised if this castle did as well.

But when I pulled the fabric back, all I found was the same stone that made up every other wall. Shoving aside my initial disappointment, I lifted the fabric higher. There. Behind the middle of the tapestry, roughly half a meter up from the floor, lay a sizable gap in the stones. I rushed back into my bedroom, grabbed a lantern from the side table, and returned, holding it up to the dark crevice. Sure enough, past the opening lay a narrow passageway.

Wherever this led, taking it would prove far more fun—and hopefully more productive—than moping about in my room.

I stepped over the short wall of stones and plunged into the cramped space, holding the lantern out in front of me. My foot knocked into something, sending it toppling over with a loud clank against the hard floor. Peering down, I noted a small lantern similar to the one I held and smiled at the memory of Calla sneaking into my room.

Shit, I wasn't supposed to be thinking of her. At least not fondly, anyway.

Forcing myself to focus, I pushed on ahead, navigating the passage and visualizing where I was in the castle as I went. At the first intersection, I turned right, confident this would take me to the stairwell, where hopefully the tunnel would follow it down to the lower floors. On either side of the passage at irregular intervals lay alcoves for hidden entrances into other rooms. I checked the first few, but finding nothing of interest, I gave up investigating the others.

Until, halfway down the passage parallel to my hallway, muffled voices caught my attention and pulled me back to the alcove I had just passed. Creeping into the tight space, I craned my neck, pushing my ear closer to the entrance, careful to keep the lantern back in case they might be able to see the light somehow.

"You were supposed to kill him," a male's voice growled, familiar, but I couldn't quite place it.

"No shit," responded another, this one easily identifiable—Korben. "It's not for lack of trying."

"He cannot win this tournament."

"So I've been told," Korben groaned. "Why does it have to be me?"

"You're the only one with a viable reason to want him dead, or have you forgotten how your friend died at the Emeryn palace?"

"It's a tournament to the death; that should be reason enough for any of us."

"Just get it done, or you might be next to have a tragic accident in these games."

Heavy footsteps stomped away, and I jumped when glass crashed violently against the wall nearby. Hurriedly I backed out of the alcove and resumed my trek onward.

So someone had hired Korben to kill me, but who? The Assembly? That made the most sense, honestly. They seemed all-too-eager to get Calla off the throne, and short of that, no doubt they'd want some say in whoever sat beside her as king. But what threat did I pose specifically?

I stopped in my tracks as a thought struck me.

I was from Emeryn. Not only that, but I had close ties to the Emeryn royals. Was that why Brennan was killed? Because of the alliance? But the alliance was intended to help both our nations stave off potential war. Who in Arenysen could be against such an arrangement?

Someone who wanted to rule.

Shit.

It had to be the Assembly. Had they killed Brennan to sever the alliance?

It was more than possible, but I needed more than mere speculation.

I took off down the passage, spurred on by this fresh trail to follow, reminding myself that this didn't clear Calla of any guilt. She could have been working with the Assembly. She could have arranged for her parents' deaths and then Brennan's.

Just the thought turned my stomach. Every interaction I'd had with her—every moment, and not just the intimate ones—pointed to her innocence, but I'd be a fool to let my feelings for her cloud my judgment.

Fuck, did I truly have feelings for her?

I shook my head and pressed on. Now wasn't the time to worry about that. Until I cleared her name—until I could prove she didn't kill Brennan—whatever feelings I'd stupidly developed for her were moot.

It took an embarrassingly long time for me to finally find where the passage led down to the lower levels. It didn't follow the main stairwell as I had hoped, and I'd had to backtrack several times and try different paths before discovering a set of narrow ladders leading in both directions. For a moment I peered up toward the dark opening that lead to the upper floors, wondering if Calla's suite lay above my head somewhere. My muscles itched to climb the rungs to see, to check on her, but with how she had fled from my room last night, she probably didn't want to see me.

No, she'd come to me when she was ready.

And if she doesn't?

I shook my head.

Then it is what it is.

But now, I need to focus.

As quickly as I could––while precariously carrying the lantern in one hand––I slipped down the ladder, one level and then another and another, noting how the air chilled as I descended.

Here there were no alcoves along the narrow passage, but in the distance came the faint sounds of chatter mixed with the dull clanks of metal and wood. I crept forward, following the noise. My stomach grumbled when the comforting aroma of braised meat and baking bread drifted toward me.

If the kitchens were that way, then the infirmary would be in the opposite corner to the left. Spinning around, I pushed forward, keeping my steps quiet as I continued. Around two corners and down one long stretch of darkness—the scents and sounds of the kitchen lessening with each step—I walked, trying to ignore the ache of my feet. The corridor then split, one path angling up, gradually rising. Leading to the outside perhaps? To the forest?

I shuddered slightly at the memory of the creeping vines and deadly trees.

The other path, unlike any other I'd traversed so far, had a dim light glowing at the end. Lowering the flame in my own lantern, I set it on the floor before slowly moving on. A crevice the same size as the one in my room was cut into the stone wall, but instead of being covered by a tapestry, it appeared to be hidden behind a large piece of furniture that stood just far enough away from the wall to allow me to step into the room.

I immediately recognized the scent of healing herbs and cleaning solution.

I was back in the infirmary.

Carefully, I shifted to the edge of the shelving and peered around it, releasing a heavy breath at finding the room empty. The lanterns—several placed throughout the space—burned low, giving it an eerie quality that tightened my stomach. I just needed to find their records, discover something—anything—that would support the queen's innocence, and get out.

What if she's guilty though?

Then I'll do what I have to, what I swore I'd do.

My job was to find the truth and act on it. I couldn't let any bias keep me from accepting whatever it might be.

On the desk in front of me, a short stack of papers crowded one side. With one final check that I was alone, I rushed forward and quickly searched through the pile. Records for Korben from when I'd brought him in unconscious lay on top, followed by an order signed by the queen and her general for the release of Oryn, complete with authorization to have him transported home to Emeryn. Below that were a few pages signed by each of the healers dictating all they'd done to aid me after I'd barely survived the first trial. There was nothing after that of any significance, only some receipts for healing supplies and a handful of memos from the other healers stationed throughout the kingdom. The rest of the desk was clear, aside from a pad of blank paper and a few ink pens laid neatly in the center.

Squatting low, I hid myself behind the desk and pulled open the top drawer—nothing but wax seals and unused envelopes. The drawer below it held several sachets of tea, spoons, and napkins. Boring and not in the least bit helpful. I was about to open the final drawer when the soft pad of footsteps hit my ears, slowly growing louder.

Shit.

Sprinting back to the cover of the shelf, I slipped into the crevice in the wall and focused on slowing my breathing and calming my pulse. Hopefully the heavy scents crowding the air would mask my presence well enough.

I held my breath as they entered the room—two sets of feet, two heartbeats—one of them speaking heatedly.

"Jocelyn, are you sure the remedy you've been providing the queen is sufficient? With the citizens' forum approaching, she can't afford to not have an adequate hold on her shadows." The harsh tone had to be the healer Ami.

Jocelyn's softer voice answered. "Yes, Ami. I am. I used the same for her mother for many years prior."

"Yes, but her mother didn't have a propensity for rage and a hidden power that could kill so easily."

"Calla is stronger than you all give her credit for," Jocelyn argued.

"That's what I'm afraid of," Ami noted darkly.

Feet shuffled, jars clinked together, and something fell onto a solid surface before Jocelyn spoke again.

"I will need more ingredients soon, though. She requires a larger dose than her mother did, and my supplies are quickly dwindling. Do we have the status of the latest shipment?"

"It's been delayed," Ami said. "Transport is taking extra precautions with the tournament. We're under a bit more scrutiny with some troubling questions being raised about the king's passing."

Jocelyn hesitated before timidly asking, "What kinds of questions? Raised by whom?"

"Some have been led to believe that it may have been poison," Ami said, her voice thick with suspicion. "Where could they have gotten that idea?"

"Possibly from their own experience?" Jocelyn offered, and I smiled at the hint of sass in her tone. "The king's family had their fair share of trouble with the poison. It would only be logical for them to consider it as a possibility."

Slow footsteps filled the resulting silence, and then Ami's voice lowered into a menacing hiss. "I never said anything about his family. Why assume—"

Jocelyn's exasperated sigh interrupted her question. "They are the only ones whose skepticism would have you worried like this. I told you we should have told them the truth from the beginning, but what are you implying? That I went behind your back and informed them somehow?"

"Did you?" Ami asked pointedly.

"And what could I possibly hope to gain by doing that?" Jocelyn asked.

Sharp footsteps cut through the uncomfortable silence that followed. Ami whispered, "A lot could go wrong if a certain neighbor of ours starts poking around in our business. What happens if they link the poison to the queen, hm? Did you ever think of that?"

"She didn't do it, though," Jocelyn protested.

Ami scoffed. "No one knows that for sure, and now that they have reason to believe it wasn't natural or an accident, they'll be ramping up their own investigation rather than trusting us to handle it."

"We should just destroy the remaining poison we have on hand, then," Jocelyn said.

"No," Ami said, her tone once again darkening. "They need it for the next trial."

"What? They can't do—"

"They can, and they will, Jocelyn. That's why I need you to make more of the antidote. You're the only one with the skills to do it."

"We should have destroyed it all before the general got poisoned," Jocelyn said. "Do we know for sure that male didn't get it from our supply?"

"General Marlowe is still investigating that, but in the meantime, we're taking precautions." Ami's voice lowered, sounding almost gentle. "All you need to do right now is worry about getting the antidotes ready."

Jocelyn mumbled a quiet, "Fine." Heavy footsteps echoed through the now-quiet room, growing louder, closer—my cue to get back to my room.

CHAPTER 51

CALLA

If Isa knew what had happened between Matthias and me, she never let on. Actually, the absence of her chastisement almost made me feel guiltier for what I'd done. Almost. For the next few days, life went on much as it had before the tournament, even before Brennan's death. Quiet time spent in the solar, poring over reports from the provinces, reading up on the grievances that I may have needed to address in the upcoming citizens' assembly.

With the next trial postponed until after we met with my subjects, there was no reason for me to see or visit with the competitors, but every night when my room was too quiet, I felt that pull to the hidden passage that would take me to Matthias's room. I didn't know if it was my shadows, my heart, or my body that yearned to be close to him, but somehow—even with the bottle of brandy I'd brought down from the solar—I refrained.

He didn't come to me, either. Not that I expected him to. Stars, he probably didn't even know where my room was—though, as a general, surely he could have found it if he wanted to.

He's probably respecting your space.

Why did he have to be so stars-damned fucking perfect?

He's not perfect, Calla.

He's just here.
And he's skilled.
That's all.

I couldn't let myself think about what would happen at the end of this tournament—couldn't worry about him winning or losing or which outcome I preferred. I just needed to get through this next citizens' forum.

❧

Standing outside the Great Hall, I listened to the quiet thrum of conversation on the other side of my personal entrance. I'd taken a double dose of Jocelyn's tea in hopes it would give me more control over my shadows than usual, but still I couldn't stop my hands from shaking as I wrung them at my waist. My heart thumped against my sternum, beating out the seconds as they passed. I hadn't met with my subjects in weeks, but it seemed more like months with how frayed my nerves were.

I straightened my shoulders, sucking in as deep a breath as I could, and lifted my chin. Exhaling through my mouth, I imagined pushing out every anxious thought and feeling. Based on the grievance reports I'd reviewed, this should have been simple enough, but with the added audience of the Assembly and my suitors, I couldn't shake the apprehension that today was more a trial for me than for any of the competing males.

I was the one being tested here––but then, every day was a test for a queen suspected of murdering her husband.

There won't be any humans here today.

They are only bringing forth the grievances I reviewed, and those are simple.

I'll be fine.

The door in front of me opened, and Isa poked her head out. Spying me, her face lit up with relief.

"Oh, good. You're here. I didn't want to have to track you down," she said, reaching for my hand and starting to drag me forward. My feet resisted, though, remaining planted firmly on the stone floor.

"Wait," I muttered, slipping my hand from hers and rubbing my temple. "Any potential surprises?"

Isa gripped both of my shoulders. "There are always potential surprises, Calla. You know this, but I'll be right there with you if they arise. Yes?"

I gave a string of small nods, though my gut was still annoyingly tied up in knots. Gritting my teeth, I drew in one last, slow breath, and muttered, "I'm ready."

Inside the hall, my throne had been set up on a long dais with two smaller chairs placed on either side for the competitors. My core tightened at the sight of Matthias seated on my left, just as he had been at dinner—a fact I had to quickly brush out of my mind before it distracted me. Phillip sat to the right, and Isa had thankfully kept Matthias and Korben apart, placing Graham beside him instead.

The males didn't turn as I approached, stepping around my throne on Phillip's side—a minor precaution to ward off any temptation. Even with hundreds present, I didn't trust myself with Matthias. From the corner of my eye, I could see him look at me, a devilish grin gracing his lips. I ignored it as best I could, pushing my attention to those gathered before me. Clasping my hands behind my back, I looked out at the crowd and greeted them.

"Good morning," I said firmly, giving them a moment to quiet their conversations and turn toward the dais. Every face looked toward me, setting off a frantic fluttering in my chest. "I do apologize that I have not been able to meet with you as often as my parents did, but I want to offer my sincere gratitude that you have been so gracious and understanding to me during such tough times."

Somewhere in the sea of faces someone scoffed. How many here today believed the rumors? How many thought me a heartless killer? If they only knew the truth about their king's death, they would understand why I'd exiled the humans, why I'd killed so many for their insolence. Or would they?

Ignoring it, I continued. "As you can see, today's assembly is a special one, as I am accompanied by the four finalists of our tournament. They will be aiding me in my judgment of your cases to assess how well we might rule together. While this is not an official trial in the games, it is a valuable exercise for all of us. I expect you to show them the same respect and courtesy you do me."

I nearly scoffed myself, given what little respect and courtesy my subjects showed me by spreading those disgusting rumors. Swallowing hard, I settled myself onto my throne and beckoned Isa and her list of grievances forward. She stepped down off the dais and stood in front of me, looking out at those gathered as she called the first case forward.

"Mrs. Mola of Leighbracht," she said in her commanding tone.

An older female hobbled forward on frail legs, supporting herself with a weathered wooden cane. She bowed her chin to me and then glanced warily at the males to either side. I searched my memory for this female's case, vaguely recalling it had something to do with her crops.

Smiling warmly down at her, I greeted her directly. "Good morning, Mrs. Mola. How can we assist you today?"

"Your Majesty, it's my crops," she said, bowing her head sheepishly again. "The season has been too dry, leaving me with little to sell at the market and barely enough to feed myself and my young ones."

I turned to my right. "Korben," I said, waiting for the male to look at me before I proceeded. He barely turned toward me, though, choosing to give only a cursory glance my way. I curled my fingers into the arms of my throne, trying to ease the anger his impertinence sparked, but pulling in a calming breath brought Matthias's familiar—and distracting—scent of woody leather.

Focus, Calla.

I eyed Korben coldly. "How would you handle Mrs. Mola's plight?"

He shrugged casually as he stared at the female. "You're from Leighbracht?" Mrs. Mola nodded slowly. "Your neighbors in Polneir have had a plentiful season, so I've heard. How is it that theirs thrived yet yours faltered?"

The female fidgeted with her fingers. "I am not an expert on the weather, sir, but it does not always bless—or curse—each part of the kingdom equally."

This earned a light laugh from the crowd which Korben brushed off. "Indeed." He paused and turned to me, fully this time. "Could we spare some of the royal stores to help her and the town out? Perhaps put in a request with the Assembly to have a donation taken up from around the kingdom?"

"Agreed," I said, nodding as I turned back to the female. "General Marlowe will give you a notice to take to the castle steward, who will issue you some food stores to take home and schedule your case with the Assembly."

"Thank you, Your Majesty," she said as she backed away.

The morning continued in much the same fashion, with my asking each male how they might resolve a dispute or address a concern. For the most part, all went relatively smoothly. I even managed to keep all interactions with Matthias as professional as possible—though that did require I refrain from looking at him directly.

There was only one instance of disagreement between a male and me. I had asked Phillip how best to handle the killing of a farmer's cow when it got off his property and allegedly trampled a neighbor's crops. While he had thought it best to fine both parties —one for negligence in containing their animal and the other for killing someone else's animal—I was all-too-acquainted with this pair of farmers. Their decades-long list of disputes over everything from trees crossing property lines to accusations of sabotage had been a nuisance for my parents when they ruled and had now apparently become mine. The cow-killer was to pay a retribution to his neighbor and reminded to stop looking for offense wher-ever he could.

I couldn't help but smile as the pair walked away, with Isa having to separate them to prevent a public squabble from breaking out between them. While so many things had changed since my parents' deaths, it was oddly comforting to have their drama remain constant. Like welcoming the horrendous winter winds simply because they were reliable.

"How do you sit through all of these for so long?" Matthias whispered from my left.

I glanced in his direction, but returned my attention quickly to the crowd. "Do the Durands not meet with their subjects?"

"Sure they do, but they travel to each town, rather than having the citizens make the trip," he explained.

"Was that due to the dangers on the roads?" I asked, still refusing to look at him.

Even so, I could picture his light shrug and down-turned smile as he answered. "Even before the rebel attacks. The king and queen enjoyed getting out of the palace."

"They'd still be sitting for a long time," I argued.

"But with ale," he said, laughing quietly.

"You often traveled with them, didn't you?"

Matthias was silent for so long, I wondered if he'd heard me or not. When I finally turned to see what had kept him from answer-ing, a smirk tugged at the corner of his mouth. "Oh, so you can look at me after all!"

My expression soured as I tried to conceal any hint of attrac-tion to this stars-damned male. "Of course I can look at you," I said, tipping my chin up as I faced our guests again. "I simply prefer not to."

His chair creaked as he leaned across the armrest toward me and whispered, "Why is that exactly? Is it that awful to remember—"

"Remember what?" I hissed as I spun around to face him, my

nose mere inches from his in an effort to keep the conversation quiet. "This is not a conversation I want to have right now."

His eyes drifted down to my lips. "Is it a conversation you want to have at all? Because I get the impression you've been avoiding me."

"Don't flatter yourself, general." I swallowed hard at my use of his title, remembering all the other times I'd used it in private. Ignoring how my cheeks warmed, I dropped my head to the side and regarded him coldly. "I didn't take you for the type to need to talk about your feelings. I've been rather busy preparing for today."

As if on cue, the main doors to the Great Hall swung open, and six of my guards marched in, escorting four hooded figures in the middle of them. The crowd parted to allow them to pass. Matthias quickly shifted back in his seat. I could feel his intense gaze studying me as I rose to my feet. Isa waited for them at the bottom of the dais. The lead guard exchanged quiet words with her, but I couldn't make them out with the muted conversations spreading through the room.

Isa's whole body tensed, and my stomach plummeted to my feet when she looked back over her shoulder at me, her face pale behind her stony expression.

This isn't good.

She whispered something more to the guard before rushing up the dais toward me. Her lips grazed my ear as she tried to keep her voice as quiet as possible, though she only uttered one word.

"Humans."

CHAPTER 52

MATTHIAS

It had to be humans.

Nothing else would have both the queen and her general as rigid as garden statues. A quick glance toward Graham further supported my suspicions, as he was sitting on the edge of his chair, his fingers drumming nervously on his knees as he watched intently. My skin prickled with unease when I picked up their faint scent. This wouldn't be good. Resting my chin on my hand, I watched, waiting and searching for any clues that might help me determine Calla's innocence— or guilt.

Isa was shaking her head vehemently, and I managed to catch some of her tense words: "No, we can't delay. It has to be now. The Assembly insists."

Calla hissed back, "I'm the queen. They are *advisors*, not rulers."

"It will look bad if you refuse. This is a chance to rebuild trust with your kingdom."

Calla's hands trembled as she clasped them tightly behind her back, as if she were wrestling with her shadows to keep them contained.

"It will be worse if I lose control," Calla seethed.

Isa flashed her signature stern, motherly look at her. "Then don't lose control."

Spinning away from Isa and pulling her hands in front of her, Calla faced her throne. She stared down at her open palms as if her shadows might be able to tell her what to do. After a few tense breaths, she turned back to the crowd and dipped her chin in a single nod to Isa.

The general, stepping to the side, gestured to the lead guard to come forward and speak.

The guard—a male about my age, give or take a decade or so, with graying hair at his temples—bowed to Calla, nodded to me and the other males sitting on either side of her, and then spoke, his deep tenor immediately silencing the crowd's murmurings.

"Your Majesty, apologies for the intrusion, but this is a serious matter indeed. We caught these individuals sneaking into our kingdom from Wrenwick, a strict violation of the law."

Calla lifted her chin once, but said nothing, and the guard immediately turned and instructed his team to remove the prisoners' hoods. A man I didn't recognize stood at the rear beside a young woman with reddish-brown hair. In front of him, the hood lifted to reveal a young woman whose face I immediately recognized.

Raven.

But my sister had said she'd slipped into Kinham, hadn't she? Thinking back to that conversation at my sister's home weeks ago, though, I realized that no, she had only relayed information passed to her through a friend, and that friend hadn't offered any description.

Regardless, Raven was here now.

But why?

I'd been searching for her—and the other rebels—for so long, a brief wave of relief washed over me, replaced instantly by a weighty worry over what she was doing here and what would happen to her now. Could I protect her against the consequences? Should I?

While I pondered those questions, the guard removed the fourth hood, and I nearly leapt to my feet.

Sera.

My sister.

What was she doing here? Why was she sneaking into Arenysen? She knew the stars-damned risk, especially for her.

Her brown eyes glided over to meet mine, widening slightly with a flare of defiance mixed with obvious fear. My mind immediately pulled up the memory of the children covered in their mother's blood. The image shifted into a pile of bodies and limbs on this floor. I hadn't needed to see it with my own eyes to know the horror Calla had caused that day—a horror I couldn't let her repeat today, for Calla's sake as much as for my sister's, Raven's, and the others'.

Calla cleared her throat, drawing all eyes to her.

"Why are you here?" she asked, her voice eerily calm, almost sweet even.

Raven stepped forward half a pace and locked eyes with the queen, no sign of fear on her face.

"The poison used by the rebels in Emeryn has been coming from Dolobare through your port in Crowmer. I came to intercept the latest shipment to keep it from getting into the wrong hands in Wrenwick."

Calla's face remained stoic, her body rigid, making it impossible to tell how she was receiving this news. Did she know the poison was coming through her country? Was she the one authorizing it? Did she believe Raven at all? She didn't ask anything more, though, and instead addressed my sister.

"And you?"

Before Sera could answer, Isa was rushing over to Calla's ear, frantically whispering words I couldn't hear. Whatever it was, though, had Calla asking, "Are you sure?"

Isa nodded, and the queen turned back to Sera once more.

"You aren't human," she said, and relief pulled my shoulders down, allowing my breaths to come more easily.

"Half," my sister said, and I could have slapped her for the confession, but admittedly it would have been hard to deny given her rounded ears.

"And why are you here?" Calla asked. "Are you, too, looking to stop this poison?"

She shook her head slowly. "No, I came to help support those who chose to remain in your kingdom despite the law."

My eyes slid closed, dread pooling in my chest as it caved inward.

"Help them how exactly?" Calla asked.

"Getting them food, namely, but also helping get their children to safety if needed."

"So they send their children away but choose to remain," Calla said. "Why don't they just leave?"

"This is our home!" The couple behind my sister voiced in unison, and immediately Calla lifted a hand and flicked her fingers in a silent command to her guards, who kicked the backs of their legs. Their knees hit the floor with a loud crack that reverberated off the high ceiling above.

"This is my kingdom," Calla said, once again in that off-putting tone. "This is my law—a law I decreed for your own safety. Humans..."

She paused, her mouth still open as if she was trying to say words that refused to come out. Calla's body tensed until her shoulders trembled while she continued to try to speak, her mouth opening and closing like a fish on the beach. After several odd attempts to finish her sentence, she let out a growl of frustrated anger.

"I cannot—I will not—rule over humans. This is no longer your home. Understand?" she asked, and the couple exchanged a wary glance.

"Does that mean you are letting us go?" the man asked quietly.

"Of course not," Calla said. "You knew the cost of staying. You knew it meant death. What kind of ruler would I be if I didn't dole out punishment fairly? And as for you two"—she pointed to Raven and Sera in turn—"You were never my citizens. Entering my kingdom unlawfully—regardless of your supposedly good intentions—makes you enemies of the Arenysen crown. And what do we do with our enemies?"

With this question, she pivoted to her right and gestured to Korben, who had a wicked gleam in his eye as he answered.

"Death is the typical punishment for spies."

It took considerable effort not to lunge across the dais and smash my fist in the male's face for trying to get my sister executed.

"Agreed," Calla said, and lifting her hand, she pulled her shadows out to swirl above her open palm.

"No," I said, pushing to my feet.

Sera was shaking her head at me. Raven seemed to notice me for the first time. Calla slowly rounded on me, her shadows still dancing on her hand while some tendrils seemed to drift toward me.

"No?" Calla asked, her dark eyes narrowing on me, a dare not entirely different from the expression she'd worn in my room the other night, though decidedly more fearsome. I risked walking toward her. Ignoring the crowd around us, I held her gaze amid the heavy silence in the room. I stopped an arm's length away from her, close enough I could grab her if she tried anything, but not so close as to betray our connection.

"Hold them for trial"—I barely stopped myself from using my nickname for her—"Your Majesty. Show your kingdom that you're just and capable of mercy, that you aren't the killer they believe you to be."

Her expression iced over. "I am just, general. But some are not worthy of mercy."

"What did the humans do to you?" I asked before I could think better of it. "Whoever hurt you, they are not here. These people did not harm you."

"They did when they chose to disobey my laws!"

"I'm not suggesting you let them go. But this is not the time to act rashly. Remind them of who you truly are—the caring, compassionate queen we all know you to be."

"Remind them?" she asked quietly, and I nodded, stupidly thinking I'd helped. Her lips curled up into a sinister grin. "Seems they need to be reminded of what happens when they defy their queen."

Before I could stop her, she sent her shadows careening toward the prisoners. They bypassed Raven and Sera to surround the young couple in darkness, their sharp cries choked off by her power. When her shadows lifted, the man and woman crumpled to the floor, lifeless.

The crowd gave a collective gasp.

She killed them without a second thought—no remorse—suffocating them with such ease, just as she had nearly done with Korben in the hallway. The scene before me vanished as a memory took its place. Gabriel gasping for breath as the Shadow Keeper filled his lungs with darkness instead. I'd been helpless to stop it, incapable of helping him, as feeble then as I was now. Calla's clicking tongue snapped me back to the present. Her shadows once again swirled slowly in front of her.

"If you wanted to stop the poison," she said to Raven, "you should have come to me or to the Assembly."

"How do you think my family got the poison in the first place?" Raven challenged. "All shipments from Dolobare require royal approval. For all I know, you're the one who has been orchestrating its transport."

"And what use would I have with a weapon against my own kind?"

"Ask your husband," Raven spat.

Calla roared—a pained, mournful sound—and threw her hands toward Raven.

No! I wouldn't let this happen again. I wouldn't stand idly by and do nothing.

I bounded forward, jumping off the dais to stand in front of

Raven, as if I could actually block Calla's powers from reaching her. Yet, that's exactly what happened. Her shadows halted, winding around my arms and legs, through my hair and over my torso, moving like a pet against its owner, who had just returned from a long absence.

Growling low, Calla glowered at me. Her face twisted in anguish and confusion as she seemed to try to get her shadows to move past me. I risked a glance at the other males still seated on the dais. Korben bore a wicked grin as if he were already picturing my execution, silently begging for her power to end me right here. Phillip's eyes were as wide as his mouth, which he tried to hide behind splayed fingers, and Graham watched all of this with a stoic curiosity.

"Move, Matthias," she hissed the command, but I stood firm, extending an arm out in front of my sister as well.

"No. I won't let you do this," I said, gently. "Not without a trial."

She sneered, baring her teeth, but pulled her shadows back into her palms. Gesturing to the guards, she said, "Then you'll go to the dungeons with them."

CHAPTER 53

CALLA

I stormed off of the dais and out of the room as the guards hauled the prisoners and Matthias away. Through the roar of anger in my ears, I could faintly hear Isa behind me instructing the crowd that the citizens' forum was ending early. Once in the royal sitting room behind the Great Hall, I threw my shadows out around me, channeling all of my anger into my power. Paintings crashed to the floor as I tore them off the walls. Cushions exploded into clouds of feathers as I ripped them apart.

The general thought he could challenge me? And in front of everyone like that?

As good as his intentions were, he had made a fool of me.

Concealed in my shadows, I moved through the castle hallways, pausing in the darkness cast by the lamp light whenever someone walked past. The air grew colder as I made my way down the spiral stone steps to the holding cells. We rarely used these, as the forest generally kept enemies or attackers from making it very far, and we'd lived in relative peace since the war ended. Though with the number of humans who'd defied my orders, the cells had recently seen more use.

At the bottom of the stairs, I paused and listened. Matthias's voice, though quiet, reverberated through the small space.

"Who is watching after Lorynne and Gabe? And the children you took in?" he asked, and my mind snagged on the first name, recalling how I had run my hand over Matthias's tattoo.

Lorynne. His niece.

Was one of the women his sister?

The demi-fae.

Of course.

There had been something annoyingly familiar about her features, and that must have been why. She was the general's half-sister. No wonder he had stepped in to protect them, though that didn't explain his connection to the other woman.

"Lottie is staying at the house while I'm away. She had planned to make this trip, but we knew the humans in Arenysen didn't trust fae, so I offered to come instead."

"That was stupid of you," Matthias said, humorlessly.

"You're one to talk, brother. What in the stars are you doing sitting by that evil queen's side?"

Before he could respond, the other woman's voice chimed in. "He's entered her tournament, competing to be the new king."

"What? Why? You've never been interested in settling down," his sister said.

Matthias gave a half-hearted chuckle, and part of me longed to hear the booming laughter he'd let out the other night. "The king thinks I work too much, wanted me to have a chance at love, I guess."

"And he thought a murderous queen was the perfect match, eh?"

"It's not quite that simple; she—" Matthias started, but his sister cut him off.

"—Murdered that couple today, Matthias! She ripped apart those poor kids' mother! Or did you forget—"

"No, I haven't forgotten."

"She's a stars-damned Shadow Keeper! The same type of monster who killed my husband, your best friend." Her voice cracked as grief took hold of her, and I winced from the pinch of guilt, as if he had died by my own shadows.

"I know, Sera. I miss him too. I know what she's done, but even monsters have their reasons," Matthias said quietly.

"You cannot seriously be defending her!"

"She's hurting," he tried to explain. "She's lost everyone she loved. Grief makes you do insane things sometimes."

"You didn't see me go on a killing spree when Gabriel died."

"It affects everyone differently. You know that."

His sister was speaking again before he'd even finished his sentence. "For all we know, she really did kill Brennan. You saw what she's capable of. You saw how little compassion she has for others. All she cares about is herself and her insane law. Why is she banishing the humans? Why?"

"I don't know," Matthias muttered.

The other woman quietly spoke. "I don't think she did it."

"What?" Sera asked. "Raven, you're the one who basically accused her to her face."

"And did you see her reaction?" The woman—Raven—asked. "That wasn't the wail of someone trying to get away with murder. That was the desperate cry of a mourning heart. Matthias is right. She's hurting."

"So you don't think she's the one ordering the poison?" Matthias asked.

Raven was silent for a moment but then answered. "I had my suspicions, but if she was the one securing it, why would she exile the very people who stand to benefit? It doesn't make any sense. The poison is being brought in to help the humans and weaken the fae."

"Only in Emeryn, though," Matthias added. "The rebels aren't targeting Arenysen at all."

"True. Seems the rebel network here was simply helping to transport it to the other kingdoms."

"Maybe she exiled them to stop the traffic of poison?"

Matthias asked, though he didn't sound convinced. "Or...I don't know."

"I can't believe you two are so willing to overlook the blood on her hands," Sera said, bitterness coating every word.

Matthias quietly responded, "I'm not overlooking anything. I just don't think it is quite so black and white."

"And what happens if you win this tournament? You just forget everything she's done and marry her?"

Matthias was quiet for so long, my insides knotted uncomfortably. He'd made a vow to be loyal to me if he won. Would he purposefully try to lose the tournament to avoid that? Had he been doing that all along? He'd come in last in the first two trials not knowing he'd end up in the lead anyway.

A quiet growl shook in the back of my throat.

I wasn't doing this in hopes of finding love. I was doing this to keep my kingdom. I shouldn't care what one male thought about me.

Stomping loudly down the hallway, I called out, "General!"

Without hesitation—as if he had known I was there listening the whole time—he answered, "Over here, Killer." His tone lacked the playfulness usually present when he used that nickname. I chided myself for missing his flirting teases.

Stopping in front of a set of bars, I looked down to see him sitting against the dank wall next to the gate, his legs outstretched before him and crossed at the ankles. In his hands he spun his father's ring, but he didn't lift his eyes to me.

"Come with me," I said curtly. "We need to talk."

"Wouldn't you know, the guards forgot to leave me the key," he said, his tone still flat.

Sending my shadows into the lock, I snapped it open and pushed the gate inward, banging the edge of it into his leg. He didn't wince or react at all. "Wouldn't you know, I have ways around locks," I said. "Now come on."

At the end of the hallway, I led him into a room with an iron door, using my shadows to slam it shut behind him.

"Your shadows work in an iron cell?" he asked with more curiosity than was comfortable.

Ignoring his question, I said, "Against the wall, arms up."

Surprisingly, he obliged, even going so far as to smirk, though the humor didn't reach his eyes.

"If you wanted to get me tied up, you could have just asked. No need to threaten those I care about," he said, not reacting at all as my shadows locked iron cuffs around his wrists so that his arms were suspended by a thick iron chain connected to the ceiling.

For a long moment, I simply stared at him, trying to pinpoint what it was about this particular male that twisted me in such confusing knots. How could one male make me hot with rage and desire at the same time? Why did I feel so drawn to him, even while wanting to strangle him? Was I being mocked by the stars? Was this their idea of a damned joke? If so, I wasn't laughing.

But Matthias was.

"What's so funny?" I demanded, forcing myself to step away from him, not trusting my hands to stay off him. He was fully clothed, but my memories needed no help in stripping him down.

Fuck. Get a grip, Calla.

Matthias's laughter faded, leaving a too-attractive half-smile on his lips. "You look so conflicted, Killer. Like you can't decide whether to kill me or fuck me."

Steeling my expression, I drew in a long breath, desperate to hide just how accurate his assessment was. My shadows itched to be freed of my palms, as if they, too, yearned to feel him again. This was a mistake. I should not have come down here, at least not alone. Looking toward the door, I contemplated leaving him here while I went to find Isa, but that would just prove my weakness, and I refused to have him think me weak or fragile.

Turning back to him, I darkened my expression and let my head fall to one side. I studied him for a quiet moment more, tapping a finger to my lips steadily as I gathered my thoughts.

"I should kill you," I said. "What you did back there? I should have strangled you where you stood."

He cocked a brow at me, his gaze falling to where I now folded my hands at my waist. His eyes flicked back up to mine. "Your shadows like me too much."

"You think so?" I asked, and I hoped he didn't sense the shaky doubt I was trying to conceal. I'd begun to think the same thing. As much as they were a part of me, they also seemed to have a consciousness of their own, and more than once they had acted as though they were connected to him as well.

How utterly absurd.

He shifted the corners of his lips down into that too-adorable frown. "You could always let them loose and ask them," he suggested.

"No." The word fell from my mouth before I could think of anything cleverer to say.

Matthias shifted his weight from one foot to the other. "Well, then, let's get on with it. What do you want to talk about?"

"Why in such a hurry?" I asked.

"Quickly losing my patience with your games, is all," he said, his face instantly dissolving into an expression of bored irritation.

"I haven't even begun to play games with you, general," I said. He didn't take the bait, though, and I had to swallow down my bitterness when he simply asked his question again.

"What do you want?"

What do I want?

Peace. An end to this madness. Freedom from this grief. To be done with all of these damned rumors. For my enemies to be punished thoroughly.

I didn't mention any of these though. What was the point of voicing them when he couldn't do anything to help me achieve them?

"I want to know why you stopped me from killing those women."

His face tightened in confusion. "No."

"What do you mean *no*?" I pinched my lips together and tried to calm my anger.

"That's not what you want."

"Well, I certainly don't want *you*, if that's what you're thinking."

This earned me a hint of a smirk. "Seems to be what you're thinking of, Killer. But no." His expression sobered. "That's not where I was going."

"So...what then?"

"You want to know what you should do with those women. What you should do with me, even."

Ignoring how he was annoyingly right, I scoffed unconvincingly. "Why would I ask you for advice when you're the reason I'm in this fucking mess to begin with?"

"Actually, you're the reason. If you never banished the humans, you wouldn't—"

"They're the ones who refused to obey the law!" I shouted at him.

"And what does that law achieve, Calla? How does it help you?" he asked, his hazel eyes penetrating the invisible shield I wanted to keep between us. When I didn't answer, he repeated his question from before. "What did the humans do to you?"

I knew Minerva's magic would prevent me from explaining, but still, I opened my mouth to answer him. As expected, silence. No matter how hard I tried to push the words out, they snagged somewhere in my throat. Growling, I threw my hands up in the air and spun around.

"You can't say it, can you?" Matthias asked, his voice surprisingly gentle, more understanding than I deserved. I dropped my chin to my chest. Fucking mage. Her spell wouldn't even let me confirm his suspicions. Perhaps I could find a way around it, but I was simply too tired to bother. No one would believe me anyway. Even if I could tell them.

Matthias sighed heavily. "Let them go, Calla. You don't want to kill anyone else. This isn't you."

I rounded on him, closing the distance between us in half a breath. I sneered, pouring all my frustration and anger out on him. "You think you know me, general."

"I do," he whispered, his eyes showing no fear, not even uneasiness.

"Just because I let you fuck me, doesn't mean—"

"Let me?" he asked, barking out a laugh. "*You* were the one who begged me, after *you* came to my room...twice."

Fuck-it-all, he wasn't wrong. I couldn't deny it either, and there was no reason to.

Drawing in a slow, calming breath, I asked through my teeth, "Why should I let them go?"

"Because Lieke is still your sister-in-law, and Raven is her cousin."

"That connection died with Brennan," I said, trying to keep my voice steady as I uttered his name.

"Lieke doesn't see it that way."

I rolled my eyes, my patience wearing thin. I should have just left, but I couldn't. "And what about the other?"

"My sister."

"And why should I care about your family?"

"Because you care about me," he said. His tone was gentle, but still his statement hit me like a bolt to the chest. I froze, trying to find the words I needed to refute it, but before I could, he continued. "You can keep pretending you don't care about me at all. That's fine. I'll play along with that for as long as you need me to, but these women shouldn't pay the price just because you're too proud to admit—"

"Admit what?" I slammed my hands against his chest, my fingers instinctively curling into him, grasping his shirt in my fists. The words tumbled out, slipping past the crumbling guard around my heart. "Admit I can't control this need to be near you? That I can't seem to escape this fucking hold you have on me? Or admit that I hate myself for having feelings for you?"

Tears crowded the edges of my eyes, but I couldn't seem to let go of him to wipe them away. My husband's body was barely cold in the ground, and I was here holding on to another male as if he could keep me from drowning in my grief.

A smile started to tug at Matthias's lips, but he hid it quickly. "I was going to say you're too proud to admit that you're wrong, but..." He paused, his hazel eyes searching mine, as if he could actually see my cracked heart and darkened soul. "I don't understand this at all."

"Understand what?" I whispered, my voice losing all strength under the weight of his stare.

"Us."

MATTHIAS

The word hung heavily in the air between us.

Us.

It was an absurd notion, and yet...

Calla's words could have easily been my own. I couldn't ignore this need to be close to her. I couldn't run from this hold she had on me. And I hated myself for having feelings for her after everything she'd done.

Despite what Sera had claimed, I wasn't overlooking the atrocities Calla had committed. I acknowledged them, accepted them, and that confused me to no end. I'd seen the power Shadow Keepers wielded, how mercilessly they took life. I'd witnessed the pain and loss Calla had left in her wake.

Stars, I should have been trying to stop her, not trying to save her or protect her or help her or whatever I was doing here.

I shouldn't have cared about her—shouldn't have cared what happened to her—but I did.

She was guilty of so much devastation and fear, but somehow, for some reason, I couldn't abandon her.

"There is no *us*," she whispered, pulling me gently out of my thoughts.

"That was almost convincing," I said, offering a slight smirk.

She dropped her gaze to my chest. "There can be no us."

"Until I win this tournament, you mean."

Shaking her head slowly, she released a long sigh and settled her forehead against her hands where they still clung to my shirt. I shut my eyes, debating what to do next.

What would Connor do?

I laughed silently to myself. He'd probably run away and sulk. *Or he'd mention some disgustingly romantic notion like mates. Mates.*

Snapping my eyes open, I searched my memories for every conversation I'd had with Connor about the stars fating souls for each other. He had noted the unnerving need he had to keep Lieke safe, but then, that was just Connor in general—the savior of his people, doing everything for everyone else and nothing for himself.

What if that had been the bond, though? What if their bond had been pulling them to each other before they'd ever kissed?

"Mates." The word fell from my lips on a rough breath, and Calla's head jerked up. Releasing my shirt, she stepped back, her eyes wide and lips parted as she regarded me apprehensively.

"What did you just say?" Her question was barely more than a breath.

"What if we're..." Fuck, I couldn't say the word again. It was insanity. There was no way the stars would play such a cruel trick. What would happen if she had, in fact, killed Brennan and I had to kill her to avenge him? Would I be able to keep my word to Connor? Would I be able to do what I was sent here to do?

Calla shook her head, slowly at first, and then faster and faster, in time with her quickening heartbeat. Lifting her hand, her fingers trembled against her lips.

"No," she breathed. "It couldn't be."

Her wild eyes darted erratically around the cell as if searching for some answer written in the air. She stilled, her mouth still hanging open in disbelief.

"It can't. We can't," she murmured, her voice growing louder as her words spilled out. "There's no way. I can't be...I can't..."

Her eyes squeezed shut, her shaky fingers pressing hard into her temples. I wished I could take back the word, go back in time and keep my stars-damned mouth shut, anything to fix this. But being strung up in these iron cuffs limited my ability to do anything useful.

"Calla, it's probably not...that. I shouldn't have even—"

"No." She started to shake her head again, her hands falling away as she slid her eyes open and lifted them to mine. The space between her brow crinkled adorably, countered by the pained fear gazing back at me. She whispered again. "We couldn't be. Could we? Is that why..."

Her voice fell away once more behind a shaky hand I wished I could hold if only to reassure her everything was fine.

"It's probably not true, but..." I started, not quite sure what I was doing.

"There's one way to know for sure," she mused quietly. Her expression hardened with dark determination.

"It's probably not," I repeated, my words losing what little confidence they'd held earlier.

She took slow, cautious steps toward me, stopping an arm's length away. Her eyes held mine captive as she lifted her hands to my jaw. Her fingers brushed past my ears and sank into my hair. I wet my lips and let her guide my face lower until our breaths mingled in the small space between us.

What did the bond feel like? My mind went blank trying to remember if Connor had ever described how it felt when it had formed. Calla sighed, her breath warming my lips, and I had to fight every screaming urge to shift forward and kiss her myself, to prove this ridiculous notion false. Before she could move any closer, though, the iron door behind her flew open, slamming loudly against the wall.

Isa stormed inside.

"Your Majesty," she said in a reprimanding tone. I winced as

Calla shoved my face away from her and dropped her hands, twisting around to face the general.

"What is it, Isa?" she asked in a shaky voice, running her palms against the folds of her dress as if trying to wipe any memory of my skin from them.

"The Assembly needs to see you. I tried to persuade them to wait, but they insisted. They're in the meeting room waiting for you."

Calla was nodding hastily, speeding out of the door without a single look my way. I expected Isa to follow her, but she turned toward me, strolling over with her hand resting on the pommel of her sword.

"General," she said. "I know what's been going on between you two."

I lifted my brows. "Could you fill me in, because apparently I don't."

She didn't seem at all amused, though I wasn't joking. I couldn't explain it any more than I could understand it.

"I can't watch her get hurt again," Isa said.

"Is this to be one of those *if you hurt her, I'll kill you* lectures then?"

A soft smile graced her lips. "Perhaps, but I don't think you need it. If you hurt her, she'll likely kill you herself."

"Fair point. So what are you here to discuss then?"

"I know you, general," she said, shifting her weight but keeping her eyes locked on mine. "You're a male of integrity, honor, loyalty. I was there at the battle when your friend fell to that Shadow Keeper. I was just a young soldier at the time. While it wasn't the bloodiest death I witnessed, it was one of the hardest, because of how it pained you and your prince."

Swallowing hard, I ignored the image that flashed in my head as I noted, "Yet you let your queen use the same power to cut down innocent—"

Her sharp stare stayed my tongue mid-sentence.

"They're not truly innocent though, are they?" She angled her head at me. "The queen passed a law with strict consequences, and they still chose to disobey. Whether we understand the reason for her exiling them matters little. They knew the consequences, and they defied her regardless."

"So you condone what she's done?"

Isa was quiet for a moment, her eyes boring into mine as if trying to detect any ill-will behind my question.

"I think she does what she has to, as queen. Mercy has its place, yes, but when so many are vying to steal her crown, she can't afford to appear weak. Those who blatantly defy the law are more likely to pose a threat of rebellion in the future. And you know better than most how dangerous a rebellion can be."

She wasn't wrong. Lieke had defied Emeryn's laws and almost ended up dead because of it. Not everyone had the benefit of a crown prince to rescue them. I shook away the memories and focused back on Isa.

"What was your question then, general? Or did you just come to flatter me and my honorable heart?"

Pausing, her brow lowered slowly over her dark, brooding eyes. "How do you do it? A Shadow Keeper killed your friend. Yet you're here, pledging your heart to one with the same power."

"Technically, my heart is only hers if I win," I corrected her, but the lie tasted sour.

"Liar," she said, one brow arching playfully, a stark contrast to the sadness in her voice. "You didn't answer the question, though."

"I pledged because I had to," I said, knowing this wouldn't appease the general but needing to buy myself time to find the answer to her actual question.

"You're no idiot, Matthias. You know what I'm asking."

"I don't love her," I insisted.

"I never claimed you did," Isa said. "But you obviously care for her. You don't see her as the monster everyone else does. Why? How? Given all you've seen and lost—"

"Because that's not her," I interrupted, hating that I was

having to discuss Gabriel's death again today. "She didn't kill my friend. She's killed because she has to. And if you think about it, so did the Shadow Keeper in that battle. That's the nature of war, of politics, of the world. We choose who we fight and who we fight for."

"And why do you fight for Calla and not against her?"

"What are you expecting me to say here, general?" I asked, growing irritated with her roundabout intent.

"I've known her my whole life," Isa said slowly. "I'm all she has left. If I abandoned her, I don't know what she would do. But you barely know her. Why is it that you are able to see past all she's done, when so many others can't?"

"Because that's not her," I repeated. Lowering my head, my gaze softened on the floor, the cell around me blurring. "She's in pain. Grief can drive anyone to do things they might not otherwise. I mean, grief led an entire kingdom to go to war, and thousands of fae and humans died because of it."

Isa regarded me for a moment, as if weighing the truth of my words. Pulling a ring of iron keys from her pocket, she stepped forward, reached up, and unlocked the cuffs from my wrists.

"If I could get you back to your room tonight without raising suspicions, I would," she said, and I wasn't about to admit I knew of the secret passageways behind the walls. "You'll need to spend the night in your cell, but I'll be down to release you in the morning for the third trial."

"And what of Raven and my sister?" I asked, stretching out my aching arms as Isa moved to open the door.

"She's your sister?" Isa half-turned to face me. I nodded. "I'll have to speak to Calla, but their infractions can't simply be ignored. I'll do what I can, though, general."

CHAPTER 55

CALLA

I rushed into the meeting room to find it dark, cold, and completely empty.

Isa had fucking lied to me.

Pulling my shadows out, I slammed them into the nearest chairs, sending them to the floor in a satisfying crash. I stalked around the room and lifted my hands to do the same to the rest of the furniture, but what was the stars-damned point? A growl rushed from my lungs as I pulled out a chair so hard it nearly toppled out of my hands. Grinding my teeth, I focused on steadying my movements and calming my mind enough for me to sit down without falling on my ass.

My elbows dug into the table while my hands cradled my forehead. Trailing the grains of the wooden table with my weary eyes, I took long, slow breaths and tried to calm my chaotic mess of thoughts.

Humans.

Assembly.

Killing.

Trials.

Matthias.

Mates.

The word swirled and swelled in my head until it crowded out everything else, like a rising river overflowing its banks and drowning everything in sight.

Why had Matthias even suspected a bond might exist between us?

What had sparked that idea in his head?

Had I done something to—

I sighed. Fine, yes, I had done quite a bit. It hadn't been him sneaking into my rooms at night to seduce me.

My lips slid into a half-smile at the thought of him doing just that, but I shook my head once and forced the smile away. That was less than helpful at the moment. I couldn't worry about that right now. There were bigger issues to deal with--like the two women currently locked in my dungeon.

And the male who made a fool out of me in front of the entire kingdom.

What was I supposed to do with him?

I couldn't just let him go, as if he'd done nothing wrong.

Weak, pitiful, small.

That's how he'd made me look when he'd intervened, and that's exactly how I would appear if I didn't do something to punish him. But what could I do?

And what if he was actually my...mate?

If Isa had arrived a bit later, then I wouldn't be sitting here wondering *what if*. Of course, had she arrived earlier, he never would have had the chance to say the word at all, and I wouldn't be sitting here fretting—at least not about a possible bond.

My head ached.

The door slid slowly open, letting in a stream of flickering candlelight from the hallway lamps. Without looking up, I said, "Thanks, Isa, for lying about—"

"Isa lied about something?" The male's question had me spinning quickly toward the door where Graham strolled in, carrying a bottle and two glasses in his hands. "Must have been for a good reason."

I dropped my head back into my hands and muttered my question. "What do you want? How did you know I was here?"

With his foot, he tugged one of the still-upright chairs closer and sat down. "Saw you stomp your way in here. I thought you could use a drink after what happened."

His cheery tone made me uneasy. I pushed away from the table and settled back in my seat, clasping my hands in my lap. My shadows stirred, though differently than usual, almost like they were trying to burrow deeper into my veins rather than begging to come out. I rubbed a thumb into one of my palms and then the other, a perhaps silly attempt to soothe the power beneath.

"You sneak into my room to grab my brandy?" I asked, though I was sure he wouldn't have the nerve.

"This is mine, actually," he said. "You aren't the only one who likes Vranić's. This is actually my last bottle. I'm hoping the next shipment isn't delayed too much longer."

As he spoke, he poured healthy portions into two glasses and slid one my way. I eyed it, but didn't reach for it. He gently swirled the dark liquid in his before lifting the glass to his lips and taking a small sip.

"You seem to be in good spirits," I said flatly. I nearly noted how far behind he was in the tournament standings, but thought better of it.

He nudged the other glass forward with his long fingers and ignored my comment, instead switching topics. "Why are you in here anyway? Meeting Isa or something?"

"Not sure I should say, Graham. You're a competitor," I reminded him, hoping his love for rules and laws would mean he'd accept this and not push. Pivoting in his seat, he leaned forward, resting his lanky arms in his lap so his hands—still holding his drink—came unnecessarily close to my knees.

"Sometimes I wish I hadn't entered this tournament so we could still talk. I miss how close we used to be, Cal."

He stared down at his hands so I couldn't read his expression. We hadn't been close since Brennan and I had married. Even when my parents had been lost at sea and I had to work more closely with him as the royal advisor, we hadn't spent as much time together as we had when we were younger.

"That's just part of growing up," I said, casually, but when he shifted just enough to look up at me from beneath his tight brow, I realized my error.

"Glad to know my friendship was so easily set aside. Just another season of life to be discarded as mere memory." He bit out the words, his features as rigid as his tone. Straightening in his seat, he threw the rest of his drink down his throat before doing the same with my untouched glass.

"Graham," I started, though I didn't make any effort to stop him when he pivoted to leave.

He pointed the bottle of Vranić's at me and seemed about to say something more when his expression started to soften, his arm falling slowly back to his side.

"I just hope you get all you deserve, Your Majesty," he said, not waiting for my reaction before rushing out of the room.

The door had barely shut when it swung open again. Soft but determined footsteps walked toward me, and I slid my gaze up to Isa, who quickly assessed the state of the room before finally looking at me.

"Did Graham try to bribe you with that fancy bottle or was he merely celebrating Matthias's failings?" she asked, crossing her arms loosely in front of her.

A heavy sigh rushed from my lips, and I rolled my head back and around to stretch out the tightness in my neck. "Not really sure. Both, maybe." I settled back in my chair and propped my feet up on Graham's empty seat, eyeing my friend quizzically. "So did you get what you wanted from Matthias?"

"More or less, I suppose."

"What are we going to do with them?" I asked.

"What do you want to do?" she asked cautiously, one eyebrow lifting.

"Well, I can't do nothing," I started, pausing for a moment

when she nodded knowingly. "I mean, they broke the law. One entered the kingdom despite the ban, and the other aided fugitives! I'd look weak if I simply let them go."

"Who said you needed to let them go?" Isa asked, though from the flatness of her tone I could tell she knew already.

"Matthias," I muttered anyway.

"And is he your new advisor?" Her face remained stoic, though a spark of humor flashed in her eyes.

"Maybe he should be."

At this she laughed, one single, dry chuckle. "As if you would be content with him in that role."

I scowled at her but said nothing.

"What will you do with him?" she finally asked, shifting her gaze from mine as she sought out a toppled chair, righted it, and sat down. Stretching her legs out in front of her, she crossed her ankles and rested her head on her crossed arms.

"I don't want to punish him," I said.

"Don't you?" she asked. "He made a fool—"

"You don't need to remind me. I was there." I scowled at my friend, but that only earned me a kind smile.

"Let him go. He's a contender in the tournament. As the Assembly wanted today to be a pseudo trial of sorts, I could always use my discretion as tournament host to determine his fate —say something like he showed great heart and strength of spirit for being willing to question you."

"Strength of spirit," I muttered. She wasn't wrong there. The male had his convictions, and damn all the stars if that didn't make him that much more attractive.

"I mean," Isa continued, "we don't want a king who lacks the balls to stand up for what he believes, right?"

"You just had to say balls, didn't you?"

"How are his, by the way?" Isa's eyes narrowed, her lips curving into an equally wicked grin.

Kicking my foot into hers, I blew out an annoyed breath.

"First you're lecturing me about messing around with him, and now you want all the juicy details."

"I never asked for *all*." She gave a single wag of her brows. "Is he better than Brennan?"

The smile I didn't remember donning vanished at the mention of my late husband's name, but the twinge of guilt that hit lacked its usual heart-crushing weight, feeling more like a light punch to my chest instead of a crushing wave.

Isa sat up, pulling her legs as she leaned toward me, concern twisting her features. "Shit. I'm sorry, Calla. That was—"

I waved away her apology, but couldn't think of anything to say in response. A long silence stretched out between us, penetrated only by the occasional soft breath and our heartbeats as they settled.

"Can I ask, though," Isa finally said, peering at me with an almost apologetic look, "what did I interrupt down there? Between you two, I mean. You leapt away from him like you'd just been caught kissing someone else's mate."

I froze as my mind started to spin out again. "What did you say?"

"Like you'd been caught kissing?" she asked tentatively.

"No. The last word."

"Male?"

"No, you said mate."

"Did I?" She seemed genuinely unsure. My head bobbed in a string of nervous nods. "If I did, I didn't mean anything by it. It's just a word."

"It's not just a word, Isa," I said, my nerves returning.

"Wait," she breathed, angling her head at me and staring. "You're not—"

"No." I shoved the word out of my mouth but then had to back track. "I mean, I don't think so. Hopefully not."

Her chin jutted out toward me, her eyes narrowing even more. "You haven't kissed?"

Slowly, I lifted a shoulder, squeezed my lips into a firm line, and shook my head.

"But you've—"

I nodded.

Isa slumped back in her chair, dropping her hands into her lap like a mother who'd given up trying to get her children to listen.

I pushed to my feet and began to pace out a small square in front of my friend, twisting my hands awkwardly in the air as I tried to explain. "We were...I was...about to kiss him to make sure we weren't... you know...but then you walked in."

"Oh," Isa breathed out.

I continued moving, pushing all my nerves down into my meandering feet.

"If you are, though...shit," she muttered. "We should have probably included a provision for that in the tournament rules, because what happens if he is...but doesn't win?"

"The stars wouldn't be so cruel, would they?" I asked, though I already knew the answer. Of course they would be. The stars didn't actually care about anyone down below as they knit together hearts and souls with their bonds. Isa rose from her seat and grabbed my elbows, forcing me to stand still and face her.

"It will all be okay, Calla."

I wished I could believe her.

CHAPTER 56

MATTHIAS

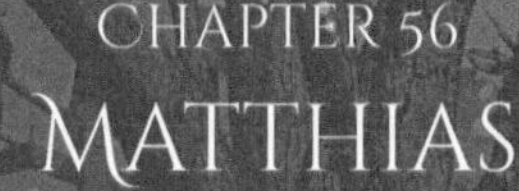

General Isa's footsteps had barely stopped echoing down the hallway after locking me back in my cell when Sera hissed out a question.

"You've already slept with her, haven't you?"

I leaned my head back against the cold stone wall and smirked, even though she couldn't see my face from her cell next to mine. Raven could, though, and she sniggered. I shrugged at her and responded to my sister.

"With the general? She's not really my type."

My sister let out an exaggerated sigh. "You know who I mean."

"It's not nice to speak about Raven while she's sitting right here, Sera."

Sera, growling, kicked the iron gate of her cell hard—at least, I assumed she kicked it. For all I knew she might have thrown her whole body against it, though that seemed unlikely.

"All these evasive answers just prove your guilt, brother."

I chuckled under my breath. "Could never hide anything from you for long, sister."

"It's going to come back and bite you in the ass," she warned.

"Some of us like that sort of thing," I joked, but she didn't react at all. I turned idly toward Raven, who was shaking her head at me, a hint of a smile tugging at her lips. "Can you blame me? I mean, I'm not one to kiss and tell—"

"You mean, *fuck or tell*," Sera muttered, but I ignored her.

"When a female like that shows up in your room, it's hard to decline."

Raven eyed me for a moment and then lifted a shoulder. "And you didn't instigate any of it?"

"Calla isn't one you want to instigate, honestly. I merely did as I was told," I said, omitting the part where I'd stepped out of the bath to keep her from leaving.

"You choose now to learn how to take orders?" Sera asked, still bitter.

"I'll have you know, sister, I've been taking orders from Connor for years without issue."

"And did he tell you to sleep with his dead brother's wife?"

Ouch.

"Not in so many words." Raven shot me a sharp look, and I corrected, "Okay, no, not at all. But he's usually okay with me doing what needs to be done."

Sera scoffed. "I doubt he will see her as *needed to be done*."

Raven laughed quietly before shifting to sit on her knees near the bars of her cell. "Matthias? What will she do to us?"

Now that was the question my sister should have been focused on. "I asked her to release you," I explained, but my voice wavered a bit, lacking conviction.

"Doubt she'll listen to you—even if you screwed her," Sera said, her tone losing some of its edge and coming out more exhausted than angry now.

"We've already established that I did, so no need for the *if* there," I noted over my shoulder. Turning back to Raven, I frowned. "She can't release you easily, because you did break the law; however, her general is smart, fair, caring, and probably the only one Calla will actually listen to. You'll probably be in here for a while, but that's better than being dead."

Sera grumbled.

Raven drew in a long breath and muttered, "Guess I might as well get comfortable. Goodnight."

Releasing a slow sigh, I shifted myself against the wall, trying to get into a more comfortable position—as if that was possible in a dungeon—and tried to keep the incessant thoughts in my head from ruining the welcome silence. I needed to be ready for the next trial and not stay up all night worrying about whether Calla would spare Sera and Raven or how Connor would react to my side activities. No doubt he and Lieke would not be happy.

But no doubt they'd be less happy if I failed.

Yes, it's always best to look on the bright side.

The next morning, I was woken up, not by the stomping of Isa's boots or the clanking of the keys in the lock, but by the sharp cramp shooting through my neck and down into my shoulder. I had apparently been spoiled by the luxury of my room upstairs, or perhaps my years were catching up with me. Either way, I felt a pang of guilt following Isa out of my cell while my sister and Raven had to remain. I made a mental note to see if the secret passages might lead down here so I could sneak them each a pillow.

Isa nodded to the lone guard as we stepped past his post at the bottom of the stairs, and Isa didn't say a word to me until we were out of earshot of him.

"Trial three will be held today. Calla and I both feel it best not to delay."

"And the Assembly?" I prodded.

Isa shifted her eyes to the ceiling briefly as she shook her head. "They want to observe this next trial, and they all happened to be visiting for the citizens' forum yesterday, so they requested it be held a bit earlier."

"How thoughtful of them," I said with a humorless laugh. We

had nearly reached the main floor when I paused and laid a hand lightly on Isa's arm to stop her. She faced me, concern filling her eyes.

"What is it?"

"How is she?" I asked.

Relief pulled a breath from the general, though it seemed half-hearted. "She's a bit rattled, to say the least. She'll be okay though. Everything will be okay."

I nodded slowly, noticing how her words seemed to be more for her own comfort than mine.

Leaning closer, I lowered my voice into a whisper. "What will become of my sister and Raven?"

"We are working on it," she said, quickly stealing glances in either direction when she paused. "The utmost care has to be taken to ensure no one can call foul."

"And releasing me? What's the official excuse?"

"That will be shared at the trial," she said, hastily pushing me to keep moving. We navigated the last several flights in silence, and she didn't speak again until we reached my room at the end of the dark hallway. "Giles should have already drawn a bath for you. Please be down in the family dining room promptly at mid-day."

Turning in my doorway to face her, I asked, "And will that be the start of the trial? Do I need to bring anything special? A weapon perhaps?"

"No weapons necessary. Just bring yourself." She bowed her head slightly and plodded back down the hallway.

Not wanting to be late, I arrived at the dining room a bit early to find the Assembly members already seated around the table, along with Phillip and Graham, the latter of whom seemed surprised—and not too happy—to see me. Unlike the last meal we had enjoyed in here, the four male competitors were all seated together, our seats indicated by ornate place markers, with two on either side of the table, near Calla's seat and Isa's beside her.

"Good day, Mr. Orelian," Ursula said, lifting her chin so she could peer down her nose at me despite the fact that I was still standing behind my chair.

Fern—seated beside the prickly female—leaned over slightly and sweetly corrected her. "I believe it's General Orelian."

Ursula scowled at her, but I offered a simple smile, nodding my thanks, even as I explained, "I'm no general while competing in these games."

"How is it you're still competing?" Warren bit out, making no effort to hide his disdain. "Did you break out of your cell?"

"You'll have to ask General Marlowe or Her Majesty," I answered, sliding into my seat across from Graham.

Graham held his usual derisive expression, his initial shock fading into renewed contempt for me. Perhaps my little stunt at the citizens' assembly negated any good graces I'd secured in the last trial. Was he angry at me for challenging Calla? For protecting the women? Or... was he simply bitter that even that action couldn't get me disciplined and removed from this competition? Maybe it was all three. It didn't truly matter. Graham was clearly not going to give me any useful information beyond what I could observe.

"You don't look happy to see me, Graham," I said, taking a sip from the glass of water in front of me.

The male's features didn't shift aside from a faint twitch of his right eye. "Just surprised to see you."

"Same," Phillip said, looking at me sidelong. He nudged my arm with his elbow. "On time, anyway."

Our laughter—though light—was interrupted by Warren's scoffing.

"And she claims no favoritism." He leaned back in his seat and exchanged a knowing look with Graham, who remained silent.

The older advisor, Yuri, did chime in though. "Now, Warren, that's rather unfair. You may not trust Her Majesty, but her general is the one running the tournament, and surely we can trust her."

Ursula dropped her elbows hard onto the table and pinned Yuri with one of her vicious glares. "If you think the queen doesn't have her ruthless fingers in every part of this mockery of a tournament, then you're as foolish as those humans were yesterday."

Graham shot to his feet, his chair grating against the stone floor so loudly most of us cringed. "I may no longer be the chief advisor"—he glowered down at Ursula—"but I won't allow you to speak of your queen in such a way."

"Settle down, Graham," Warren cautioned.

"I don't take orders from you," Graham said, though he still returned to his seat, where he stewed silently until Korben walked in a few awkward moments later.

He grunted in way of greeting, heading straight for his seat without affording anyone a glance. Once he was seated, though, he spotted me and froze, his hand lifted halfway toward his water glass.

"What the fuck is he doing here?" he spat, not taking his wild eyes from mine.

"Nice to see you too," I said around a demure smile.

"Seems some are immune to the queen's deadly outbursts after all," Ursula stated. "I am curious, *General* Orelian, how did you convince Her Majesty to spare you?"

"And those women," Warren added, waving his hand in the air toward the female advisor. "I hear they're still alive and well down in the dungeon."

"About as well as one can be in such a place," I said. "Respectfully, I must defer to General Marlowe and the queen, as it was their decision, though I am incredibly honored that you think me persuasive enough to sway their judgment in my favor."

"So many words from such an insignificant male," Korben said.

I shrugged. "I mean, being tied for the lead in this competition seems far from insignificant, especially given how far behind I was in both the first two trials."

Graham narrowed his eyes and eyed me thoughtfully. "Do you ever think you'll win a trial by actually performing well in it? Or will you merely get lucky every time?"

"Good questions," I said, nodding for a bit before continuing. "Though I would argue it takes more than luck to befriend a dragon shifter—and in such a short time, too. I do concede that it may have been pure dumb luck that the general happened to be judging that second trial in such a way. Still, winning by luck is still winning, so I'll take it."

"You haven't won yet," Phillip noted through his wry grin.

I laughed—the only one in the room to find that funny, apparently. Before I had time to formulate a response, the door opened and Calla strode in with Isa close behind her. Calla merely nodded to the room, not making eye contact with anyone as she took her seat.

Isa remained standing and rested her hand lightly on her chair as she addressed us. "Thank you for being here. Shortly, the staff will be bringing in the mid-day meal. I believe it's a baked fish and vegetables, with a honey custard for dessert. We ask that you all stay seated following the meal, so I can introduce the third trial. Are there any questions before we eat?"

Korben, Graham, Warren, and Ursula all began to speak at once, but they didn't manage more than a couple words each as Isa snapped her hand up to stop them.

"Yes, General Orelian remains in the competition. Despite your request that the citizens' forum be akin to a trial, it was still not an official one. As the primary adjudicator of these games, I have personally assessed the situation. While the general did challenge the queen—at considerable risk, I might add—we are not here to select a king who will agree with Her Majesty all the time, even if she might prefer that. Arenysen needs a ruling pair who can work together, who complement each other, and whose strengths offset the others' weaknesses. The general's actions yesterday may have, on the surface, seemed out of line, but I found it admirable that he would risk disagreeing with Her Majesty in order to save others."

"To save spies, you mean," Warren hissed.

Isa's sharp eyes swung to the male, narrowing on him. "Were you not one advocating for proper trials? Of all on the Assembly, I would expect you to appreciate the general's actions in demanding a hearing for the accused."

Graham lifted a hand, but didn't bother to wait for Isa's approval before he spoke. "While I agree we want a king willing to challenge Calla as needed, doing so in front of so many yesterday was less than ideal."

Isa nodded slowly. "Agreed. Normally I would prefer for these disagreements to be addressed privately before being debated before the public; however, as tense and"—she glanced down at Calla almost apologetically—"volatile as the situation was, I believe the general acted accordingly to stop further bloodshed."

Ursula cleared her throat. "Thank you for that explanation, general. I believe that will suffice." She glanced around at her fellow advisors, who all gave nearly imperceptible dips of their chins. "Now, let's eat before the fish becomes overcooked and inedible."

CHAPTER 57

CALLA

*V*olatile.

The word reverberated in my head, pricking my conscience with every mental bounce and spin and turn. Isa wasn't exactly wrong in using it, but still. I wasn't particularly proud that I'd created such a situation last night.

But I didn't create it. The humans did.

The meal was uncomfortably silent, and the clinking of the silver utensils on the dinnerware began to grate on my nerves before the first plate had been cleared away. The tension among the males only increased as time went on, Korben regularly glaring at Matthias with his loathing on full display. Graham at least seemed to attempt to hide his occasional scowls across the table. Matthias, as expected, pretended not to notice their animosity, even going so far as to smile at them in turn. Phillip shifted in his seat throughout the entire meal, so much so I half-wondered if he hadn't had too much water and needed to relieve himself.

I could barely even enjoy my dessert—though, to be honest, it wasn't one of my favorites from Chef Xavier's repertoire—as we neared the kickoff of the third trial. This trial had seemed like a grand plan when we'd initially designed it before the males had arrived—before Matthias had ridden in and mucked up all of my plans for an emotionless, empty match. Now, even if he didn't win, I'd be stuck in a dreadful marriage pining after someone else.

Matthias hadn't actually performed well in the last two trials—though he'd come out on top regardless. There was little Isa could do in this next challenge to sway it in his favor if he didn't succeed.

I stole a glance his way, only to meet his gaze. My shadows danced against the surface of my palms, but I held them steady. Smiling, I dropped my eyes back to the half-eaten honey custard. I should have probably warned him last night of what was to happen today. In fact, I had intended to after the citizens' forum, but with the humans' arrival, my *volatile* temper, and that whole worry over being mates, I'd all but forgotten.

Until now.

Could I watch him do this trial?

Could I witness him try to outwit death?

Did he have the knowledge he needed to beat this test?

Trust him.

I do, but I don't trust these other males.

Or the vindictive assholes at the other end of the table.

I shot a wan smile at Ursula before sliding the last spoonful of dessert into my mouth. Something about the way she smiled back sent a cold jolt through my veins.

As one set of staff members cleared away our dessert bowls, another brought in a tray of wine goblets, placing a drink in front of each of us. Four more of my staff followed after them, each balancing a silver tray and stopping beside the competitors. All at once, they took four identical cordial glasses from their trays and placed them in front of the males.

My gut writhed at what was to come. Isa nudged my leg with her foot, a concerned look on her face. Mouthing the words "I'm fine," I reached for my wine and took several hearty gulps.

Bracing her hands on the table, Isa started to rise but stopped at the sound of Ursula's chair sliding back noisily. The bitter female stood, clasping her hands at her sternum as she stared down Isa.

"There's been a change of plans, general."

CHAPTER 58

MATTHIAS

That meal had certainly been uncomfortable, but that compared little to the tension coursing through the air when the advisor cut Isa off. Isa noticeably fought to keep her features calm, though it wasn't hard to recognize the fury burning in her eyes, whitening her knuckles as she clenched her fists.

"What do you mean *changed*?" Isa demanded, pushing to her feet. "What did you do?"

Korben's gaze darted between the two females. He sunk lower in his seat as if expecting them to throw punches any moment now. Graham, however, had his eyes locked on Calla.

Calla's hand started to tremble as she lowered her wine back down onto the table. "Isa," she said weakly, and her general spun around and leaned over.

"Calla, look at me," she said, gingerly lifting the queen's chin when she didn't comply, but Calla's eyes had already glazed over, turning distant and unseeing.

"What did you do, Ursula?" Isa growled, not taking her attention away from Calla, whose head began to sway from one side to the other until Isa cupped her cheeks with both hands. "Calla, are you okay?"

Ursula's harsh voice cut through the thick air. "The Assembly decided to amend your third trial, General Marlowe."

Isa's eyes widened in horror, her face slashing around toward the Assembly members. "You had no right!"

Ursula shrugged. "Regardless, what's done is done. The trial remains the same; the only change is who drank the poison."

Poison? Fuck.

My focus shifted back to Calla, her face still cradled in Isa's hands, but her eyelids blinked lazily, her lips forming silent words. On the table her hands fell open, her shadows flashing erratically in her palms like a monster trying to break loose. Then she stilled, and my heart fell into my stomach like a lead weight, cold and heavy.

"Calla! Calla!" Isa called out to her friend, gently tapping her cheeks, squeezing her hands, shifting her head, anything to try to rouse her. Angling her chin over her shoulder, she screamed at the Assembly. "Why would you do this?"

None of them answered. Even the sweet-looking Fern remained quiet, though she at least seemed somewhat uncomfortable with what they'd just done. Their silence was met by a deadly glower from Graham whose panic—while less obvious than Isa's—was evident.

"What were you thinking?" He hissed the question at Ursula, but then swung his gaze across all of the advisors. "Whose fucking idea was this? And the rest of you just went along with it? You spineless—"

"It was a collective decision," Warren said in an irritatingly calm tone. Graham tensed, leaning forward suddenly as if he'd been about to lunge across the table at him.

"I bet," Graham muttered, though he relented and slowly returned to his seat.

My muscles itched to leap up from my seat, grab Calla, and somehow save her, but they'd said they'd only changed one piece of the trial. All I had to do was win the trial. Win and save her.

Drawing in a deep breath to calm my nerves, I called out to

Isa. She didn't look at me, didn't respond, so I said her name a little louder. Surprisingly—and rather uncharacteristically—Korben reached a hand out and tapped her on the back. Jerking around, she stopped short when she found me staring intently at her.

"What is the third trial? What do we need to do?" I asked as coolly as I could with Calla's head lying limply in Isa's hands.

At first, I thought she wasn't going to respond, or maybe she hadn't heard me through the fog of panicked grief, because she slowly turned back to Calla without a word. A hush fell over the room as she laid Calla's head against the back of her chair and folded her hands in her lap. Isa's own hands shook as she turned back to the rest of us, not looking at anyone in particular when she spoke.

"This trial was—is—to test wisdom," she said. Her voice came out much weaker than usual. Slowly she brought her eyes up to mine, her distant gaze slowly finding its focus as she spoke. "Use whatever knowledge, prowess, and experience you possess to determine which of the four glasses in front of you contains the antidote to the poison."

"And who was to be poisoned originally?" Phillip asked.

I leaned over to him and said—loudly enough for everyone to hear—"Us, I assume."

Ursula clapped her hands once, a wicked smile spreading across her lips. "Perfect display of that wisdom we want to see, General Orelian."

"Yes, it was to be you four," Isa admitted more shamefully than seemed necessary. "You were to choose one—and only one—of the four glasses and see if it was the antidote. The first one to find the correct glass would win."

"And what if we chose wrong?" I asked. "Would you just leave us to die?"

"No, you all would have been administered the antidote before you died."

"And now—" I started, but Ursula finished my sentence for me.

"You must choose one—and only one—from your four, to see if it cures the queen. Before she dies."

"Is this the same poison used on Matthias?" Phillip asked.

Warren released an obnoxiously loud sigh. "How many questions do you usually let them ask before a trial, General Marlowe?"

Isa shot him an icy glare. "As many as I damn well please, Warren." She turned abruptly to Phillip. "It is similar, but not exactly the same—assuming the Assembly hasn't changed that part of this trial as well, that is. The four cordial glasses are in no particular order, to prevent you from learning anything by watching your competition."

I glanced at Calla, hoping to the damned stars that it was similar enough to the poison Korben had used on me. At least then I could be assured she was in no pain right now but in a peaceful darkness. Though who knew how the shadows in her blood might alter that.

"How much time do we have?" I asked, keeping my attention on the queen. "Until she...until *we* are too late?"

"Two hours, I believe," Ursula said flatly. "If the healers are to be trusted."

So little time, and I know nothing of fucking poisons aside from my own personal experience. Which won't exactly help me here.

"And we can only try one?" Graham asked.

Isa nodded.

"And how are we supposed to give her the antidote when she's obviously unconscious and can't swallow anything?" Phillip asked with more indignation than I'd ever heard or expected from him.

Isa breathed out a sigh, dropping her chin to her chest. Pulling in a long breath, she started to answer before she ever looked back up at us. "It should not have taken such quick effect. Originally, you would have been given a dose that would keep you conscious at least for half an hour. As you can see"—she shot a glare toward Ursula and then Warren—"Calla was poisoned with a larger dose. Still, the antidote does not need to be swallowed to be administered. While drinking is most effective, the plain truth is, sometimes that is not possible. The next best thing is to be absorbed through any bodily fluid: blood, saliva, etc. The antidote —should you find it—should show signs of efficacy within a minute or two, if not sooner."

"General," Warren groaned. "Seems like you're giving a lot of information that should be better left for the competitors to figure out—or to know on their own. Hence the *wisdom* part of this trial?"

Isa ignored him, turning to Phillip to say more, but Korben's voice boomed through the room, forcing Isa to snap her mouth shut.

"Aren't we wasting time asking all of these questions?" he asked, already bringing his four cordial glasses closer to him.

"I have one more though," Phillip said warily. He drummed his finger nervously on the table, eyeing his four options as if they might leap up and bite him.

"Yes?" Isa asked, ignoring how Korben and Warren both groaned in unison.

Phillip peered up at the general sidelong. "What's in the other three glasses? The ones without the antidote? Are any of them... dangerous themselves?"

"Water, I believe," she said. "The antidote is colorless, flavorless, with no aroma—as undetectable as the poison itself."

Graham shook his head slowly, his hard gaze landing on Warren across the table. "And we are just supposed to trust the Assembly to not have added this invisible poison to any—or all— of our glasses?"

"What would that achieve, Graham?" Ursula asked.

But I answered before he could. "Kill off a competitor you don't approve of, for one."

The female clicked her tongue as she shifted her head to one side. "Come now, general. We only want to find the best king for our kingdom—and for our Calla."

"For the queen you tried to strip of her crown?" I asked, curling my toes inside my boots to keep from jumping to my feet and strangling her.

Ursula softened her features into an innocent expression. "We were merely adhering to the laws *her* parents insisted on. Now you're welcome to keep arguing with me, general, and you can think all manner of awful things about me, but time is slipping away with every barb you cast."

I started to pull the small glasses closer when Isa cleared her throat.

"There is one more stipulation," she said. "You cannot mix the glasses into one. They must remain separate."

Well, there goes my first plan.

My heart pounded gradually faster and faster in my chest as my doubt gathered strength. I should have asked more questions when I'd been healed. I should have looked for more information when I had been sneaking around the infirmary. Never mind that my search that night had been interrupted.

Phillip arranged the small glasses in front of him quickly, his once shaking hand now scratching at his jaw as he considered the four options. Lifting his chin slightly, he asked, "Could I get four empty glasses, by chance?"

Isa quickly looked over her shoulder to the staff person standing by the door behind her and waved her forward with a flick of her fingers. She whispered quickly to the young female server, who dashed away with a sharp nod, leaving Isa to address the table.

"Yes, you will each get a number of empty glasses for any tests you feel would be helpful in your decision. Remember, though, that you may not mix them."

While we waited for these to be brought out, Korben seemed

to be using some sort of nursery rhyme to select his choice. His mouth moved silently as he tapped his finger on each glass, making several passes through all of them before finally settling on one, which he gingerly slid away from him. He did this a few more times, until he only had one remaining. We all watched him —curious looks on all our faces—as he picked up the final glass and walked over to Calla.

Isa stopped him, though, laying her hand flat against his chest.

"You've made your selection?" she asked. He nodded crisply, and she held out her hand in silent request for the glass. "I'll be administering each."

I couldn't blame her for that decision, given that the queen's own advisors had poisoned her. I wouldn't want to let the contestants near her either.

Korben, however, pulled the glass closer to his chest and shook his head. "That wasn't stated in the initial rules of the trial, general."

Isa started to protest, but Ursula argued first. "He's right, general. Each competitor should be allowed to administer their selection themselves, to ensure no...interference."

Isa's hands tightened into fists at her sides. She slammed her teeth together, but she stood firm, refusing to step aside until Ursula cleared her throat loudly. Snarling, Isa slowly pivoted out of her way, her muscles remaining taut.

"Sit down, general," Warren insisted, gesturing smoothly to her chair. Again, she remained where she was, but the advisor brought his fist down so hard on the table that the glasses trembled. "NOW!" he barked.

Isa lowered herself to the edge of her seat, though I noticed her hand shifted to the dagger at her hip as she slid her gaze back to Korben. He approached Calla lazily, as if he were being forced to do some mundane chore rather than competing to save the queen's life. I leaned forward, watching intently to see if his choice would have any effect on her.

He didn't lift the cup to her lips though.

Instead he knelt down in front of her and reached for her hand.

What is he—

In a flash of movement, he produced a knife from his sleeve and sliced the blade across her palm.

"What the fuck are you doing?" Isa yelled, leaping up from her seat and shoving him away from Calla.

Korben didn't seem at all bothered by her reaction, his face the epitome of calm. "You mentioned blood, so that's what I chose."

Isa looked about ready to punch him in the face, but instead she merely growled, crossing her arms while she hovered over him to observe his every movement. From where I sat, I didn't have a clear view of it and didn't know he had finished until he placed the empty cup upside down on the table.

Everyone craned their heads to see—even those who had an unobstructed view of the queen. I tried to pinpoint her pulse, but with so many of us in one room, it was impossible to identify hers.

Several breaths later, there was still no noticeable change in Calla's state.

Isa pushed Korben out of the way with her hip, dragging Calla's napkin off the table and wrapping it tightly around her limp hand. Tenderly, Isa brushed Calla's hair out of her face like a fretting mother waiting for her child's fever to break. She had barely rested the queen's hand back down when she spun back around and slammed her hands onto the table, leaning forward and piercing each of us with a murderous glare.

"No. More. Blades," she growled, hitting the table with her palm on each word. "Saliva only. Not blood. Understand?"

Warren threw out a condescending sigh across the room. "Stop being so dramatic, general. She's a fae. She will heal."

"You fucking idiot! The poison hinders her ability to fucking heal!" Isa screamed, flinging her hand into Calla's water glass and sending it flying into the rest of Korben's cordial glasses, which fell to the floor with tiny crashes.

Warren shrugged, donning a smirk I was about ready to punch off his smug face. "A few cuts are not going to kill her, general."

I turned to the male and narrowed my eyes at him with feigned concern. "It may not be wise to patronize the heavily-armed female."

He looked right past me, staring at Isa, and scoffed lightly. "She wouldn't risk it. She can't leave the queen's side, and she knows coming after me—or any of us—would earn her a swift trip to the executioner."

Shrugging, I turned away from him as servers brought in the empty glasses Phillip had requested and placed them in front of us.

What was I supposed to do with these? What *could* I do at all? Pick one randomly like Korben? That gave me slim odds for selecting the right one.

Phillip shifted away from me, reaching down the table toward Calla's wineglass.

"May I?" he asked Isa, and she nodded.

He slid the glass toward him and proceeded to pour a little into each empty glass. Across from us Graham was studying each cup of potential antidote. What he was looking for, I couldn't fathom. They said it was basically undetectable. Beside me, Phillip now poured a bit of one possible cure into a glass with the poisoned wine. Swirling it around, he peered into the cup— brows lifted high with hope—and waited. After a long moment, his face fell and he set it down, moving on to the next potential antidote.

It wasn't a bad method, to be honest, but there was no way to know if the cure would react with the poison in any observable manner.

What if...

I shook my head, as if I could dislodge the insanity from my mind.

It was a risk, but a worthwhile one. It would only require a sip. I would just need to find the cure as quickly as possible before the poison could pull me into that peaceful darkness. With a glance toward the queen, verifying she was still unconscious, I reached for her wineglass from in front of Phillip and lifted it to my lips.

CHAPTER 59

CALLA

At first their voices were muffled, distant, but they faded away, leaving me with nothing but dark emptiness.

No pain. No anger. No loss. Nothing.

Peace.

Rest.

Was this what death would be like? Was this what death had been like for Brennan? For my parents?

I hoped so. On all counts.

Unlikely, though, given my misfortune. Nothing would ever be as I hoped.

Peace.

Rest.

Love.

These weren't mine to have. This darkness was an illusion, a void to mirror my hollow chest.

I wasn't destined for good things, only destruction and misery, blood and chaos.

I opened my palms, but my shadows had become light— wafting through the abyss around me, like smoke with no flame. It swirled and danced against the black backdrop, circling around me, caressing my cheek, and then seeking something apart from me, drifting further and further away, though illuminating nothing.

I was about to follow it when a sharp pain in my right hand recalled the light, pulling it back to me. The light wrapped around me as if to shield me, but it couldn't stop the blood that welled up in my palm or the panic the sight triggered in my heart. What were they doing to me? What was happening to me while I was here? Why wasn't Isa stopping this? Where was Matthias?

Surely he would ensure I survived this.

CHAPTER 60

MATTHIAS

The small bit of wine was still enough to coat my tongue before sliding easily down my throat.

Nothing happened.

Aside from Isa's scolding voice booming toward me, "Matthias! What in the stars—"

A single cackle from Warren cut through her words, followed by a collective gasp from the rest of the Assembly. Isa once more leaned over the table—much further this time, with her entire torso barely hovering over its surface. Her hand shot out in a silent demand for the wineglass.

I hesitated, taking a moment to assess my well-being. Fingers. Hands. Feet. Legs. Head. Nothing seemed out of the ordinary. Everything was in working order. Perhaps I needed to take another sip.

I started to lift it to my mouth again, but Phillip reached his hand over and grabbed it.

"Don't," he said, though he made no move to actually pull the glass away; he simply held his hand firmly in place, blocking me from another dose.

Korben laughed. "Let him drink more if he wants. Narrows the competition."

Ignoring him, Isa moved closer. "Hand it over."

As I moved to relinquish it, Phillip pulled his hand away and waited for a tense moment, studying me. Isa clutched the glass and awkwardly scooted backwards. Wine sloshed out and splashed onto the table, leaving deep red spots that might have resembled blood perfectly had it been thicker.

"What were you thinking?" Isa asked, smoothing down her jacket and checking to make sure her dagger was still secure.

I opened my mouth to answer, but the room flickered around me, like someone had extinguished all the lamps and relit them immediately. Looking around, I tried to focus, but ribbons of darkness danced across my vision, reminding me of the queen's deadly, elegant shadows.

Hurry up.

She's dying.

My thoughts nudged me in hissed whispers.

I pushed my fingers through the smoky strands, mesmerized by how my hand seemed not my own, like I was watching someone else choosing the glass and pulling it close. Darkness bathed the room once more, still brief, but longer this time. Tremors coursed through my arm, shaking my fingers.

Steady.

Little closer.

My lips could barely sense the glass against them, only aware it was there by the pressure of it as I tilted it back. The cool water cleansed away the taste of the wine, and I slowly set the glass down and began to count my breaths. Turning my head, I searched for Isa's face. The room seemed to stretch out away from me, and I could barely make out her outline, let alone her expression.

Not it.

The black ribbons swelled as they continued to swirl.

That is definitely not the one.

Voices echoed around me, but I couldn't make out any of

their words, only their tones. Anger. Confusion. Laughter. A crash.

Through it all I narrowed in on the next glass, but it was now sitting so far away from me. Time seemed to lengthen, slowing. Or maybe it was me who was sluggish, but the glass was in my hand and to my lips before I even realized I was holding it.

Was I the one holding it?

Does it matter?

Just drink it.

The glass tipped up. The water cooled my senses, temporarily slicing through the dark patches and sparking a sliver of hope when my surroundings came back into focus. Within moments, though, everything faded, the inky streams trailing through my vision again, thicker this time. Silence settled around me, but I doubted everyone had stopped talking.

Why was my hand moving so slowly?

I opened my mouth—I thought—to ask Isa if Phillip or Graham had found the antidote yet, but snapped it shut again. I couldn't waste time with that. If they'd won, they'd be giving me the antidote already. If Isa didn't make sure of that, then Calla surely would.

A pained howl pierced the quiet of my dimming consciousness, and I jerked my head up despite not being able to tell which direction it came from. The room had shifted to dull shades of brown and gray, and it took my full attention to nudge both of my hands toward the remaining two glasses. They floated to me, the only indication that I was the one moving them being the sight of my own hands gripping them tightly in my shaky fingers.

One of these was the antidote.

Something bumped into my leg, and I barely held them steady. I brought one up to my mouth as fast as I could before anything else could fuck this up. I couldn't take them too closely together, because then there'd be no way to know which actually held the antidote. Carefully, I tilted the glass up, pouring some of the liquid past my lips.

There was no refreshing sensation this time, and while the water itself wasn't actually hot, a searing pain shot through my tongue and throat, as if burning away the poison.

I hoped.

Clenching my eyes tightly, I willed myself to remain silent, swallowing back the agony.

This is temporary.

Only temporary.

I'll either be cured soon.

Or dead.

The pain ebbed, fading as quickly as it had come on. I opened my eyes. The shadows had dissolved. The room had returned to its original state, except...not. I had emerged from my poisoned stupor to utter chaos.

While Calla still sat, unconscious, dying in her chair at the end of the table, Korben stood in the far corner, holding Isa's arms tightly behind her back. She struggled to get free, and he sneered as he hissed in her ear, convincing her to still. Graham stood—his chair toppled over on its side—screaming at Ursula and Warren, who had joined her on the other side of the table.

"You can't have him restrain the fucking general!" Graham shouted, throwing his arms out to the sides. Ursula shrugged while Warren waved a placating hand in the air.

"The *fucking* general shouldn't try to interfere with official trials. She'll be released once the trial is complete. No harm done."

"No harm done?!" Graham's eyes flew open even wider. He pivoted around and tossed his hand toward Calla. "The queen is dying because of you assholes."

His words hit me like a bucket of cold water after a night of too many drinks. Pushing away from the table, I turned, ready to take the antidote over to Calla, but I stopped short. Phillip lay on the floor, eyes closed but still breathing. At first I wondered if he'd taken the poison, too, but the eight glasses that had been in front of him were now scattered around him, water and wine spilled across his shirt. Kneeling beside him, I pressed my fingers to his wrist. He still had a pulse, though slower and weaker than normal. I rose, determined to get to Calla. As I stepped over him, Phillip must have come to, because his hand reached out for my ankle, tripping me up enough that the remainder of the antidote spilled from the glass.

A growl erupted from my chest.

I'd fucking poisoned myself and for what? Only to have it spilled and wasted?

Pulling my leg back, I prepared to kick the poor male on the floor, but I slammed my boot down onto the stone instead. It wasn't his fault. He hadn't intended to do that.

I spun around, my balled fists restrained at my sides.

Graham froze, half-turned toward me. His eyes drifted down to the four glasses still sitting at his place.

"Which one is it?" I bellowed, but he only shook his head, one shoulder lifting shakily.

"I don't know. I'm not sure."

"Pick any of them!" He hesitated, biting his bottom lip hard while he studied his options. Slamming my fist on the table, I snarled at him. "Who gives a shit about winning if she fucking dies?"

I just needed him to pick one. Even if it was only water, the trial would be over and they'd give her the antidote to revive her. Still he hemmed and hawed, though, his hand now rubbing at his jaw.

"Just pick one, Graham," Isa yelled from the corner, but Korben rewarded that with pulling her arms tighter behind her.

"For fuck's sake." I charged around the table, ready to snatch one up and force it into his pathetic hand, but having poisoned myself like an idiot, I wasn't as fast. Warren darted around Graham, stopping me with his finger jabbing into my chest.

"No. No helping each other in this trial," he warned.

I screamed in his face. "I don't give two fucks about him; I just want to save her!"

Graham gingerly lifted a glass and started to move around us.

I might have sighed in relief that the prick had finally found his nerve, but I didn't know how long it had taken me to find the antidote and how much time Calla had left. With Graham on his way toward Calla to test his pick, I attempted to push past Warren to grab the remaining three, but the fucker stopped me.

His hand came down hard on my wrist, his fingers tightening around it. He started to force my arm away from the table, but Ursula stepped forward and laid a gentle hand on his shoulder.

"Graham has made his choice, Warren. Certainly there's no harm in letting this general take the others over? If Graham fails, we will want the antidote close by, no?"

Warren glowered at me for a long breath before finally pushing out a sigh and muttering, "Fine." He didn't release me until Ursula pulled away, but she dropped her hand too low, conveniently crashing into the glasses, spilling them.

"Fuck!" I growled, shoving Warren back. He stumbled into Ursula, who looked about ready to come at me herself, but she decided against it. The other four advisors all sat at their end of the table, hands covering their mouths, eyes wide, but they did nothing to actually step in.

"You are all worthless," I said, and turned away from them.

Graham set the glass he'd tried upside down on the table. His head dropped to his chin, and he crumpled into Isa's chair. A furious scream burst from him, and he thrust both his hands angrily out in front of him, sending Calla's cup of poisoned wine flying, splashing across the table.

The worthless prick. Was he just going to give up? Wait for one of these other fuckers to save her? The only one here aside from me who cared about Calla was Isa. I snapped my eyes up to her, where Korben still held her tightly.

"Let her go. It's over!" I said, but Korben didn't until he shifted his gaze to the Assembly, who presumably nodded.

As soon as he released her, she twisted around, and before he could react, she reached up, grabbed him by his hair, and pulled his face down into her raised knee. His pitiful groan filled the room, and Isa shoved him down into the corner before turning back to me.

"Where's the antidote?" I asked her. Isa scanned the table, and then all color drained from her face.

"Gone," she mumbled. That couldn't be right.

"What do you mean gone?" I asked, grabbing her arms and forcing her to look at me.

"I mean"—she threw a hand out toward the table—"there's none left. It's all spilled."

"You didn't have any extra on hand?" I couldn't believe this. Who the fuck planned this trial?

"All the extra was supposed to be in Calla's water glass, which isn't here."

I could face the Assembly, demand to know where the rest of it was, but we didn't have time. They wouldn't give me any useful information anyway.

Slowly, I turned to Calla, lowering myself to kneel beside her and lifted my hand to her face. I brushed my thumb over her cheek, desperate fear causing it to shake. My chest burned, a dark fire consuming me, searing my heart, eating away at any hint of hope I had left.

I stilled.

Burning. Searing.

The cure.

The cure had burned away the poison when I drank it.

No.

This was insane.

Then again, poisoning myself to find the antidote had also been insane, and it had worked.

Maybe this would too.

Lifting myself up off the floor, I cradled Calla's face in my hands and brought my lips to hers, hoping against all fucking hope that some of the antidote lingered to save her...and that she wouldn't kill me for this.

CHAPTER 61

CALLA

One moment there was dark emptiness, a hollow peace. The next moment my world was on fire. Brilliant white light chased away the darkness. A breath so pure, so fresh rushed into my lungs, so different from anything I'd ever experienced I wondered if I had ever truly been living before now.

Had someone done it?

Had they found the cure?

Someone must have.

But all I saw around me was a white expanse that both delighted and terrified me at the same time. I tried to open my eyes, but no matter how many times I blinked, I was still here. Alone.

Yet...not.

There, pulsing through my confused elation, was something else.

Panic, but not mine.

I closed my eyes again, and Matthias's face flashed into focus. That smirk. That mischievous spark in his eye.

Neither were present now.

He stared at me so intensely, like he was seeing me—really seeing me—for the first time.

My chest caved inward one final time, as if saying goodbye to the hollowness I'd nurtured these past months. No, my whole life.

Gasping for another breath, my heart burst from where it had lain shattered and broken, not simply healed, but new. I had loved Brennan—of course I had, but only as much as a flawed heart could.

This...this was something different, something incredible, something impossible.

Like having every dream fulfilled, every wish granted, every hope realized.

My heart pounded furiously against my sternum, filling my ears, as if it were trying to reach him.

I needed to find him.

I needed to wake up.

I needed to get back to him.

Back to...my mate.

My world imploded the moment my lips touched hers. Everything I'd ever known, ever desired to know, and ever yearned to forget vanished—all replaced by one single thought: Calla.

I'd thought myself whole, but I'd been a fucking fool. I'd been happy, content, but I'd been blind to the cracks and crevices and hollow spaces of my soul until she filled them all—like parts of me I'd never known were missing had finally been restored to where the stars had always intended them to be. I had spent my whole life loyal to my friend and his kingdom with the sole purpose of serving them, and while that duty remained, she dwarfed them all.

I couldn't let her go even if I'd wanted to, and I never wanted to.

How in the stars had Connor run away from Lieke in that moment? How had he released her, let alone abandoned her?

I clung to Calla with desperate hands, my lips silently begging her to respond, to return my kiss, to wake up. Softly, I parted her lips, sweeping my tongue against hers, mentally screaming at the stars for there to be some of the antidote left there to save her— my mate.

Reluctantly I pulled back as far as I dared, nuzzling my nose against hers as I opened my eyes. But no deep brown stared back at me. She was as motionless before.

Had she felt the bond? Had she sensed even a sliver of what I had in that kiss?

Her face gave no indication she had.

What if the poison numbed her senses so much not even our stars-fated bond could reach her?

No. I refused to accept that.

She knew. She had to know. She had to come back to me.

Lowering my hands, I gripped hers in mine and squeezed gently. Her shadows tickled my palms, and I peered down to see them slipping between my fingers, wrapping around our hands like an ancient ceremony binding us to one another.

Through weary eyes, I studied her face again, but she remained torturously still. I rested my forehead against hers and pressed my eyes closed.

"Don't worry, Killer," I whispered. "I've got you."

Slipping my arms beneath her legs and shoulders, I lifted her up and stood, prepared to argue with anyone who tried to stop me. I turned. Everyone simply stared at us, their mouths agape, some hidden behind splayed fingers, others displayed like prized fish on a tavern wall. Isa's hand hovered in the air, pointing at me, as if the moment I'd kissed Calla had frozen her in mid-scolding.

"I'm taking her to the healers," I declared, daring any of them to argue.

They didn't, but behind Isa, Graham shifted, the first to move. Anger flashed in his eyes under bitter brows, while his lips twisted into a sneer, but the expression dissolved so quickly—settling into one of disappointed acceptance—that I half-wondered if I'd imagined his rage. Before he could say anything, though, Isa rasped out, "You're..."

I waited half a breath for her to say it, but when she didn't, I did it for her.

"Mates. Yes."

"But..."

"How…"

"What…"

Their hushed voices all chimed in at once with unfinished questions, but I ignored them all, lifting my chin and pivoting toward the door. Korben slid in front of it to block my way.

"Being mates doesn't mean you win," he taunted.

"And winning won't be worth shit if she fucking dies. Move."

He refused but dared to lean toward me. "Who would want to marry a shadow bitch anyway?"

If only I had my own set of shadows, I'd have had them gut the male right where he stood.

Cackling to himself, he threw his head back and stepped out of my way, directly into the path of Isa's dagger. It struck him hard below the collar bone, burying deep into his chest. He looked down, perplexed, his hands floating up to the handle sticking out of him as if he didn't quite believe it was there.

"Go!" Isa shouted, running up beside me to open the door. "Get her to the infirmary. Now!"

I didn't need her to shove me out of the room, but she did all the same.

The journey down to the healers took far longer than I wanted, and I nearly slid onto my ass several times trying to round the stairs too quickly. By the time I reached the lower level, my lungs heaved, my legs burned, and my arms and head throbbed, but I'd have suffered far more than this to heal Calla.

Jocelyn waited at the door before I'd even turned the corner.

"I can't believe they poisoned her," she said. I shot her a confused look. "You know staff gossip. Bring her inside."

I tried to catch my breath as I laid Calla gently on the bed that had been mine.

Jocelyn checked her pulse, her eyes, her breathing, not looking at me as she asked, "How long ago was she given the antidote?"

"She wasn't," I choked out, guilt flooding my chest.

The healer's head snapped up, her eyes wide. "What do you mean?"

"There wasn't any left," I said. "But you have some here. Get it for her."

Jocelyn rushed back to the large hutch against the wall. The bottles and jars clinked and thudded as she shoved them around, knocking them into each other and sending others toppling.

"Where is it?" I asked, though I knew my badgering her wouldn't help.

"It should be here," she muttered, but the next shelf down didn't offer any hope either. She slammed her hands down the hutch, sending more glasses rattling. "I just made more."

Despite the agony of it, I rushed from Calla's side to help Jocelyn search.

"It should be right here," she said, her voice cracking. She shook her hand at one of the shelves. "But it's gone."

"How can it be gone?" I asked.

She didn't look at me, but continued to stare at the shelves, bringing her trembling hand to her forehead. "We don't have any."

Grabbing Jocelyn's elbow, I swung her around to face me, but she looked right through me, her eyes glossy.

"Jocelyn! Are you saying there's no way to heal her?"

She didn't respond.

I shook her just hard enough to force her to focus on me and bent lower to look her in the eye.

"Can you make more?"

"Yes—wait, no. I can't." Her shoulders lifted high and shook. "We used most of the poison to make the antidotes for the rest of you. The rest was supposed to be used to poison your wine, but..."

"They gave it all to Calla? There's no more?" I asked, the bottom of my stomach dropping out. I was going to be sick. I was going to lose her. I was going to fail her.

I couldn't.

"If we had a little bit of poison, maybe—"

I straightened, my thoughts spinning furiously.

"How much do you need? Does it need to be the *exact* same poison?"

"Well, it can't be a completely separate poison."

"Obviously. What about the same poison, just a different concentration? Say, one that could kill a fae within seconds? Would that work?"

Suspicion clouded Jocelyn's expression, and she let out a slow, "Yes, but...when did she drink the poison?"

"An hour ago. I think. How long does it take to make the antidote?"

"Depends on its potency." She fumbled with her hands in the air as if doing mental calculations. "But I'd need it now."

"Give me a few moments. I'll be right back."

I dashed out of the room, allowing myself one lingering glance at my mate before I left her. If she didn't end up hating me for kissing her, she would when she learned how I saved her. But I'd gladly accept all her wrath and endure a lifetime of her hatred if it meant she lived.

CHAPTER 63

CALLA

I didn't know how long I'd been stuck in that white emptiness, but when everything began to dim, panic gripped my heart.

The poison had killed me, the Assembly had won, and I would die without ever hearing my mate's voice again.

The stars were cruel indeed.

Something sharp pricked my arm, and I recoiled from the pain.

Pain.

I'd felt it. Hadn't I?

Calling to my power, I waited for it to answer, but my palms remained empty. My heartbeat quickened as the bright white faded into complete darkness that didn't bring the same comfort as my shadows.

Until I heard him.

"Killer, I'm here."

Where?

The question whimpered in my thoughts, but my body refused—or couldn't—give it a voice.

This new darkness closed in around me, keeping me from seeing him.

"Can you hear me?" he asked softly, and I could almost imagine the warmth of his breath on my ear.

Still, my reply remained silent. *Yes, I hear you.*

"Are you sure it's working?"

I pinched my brows together. Who was he talking to? Where was I? Was I still in the dining room? Who else was with him?

"She might be out for a few days," another voice—a female—answered him.

A few days?

It might be days before I can see him?

No. I needed to get up now.

Despite the black void surrounding me, I called for my shadows, hoping perhaps they could speak to him when I couldn't. They slipped from my palms, though blind as I was, I had no way to confirm they did as I commanded.

"Whoa there, Killer. We're not alone here," he said huskily in my ear. His deep rumble of a laugh warmed my heart. "We can do that when you wake up, but not until then."

Directing my shadows up toward his face, I hoped he understood how I longed to get back to him.

"Matthias," a voice, soft and distant, called to him.

Isa! She would make all of this right. She would help me against the Assembly.

My shadows snapped back into my veins of their own accord, as if frightened by my friend. I strained to make out what she said, but it was so quiet.

"Where did you get it?"

Get what? What was she talking about?

"Can we speak somewhere else?" Matthias asked.

No! I growled, but no one heard me. They couldn't leave. I was still here. I could still hear them.

Don't leave me, I silently begged.

Matthias's voice came closer. "I'll be right back, Killer." Peace washed over me, soothing my panic, until he added, "I hope."

The darkness finally lifted, reality drifted back into my consciousness, and the strong scent of herbs hit my nose with a hint of woods and leather. When I opened my eyes, though, Matthias wasn't there, and I couldn't hold back my frown.

"Don't look so happy to be alive," Isa joked, though there was an empty shakiness to her tone.

"What's wrong?" My weak voice was further strained as I tried to push myself up onto my elbows.

My friend shifted forward to help me. "Steady, Calla," she warned. "Let me help." Before I could protest, she was fetching another pillow to place behind me so I could sit back against the wall.

When I was finally settled—my breath ragged from such little exertion—I shot Isa a sharp look. "What happened? Where is he?"

Isa's gaze plummeted to her hands, taking my heart along with it. "The dungeons."

My shadows were out of my palms before I'd even sat up fully, but I reined them back in before they could grab Isa's chin and force her to look at me. Slowly they settled into my lap like a guard dog reluctantly lying down by its master.

"Why?" I growled, though I knew from the regret on my friend's face that this hadn't been her doing.

"You're lucky they didn't immediately execute him, Calla."

"Don't make me force the words out of you, Isa, because I will. Now, speak!"

"There was no antidote left at the end of the trial," she explained as quickly as she could in the meekest voice I'd ever heard from her. "And there was no poison left to create any more."

"How am I alive then? What does this have to do with—"

It wasn't the speed with which she looked at me that stopped me mid-question, but the tears lining her eyes. Isa never cried, at least not that I could ever recall.

410

"You're scaring me, Isa," I whispered. "What happened?"

She shook her head, her lips pressing tightly together for a moment before she sucked in a deep breath and answered.

"He had poison with him, Calla. He brought it with him from Emeryn, embedded in a dagger's blade."

The room spun wildly as my thoughts swarmed in a confusing mess.

"Why would he have—what was he going to—it must have been for the tournament," I concluded finally, but Isa was shaking her head again, more resolutely this time.

"He won't tell me," Isa said. "He refuses to talk to anyone but you."

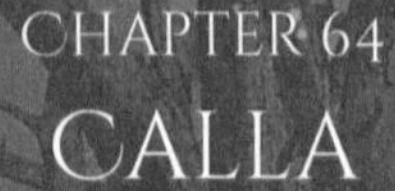

CALLA

He had poison. From Emeryn.

Isa's words repeated on an endless loop in my head as I slowly paced up and down the rug in the solar, swirling the brandy in my crystal glass. Surprisingly enough, Isa hadn't fought me on my demand to immediately leave the infirmary, but when she'd asked if I wanted her to come to the dungeons with me, I had declined.

As eager as I had been to see Matthias, to talk to him about this whole bond thing, I couldn't face him yet. Not now.

Mate or not, he'd lied.

He'd pretended to care about me to—what?—get close to me? To avenge Brennan?

The bitterness of betrayal coated my tongue. I'd tried to wash it away with the Vranić, but that first sip had only reminded me of him, stoking the burning embers in my chest.

What would I say to him?

What possible excuse could he have?

What if the Durands truly believed I'd killed Brennan? Matthias had certainly been a convincing actor, pretending to understand how hard it was to lose everyone.

He'd lied.

He'd played me for a fool.

He'd tricked me into thinking he gave a shit.

I'd thought the stars cruel before—keeping me from him as I lay there dying—but now I had proof they were: they'd dared tie my soul to the one sent to kill me.

I fell into one of the armchairs, realizing only too late that it was the one he'd sat in.

Leaping back to my feet, I pivoted, and a roar burst from my lungs as I heaved the glass at the wall. It shattered in a satisfying crash, sending millions of tiny shards sprinkling to the floor and brandy splattering across the stone. My knees buckled beneath me, and I crumpled onto the area rug, bracing myself with my palms. Curling my fingers into its soft fibers, I squeezed my eyes shut and let another growl rush out of me.

My shadows pooled out from under my hands, weaving around my arms and pressing against my chest as if to stave off the invisible wound Matthias had left.

The liar.

The fucking liar.

I didn't want to hear his excuses. I didn't want to know why he'd been sent. I didn't want to be anywhere near him.

But the thought of sending him away brought back the same rush of fear I'd experienced when he'd walked away from me in the infirmary—a terrifying emptiness with flames encroaching, threatening to consume me from the inside out. I thought I'd been hollowed out by Brennan's death, but that was nothing compared to the mere prospect of abandoning my stars-damned mate.

Were these my only options? To live the rest of my life with the male who turned me into a fucking mockery in front of my subjects or to suffer an eternity of agonizing loneliness?

Fuck the stars and their damned bonds!

Slowly, I pushed myself up off my hands so that I sat on the floor. Leaning against the side of the sofa, I pulled my knees up to my chest as my shadows settled around me to wait patiently for my command.

I would have to see him—eventually—but first I needed to sort through the knot of thoughts tangled in my mind. Isa's debriefing of what had happened while I'd been unconscious left me with so many questions and so much confusion.

Matthias had poisoned himself to find the cure.

If the Durands had sent him with that poison to kill me, then why would he do that?

Why would he risk his own life? So he could ensure he was the one to take mine?

What if the poison wasn't for me?

What if it was merely a precaution?

There's only one way to know the truth.

Talk to him.

The thought triggered the image of his face in my mind, and I snapped my teeth together, clenching them as hard as I could to keep my anger constrained. No, I wasn't ready.

I needed time, but I had so little of it. He'd hang if I didn't do something, and while part of me would have relished placing that noose around his neck, another part cowered at the prospect of the torture my heart would face if he died. I'd already endured so much. Could I bear to lose someone else—and not just anyone, but the one whose soul had been seared to mine?

Life was one misery after another, heartbreak after stars-damned heartbreak, and I was tired of being broken again and again and again.

I had barely closed my eyes when a faint knocking pulled them wide. My shadows crept back into my palms when the door slid open.

"Calla? Someone would like to speak to you," Isa said timidly, as if she expected me to bite her head off in response.

Without looking her way, I bit out the words—for what felt like the hundredth time—"I'm not ready yet."

"It's not Matthias."

Jerking my head around to look at her, I winced at the sharp pain that stabbed my neck from moving too quickly. Isa stood just inside the room with the door nearly closed, her hand resting on the handle like she was prepared to bolt.

"Who then? If it's Graham—"

"It's Raven," she said, her tone still cautious.

"The human? You didn't bring her up here, did you?"

"Of course not. She's still a prisoner awaiting trial. I put her in the interrogation room."

Slowly, I pushed to my feet, swallowing the annoyed groan that tried to escape my chest. "Do you know what she wants?"

"To plead her case, perhaps? To plead for Matthias's? She didn't say. Everyone seems reluctant to tell me anything lately," she joked, though her half-smile didn't meet her weary eyes.

Assessing the apprehension on her face, I asked, "Afraid I'm going to lose my temper and murder this woman?"

She cast her eyes down as she answered. "He's your mate—"

A deep growl vibrated in my chest, and my fingers flared open as my shadows burst from my palms to wrap around my midsection like a coiling snake prepared to strike where I demanded.

"I know he's my mate," I bit out.

"And you're just going to let him—"

Spinning away from her, I dropped my chin to my chest and pressed my shaking hands to my temples. When Isa reached for my shoulder, I threw my arms back down to my sides, but I didn't face her, keeping my eyes slammed tightly as I tried to compose myself.

"I don't know," I seethed. After a few calming breaths, though, I was able to steady my heart enough to turn toward my friend. Lifting my chin, I slowly opened my eyes and—recalling my shadows back into my veins—I said, "But I'll see Raven now."

CHAPTER 65

CALLA

Isa accompanied me in silence to the dungeons but departed once I stepped inside the room where Raven waited. The woman wasn't chained to the wall as Matthias had been, but that was an unnecessary precaution with an unarmed human. Still, Isa had restrained her, cuffing her wrists behind her back and binding her ankles together with a hefty chain.

"You wanted to see me?" I asked gently, and the woman lifted her chin, a knowing smile spreading across her lips.

"I did," she said, though she didn't elaborate.

I studied the woman who appeared to be around Lieke's age, though she had a few more visible scars than my former sister-in-law.

"Why?"

Angling her head to one side, she lifted a brow. "When I last saw you, you were ready to strangle me with your shadows."

"Your point?"

"Where is that anger now?" There was no challenge in her question, only genuine curiosity.

"Directed at Matthias," I said easily, though I had expected it to elicit some sign of surprise in the woman.

Instead she offered an almost-sweet smile. "But not toward me?"

I was about to ask her what she was getting at when I realized she was right. Ever since Minerva had revealed that someone in Wrenwick's royal family had killed Brennan, I had placed the blame—and directed all my fury—at the humans. I hadn't been able to face a human—except Asher, though he was only half—without my boiling blood calling for revenge.

But now...

A human was still responsible for taking my husband from me.

I still grieved for him, still missed him.

But now...

"I...I don't know," I stammered, unable to look up at her again as tears threatened to surface.

"The bond," Raven said quietly.

My fingers quivered against my lips, and my shadows peeked out slowly of their own volition, as if checking to make sure I was okay. How could the bond have done this, though? It bound me to Matthias, sure, but how could it change my attitude toward the humans?

I glanced up at her through my lashes. "What about the bond? How do you know about it?"

"About your bond with him or in general?"

I risked lifting my face a little higher. "Both."

"Your staff talk, and it's easy to forget that Sera is part fae. Good hearing and all that."

"But how could the bond change...this?" I waved my hand between us. "How did it curb my anger?"

Raven shifted her head to the other side and pursed her lips for a moment before finally speaking, but she answered my questions with one of her own. "What do the humans have to do with Brennan?"

My head jerked up, eyes flying wide. I parted my lips to speak, though there was nothing I could say that wouldn't be hindered by Minerva's magic. I couldn't even explain to the woman why I couldn't answer. Her brow flinched at my silence.

"So they *are* related somehow," she muttered, more to herself than to me. Her expression softened then, her eyes brimming not with pity, but empathy, as if she actually understood me—though that was preposterous.

Softly, she asked, "How do you feel about Brennan?"

"I love him," I snapped.

"I never claimed otherwise," Raven said, her tone still patient, calm. "I'm sure you still do—in a way. Has it changed at all? I don't mean over time, but suddenly—drastically."

I started to shake my head and deny it, but my gaze shifted away from her as I forced myself to truly consider it. As soon as Matthias had kissed me and the bond had formed, something else had been severed, like my connection to Brennan had been a simple thread. So easily broken when my heart had been pulled toward Matthias's.

"How?" I asked, barely over a whisper.

Raven raised one shoulder. "From what I've pieced together —talking to folks here and there over the last few years—when mates find each other and their bond forms, all former connections fade, and any connections they might try to forge in the future will never be as strong as the one with their mate."

"So, you think because I don't feel as strongly for Brennan as before, I—what?—no longer care about punishing the humans?"

"Do you have a better explanation for why you don't want to kill me?"

"I could still kill you," I noted.

Her expression didn't shift at all. "Undoubtedly, but that's not really the point, is it? You don't *want* to kill me now."

I twisted my lips into a small smirk. "Keep testing my patience and I might soon."

Chuckling quietly, she flashed me another smile. "Can I ask you something though?" I nodded, and she continued without hesitation. "What will you do about the bond? Will you choose it or walk away?"

The last two words stung like sharp barbs in my chest. It was none of this woman's business what I did, but for some reason, I found myself choosing to answer her. "I don't think I can. Walk away, that is."

"So why are you hesitating?"

Pressing my lips firmly together, I shook my head before letting it drop wearily to my chest again. "I'm so tired."

"Of what?"

"Being afraid." Why was I admitting this to her? I didn't know this woman, and I'd never even spoken to Isa about this. Fear was weakness. Weakness was unacceptable. But now that I'd said it, I couldn't seem to stop the rest from spilling out. "I'm afraid that no one would ever believe me—believe my..." I tried to spit out the word *innocence*, but Minerva's curse stanched my voice. "That everyone would believe the rumors, believe me unfit to rule. That I'd lose my kingdom and my crown. And not simply that I'd never want to love again, but that I'd never be *capable* of loving again."

"What would Brennan want for you?" she asked.

Instinctively a part of me balked at her candidness, to ask such personal questions, but another part— smaller, more fragile—was grateful she did. Isa knew me too well; she was too close to me to ask me the hard questions she knew I'd never want to face. She could give tough love when necessary, but sometimes she shied away, caving to my need to be strong and in control.

"You don't have to answer," Raven said when I remained quiet. "But it is something to think about. I won't ask what your feelings are for Matthias, but I do hope you'll give him a chance."

"Why?"

"He's a good one," she said. I nearly argued with her, to point out how he'd lied and manipulated me, but her next words stayed my tongue. "He's not perfect—no one is—but he means well, and as much as he'll claim to not be a romantic like Connor or my cousin, he serves with his whole heart. Always doing what he feels is right, even when it could cost him everything."

CHAPTER 66

MATTHIAS

I couldn't hear anything in this blasted room. The Assembly had ordered Isa not to put me with the other prisoners, fearing what I might say to my sister and Raven, I supposed. At least Isa had done me the favor of not chaining me to the wall as Calla had the last time she'd visited me down here.

Still, with no windows and no sounds, it was impossible to know how much time had passed aside from pacing along the walls. I'd made the small loop at least seventy-eight times before I'd given up counting and resorted to sitting on the floor. Eventually, Isa herself brought me a meager dinner of bread, cheese, and water, apologizing that she couldn't get me anything more.

"Are you sure you won't tell me?" she asked, looking over her shoulder at me from where she stood at the door, about to pull it open.

I forced my bite down and followed it with a small sip. "I'd rather she hear it from me first."

"Even if I promise not to tell her?"

"Sorry, general," I said. "Can you just let her know I'm here when she's ready?"

"I will," she said, turning to pull the door open. She stepped one foot out into the hallway before pausing to glance back. "I just hope she's ready before the Assembly hangs you."

"Me too."

Another eighty-four times around the cell I paced, and Calla still hadn't shown up. Unable to fight the exhaustion any longer, my sigh shifted into a yawn, and I settled down on the cold stone floor. Leaning my head back against the wall, I let my eyes drift closed and welcomed whatever dream my mind created.

&

Of all the places I could have landed in my dreams, the edge of Calla's demon forest was one of the last I would have chosen. Looking down, I noted the black cord around my neck and plucked the vial up from where it rested against my chest. Hopefully I wouldn't need to fight off the forest in this dream land, but just to be sure, I tucked the pendant back into my shirt and adjusted my collar to hide it.

Glancing around, I shivered at the eerie feeling that I'd been in this very spot before.

Of course, I had been here. This was where I'd brought Oryn, hoping to find a guard to save him.

But at my feet there was only grass and leaves and dirt, no sign of my friend. For a moment, I wondered if he'd passed already, hoped I'd make it back to Emeryn for his burial. If not, I'd need to ensure I visited his grave once I completed this tournament.

Assuming I survive this tournament at all.

Cautiously, as if this wasn't a mere image painted from my memories, I stepped out of the forest, half-expecting Asher or one of the other guards to rush at me and punish me for breaking the rules of the trial. But no one came. The sunshine warmed my skin, and I lifted my face, closing my eyes as I soaked up its heat.

"You're not supposed to be here."

The voice pulled a smile to my lips, but I didn't move, as if I could savor the feel of the sun on my face and the sound of her voice in my ear as long as I remained still.

"Hello, Killer," I said around my grin.

"Why do you call me that?" she asked. When I shifted my head up to look at her, she wasn't where she had stood with Asher during the trial. Instead, she was inside the forest, leaning back against a large tree.

"It sounds a bit like your name. Killer—Calla," I said, pulling my mouth into an upside down smile while I shrugged.

Calla lifted a brow. "And my being accused of killing my husband has nothing to do with it?"

I waved a hand in the air, dismissing the comment. Gingerly, I took a step forward. "And why am I not supposed to be here? This is my dream, after all."

Her entire body went rigid—not blinking, not breathing, nothing. Leaning closer, I waved my hand in her line of sight, and she finally blinked rapidly until her eyes focused on me again.

"This isn't your dream," she said, frowning when I started to laugh quietly to myself.

"You're right," I said, fighting not to smile when I noticed her relax a little. "I mean, technically it's *our* dream."

Her eyes widened slowly. Her lips parted, but she didn't say anything. Daring to move closer still, I surveyed the surrounding forest as I continued to speak.

"I didn't expect it to be here, of course. Thought surely our first shared dream would involve a bath."

Calla shook her head slowly, and a silent "no" formed on her lips.

"Did Brennan never tell you about this little trick?" I asked, curious about how different their marriage had been compared to Lieke and Connor's. Those two told each other everything.

"Shut up. Don't say his name." Calla bit out the words. Her lip curled into a sneer, matching the animosity I sensed as clearly as if it was my own.

I held my palms toward her in silent apology, but I didn't retreat.

"Can you feel that?" I asked her, letting my humor fade from my voice.

"Feel what?"

"My remorse? My regret? My concern?" With each question I risked another step closer. Another few steps and I'd be within arm's reach. Her anger, while still as clear as the guilt and shame swirling in my own veins, mixed now with a hint of doubt and a bitterness so stubborn, it was almost cute.

When she remained silent, I softened my expression and said, "You do, don't you."

"So what if I do," she said, lifting her chin. "It doesn't change the way I feel."

"And what is it you feel?" I asked, despite my sensing it all already through our bond.

Calla's deep brown eyes darkened as she tightened them, threatening to drown me in their intensity. Her mouth twitched before she finally said, "I hate you."

As my eyes fell closed, I let a smile creep onto my face. Her words pricked me square in the chest, yet I cherished their bite—because they'd come from her.

"Why are you smiling? Did you not hear me? I hate you, Matthias."

She drew out the last words, but it was my name on her tongue—even said in that context—that made every stab of rejection worth it. She'd never called me by name before, always using my title instead. When I opened my eyes again, I found hers glistening with heated tears. Two more steps nearer, and I lifted my hand to her face, noting how she didn't recoil as my fingers grazed over the line of her jaw. My thumb traced her scowl, brushing lightly over her lips.

"I'll take your hate, Calla. I'll take anything you're willing to give me. And if hate is all you can offer, I'll take it a million times over, because an eternity of your hate is better than a lifetime without you."

"I hate you." She repeated the words, but already the anger behind them was wavering, making room for something else. "Why did you lie to me?"

Tucking a lock of her hair behind her ear, I yearned for her to sink into my touch, but she didn't. Still, I kept my thumb lingering at her cheek, ready to catch her tears if they spilled over.

"I'm sorry." My words fell out on a rough breath.

"Fuck your sorries," she growled as she thrust her palms against my chest. "You lied to me!"

I surrendered, letting her shove me back. My hand fell to my side, but I approached her again.

"I know, Calla, and I'm so sorry."

"No," she whispered, but she didn't stop me as I once again brought my hand up to her neck, following its curve until I cradled her jaw gently in my palm. She didn't lean into me, but she didn't pull away either. Drawing in a long, slow breath, she fisted her hands at my chest.

"I trusted you, and you tricked me." She hissed the words as she beat her fists over my fractured heart. I didn't try to stop her, didn't grab her wrists, but stood there and took each deserved blow. Brushing my fingers past her ear, I buried them in her hair, fighting the urge to pull her close.

"I'm sorry. I had to. It was the job," I said.

She lifted her fists to her forehead, driving my hand away from her and blocking her face from view. She shook her head, and her shoulders quivered with quiet sobs that pulsed through the bond, splintering my heart to match hers.

"Is that all I was?" she asked, her words muddled from her tears. "A fucking job?"

I couldn't lie to her. Not again.

"At first, yes," I admitted. As expected, she began to crumble, her shoulders curving forward as she tried to back away, but I couldn't let her go without her hearing the whole truth. Wrapping my arms around her, I drew her to me, and with every squirm, every whimpered "Let me go," I held her tighter, listening to our bond and the need she couldn't—wouldn't—voice.

"Stop, Calla, listen to me. Breathe, please, and listen."

Her shallow breaths deepened as she stilled, yielding to me little by little. Loosening my hold on her, I stroked her hair with my hand, thankful when the bond quieted and her pulse slowed.

"You were the job, yes, but the more time I spent with you, the better I got to know you, the clearer it became that I'd royally fucked it up."

She lifted her face, tucking her hands between us to peer up at me. "How?"

Pulling back slightly, I slipped my finger beneath her chin and angled her head so I could see her more clearly. I took a deep breath as I studied her face, etching every curve, every freckle, every line into my memory. I bit the inside of my lip to fight back the nerves, knowing once this was said there was no turning back, no walking away, at least not with my heart intact.

"I let myself care," I whispered. Grabbing her hand, I pressed it against my chest. "You feel that, don't you? Through the bond? My heart is yours—if you'll accept it. Fuck, even if you won't, Calla, it is yours. Completely and eternally yours."

Her tongue slipped out to wet her lips as she searched my eyes for several agonizingly long moments. Pulling her bottom lip between her teeth, she held my gaze even as her tears returned, but when she finally spoke again, it wasn't the words I'd hoped to hear. "But...why did you have that dagger? The poison?"

I choked down my dread. "You know why," I whispered.

A single tear escaped, sliding down her cheek. Her mouth pressed into a thin line. "I want to hear you say it. Why were you really here?"

Swallowing hard, I grazed her cheek with my thumb a few times. The answer could drive her away from me forever, but worse than that, it would hurt her more than I already had. But there could be no more lies.

"I was to kill you," I said, struggling to get the words out past my tightening throat.

"They think I killed him?" Calla's voice was so quiet and meek, more like a frightened child than a terrifying queen.

I forced myself to hold her stare and face the pain I'd caused her. "They didn't want to believe it, but with the rumors, they had to at least consider the possibility. So they sent me to learn the truth."

"With the command to kill me if the rumors proved true," she noted. I hummed my assent. "So what did you learn? About the truth, I mean."

"I learned you have a temper," I said, tugging playfully at a lock of her hair. "And you are strong, passionate, determined, but also broken. You don't want anyone to see it, can't let anyone see it, but I did. I see you, Calla, and I don't believe the rumors. I don't think you did it."

"Because I didn't. I didn't kill him," she said, and her eyes widened in surprise, her fingers flying to her lips. "I said it," she whispered.

I lifted a brow. "You've never said it before?"

She shook her head, and a long-overdue smile lit up her face. Wiping the last remnants of her tears away, she explained, "I couldn't. Minerva. Silence was the price I paid for her magic."

"What did you get in return?" I asked, hoping it was worth it.

"Brennan's true killer. I asked Minerva to reveal the ones behind his death. It was Wrenwick. The Olanders." She dropped her gaze from mine, a wave of shame thrumming down the bond as she said, "Humans."

"And this is why you banished them? To protect them?" I asked.

She nodded. "Yes, as backwards as that sounds. I didn't want to hurt them, but every time I looked at them, I saw Brennan dying on that floor. I couldn't serve them."

"And you couldn't tell anyone?" I asked, brushing her hair away from her forehead.

"No one. Not even when I was alone. I wonder if the old witch knows the bond is immune to her magic."

"Well, let's not go telling her. She may have helped save Connor, but she's a tricky bitch I'd rather avoid. What had you hoped to do with her information? If you couldn't tell anyone, why bother knowing? Just for your own peace of mind?"

"I may have also had Minerva curse his killer."

I froze. "What? And what did that cost you?"

She shrugged, her smile wavering only slightly. "Just a bit of my shadows."

"And do you know what the curse was?"

"No. I didn't care. I just wanted them to suffer as I had."

She remained quiet for a long moment, staring at my chest. Her smile slowly faded, though.

"I can't believe Lieke and Connor actually thought I could... they know me. They had to know how much I..."

"Grief can push us in directions we wouldn't otherwise go. Even someone as noble as Connor."

Calla didn't respond except to slide out of my embrace. Turning, she started to walk deeper into the forest. She'd gone a few paces when she stopped and glanced back at me.

"You coming?"

"That depends," I said, smirking. "Do you still hate me?"

I didn't answer Matthias, except to lift a quizzical brow before turning away again.

He was at my side so quickly it startled me until I remembered this was a dream where poison didn't slow our movements and time didn't matter. In silence we walked deeper and deeper into the forest. Occasionally, I stole a glance at him, shifting my eyes quickly when he caught me. I expected some teasing response, but he said nothing.

The quiet was oddly refreshing, though, and I focused on the muted thumping of our boots against the soft ground as it blended with the pulse in my ears.

Not two pulses, but a *single* pulse.

I stopped mid-step and pivoted toward him, laying one hand on his chest and the other on mine. My mouth fell open at the impossibility, but there beneath my fingers our hearts—bound by the stars—beat as one. Lifting my eyes to his, I started to remark on it, but he vanished along with the entire forest, leaving me in a dark emptiness. The uniform beat of our hearts was replaced by a steady, incessant pounding that pulled me reluctantly out of my reverie and back to my cold, lonely reality.

My gut hollowed as I slipped my feet off the sofa and down to the floor. I wanted to lie down, to find my way back to that dream, but the knocking at the door only grew louder and more impatient with every breath I drew trying to find the energy to stand.

There'd been so much more to say to Matthias, so much more to discuss and to argue about.

Like why he'd taken the poison himself, why he'd kissed me while I was unconscious, and what in the stars-damned fuck I was supposed to do now that we were mates.

"Calla!" Graham's muffled voice shouted from behind the door, pulling a soft groan from my chest. Here I'd foolishly hoped it was Isa.

"I'm coming," I muttered as I stomped to my feet and trudged to the door. I half-expected him to barrel in as soon as I answered, but he was leaning against the door frame, his head rested against his forearm as he struggled to catch his breath.

"What is it? What's going on?" I asked.

"The Assembly is sending the guards up here," he huffed, his eyes wild with panic.

"Why? Where's Isa?"

Graham shook his head as he pushed away from the door-frame and moved into the room. His eyes darted around errati-cally, as if he were trying to find the answers to my question on the dust motes floating in the air.

"Where is Isa?" I repeated, more sternly.

Wrapping his arms around me, he pulled me close and repeated the same words over and over. "I don't know. I don't know."

I'd never seen him in such a state, not when my parents died, not when Brennan had been killed. Slowly, I leaned back so I could cup my hands around his face and force him to look at me.

"Why is the guard being sent, Graham?" I asked, stepping back to force his arms to pull from around my waist.

"You need to leave. Now," he said.

"Fuck it all, Graham. Why!"

"They're arresting you for the king's murder!"

My hands shook as they fell, lifeless, to my sides. My shadows, awakened by the jolt to my heart, burst from my palms and swarmed around Graham, slowly spiraling around his body, higher and higher. He eyed them as they crept closer to his throat.

"They couldn't find Isa. I thought she might have come to warn you, but I came up here in case she hadn't. We need to leave, now."

"No, no, no," I mumbled. The tremors moved from my hands up my arms. "They can't. They couldn't. I..."

But I couldn't utter the word. I couldn't even mutter to myself that I didn't kill him, thanks to the damned mage.

"Calla, can you...please..." Graham choked out the words, and blinking, I realized my shadows had begun to tighten around his throat, as if he were the one trying to detain me. I called my power back, surprised at the effort it took to force them to ease away from my friend.

Footsteps—faint but steady—had us both snapping our attention to the open doorway. They were almost here.

Graham spun back around to face me, taking both of my hands in his and giving them a squeeze.

"Do you have another way out? I'll buy you as much time as I can, but is there a place you and Isa might meet?"

The room began to tilt and rock, but I managed to offer the quickest of nods.

"Good," Graham said, lifting a hand to my cheek. "I'll—"

"Matthias," I blurted out.

Graham's brow wrinkled. "What? There's no—"

"Save him, Graham. Before they can hang him. I need you to save him."

"He had poison—"

I waved my hand frantically between us. Couldn't he hear the guards?

"Promise me!" The words were a desperate hiss.

"Okay. I'll get him out. Now, go!" He whispered the command and shoved me back into the room. Spinning quickly away from me, he darted out into the hallway.

I ran into my bedroom, grabbed my boots from beside the wardrobe, and ducked inside, pulling the double doors closed behind me. Shoving back through the hanging garments, I slipped into the tunnel entrance and stopped. My heart thundered inside my ears, so loud and fast I couldn't listen for anyone approaching.

"She's not here, I told you that." Graham's muffled voice stilled my breath. "Look for yourself."

If I stayed much longer, they'd hear my pulse or my footsteps as I fled.

Not waiting to hear any more, I took off through the tunnel, navigating the darkness from memory, grateful my mother had insisted I learn these passages by feel. At the first turn, I paused long enough to slip my boots on. Any lost time would be made up by being able to travel quicker.

I started to take the path that would lead out to the forest. If Isa wasn't in the castle, she was probably waiting for me at our contingency location. But a single thought gave me pause.

Was I truly allowing the Assembly—who had the gall to poison their queen—run me out of my own castle?

Turning on my heel, I retraced my steps and turned down another passage. Picking up speed, I ignored every scrape of my arm against the stone walls and bit back a curse every time I stumbled over my own feet. It was so dark in the tunnel, I had to slow my pace when I made the final turn. Gingerly, I felt my way toward the end of the corridor, and a spark of hope lit in my heart when the wall abruptly turned. I reached out to my left, my fingers fumbling for the crevice and the rough fabric that covered it.

Holding my breath, I paused to listen. Silence. No one waited on the other side.

No breaths. No whispers. No heartbeats.

Still, I beckoned my shadows out of my palms, concentrating on concealing myself in their darkness. Slowly, I pushed the tapestry away from the wall and stepped out into Matthias's empty room.

MATTHIAS

No sooner had Calla disappeared than the entire forest started to fade around me as our shared dream gave way to my own solitary consciousness and the bleak emptiness that it now held. I'd been happy with my life—content.

And now I have a mate.

The cold of the dungeon seeped under my skin, and I slowly blinked as I woke up. Everything ached, but my fucking heart worst of all. She hadn't forgiven me. Not that I had expected her to, but I had certainly hoped for more time.

Or for her to at least speak to me face-to-face.

I should have said more while we were together.

I should have... No.

Calla needed time. She deserved that much. Unfortunately, given how the Assembly had reacted to my providing the poisoned dagger, time wasn't a luxury I possessed. As if to illustrate that point, the door to my cell flew open, scraping loudly against the stone floor. Two guards stomped in. I eyed them lazily.

"On your feet," one of them ordered.

Stretching my arms overhead, I yawned and took my time getting up off the floor.

"Time for my trial already?" I asked.

The only answer I received was another command. "Hands behind you."

I complied, craning my neck to peer behind me as one of them slid around to clasp cuffs on my wrists.

"Where's General Marlowe?" I asked, but again they ignored me, taking me by the arms to escort me out into the hallway. "You two can hear me, right? I haven't lost my voice, have I?"

"Matthias!" Sera called down the hallway. "What's happening?"

Raven tried to hush her from her cell. Before I could respond, the guard on my right yelled at her as he yanked me forward. "Shut your mouth, woman! This doesn't concern you."

We had barely passed out of my sister's sight when Graham came bolting around the corner, his face heated with sweat beading along his hairline. He straightened as soon as he saw me in the arms of the guards. His lips twitched as if trying not to smile at my predicament, which seemed fitting given how he'd nearly beamed at my arrest after I'd handed over the daggers.

I offered a friendly smile—just to irritate him. "Come to gloat, Graham?"

"No," he said, his expression stiffening as he worked to control his ragged breaths. His eyes glanced from one guard to the other. "Where are you taking him?"

I expected them to reprimand him as they had my sister, but instead the guard on my left lifted his chin and replied, "Assembly's ordered him be taken upstairs. Hoping to lure out the queen."

Bristling, I worked to keep my features neutral as I watched for Graham's reaction.

Graham sighed heavily and dug a piece of paper from his pocket. "I just spoke with them," he said, handing the paper over.

The guard read it over quickly before thrusting it at his counterpart. They shared a skeptical look around my head, but when they straightened, their hold on my arms tightened.

"How do we know this is from Ms. Ursula, and not a trick of yours?"

Graham stepped forward, reaching his hand out to take the paper back. "Fine. I'll just return this to the Assembly and explain how you declined the order. They're a little on edge at the moment, but I'm sure they'll understand."

The guards both went rigid, their hands loosening slightly. Another shared glance later and they marched me forward, passing me off to Graham before dashing up the stairs. Graham peered after them, and I released a tense breath.

"Did they really send you down here?" I asked. When he turned back to me, he lifted a shoulder and smirked. I couldn't help but laugh. "Mind taking these cuffs off?"

Graham shook his head and wrapped his hand around my arm as he turned to stand beside me. "Better keep the pretense up in case we run into any of the other guards, or worse, one of the Assembly."

"Can I assume you're not delivering me to them then?"

"You really think I'd do anything for those fools? We do need to get going though, before they realize what I've done," he said, nudging me toward the stairs.

Refusing to move just yet, I tossed my head back toward the hallway behind me. "Mind if I say goodbye to my sister first?"

His eyes darkened over his scowl. "No time. Calla told me to get you out, so that's what I intend to do."

"It'll only take a moment," I argued.

"And a moment is more than I have to spare with how far we need to travel," he insisted, but I stiffened in my stance and glared at him. Finally, he sighed and gestured with his hand for me to go ahead.

I hadn't even gone two steps toward their corridor when Graham let out a growled curse behind me and something pricked my neck. I tried to twist around to see what had happened, but darkness closed in, leaving me with nothing but the sound of my sister shouting my name as I fell to the floor.

CHAPTER 69

CALLA

Despite it being mid-morning, Matthias's room was as dark as nightfall with the drapes drawn tightly closed over the single window. My shadows darkened my vision further, making it nearly impossible to see where I was going as I moved further into the room. Slowly, I pulled my power back into my palms, releasing a breath as the room came into better focus. My fingers grazed the edge of the now-empty tub as I stepped around it, surveying the space and savoring his comforting scent that still remained on the air despite his absence.

Stars, I hoped Graham had been able to get him out in time. No doubt the Assembly would seek his suffering simply for being my mate. The six fae appeared in my mind's eye, sending my teeth grinding together. My hands formed tight fists at my sides, shaking with the need to do something other than hide here.

I needed Isa.

Where are you, Isa?

The door opened behind me, and I spun around, hope igniting in my chest that my friend had somehow heard my silent call and arrived, but it wasn't Isa.

Six members of the guard rushed in, their boots thundering against the floor as they circled around me. My mind raced through my options. My shadows itched to be released, to help me, but these were my guard, my protectors. I didn't want to hurt them, though I would if I absolutely had to.

"Where's General Marlowe?" I asked, looking into the face of each of the armor-clad fae. None of them met my gaze, the fucking cowards.

"We thought you might know that," a female replied from the doorway in a recognizable, pompous voice—Ursula. She strolled into the room, her slim figure silhouetted against the dim lamplight in the corridor. I wanted to send my shadows toward her, but I forced myself to remain patient. If I was going to learn anything, I needed her alive, at least for a little while longer.

"Under what authority do you command my guard, Ursula? The Assembly holds—"

"Holds all of the power should our king or queen be found incapable of ruling," she offered. "And unfortunately for you, the evidence against you is substantial enough the Assembly has assumed control."

"What evidence?"

"The healers went back over their records from the king's death per your request, and they discovered he was, in fact, poisoned."

"How does that point to me exactly? After all, you and the Assembly just had me poisoned. Why aren't you suspects?"

"Because your signature is on the shipment orders from Dolobare."

"Of course they are, but I never approved poison on those manifests," I explained.

Ursula produced a well-worn piece of paper from behind her back and brought it closer for me to read. She pointed to a line in the list of items.

"This, right here. What is it?"

I narrowed my eyes and read aloud: "Shadowsong, liquid." I peered up at the advisor. "I have never heard of this before. I

438

certainly didn't put it on this list. And why would poison be listed so clearly? Do you even know that's the poison?"

"Yet you signed your name to have it shipped here, without knowing what it is?"

"I approve a lot of items requested by the healers—from those at the castle and throughout our kingdom—"

"And you never thought to ask what this was?"

"I trust our healers, but unless you know for certain that this *Shadowsong* is the actual poison used on my husband, you have no reason to arrest me simply for an unknown substance on a manifest."

Ursula angled her head, her brow lifting crookedly. "Your own healers had poison available for the trials."

I wanted to remind her that was the poison she'd just used on her queen, but I held it back. Barely.

"The poison in the healers' possession was from a small stash retrieved from a group of rebels we caught years ago in our efforts to help Emeryn."

Ursula's chin lifted, her eyes darting to one of the guards as she flicked her fingers in the air. "Check her pockets."

The guard on my left stepped toward me, and my shadows—spurred on by my sudden burst of anxiety—flew from my palms, splaying my fingers. They shot straight for the guard, burrowing into his nose and ears. He opened his mouth to scream, but my shadows extinguished any sound, drowning him in darkness as they traveled through his body, wreaking havoc on his organs until he fell in a lifeless heap at the floor.

It took the span of a single breath to fell one guard, and I was foolishly so transfixed on my own power I didn't notice Ursula flick her fingers again.

Arms wrapped around my shoulders and pinned my arms to my sides. Two guards moved in, holding large pieces of metal connected together by hinges. I tried to redirect my shadows, but I wasn't fast enough. Two more guards approached, each taking hold of one of my forearms, using both hands to hold me steady.

My shadows finally reacted, swirling around my attackers' heads, trying to obscure their vision, but somehow this didn't hinder them from clamping the metal—iron—contraptions on my hands.

No!

My shadows vanished at once, recoiling.

With all my strength I thrust my knee into the groin of the male in front of me. He doubled over but recovered quickly, bringing the back of his hand to strike me across the face as if I were some common criminal and not his queen. The strike sent my head flying to the side, but I refused to cry out in pain. Instead, a growl erupted from my chest, and I put all my strength into getting free.

"Seriously, three of you should be able to hold her," Ursula chided, smirking at me as I twisted and pulled and kicked to get away. "Someone check her pockets."

What did she think was in my pockets? This was ridiculous. What could they possibly expect to find?

One of the guards came forward and almost seemed apologetic—the only thing that kept me from kneeing her in the face as she reached her hand into one pocket and then the other. I was about to gloat over them finding nothing when the guard lifted a clear bottle I'd never seen before.

I stilled. My blood froze with dread only to shift in the next breath, my growing rage heating it to near boiling as I watched Ursula stretch out her hand for the vial. She held it up to peer through it.

"Seems we have every right to arrest you, Your *Majesty*."

"I don't even know what that is!" I spat at her, but somehow I knew it was the poison. Even if it wasn't, they would force the healers to declare it was just to rip me from power.

I threw all my weight forward as if to attack her, but the guards held firm, and all I achieved was to cause a searing pain in my shoulders as my arms were held behind me. Cuffs slammed onto my wrists below the iron gloves. The chains rattled as I continued to struggle to get at Ursula.

How did it get into my pocket?

Who had been close enough to—

Graham.

My whole body froze except for my chest, which heaved faster and faster as this new betrayal took hold of my heart. I wanted to double over and retch, but the guards held me upright.

No. He'd been my friend for years. Decades! He wouldn't.

I glared at Ursula through hot tears.

"How?" I hissed out. "How did you threaten him to get him to help you?"

Ursula's empty hand flew to her chest. "Threaten? Threaten whom exactly?"

"Graham." His name was ash on my tongue.

Ursula's dry cackle rent the air. "Oh, Your Majesty, this was his idea."

My eyes closed as my head dropped to my chest, but I refused to shed a fucking tear over that traitor, instead clinging to the bitter hatred brewing in my veins. The bastard would die for this —painfully and slowly.

I barely listened to Ursula's prattling. "This holds a striking resemblance to the poison used in the trial," she said, clicking her tongue at me. "We'll have the healers determine what it is just to be sure."

Ursula's lips curled into a sneer as she stepped closer, and she dropped her voice into a whisper. "I wonder, though, will you choose to die by poison like your husband? Or to hang like your mate?"

CHAPTER 70

MATTHIAS

If I never got poisoned again, it would be all too soon. How much poison could someone take before it eventually killed him? Or could I potentially develop an immunity to it? That would be decidedly better, but that was not at all helpful to me now as I sat here in a dark, dank prison cell. From the pitching and rolling of the floor, and the water seeping in through the wooden wall opposite me, it wasn't hard to conclude I was on a stars-damned ship.

Which meant we probably weren't heading to Emeryn, leaving only one likely destination: Dolobare.

Stretching, I winced as the metal bars of my cage dug into my shoulder blades.

"Ah, you're finally awake," a voice noted from behind me.

I peeked over my shoulder at Graham, who leaned against the ladder that led to the upper decks. "So Calla asked you to poison me and throw me into the belly of a boat?"

"Ship," Graham corrected under his breath. "And no, I don't answer to Calla anymore. Soon, no one will."

I stilled, studying the fae, trying to piece together his plans. The lingering poison, however, fogged my brain and made it nearly impossible to follow one train of thought through to completion.

"So, you're giving up and running away?" I asked, cringing at the throbbing ache sitting behind my eyes.

Graham sneered. "Hardly."

I waited for him to elaborate, raising a crooked brow at him in hopes of spurring him into saying more, but he didn't. Sighing, I turned back around and laid my head against the bars, letting my eyes drift closed. "Why don't you wake me when you're ready to talk."

Sucking in a loud breath, Graham slowly approached. "As if I owe you any sort of explanation."

"You're right," I said around a half-hearted smile. "You don't. So if you don't mind, I'd like to sleep off the last bit of this fucking poison you jabbed me with."

"I don't answer to you either," Graham snarled, and I nearly laughed at the annoyed expression I envisioned on his face.

"Fair," I mumbled. When he didn't leave, I shifted my head against the bars and asked, "Aren't you the slightest bit worried about what Calla will do when she learns you've kidnapped her mate?"

"Not if the Assembly follows my orders."

My eyes popped open, my jaw tensed, and I slowly shifted around to stare up at him through the bars.

Graham scoffed lightly. "What? No pithy remark now?"

"*Your* orders," I said.

Graham nodded smugly.

"Have to admit, you had me fooled," I said, my mind racing through all of Graham's actions during the trials. "Here I thought you were just bitter from unrequited love—broken-hearted and wracked with jealousy."

"Jealous of what—you?"

I ignored his question. "I mean, is all of this because Calla rejected you—repeatedly, I assume?" I paused to note the way his jaw pulsed and his lips pressed together. "Or was she always just a means to an end, an easy path to power and prestige?"

"Why does it matter? Either way, I'm winning." His smug smile tried to return, but it was marred now by his obvious irritation.

"I merely wondered why. Seems like quite the complicated endeavor just to steal a throne, no?"

"None of this had to happen," he seethed. "No one had to die. Their blood is on *her* hands, not mine. I simply wanted the status and power that was owed to me—that was denied me."

"Ah. Of course. Everything is everyone else's fault, right? Your life is so hard, so unfair." Angling my head, I regarded him curiously. "Aren't you tired of always being the victim?"

A sneer curled Graham's lips. "Says the one who's been poisoned...how many times now?"

"A few, but remember, one of those was self-inflicted," I reminded him, pleased by how my attitude crept under his skin, his eyes flashing with anger beneath deep creases in his brow.

"And aren't *you* tired of always failing?" Graham spat out the question, but I found it hard not to chuckle.

"Failure brings growth," I said, shrugging.

"Will you still feel that way when your mate is dead? When you fail to save her?"

Against my will, the memory of Calla slumped in her chair swarmed me, and I recalled the panic that had flooded my veins when she didn't wake up after I'd kissed her. Drawing in a breath —and trying not to gag on the putrid scent riding the air—I calmed my nerves and my heart as best I could. Turning my face back around to stare at the wall, I pulled in one more breath and let it soothe away the tension until my shoulders slumped and my jaw relaxed.

"You underestimate her. Everyone does. She won't be that easy to kill, and I think you know that."

"The rest of her family died easily enough. She will too."

This pulled another laugh from deep in my chest. "If you

truly believed that, then you wouldn't be fleeing across a fucking sea."

Graham's scoff gave way to a low growl, a hint of fear sparking in his expression, but he said nothing.

"No. You're scared of her."

"Don't be—"

"And you fucking should be."

CHAPTER 71

CALLA

Isa still hadn't come for me.

Granted it had been only a handful of hours, but that was longer than I'd expected from my best warrior...my best friend.

What if she betrays me like Graham did?

The thought pinched my heart.

How many betrayals could someone endure before the pain charred their heart and they decided to burn the whole world? Of course, at this moment in this iron room with nothing but a bucket in the corner, I couldn't do anything—let alone destroy everything. Stars, I could barely use that damned bucket with these iron gloves on my hands.

Ursula hadn't said how long I would remain here, claiming my trial was still being debated by the Assembly. Whether that debate was to determine the date of said trial or to have a trial at all didn't matter much to me. The one consolation I had was the shocked hurt that had played on Ursula's face when we arrived in the dungeon to find the door to Matthias's cell open and the room empty.

Ursula had screamed at the guards holding my chains, as if they could have possibly known what had happened when they'd been with her arresting me the entire time. It had been Sera who had blurted out a single word from her cell down the hallway.

"Graham."

Graham.

The bastard.

I spent the first hours in the dungeon wondering where Isa was, how Matthias was doing, and what I would do to Graham when I finally got a hold of him.

I simply needed Isa to get me out of here.

Until then, all I could do was wait.

❧

After the pair of guards left with my empty supper plate—and I recovered from the humiliation of having to be fed by them—I settled myself on the floor and counted the rivets on the cell door until exhaustion finally claimed me.

At first there was only darkness, but just as disappointment kicked in, the void around me faded slowly until I was surrounded by the forest once again. I wasn't near the edge of the forest as I had been in that last dream. Instead, I was kneeling in the mud and leaves, the rhythmic pounding of a horses' hooves pulling my gaze over my shoulder, where my horse's tail disappeared into the trees.

"Matthias?" I queried the stillness, my voice so meek and piti-ful, I cringed. Pivoting onto my backside, I brushed the muck from my hands as I surveyed the forest.

Please be here. Please be here.

How were these bonded dreams supposed to work anyway?

They seemed highly inefficient and pointless—no different than mediocre, single-minded dreams if I couldn't call to him to meet me. I hated waiting.

Waiting in my dream.

Waiting in the dungeon.

Heaving a sigh, I slammed my palms back into the dirt to push myself to my feet when a hand appeared before my face.

But it wasn't Matthias's eyes peering down at me. Brennan stood over me, that mischievous smile of his beaming. My heart lit up at the sight of him, but not in the way it had before. Raven was right. The bond had altered my feelings.

Slipping my hand into Brennan's, I let him pull me to my feet. "How are you here?" I asked, dropping my eyes to his chest.

When he spoke, though, it wasn't his voice. It was Graham's.

"It didn't have to be this way. You could have just picked me."

My whole body trembled as I yanked my hand from his and retreated backwards, shaking my head. This wasn't real. He wasn't really here. This was just a regular, run-of-the-mill bad dream. Glancing around, I searched for any sign of Matthias, any hint he was sharing this dream with me.

"Matthias!" I called, spinning around in the trees, the forest becoming a blur as I turned and searched.

"Calla, wake up." A voice pierced my consciousness, but it wasn't his, and I resisted its command, desperate to remain in the one place where I could find my mate and talk to him and make sure he was okay.

"Calla, wake up," the voice repeated, and something gripped my shoulders, shaking me as I clamped my eyes closed, not wanting to see anyone but my mate. "It's me, Isa!"

Her name yanked me from my dream, and slowly I opened my eyes to find myself back in my cell and staring at my best friend.

"We have to move." She started to haul me up to my feet, but then stopped, noticing my iron-clad hands.

"Where have you been?" I asked as she studied the contraptions encasing my hands and shadows.

"Explanations come later." Her eyes snapped up to mine. "How do we get these off?"

I shook my head. "I don't know. The guards might have the keys? Who keeps the keys to the cells?"

"They wouldn't make it that easy. You can't conjure your shadows to help break free?"

"First thing I tried, and no, not without blinding pain. Even with the pain I don't know if I can hold them steady long enough to free the lock."

"Ursula?" Isa asked.

"Her or Warren maybe?"

"Okay," she said, lowering my hands back into my lap and gripping my shoulder reassuringly. "I will find the keys, but until we can get those off, I want you to stay here."

Before I could protest, she was at the door and slipping through the tight opening.

"Isa," I called after her, and she poked her head back inside. "Where is he?"

My friend swallowed hard, her eyes darting back to the corridor. When she turned back to me, she didn't meet my stare, shame pulling at her features as if all of this was her fault.

"Graham is taking him to Dolobare."

CHAPTER 72

MATTHIAS

I didn't know how many dreams I spent searching for Calla, but she never appeared. Did the bond have some sort of range? Maybe we simply weren't catching each other at the same time. That was a far nicer idea than the alternative: that she simply wasn't thinking of me.

We'd been sailing for what seemed like a fortnight, but based on the number of meals one of the crew had brought me—if one could call maggoty bread and flat ale a meal at all—it was no more than a few days. Four, at most.

Graham didn't visit me again, which might have offended me had I not wanted to gut him with my bare hands. It was a colossal waste of energy to imagine all the ways of killing him, and it did nothing for my plummeting morale, so I tried to focus instead on Calla.

My mate.

Shadow Keeper. Queen.

My best friend's brother's widow.

I cringed every time I reminded myself of that fact, and no matter how often I tried to shrug it off as the stars' bad joke, the awkward discomfort remained. Would Connor and Lieke understand? They had to. They were the most hopeless romantics I'd ever met. If anyone could understand, it would be them.

An intense rumbling vibrated the entirety of the ship, pulling me out of my thoughts. Pushing to my feet, I steadied myself against the bars. The ship was slowing. They must have been lowering the anchor—my best guess, as someone who knew little-to-nothing about ships.

A moment later, Graham was stepping down the ladder, a set of chained cuffs in one hand.

"Time to go," he said. "Give me your wrists, and don't do anything stupid. The entire crew has orders to kill you if you arrive above deck without me."

Obliging, I allowed him to bind my arms together and lead me up out of the ship's belly. I squinted against the drastic shift in light despite the overcast sky. Dark gray clouds hid the sun and made it impossible to determine the time. The small crew—a rough and haggard group who rivaled even the surliest of crowds Connor and I had met in the taverns around Emeryn—filled the deck, hands either gripping their weapons or hovering at their hilts. Graham said nothing to anyone, only nodded at a male sporting an impressive hat and an even more impressive beard before dragging me across a wide plank that connected the ship to the simple, narrow dock.

It wasn't until my feet were on solid ground again that I got a good look at my surroundings, and I couldn't tell which dropped lower, my jaw or my stomach.

The land—Dolobare—was like no place I'd visited on Sandur-dam. Steep cliffs of jagged black rock lined the coastline, their peaks lost in the thick mist high above. In the distance, white falls cascaded down narrow crevices along the mountainsides, only to disappear into the rock. Cold and desolate, the land appeared devoid of any vegetation, and if not for the dock beneath my feet and the few buildings dotting the black sand beach, I would have assumed it was devoid of life altogether. Though, as we neared the end of the dock,

I realized the buildings were in various states of disrepair with roof thatching caving in, doors hanging askew, and glass in the windows cracked or shattered. Further down the coast, rock and timber littered the sand, possibly the ruins of the rest of the village.

"A bustling port of trade, I see," I said, hoping my sarcastic tone was sufficient to hide the apprehension swirling in my gut.

"Once was," Graham noted. "At least, so I'm told."

"What happened here exactly?"

Graham whispered a single word, "Nightwalkers."

I swallowed hard. "Are they still here?"

He shrugged and continued walking up the beach toward the cliffs, yanking hard on the chain so that I nearly lost my balance. The chilled air nipped at my skin as we trudged on.

"Where are these human friends of yours anyway?" I asked, though I expected him to ignore me.

He ignored my question. "What do you know of the island?"

"Only that the nightwalkers—who make exceptional brandy —fled here when the war broke out, while the humans—who presumably create the poison wreaking havoc on Sandurdam— aren't happy to share the island with their new neighbors."

"And why should they, when those neighbors use them as food?" Graham asked, a hint of humor present, as if he held the humans in such little regard as to ridicule them for not wanting to be drained of their own blood.

"The island is ruled by the nightwalkers, though, and—like us in Emeryn—they've been struggling to eradicate the human rebellion."

Graham was silent for a bit as he led me into a narrow canyon barely the width of three males standing shoulder-to-shoulder. Staring up the sheer rock faces towering over us, I shivered at the expanse of mist that seemed to be closing in on us from above. The ground slowly shifted from sand to rocky soil, though I still found no sign of any flora.

"Funny," Graham said. He kept his voice low, but it did little to prevent it from echoing around us. "All the benefits we immortals possess have mattered little in this war against the humans."

"Who said it was a war?" I asked. "It's not—"

"Perhaps that's why you're losing, general."

I sucked in a sharp breath. Was this pitiful excuse for a fae actually right? Were we—both fae and nightwalker—failing to overcome the rebellions because we didn't take them seriously enough?

"You think Calla had it right then? Exile or kill all of them?"

Graham wrinkled his nose at me, not out of disgust, but as if he were legitimately pondering the question. "I don't know. Maybe. But then again, the humans have proved rather helpful for my ambitions."

This nearly had me stopping in my tracks, but pretending to stumble, I forced myself to keep up with my captor. What were his ambitions? The way he'd said that implied the humans had done more than simply provide him with the poison, but what else had they done?

Wrenwick.

I'd nearly forgotten Calla's words from our dream. The humans in Wrenwick had killed Brennan, and they could have quite easily done that at Graham's behest. But then wouldn't Minerva's spell have pointed to Graham instead of the Olanders?

Tricky mage.

It was like that old myth the humans once believed about not making deals with us fae, as though we all took some wicked delight in toying with mortals. Of course, there were some delights to be had with them—some of them, perhaps, even a little on the wicked side—but not in the sense the humans believed. No, it wasn't the fae that deserved such suspicion; it was the mages.

Or rather, *the* mage.

Minerva was the only one I'd ever heard of, though she had mentioned a sister once. Something about her being lost in time and space, but that seemed nothing more than the nonsensical ramblings of a psychotic recluse.

Pulling my mind back to the present, I followed Graham further and further into this trench. After several minutes of nothing but our boots scuffing against the ground, I sighed loudly, if only to irritate my companion.

"If I'd known we were going on such a long hike, I would have requested provisions," I said.

Graham didn't look back at me but tugged on the chain lead once more. "As if you were in any position to make such a request."

"Whether you listen or not, there's nothing to stop me from asking."

This time he did peer over his shoulder, a smirk creeping across his lips. "A swift punch to the face? A gag? More poison?"

"I could still talk with a swollen lip, can make obnoxious noises around a gag, and, well, rendering me unconscious doesn't seem a viable option. Would be a shame for you to hurt your back trying to carry me."

"You do love the sound of your own voice, don't you?" He snapped his head back around.

"It is pretty nice. I mean, Calla seems to appreciate it." I watched Graham's back as I mentioned the queen, but he neither tensed nor bristled in response, two reactions I would have expected if he were doing this all out of jealousy.

"Too bad she'll never hear it again," he said.

"You don't expect her to find me? I am her mate after all." Again, no reaction, except a slight tremor through his shoulders when he laughed.

"It will be rather hard for her to reach you here—at least in time to do anything to save you."

"Is that why—"

Graham held up a hand, his feet skidding to a stop, and I clamped my mouth shut on my unfinished question. His head shifted to the left and then to the right.

"What is it?" I hissed.

Before he could answer, a tall figure seemed to slip out from the rock fifty meters ahead of us. He didn't approach, but remained standing, his feet set firmly and arms crossed at his midsection. A sentry of some kind. He had to be a good half-meter taller than either of us, his black eyes glaring down at us as if we were nothing but inconsequential vermin about to be exterminated. From this distance I could see the ink that decorated his hands and neck, but I couldn't make out what the designs were. His rounded ears indicated he was no fae—at least not a full fae.

Graham took a bold step forward, which pulled the chain between us taut so that my arms extended out straight in front of me.

"Alek," he said, and the stranger dipped his chin slightly in recognition. "I'm here to see the Lassiters."

Alek started to shake his head before Graham was finished. He pointed a long, slender finger my way. "Not with him."

Now Graham bristled. I nearly chuckled at seeing him so perturbed.

"He's a gift, a fae. Thought they could use him."

"Perhaps you should have checked first," Alek said, and I might have liked this guy's matter-of-fact handling of Graham if it wasn't for the discomfort he sent shooting through my veins.

"Can I at least plead my case before they decline?" Graham asked.

"Not with him," Alek repeated. His dark eyes flashed to mine, and despite my longing to look away, I couldn't.

Graham huffed out an impatient groan. "Can you watch him?"

"I'm not a babysitter," he said, and I could have sworn a smile almost cracked through his cold demeanor.

"Last I checked, that was exactly what you were." Graham sniggered.

In a flash, Alek was standing in front of Graham, looming

over him. His spindly fingers snatched Graham up by the neck and lifted him off the ground until their eyes were level.

"Careful how you speak to me, worm," Alek hissed. Graham tried to speak, but only rasped groans escaped him. "You aren't the only contact we have on Sandurdam. You are replaceable, and you only draw breath right now out of my good graces. Understand?"

He maintained his hold on Graham's throat as his black eyes shifted to mine again, but this time he looked me over like he was assessing a cow at the market.

"Who is he anyway?" When no response came, he slid his gaze back to Graham and released him, letting him fall to the ground in a gasping heap. I winced at the crack his knees made against the rocky ground. Graham's head hovered low as he struggled to catch his breath.

Without looking up, he answered Alek in a rough whisper. "No one of consequence."

Alek's laughter boomed through the pass. "If he is so inconsequential, why not throw him into the Laraburn? Why keep him alive?"

I had to admit, it was the question that had bombarded me since he'd taken me from the dungeon.

Graham, still bent over, shook his head slowly. "Pain. He deserves pain, as does his mate."

Crooking a brow at me, Alek frowned as he pondered this. "There are painful ways to kill him without bringing him here."

"Nothing compares to what the Lassiters could inflict on him," Graham explained, groaning as he pushed up to his feet.

Alek didn't disagree but simply lifted one shoulder. "Very well then. I can take you to West Peak--until they decide what to do with you both."

CHAPTER 73

CALLA

Every time my door opened, my heart spiked with foolish hope, but it was never Isa. Three times a day it was the same pair of guards delivering—and feeding me—my meals. Each morning and evening, Jocelyn arrived with an escort to administer my tonic. Apparently, the iron gloves weren't enough to put the Assembly at ease; they needed to ensure I was emotionally stable, to the point that they even insisted the guard verify I had consumed the entire mug before they left me alone again. The guard's constant scrutiny prevented me from ever asking Jocelyn if she'd seen Isa.

By the third day, my hope had dwindled to a mere sliver—that was promptly crushed that morning when my usual guards didn't come to deliver my breakfast. Instead, four new guards arrived—two with swords drawn, one carrying a piece of black cloth, and the last holding an iron collar.

"Where are you taking me?" I asked. Lifting my chin, I fought to maintain my regal stature, but my stoic expression was slipping before I could even get the first words out. If the guards noticed the fear present in my eyes, they didn't let on, graciously allowing me to hold on to some bit of dignity.

The guard who responded—a male whose name I didn't

remember—seemed almost apologetic as he said, "To see the Assembly, Your Majesty."

Part of me relaxed at not hearing the word *gallows*, but the practical part of me wasn't so easily fooled. The gallows could quite easily be the next stop after those wretches.

"Is that"—I pointed a stiff finger at the collar—"entirely necessary?"

"Only if you resist," the male said, shrugging. "We do need to use this, though."

He lifted the black cloth up, pulling his hands apart to reveal it was a hood.

"Why? Where is the Assembly that I'm not allowed to know their whereabouts? Are they not in the castle?"

The guards exchanged timid looks but provided no clarification.

"Fine."

No sooner had I uttered the word than the two armed guards stepped forward and took hold of my elbows, aiming the tips of their blades at my neck and gut. Sucking in a deep breath, I summoned every bit of courage in my veins as the male stepped forward and lifted the hood up over my head. I remained relatively calm until he cinched the opening of the hood closed loosely around my neck, preventing any light from entering. Swallowing hard, I attempted to maintain control over my thumping heart and quickened breaths.

The door to my cell slid open—known to me only because I'd grown accustomed to how it roughly grated against the stone floor—and the guards marched me out. The dungeon was quiet aside from the steady footsteps of my procession, until Raven's voice echoed off the walls.

"Fight, Calla! Do not let them win!"

I allowed myself a small smile. One of my guards diverted down the hallway, and I flinched at the loud clang as they struck the bars.

"Quiet, woman," the guard snarled, but Raven called out again all the same.

"He needs you!"

Matthias's face flashed in my mind. Dread pooled in my empty stomach.

How could she expect me to save him when I couldn't even free myself?

After being cooped up in the small cell, even for only a handful of days, my legs and feet fatigued faster than usual. Thankfully, they weren't leading me to the assembly room on the upper floor; one more flight of stairs and I likely would have collapsed. Where *were* they taking me, though? Where else could the Assembly possibly want to meet?

A door creaked quietly open, and I nearly tripped over the threshold as they led me outside where the sun warmed my arms. Closing my eyes, I focused on my other senses, desperate for any hints of what awaited me. No scent of hay or stamping hooves—meaning no carriage.

"Stairs down," one of the guards warned quietly, and to my surprise, they slowed our pace to help me navigate the steps.

Gravel crunched beneath our feet, and I envisioned the castle grounds in my mind in a desperate attempt to map our movements. Continuing straight, we were obviously traveling down the long driveway. Through the hood, I caught the faint scent of decaying leaves and soil coming from the forest on either side of us.

When we finally turned, shadows engulfed us, chilling my skin. I scrambled to a stop and tried to pull my arms back to keep the guards from venturing too far into the forest.

"We can't," I said. "You can't."

The two guards on either side of me hauled me forward by my arms. Fingers pressed between my shoulder blades, nudging me to keep moving.

The fourth guard—who seemed altogether too nice to be doing the bidding of the Assembly—gently explained. "We would not enter your woods unprepared, Your Majesty. Keep moving. It's not much further now."

"It's not like she cares about us," the voice behind me grumbled. "If she had her hands free, we'd all be dead in that dungeon."

I didn't bother to correct him, because if I was being honest, I didn't know what I would have done to them if I had access to my shadows.

The kind guard, though, did respond. "Careful how you speak about her. She could kill you yet."

I didn't hear how the other three reacted to that, because a new sound caught my attention: whispered voices and pounding heartbeats—a lot of them. I couldn't quite make out what they were saying, but underneath it all. The forest remained relatively still and quiet. With this many bodies gathered, the trees and vines should have been far more active. Instead, I could only catch the barest rustle of vine against dirt and the slightest creak of shifting bark.

"Ah, you're here." My stomach turned at Ursula's pompous tone. All whispering died away, but a muted grunting persisted.

"Am I to stay in the dark then?" I asked.

Ursula cackled. "Of course not. Your reaction is half of the fun, after all."

While she spoke, the guard worked to loosen the hood's opening. It didn't take long for my eyes to adjust to the dim forest light when the fabric lifted away. The Assembly—all six members—formed a semi-circle around me, with Ursula and Warren standing in the middle studying me with wild anticipation. The other four fidgeted uncomfortably but didn't bother to protest what was happening either.

Warren gestured to the two guards still holding me. "Secure her."

My gaze dropped to the forest floor, where two iron anchors had been driven into the ground on either side of where I stood. I didn't fight as they disconnected the chains binding my hands and attached them to the anchors.

"Is this truly necessary?" Fern asked timidly, peering up at Ursula on her right.

Yuri chimed in, noting, "She was given her tonic, yes?"

Warren's dark eyes continued to burn into mine as he answered, "The tonic only helps to subdue her powers and prevent them from going rogue when her emotions spike. Unfortunately, it doesn't actually stop her from using them."

No one else spoke, though Fern and Yuri did offer me sympathetic looks—as if that was enough to garner mercy from me. No, I'd remember how they stood here and watched their peers attack me. No one would escape my justice.

The other advisors stood triumphantly, as if they'd already won, but chained or not, I wasn't beaten yet.

Failure wasn't an option.

Giving up wasn't an option.

Dying wasn't a stars-damned option.

Warren and Ursula glanced at one another, brows crooking and lips curling as they held some silent conversation. When Ursula gave an almost imperceptible nod, they pivoted away, watching me intently as they instructed the rest of the Assembly to step aside to reveal Isa's limp form suspended above the ground by the forest's vines.

CHAPTER 74

MATTHIAS

Alek led us to the West Peak, which turned out to not be a peak at all, but a series of caverns tucked into the black rock of the canyon, accessed by a near-invisible crevice I never would have noticed had I not watched the man disappear into it. The first room held little more than a small desk, a chair in the center, and a simple cot against one wall.

"Stay here," Alek commanded. As he turned to leave, Graham grabbed his arm but pulled his hand away quickly when Alek's stony glare dropped to where he'd dared touch him.

"What am I to do with him?" Graham asked.

Alek dropped his head to the side to survey the fae. "I don't care what you do, as long as you don't leave these rooms."

Something the man said piqued Graham's interest, and his head whipped around toward the archway in the back wall. He thrust my chains into Alek's unwilling hands and rushed around the desk. After he had disappeared into the next room, Alek cast a disinterested look my way.

"Why does he want to hurt you so badly?" he asked, sliding his tongue along the edge of his top teeth.

"I didn't think you cared," I said with mock endearment.

"I don't," he said. "But it's good to have as much information as possible when fae scum arrive unannounced."

I nodded at his explanation. "I'm not entirely sure."

"But if you had to guess?" I shrugged, spinning my ring on my middle finger as I pretended to think, not sure how much information I wanted to share with this stranger. He pursed his lips thoughtfully. "Steal his lover? Seduce the queen? Or..." He leaned in closer and raised an amused brow. "Did you reject his advances?"

A quiet laugh escaped me. "More or less."

I was about to ask what was in the other room when Alek straightened, turning his gaze back to where Graham had reappeared with a wicked glint in his eyes.

"Can you help me out before you go?" Graham asked, gesturing toward the back room.

I lifted my shackled hands to my chest. "I don't—" I started, but Graham scowled. Pulling my eyes wide in feigned embarrassed shock, I shoved my hands toward Alek. "Oh, you mean him. Right. Of course. That makes more sense."

"Do they find you funny back home?" Graham asked, still frowning.

I didn't get a chance to answer that obviously rhetorical question, because Alek was already leading me across the room, though he didn't hand me over to Graham like I expected him to.

"No," Alek said flatly.

Graham scoffed, pivoting around to throw his hand toward the other room. "All I need is help restraining him."

Alek didn't move except to say, "You should have thought of that before you brought him here."

"Fine," Graham grumbled, snatching the chain out of Alek's grasp and yanking me forward. "How long do you think it will be?"

"I don't know," Alek said, his empty response irking Graham so much I barely contained my laughter.

Rolling his eyes like an irritated adolescent, Graham let a growl escape and dragged me into the other room.

"Good luck," Alek muttered, and I shot him a curious glance.

"Thought you didn't care."

"Still don't," he said and turned on his heel, leaving me alone with Graham and whatever was in this back room.

CHAPTER 75
CALLA

Tree roots shifted around Isa's feet, slowly pulling her into the ground like a snake swallowing its prey. Vines, though, kept her upright, wrapping around her arms from shoulders to hands where they had pierced her palms, their spiked ends wriggling in the air as if inviting me to come free her.

Ice shot through my veins, pulling all the color from my face. Heaving, I nearly doubled over as my stomach lurched, sending bile up into my throat. I fought it back and focused instead on stoking the fiery rage they'd kindled

Someone was speaking, but I couldn't hear their words. All I heard was Isa's thready heartbeat. Her eyelids fluttered, but didn't open completely. She wasn't dead. Yet.

Each breath fed the flames in my chest. My shadows curled and writhed within me, like they were gearing up for battle.

"Hang on, Isa. I'll get you out of here," I said, only realizing I'd uttered the words aloud when the Assembly began to laugh. Ursula's cackle broke through my muffled hearing, so I heard her response clearly.

"How are you going to do that, *Your Majesty*?"

Her mockery of my title only served to feed my fury. I shot my hands out at her, a silent scream escaping my lips, but the chains pulled taut as the anchors held fast. Searing pain engulfed my palms as my shadows met the inside of the iron gloves. My fingers clawed against the metal, agony tearing through my hands. Still I persisted, spurred on by Ursula and Warren's jeering.

"I think she's actually trying to free herself," Warren noted.

Fern's hand lifted to her mouth, her eyes tearing up, though still she remained silent. The entire Assembly—aside from Ursula and Warren—simply stood there, watching, letting this happen.

Warren, chuckling haughtily, strolled forward to peer up at Isa's slackened face.

"Wake up, general! Would be a shame for you to miss this display of affection from your queen." He glared at me over his shoulder, but continued to speak to Isa. "You should really see her try, though. She must actually care about you. Too bad it won't work."

As if on cue, another vine dropped down from the canopy and began to wind itself around Isa's throat.

Ursula turned to Warren, shaking her head. "This is so much better than having to rely on others to kill the king and queen, isn't it?"

My parents? Did they know who—had they been the ones to—

I tried to push more of my energy into my hands, but the excruciating pain threatened to blind me as my vision started to warp at the edges. My shadows pushed back against me, crawling back into my veins.

No. They couldn't retreat. They couldn't give up.

My hands fell to my sides. My chin dropped to my chest. My whole body trembled.

Silently, I pleaded with my shadows. With each ragged breath I begged them to listen, to regroup, to try again. I tried to lift my hands, but they seemed so heavy now, like the earth had a hold of my chains and was fighting me. I peered down, sure I would see the vines working against me, but there was nothing there except the dirt and leaves beneath my boots and my chains secured to the anchors.

My shadows gathered in my chest, embracing my heart, as if promising me it would all be okay.

Ursula leaned forward, bending down as if she were speaking to a child and not her queen. "Just stop, Calla. We all know you can't win here. Stop fighting it."

Do not let them win!

Raven's words roared through my mind, and my shadows reacted. Releasing my heart, they billowed into a savage tempest, but instead of rushing to my palms, they flooded my lungs, choking off my breath. My head snapped up, and my eyes met Ursula's. Fear flashed in her expression when my jaw fell open and my shadows surged from between my lips, heading straight for the female.

Ursula tried to scramble backwards, but my power punched through her body, impaling her as effortlessly as if she were mere shadow herself. Blood gushed from countless wounds, soaking through her bodice. Her hands clamped down over her stomach in a futile attempt to staunch the bleeding. Falling to her knees, she gaped in terror as my shadows gathered around her.

"Stop her!" Warren screamed, but he made no attempt to help his fellow advisor. My shadows, however, were no longer tethered to me as they normally were, and the guards shifted nervously beside me as I stood calmly watching my enemy's demise.

"Call them back," one of the guards—the nicer of the lot—requested.

"Not yet." I bit out the words and pursed my lips, refusing to glance away from where my shadows now poured down Ursula's throat, flowing into her ears, drowning her in my bitter darkness and sweet revenge.

In my periphery, Warren crept backwards, foolishly thinking I wouldn't notice him trying to retreat. He was behind two of the other Assembly members when I jerked my head in his direction. Whether some invisible connection still existed between my shadows and me or not, they heeded my command regardless, abandoning Ursula to chase down the fleeing male.

Two other Assembly members darted forward to avoid my shadows' path, but I wasn't after them—not yet, anyway. The darkness coiled around Warren, lifting him off the ground and whisking him back to face me. They held him tightly, a little more than an arm's length away. Though the stench of his fear hovered in the air around us, he glared at me with burning defiance.

"Kill me. Kill us all. But you won't reach him in time. He'll die across the sea, just like your parents."

The shadows tightened until he gasped painfully for air. Still, he sneered at me.

"No amount of spilled blood will fix your failings. They'll still be dead, all because you—"

I lifted my chin and gulped down a deep breath, and I couldn't help but smirk at the traitor as my shadows flooded his yapping mouth. Choking, he lifted his hands to his neck, clawing at his throat as if he could somehow rip the darkness out of himself. Suffocation alone was too good for him, though. My next command rumbled in the back of my throat like a feral growl, and jerking my chained hands behind me as far as they would go, I summoned them.

Bursting outward, my shadows ripped through Warren, leaving no piece of him untouched by my power, reducing him to ash floating down to the forest floor.

The surviving advisors and guards all took an instinctive step back, and some looked ready to scurry away like hares preparing to outrun a fox. My shadows swelled in front of me, ready to be sent after the rest of those responsible for this, but my eyes fell on Isa, still caught in the forest's vines. Silently, I beckoned my powers to me, and they slowly gathered around my feet like a dark fog.

"Guard," I said, quietly, taking stock of where the remnants of the Assembly remained frozen. The kinder male cautiously stepped closer.

"Yes?"

"Do you have a knife?"

His face twisted as he stammered out, "Yes."

I shifted my gaze to his and lifted my arm nearest him. "I need you to draw some of my blood and take it to the general. It doesn't need to be a lot, but she needs a few drops placed anywhere on her."

He hesitated, as if this was some elaborate ruse to get him to come even closer.

My husband was dead. My parents were dead. Maybe Matthias, too. But I could still save Isa, if he would just listen to me.

Swallowing back my grief, I forced the words out on a hoarse whisper. "Please. Save her."

The guard studied me with narrowed eyes, and I closed mine. Isa would die because of me, because I'd let myself become such a monster that my own guards didn't trust me.

A blade hissed out of its leather sheath, and then I felt a sharp sting as it sliced against my upper arm. I opened my eyes in time to see the guard collecting deep red drops on the flat of his blade. Without another word, he jogged over to Isa, leaped onto the still-writhing roots, and wiped the blood on her neck.

He was still standing on the roots when they retreated, along with the vines. Jumping back down to solid ground, he reached his arms forward to cradle Isa as the forest released her.

"Take her to the infirmary, find Jocelyn. If she's been given any poison, Jocelyn is the only one who can help her."

The guard transferred her into the arms of one of the others, reiterating my directions and adding the command to hurry. I turned as they carried her away, back through the dense forest.

"I can't let you hurt the others," the guard said, pulling my attention back to him.

"I don't intend to," I said. "Not yet, anyway."

Suspicion once again crossed his expression. "You're not

going to slaughter them like you did those two?" He gestured to Ursula, who now lay in a crumpled heap.

I shook my head slowly. "A month ago—stars, an hour ago, even—I would have." The words surprised me as much as they evidently did the guard, but his eyes still held a hint of skepticism.

"What changed?"

Surveying the faces of the remaining Assembly members, I searched for the source of this shift. Mere moments ago, I was prepared to show no mercy to any of them. Now? The anger remained. They'd been weak, unwilling to stand up to their own and do what was right. Yet, that vengeful urge I'd become accustomed to chasing had dampened.

Maybe it was finally knowing my parents' fate. They'd been killed by the Assembly, even if not directly. I'd spent months pushing away my memories of them, trying to rule my kingdom without having to see their faces in my mind. When I finally allowed the image of them to surface, it became clear I couldn't ignore their silent guidance.

"My parents—" I barely got the two words out before my voice gave out, overtaken by a new flavor of grief I hadn't experienced since they'd died, like I had finally found a small semblance of peace with it. They were still gone, but somehow knowing who was responsible for their deaths had granted me a sense of closure, acceptance. I might not have that with Brennan's death yet—despite knowing who was responsible—but every step forward was movement in the right direction.

The guard nodded slowly, as if he understood my unspoken explanation. "So, what do you propose?"

"A trial," I said, once again looking around at those gathered. "While they might not have instigated all that has happened, they appear to have been complicit in the efforts to steal the crown. They will have their chance to stand before the citizens and have their fates determined by the law of our land."

"You expect us to just release you?" one of the other guards asked, scoffing. "How do we know you won't rip us apart as soon as we remove the gloves?"

"If I wanted to rip you apart, I would have already done it," I said. To emphasize my point, I dropped my head to the side as I called my shadows up from the ground. They hovered between the guard and me, swaying with anticipation. His eyes widened, but he clamped his lips shut as if that would help him withstand my powers. I offered a small smile and pulled the shadows back down to my feet, hoping I'd sufficiently convinced him.

He shook his head slowly, but didn't offer another word of protest as the other guards moved forward to unlock the gloves. Turning my hands over and over, I searched for any sign of damage from the searing pain I'd suffered earlier, but aside from a bit of dried blood at my fingertips from my clawing at the metal and some red, blistered burns on my palms, they were unscathed —far better than the melted skin and mangled flesh I'd envisioned.

My shadows instantly drifted up to my hands, pouring back into my veins where they belonged—where they would wait, until I could find Graham. I might have had a change of heart regarding the others, but if this had all been Graham's plan, then he deserved the same trial by shadows as Ursula and Warren had faced.

That bastard would suffer.

For my parents...my husband...my friend...and my mate.

CHAPTER 76

MATTHIAS

Of all the messes I'd gotten myself into—or been thrust into by others—this was the first I faced with more regrets than hope. My life had always been one of danger and risk. Death had come knocking many times, and I'd always jumped in, ready to face whatever happened, knowing that if it was my time to go then so be it.

Walking into this room, though, where the stench of death permeated the stones, I wasn't ready.

There was too much left unsaid, too much left undone.

Calla might have already been dead—unless the bond would have alerted me—and even if she wasn't, the likelihood she'd get here before Graham killed me was next to impossible, assuming she even knew where he'd brought me. Connor and Lieke wouldn't know what happened to me, and...

Stop!

I silently screamed at myself, desperate to keep from falling headlong into despair. It would do no one—not me, not Calla, not the Durands—any good if I let my confidence drown completely. If I was going to fail here, it was not going to be because I'd given up.

Graham pulled me to a stop in the middle of the room, which

was barely bigger than my suite back at the castle. Unlike that suite, though, this one offered no luxuries. Quite the opposite. A large worktable covered in dust ran the length of the far wall. Cobwebbed chains hung from anchors lodged into the walls, suspended from the ceiling over an ominous looking drain in the center of the floor.

Shoving me forward, Graham roughly grabbed my cuffed hands and shot me a warning glare.

"Don't do anything stupid," he growled. I made no move to respond, except to force a smirk. That, apparently, counted as something *stupid*, because he repaid it with a swift hook into my cheek. I bit back the urge to laugh, knowing I needed to pace myself—especially since my body would not be healing itself as quickly as usual, and even less so now that I'd taken two extra doses of the stars-damned poison since Korben's attack in the first trial.

I exaggerated a pained wince as I dropped my chin toward my chest in defeat. Graham chuckled triumphantly and lifted my arms to attach my cuffs to the chain dangling from above. Graham stepped back, angling his head to marvel at his work. My hands were already growing cold from the blood rushing down through my veins. Soon they'd go numb from being suspended like this.

I rolled my head to one side and then the other, working out the stiffness that had settled in. "So, your friend seemed nice."

Graham lifted a brow. "It's just us here. You can drop this act."

"What act?"

He gestured to me, waving his hand lazily between us. "This whole *nothing-bothers-me-I've-got-nothing-to-lose* act."

"Who said it was an act?"

"Maybe not before, but"—he paused to bend his lips into a crooked smile—"ever since that bond formed...well, I'd say you have quite a bit to lose."

My stomach tensed, and I had to concentrate more than usual

to keep my features still when Calla's face flashed into my thoughts. The last time I'd seen her had been in a fucking dream, and that's how I saw her now—livid and on the verge of tears as she yelled at me, pounding her hands against my chest.

Graham leaned in slightly, circling his finger inches from my eye. "There it is. The shame, the cowardice, the regret."

"Are you sure you're not just seeing your reflection?" I asked, trying to push Calla's image to the side so I could focus on dealing with this worm of a male.

He stiffened but didn't retreat, clearly debating whether to punch me again or not. I hoped not, but not knowing what other surprises he had in store for me, perhaps that would have been the better option. He shifted even closer, his stale breath causing my nose to wrinkle involuntarily.

"I'm going to enjoy breaking you before we're done here," he sneered. Patting my cheek, he straightened and retreated several paces.

Shifting my feet, I pivoted around to search for any sign of weapons or tools often used in rooms such as these. There was nothing here, but then again, one didn't need much to get people to talk. Only a couple months ago I'd managed to do well enough with nothing but a bar top for Mr. Marstens. I turned back to find Graham watching me as he retrieved a small blade from his belt.

Graham pursed his lips, studying me for a few more breaths before finally saying, "I'll be nice and let you choose the first cut. What do you think?"

I looked down, peering at different parts of my body and humming as if actually pondering his ridiculous suggestion. "How about you cut..." I dragged the last word out as I lifted my eyes back to his. "Your own throat."

He let out a slow laugh that was more obnoxious than terrifying. "Unfortunately for me, demi-fae don't heal quite as easily or quickly as the rest of you."

Demi-fae?

My gaze darted to his pointed ears, pulling another laugh from him.

"Too bad your sister didn't have the good fortune of inheriting the pointed ears. Then maybe she wouldn't be forced to hide in the woods."

Leaning back slightly, I scrutinized the half-fae male. I frowned at him and lifted my brows. "Is this where you share the intricacies of your schemes and boast of how you finally bested me? All while torturing me, of course?"

A bark of laughter echoed through the room, though Graham's face showed no sign of amusement. Without a word, he paced around me as he tapped the end of the blade against his lips and hummed quietly. He stopped behind me, moving unnervingly close.

"What's this?" he asked, slipping the knife into the back of my collar. The cold steel scratched my neck, though not hard enough to break the skin.

"A shirt?"

Graham said nothing as he jerked the knife down, slicing through the cloth and exposing my back. I shuddered against the sudden chill.

"Well, it *was* a shirt," I muttered.

"Not the fucking shirt," Graham growled. He pressed the tip of the blade into my back between my shoulder blades. "This."

I opened my mouth to give a smartass remark but thought better of it. As much fun as it was to get under his skin, I needed to keep him from killing me for as long as possible. Pulling in a slow breath, I lowered my head slowly.

"Do you have any family, Graham?" I asked, immediately regretting not coming up with a lie.

He dug the knife in until warmth trailed down my skin, and I winced as the pain shot through my nerves, making it feel like he was cutting in multiple places at once.

"What does that matter?" he asked, his delight at my pain evident in every syllable.

"Just curious," I claimed. Perhaps I could fix my mistake and direct him away from the truth.

"Why do I not believe you?"

"Because you're a cynical prick?" I guessed. Craning my head back to speak over my shoulder, I added, "Could be why you have no friends."

Graham didn't react except to press the knife into my skin once more and drag it slowly down through my flesh, pulling my face into a deep wince, though I suppressed any sound from escaping.

"Who is G.H.?"

I dropped my head against my arm, and a pained chuckle fell from my lips. "Someone who definitely would have killed you already if he were here."

"Doubtful, but sounds like you two were close? How did he die?"

"Who said he was dead?"

Graham clicked his tongue. "No male immortalizes a living friend with a tattoo."

This time when he drove the knife into my back, I couldn't keep the growl of pain contained.

CHAPTER 77
CALLA

For about the next eight hours I remained at Isa's bedside in the infirmary, only taking necessary breaks when Jocelyn forced me to, though I noticed she took far fewer herself. Jocelyn had administered a tonic that would keep Isa asleep and allow her body to focus on healing her wounds. With no poison in her system, her wounds healed relatively quickly, though it took longer for her to finally awaken.

Isa slitted her eyes against the lights in the room, but then widened them when she noticed me.

"Calla?" She croaked out my name on a parched breath, and I quickly retrieved a mug of water for her, helping her to sit up so she could drink.

"You didn't think I'd let them win, did you?" I asked, trying to laugh, but it came out hollow.

Her eyes fell closed as she took several small sips. Falling back down on the pillow, she shifted her head to look at me.

"I'm so sorry." Her apology tumbled shakily out of her, and I shook my head.

"No. You have nothing to apologize for. They were traitorous bastards. This is on them. Not you."

Her brow tightened with concern. "Did you kill them all?"

Again I shook my head, trying to ignore how her expression so quickly shifted with shock. "Only Ursula and Warren. The others are being held for trial, charged for their complicity. They didn't even try to stop them, though I suppose I can understand why."

"Seriously?"

"Despite what many may think, my heart hasn't charred completely. It's just singed, significantly."

"Was this show of mercy because of him?" she asked, noticeably cautious with her words, as if afraid I might strike her for saying them.

"Matthias?" I rolled my eyes dramatically. "I didn't take you for being the sentimental type. Why is it that everyone always assumes it's love that so drastically changes us?"

Her lips pulled back into a smirk as she breathed out a small laugh. "You love him?"

Shit.

"I didn't say that."

"Whatever you say. So, was it because of him?"

"I'll have you know, it wasn't. It was actually my parents. They would have wanted it handled this way, I think."

Isa breathed that in before sighing contentedly, but her expression tightened again, her eyes shooting to mine. "Graham."

Nodding, I muttered, "I know. We need to find a way to Dolobare before—"

"No, we don't," Isa chirped.

"We can't just leave Matthias to..." I paused as realization sank in. "You've already got a plan, don't you?"

"Indeed," she said, donning a smug smile that did not suit my normally stoic friend. "How long was I out?"

"Half a day, maybe less."

Isa bobbed her head approvingly. "Assuming the falcon I sent arrived safely, I expect them to arrive tomorrow, maybe the day after."

I started to ask her who in the stars she was talking about

when it dawned on me—the only friends who could help us in such a predicament, who were always willing to take on last-minute jobs. "You're a genius."

"It's why you keep me around."

"Only one of the reasons." I quickly scanned her limbs and hands for any sign of lingering injury. "Can you walk?"

Isa responded by slowly swinging her legs over the side of the bed. "Probably. Are you planning to wait for them outside on the front steps like you used to?"

"Of course. Watching dragons fly in for a visit never gets old."

While we didn't expect Asher and his brothers to arrive until the next day, Isa still humored me, sitting with me in silence in front of the castle entrance until the sun had long since retreated for the night. By my third long yawn, Isa insisted I retire for the night, and I was too exhausted to protest.

For so many nights, my mind had swept me away to desolate darkness devoid of dreams or any memorable locations where I might find Matthias waiting to meet me. When I dropped my head to my pillow, I expected yet another night of disappointing emptiness.

Instead, I found myself back in those foreign woods, standing atop a wooden platform beneath lit lanterns suspended in the trees. My heart jolted at the memory, tears rushing to my eyes, but not for the same reason they had the last time I'd relived my friends' wedding.

Spinning around and around, I searched for Matthias, my pulse pounding in my ears as if my heart was frantically trying to call to him. No one was here, though. Not Connor nor Lieke. Not the king or Brennan or...

"Killer?" Matthias's voice cut through my thundering heartbeat, pulling my head around so quickly I lost my balance and nearly fell. I expected him to catch me, but he stood across the clearing, among the trees, his boots sinking slowly into the mud that covered the forest floor.

I hesitated. Why in the stars did I hesitate?

But for some reason, I couldn't move. I couldn't speak. I couldn't think of anything beyond the sheer relief of finding him here. I merely stood there, staring at my mate through my gathering tears, until he took a step forward, his expression shifting slowly into one of desperate relief as he walked toward me.

I opened my mouth to speak, but before I could utter any sound, he vanished, leaving me alone again with only my tears and my dark dread.

"I'll find you, Matthias," I whispered to the empty forest.

CHAPTER 78

MATTHIAS

I'd seen her—I'd finally seen her—and I only managed one word, one step closer, before I was violently ripped from the dream with a splash of cold mountain water in my face. I spluttered, shaking my head and silently cursing this painful reality I'd been thrust back to.

Graham's rank scent of sweat and dirt chased away any relief I'd found in that brief amount of sleep. "Wakey, wakey, general. You'll have plenty of time with your mate when you're both dead. For now, though, I need you to stay with me."

I had no energy to respond, and he almost seemed disappointed when I merely blinked at him. Shrugging, he started whistling as he walked slowly around me. When his knife dug into my flesh again, I squeezed my eyes shut and forced the image of Calla to my mind to help me endure. By the time he cut away the last bit of tattooed skin from my back, my hands had lost all feeling, my arms ached, and my legs wavered, each one buckling in turn as they struggled to hold me upright.

I tried to mentally prepare for spending the next several hours —if not days—in this position, wondering how long it would take for my legs to give out completely and my shoulders to slip out of place. Directing all my energy toward keeping my feet under me, I let my head drift down, but struggled not to close my eyes lest I lose my balance. Graham appeared in front of me, but I was too exhausted to worry about where he'd strike next. Faintly aware that he was reaching up to the chain above my head, I still didn't expect him to actually unlock my cuffs and let my arms slump down between us.

The sudden shift in weight sent my legs caving, and sleep—blissful but unfortunately dreamless—took me before I ever hit the ground.

How long I was out, I didn't know, but a friendly kick between my shoulder blades, directly onto the slow-to-heal wound, roused me from my slumber. The cold stone floor bit into my bare shoulder, and it took me several breaths to realize I was lying on the ground. A small twist of my wrists produced the now-familiar clink of my chains.

"On your feet," Graham ordered. When I didn't oblige quickly enough, he snatched my arm and yanked me up to sitting, though my body immediately tried to crumple back down when he let go. He tried to haul me back up, and his growls of exertion soon gave way to muttered curses. I could have sworn he mentioned Alek and the word human at some point in his private tirade.

My eyes refused to stay open, and when he slapped me again, I was back in the center of the room with my hands once again secured to that fucking chain. Before I was ready—as if that was even possible—he pulled out his knife and resumed carving up the rest of my back, like some masochistic painter creating a bloody work of art with me as his canvas.

I forced myself to swallow every pained sound my body wanted to release, and as time passed—by some small miracle—each sweep of his blade began to blend into the next one until their sting faded into the background of my consciousness. Graham must have noticed my body relax, though, because he paused. I braced myself for the impact—whether from fist or his knife—but instead the metal of his knife was replaced by a dry cloth. He dragged it across my skin, wiping away the blood and grating at the fresh incisions until I sucked in a sharp breath that whistled through my clenched teeth.

As if my body suddenly remembered where I was and what was happening, my legs, barely holding me upright as it was, started to shake. Despite the frigid air inside the cavern, sweat beaded along my forehead, trickling into my eyes and down along my nose. My attempts to wipe it away on my arms helped minimally.

"Hanging in there?" Graham asked, his tone light like he was asking if I wanted another macaron.

An agonizingly dry cough erupted from my throat.

"Not much else to do around here," I rasped.

He chuckled quietly as he walked away, coming back moments later. My body jerked away from him as he dabbed something onto my wounds. Its scent reminded me of the healers' infirmary, though not nearly as pungent, meaning it was probably less than fresh. If the bastard was taking the time to heal my wounds, it wasn't out of any goodness in his deranged heart. More likely he was drawing out the pain, making it last as long as possible, like a lover who eases away right as you reach the fucking precipice.

Graham hummed—almost cheerfully—as he applied the salve.

"Is that poisoned by chance?" His face appeared from around my arm, and I flinched, nearly choking on my next breath.

"Why? Are you hoping for death already?" he asked beneath raised brows.

"Just wondering if you understand how this whole torture thing is supposed to work."

Graham's dark laugh filled the room. Returning to his task, he continued smearing the medicine over my wounds, albeit not quite as gently as before.

"Playing dumb doesn't suit you, *general*."

"Neither does having my back used for whittling, yet here we are."

Graham didn't respond, but at least he ceased that infernal humming.

CALLA

I got no more sleep that night but lay awake, staring at the ceiling above my bed for hours and trying not to imagine all the ghastly things Graham—or the humans—could be doing to Matthias. The only thing holding me together, keeping me from completely falling apart, was the assurance my mate was still alive. As long as he was still breathing, I still had time; though how much, I couldn't know.

The sky outside had barely lightened when Isa showed up looking as though she hadn't slept much either. We spent the entire next morning and afternoon back on that stairway, taking our meals under the sunshine like we used to when we were younger and life wasn't quite so depressing and complicated.

Swallowing the last bite of bread from lunch, I looked up as three figures drifted over the treetops and into view—massive creatures with scales of various hues and immense clawed wings, though I tried never to compliment those, lest it go to their heads. Isa and I rose to our feet to watch them circle above the castle twice before swooping down onto the gravel driveway.

Asher landed in the front, the sun reflecting off his bronze and gold scales as he stretched and brought his wings in close to his sides. Behind him, his two brothers, Dax and Kai, mimicked his movements. By contrast, their darker scales—one a dark blue, the other a deep purple—seemed to swallow the sun's light as it hit them.

They strode forward, their razored feet grating against the gravel, each step made slightly lopsided by the bundles they each carried in one of their front feet. I smiled warmly at them as they dropped the bundles to the ground beside them, but they made no move to shift.

"It's going to be a bit difficult to plan with you in this form, no?" I asked Asher. His giant eyes rolled in annoyance, a sight that never failed to amuse me, even now.

Dropping his head low to the ground, he gave a massive shake from snout to tail. His wings shrank down, folding into his back as the rest of him seemed to melt away until he stood before us in his fae form. His clothes—which I never fully understood where they exactly went when he shifted—looked more suited to a leisurely holiday trip instead of the battle that likely awaited us across the Laraburn Sea.

"Thank you for coming so quickly, Asher," Isa said from beside me. She dipped her head low to emphasize her gratitude.

"Honestly? I was looking for an excuse to get away from my current job," he said. His brothers, still in their dragon forms, seemed to be struggling to stifle laughter, and Asher quickly glared over his shoulder at them before bounding up the steps to join us. "Never mind them. So, that Graham prick ran off with Matthias?"

I bristled, but when Asher's brow shot up in intrigue, I tried to play my reaction off with a joke, grimacing as I said, "You make it sound like they eloped."

Asher looked from me to Isa and back again. "So which one of you is going to tell me exactly why we're all risking our lives for one male?"

"You said yourself he was a good one," I noted.

He bobbed his head to the side and frowned. "True, but if

you're calling on us and risking war with Dolobare to get him back, I have to assume—"

"He's my mate." I spit out the words like they were burning my tongue, but Asher didn't laugh or make some quip at my expense. His eyes widened ever so slightly, before warming with affection again.

"I had a hunch."

"You did not," I grumbled. Not wanting to have to answer any prying questions, I clapped my hands and turned to Isa. "We're wasting time."

Isa shifted her gaze to Asher. "When can you be ready to go? Do you need to rest? Eat?"

Asher pivoted around, and after a brief moment, his brothers each nodded their giant heads to whatever he'd asked them.

"I'll never get used to that dragon telepathy," I muttered to Isa.

Giving one short burst of laughter, Asher said, "It's not any weirder than that bond you have with our male in distress, is it?"

Male in distress.

I groaned quietly. "So? When do we leave?" I prompted Asher when he remained silent waiting for me to answer his dumbass query.

"We could leave now, but that would have us arriving in that barren-ass land in the middle of the night, and we wouldn't be at our most energetic should we run into any trouble searching for him."

Isa's hand shot out to grab my wrist, squeezing hard. "I only thought of how to get us there quickly. How are we going to find him in all of those mountains?"

Shit.

I was about to echo the thought aloud when a thought struck me, and I angled my head at Asher.

"I have an idea," I said.

CHAPTER 80

MATTHIAS

Much like in the dungeon back in Arenysen, time ceased to matter in this stars-awful room.

Well, that wasn't completely true. The breaks Graham provided were welcome reprieves that seemed to be over too quickly, though with nothing but stone and dust and chains surrounding me, I had no way of knowing exactly how much time passed. At least the asshole found it worthwhile to give me breaks to relieve myself—a courtesy I assumed was more for his comfort than for mine, so he could continue to slice and jab and carve away at me without a foul stench clinging to my body. He also offered water and food regularly, though like the salve, this was likely only meant to keep me alive for as long as he needed.

I just needed to survive long enough for someone to find me.

In the rare times my sleep brought dreams, Calla never reappeared, and her absence fed my growing despair. The last dream we'd shared, she hadn't come to me, hadn't spoken, and I started to doubt the relief I'd seen in her eyes. Could she get here in time? Could she find me in this hidden hole in the rock? Would she even want to?

These questions haunted me, swirling around my head with the memory of her hatred thrown at me—the only words of hers I could seem to remember. *I hate you, Matthias.* As time dragged on in its imperceptible increments, those once-welcome breaks from Graham's abuse gradually became less and less desirable as it provided my mind nothing to focus on other than my numerous failures and eventual demise.

Even if Calla were to save me—even if she did forgive me—she deserved far better than a washed-up, has-been general who did nothing but get himself nearly killed. I hadn't survived this long because of my own prowess or ingenuity. It had been luck. Always luck.

Luck that Asher had saved me in that fucking forest.

Luck that Calla had protected me in that hallway.

Luck that Phillip had rescued me in that stars-damned lake.

Even before this tournament, it had been luck that brought Gabriel between the Shadow Keeper and me on that battlefield, and it had been luck that the rebel's arrow at that barn in Emeryn had not been poisoned at all—and that their archer had been a stars-awful shot.

No, I never saved myself.

What kind of mate could I be to Calla? What kind of king to Arenysen?

Calla deserved more than a lucky bastard—more than a fuck-up.

Spiraling down and down into these thoughts, I let my will to keep going slip away and my hope of surviving fade into the darkness of my mind.

A hand grabbed my jaw and lifted, thrusting my head back into the stone wall I sat against, but I kept my eyes closed, my focus fixed on the last image of Calla that played on the back of my eyelids.

"Told you I'd break you." Graham's oily voice slithered into my ear. "Now the real fun begins."

CHAPTER 81

CALLA

The last time I traveled to Dolobare, I had taken a ship with my parents. The war had barely concluded, and our kingdom was newly established. My parents insisted on reaching out to the nightwalkers, who had fled to the island at the first threat of war, wanting nothing to do with a conflict between human and fae. At the time of my first and only visit, the nightwalkers—or vampires, as the humans called them—and humans had found a way to coexist, working together to ensure both survived. The humans provided sustenance while the night-walkers' blood healed a myriad of ailments for the mortals.

At some point in the last two decades, though, something had changed, dividing the two races, leaving the island reeling. With the humans going underground, masking their scent somehow, the nightwalkers were forced to adapt to animal blood—which Arenysen helped provide as part of our trade agreement.

I had planned to visit the ruling nightwalkers—the Vranićs—sometime after my parents' death, but the thought of crossing the same sea that had claimed their bodies had been too much to handle. Now it stared up at me, a dark abyss peppered with white-capped waves hundreds of meters below where I sat nestled in my harness and saddle strapped to Asher's broad back. While it was mid-morning, thick, dark clouds hung low in the sky, hovering just over our heads and blocking out much of the sunlight.

Conversation was impossible as we flew through the gloominess, but thankfully the brothers were navigational experts—perfected through their years of mercenary work—and once I'd explained where we needed to go, they simply required us to hold on and not fall into the sea.

I glanced over at Isa strapped onto Dax's back, but she was dozing contentedly. Perhaps I should have done the same, especially since sleep might have connected me to Matthias again so I could let him know we were on our way—assuming I could find my voice quicker—but he had been in none of my dreams since.

For all I knew, Graham had already killed him.

No, surely I would feel something if that had happened.

If only the bond could have helped me find him, but so far it seemed to do nothing more than complicate life. Thankfully neither Isa nor Asher hounded me about whether I was accepting the bond or how I felt about Matthias. Fact was, I didn't know myself. All I knew was I couldn't let his death make that decision for me. I hadn't wanted to choose my next husband before, but everything had changed with this tournament and that kiss—a kiss I couldn't even remember.

Snorting, Asher swung his head around to look back at me, catching my attention before he gestured ahead with his snout. Black mountains loomed in front of us, the white spray of the gray sea crashing against them. As if they were of one mind, the three dragons angled to the left in unison, swooping down toward the northern mountains. My breath caught as the cold air rushed past us and we soared between the massive peaks, flying so close I swore I could have touched them if I dared reach an arm out.

A dull ache pulsed through my fingers as I clutched the edge of the saddle. I had taken the last of my tonic this morning before we departed. Of all places to lose control of my shadows, the

Vranićs' court was one of the least desirable. Trade agreement or no, they wouldn't tolerate my powers being unleashed in their walls.

My stomach lurched and heaved and rolled as Asher glided around the twists and turns toward their lair nestled among these dark mountains. As sick as this journey was making me, it was decidedly better than traveling by sea which brought the same gut-churning movement but for much longer. Then, from their port village of Novibel, the road inland to visit the royal family was difficult to traverse with its narrow passages and regular cuts through dark tunnels carved into the stone, not as easily navigated by those of us lacking the nightwalkers' keen eyesight.

I tried to close my eyes against Asher's neck, but that only made the nausea worse. I was about to tap him and request he slow down so I wouldn't vomit all over him when he swept around one final turn and landed lithely on the large terrace that jutted out from the mountain. When Isa had sent the falcon to the three Starck brothers, she had sent a second across the sea to the Vranićs, two of whom now stood before towering gilded doors set in the mountainside, watching us as we landed.

Isa—likely roused from her sleep when we started our descent —unharnessed quickly, accepting Dax's raised front leg to help her down. Nodding to him, she waited for me to do the same so we could approach the intimidating pair together. A male and female, their pale skin shining against the obsidian backdrop of their home as if lit from within, lifted their chins. I nearly stopped short when I recognized them as Master and Madame Vranić themselves.

"Queen Vael," Niko Vranić greeted me in a voice that reminded me of the spiced brandy his family made—smooth and oddly warm, given his cold surroundings, but with a hint of bite. Though, his tone was as impossible to read as his expression.

Bowing my head slowly, I looked from Niko to his wife, Sasha. "Master Vranić. Madame. You have my deepest gratitude for agreeing to meet with us."

Sasha eyed me coldly and spoke in a matter-of-fact manner. "We did not agree to anything...but, as your parents died while traveling home from our island, we will at least hear your plight."

"However," Niko said. "We do not guarantee our approval or aid."

They did not wait for us to answer but rather pivoted on their heels to march through the doors, which swung open for them as they neared. Asher nudged me, nearly toppling me over. He gestured to the buckle for the saddle, and I quickly released it. I'd barely slipped it free from his back when he shifted back into his human form.

"Should your brothers shift too?" I asked him quietly, but he was already shaking his head.

"They're not a fan of nightwalkers. Or meetings," he said around a smirk. "Plus, it'll be better to have them here ready to leave in a hurry if needed."

Niko and Sasha had paused inside the door. Half-turned toward us, they waited with those same bored expressions on their faces. The three of us hurried across the terrace, leaving Dax and Kai to stand guard outside. The doors shut ominously, throwing us into near total darkness.

"Come," Sasha said from somewhere in front of us.

"One moment, please," I requested. "Our eyes could use time to adjust. I'd hate to step on you."

Someone chuckled in the darkness, but a snap echoed through the chamber, and flames flickered to life as torches ignited, lining the walls of the grand cavern. We stood in an antechamber of sorts, unfurnished but decorated with ornate tapestries and plush rugs that made the space warmer than expected given the location.

Several guards stepped in front of us, and from behind them Niko said, "My guards will take any weapons."

Isa cast a wary glance my way as she complied, slipping her sword and daggers from her waist, while Asher and I each handed over a small knife. We followed the royal couple down a long, winding corridor and into a more intimate circular room dominated by a round table of rich wood that seemed to be made from a single slice of an ancient tree trunk. Wooden armchairs, upholstered in a deep red velvet, surrounded the table. Similar to the first room, rich tapestries adorned the walls with torches encased in iron and glass hanging between them.

Niko and Sasha each took their seats, motioning for us to do the same.

"What is this emergency that brings you to our isle, Your Majesty?" Niko asked.

Sasha lifted a brow as she added, "And with dragon escorts, no less."

Clearing my throat, I folded my hands in front of me on the table to steady myself as much as my shadows. "My former advisor has betrayed me and fled to your shores. I need to find him immediately."

"Why the urgency?" Sasha asked.

"He has my mate," I stated, surprised that the word didn't taste quite as bitter and wrong as it used to.

Niko and Sasha shared a knowing look, both sighing as if endeared by the news I had found my mate. "What do you need from us?"

"Permission to hunt on your island."

"And where do you think he is?"

"I believe he is with the humans, though I cannot be sure."

The pair stiffened, and tension rippled through their shared glance.

Niko pursed his lips before asking, "What do you intend to do?"

"Kill anyone who gets in my way," I said, unblinking.

"We can't allow that," Sasha said quietly, and I snapped my attention to her. Her features softened, seeming almost sympathetic—the most emotion she'd shown during this visit.

Asher dropped his clasped hands on the table and leaned

forward. "Why not? I thought there was no love lost between your kinds. Or am I mistaken?"

Another anxious look passed between the couple. Niko spread his hands in front of him as if physically offering his explanation. "You are not mistaken. We are indeed at odds with the humans here, and have been for some time, but the situation is... delicate."

Sasha touched a hand to his forearm but kept her gaze locked on mine. "There are two individuals of importance among the humans, and we cannot risk their lives for your vendetta."

Shrugging, Asher said, "Easy. Tell us who they are, and we'll be sure to spare them."

Sasha's throat bobbed as she swallowed hard.

"You can't, can you?" I asked.

The female offered a small shake of her head, her eyes dropping to the table.

Niko breathed out a sigh. "I'm sorry. We have spent too many years—sacrificed too much—to put it in jeopardy now."

Isa spoke for the first time since we'd arrived. "Put *what* in jeopardy? What are you trying to accomplish with the humans?"

Niko nodded but avoided answering her questions. "I truly am sorry we cannot allow you to go rescue your mate."

My shadows shifted in my palms, and I closed my hands tighter to hold them back.

"I'm not leaving without him," I said, fixing a hard stare on him. "I will, in fact, kill anyone who stands in my way—even you."

The pair pushed to stand, their fangs slipping out over their bottom lips as they snarled, but I was on my feet just as quickly. Opening my palms, I released my shadows, sending them across the table with a silent command. I stopped them in mid-air but left them hovering close to the nightwalkers' faces. In my periphery, Isa and Asher remained seated, but noticeably on edge, their eyes shifting between the vampires across the table and me.

"You dare threaten us, Ms. Vael?" Niko hissed out. Snapping his fingers high above his head, six nightwalkers materialized from the dark edges of the room and took their places behind each of us. "This behavior will not earn you any favor with us. Put your shadows away before my guards snap your necks."

Easing my shadows back into my hands, I settled into my chair, gesturing for my hosts to do the same. They didn't move.

"Master Vranić," I said as respectfully as I could. "There must be a way to work together here so I'm not forced to sever our years of partnership. Yes? So, what *can* you do to help us?"

It took them several breaths before they finally lowered into their chairs. Their fangs slipped from view again, but they remained quiet with a wary gleam in their eyes.

Isa peered up at the two nightwalkers standing behind her as she asked the royal couple, "If you can't name the individuals, can you describe them for us?" They remained quiet, the only sign they'd even heard her being a tightening of their features as they—hopefully—contemplated her suggestion.

"Or send someone with us," Asher commanded, not bothering to phrase it as a request as Isa had. "We have an extra mount."

I snapped my head around to stare at him. That third seat was to bring Matthias home, and I was about to remind Asher of that, but his confident gaze and faint smile assured me he had already considered this.

"And have them do what, Mr. Starck?" Sasha asked. Her brows fell low over her cold eyes. "Shall they point out the ones we need protected? Risk exposing them? I don't think so."

Niko shook his head slowly. "Agreed. We can't send anyone with you, nor can we provide names, but"—he caught Sasha's uneasy gaze, and they had a brief but intense, silent conversation before he snapped his attention back to Asher—"we will need time to deliberate."

Sasha scowled, clearly over this meeting, but she added, "There is one other issue with your plan. *We* don't even know where they are located. The humans are able to mask their scent, their heartbeats. It took our man years to successfully infiltrate them, and even then he had to entice them to come to him. How do you plan to succeed where we have not?"

"With this," I said, pulling a gold coin from my pocket.

CHAPTER 82

MATTHIAS

Fire tore through my throat as I released another ragged scream, sending the sound past flesh worn raw by hours of ineffectual, inevitable wailing as Graham unleashed his quiet wrath on me. He'd ceased providing water, leaving me weak and dried out as if I were a corpse dug up from the ground. Where his tools came from, I didn't know, and at this point, it didn't fucking matter. He could have conjured them out of the stars-damned air. Knowing how he'd gotten them wouldn't help me endure the torment any easier.

The clank of metal falling to the stone floor drew my eyes open, and I waited for the haze to clear from my vision, thankful for even the slightest of reprieves. My fingers burned—shooting sparks of pain into my hands—as I tried to move them against the arms of the chair I was now chained to. Even through my blurred sight, I noted the slick darkness at the end of each finger. The faint sound of blood dripping to the stone floor hit my ears, pulling my gaze down to my fingernails dotting the floor.

"You know, general," Graham started from beside me, wiping his bloody hands on his trousers. But I didn't turn toward him, my attention locked firmly onto the pieces of me he'd strewn about like bread tossed to birds. "I had almost thought you incapable of feeling pain with how little noise you made before. I have to wonder—is this that much more painful? Or does the lack of all hope simply make it seem so?"

Ripping my chapped lips apart, I rasped out my answer. "Fuck... you..."

Graham let a single laugh escape before he grabbed my hair and yanked my head back. "That's not on the agenda, I'm afraid. But just wait—"

Heavy footsteps echoed around us, and Graham shoved my head forward again.

"About time," he muttered, turning for the doorway behind me. "I hope you have good news for me, Alek," he said, even before he'd left the room.

My head bobbed from side to side for a moment, my eyes struggling to remain open, until I forced myself to turn an ear toward the other room. As pointless as it was to expect any help, some small part of me insisted on staying in this doomed fight and pushed me to listen for any hint of what was happening outside.

"What do you mean she's not dead?" Graham's low frustrated hiss blew a hint of life into my dying hope, like a breath resurrecting a flame from glowing embers.

A familiar but hard-to-place voice answered his—a female whose irritability matched my captor's. "I mean she slaughtered two of the Assembly and threw the others in the dungeon. I left immediately—didn't trust a falcon to deliver the message to you here. Worried it would be intercepted."

I cringed at the slap of flesh against flesh that cut through Graham's distinctive growl.

"If they didn't suspect your involvement before, they certainly will now," he reprimanded.

The female responded bitterly. "The surviving advisors will betray us eventually, regardless. We felt it more prudent to warn you as quickly as possible. And I left my sister behind to cover for me. It will be some time before they realize I've left."

"Does she know where we are?" Graham asked, a hint of

worry creeping into his voice. When she didn't answer readily, he issued a warning. "Don't make me hit you again, Ami."

My eyes jolted open. Ami? The healer was here? She'd been working with Graham?

"I don't know," the healer said with far more defiance than expected. "I think you should assume she does."

"Fuck." Graham bit out the swear, but when he spoke again, his eerie calmness had returned. "Having you here could actually help me, though."

"Help you how?" Ami asked, her voice quavering slightly.

The resulting silence was punctuated by slow steps growing louder.

"What are you—" she started, but Graham didn't let her finish.

"What I need to. What he deserves."

"This isn't what I agreed to."

"You took no issue with him dying during the tournament," Graham reminded her.

"Yes, but that was a known risk. This...this is torture. It's not right."

"What are you going to do about it? Stop me? Turn me in? To whom exactly? The humans won't care. The vampires don't know where to find us. Stars, you wouldn't have found me if I hadn't brought you here before. And Calla? *If* she knows where we are, it will take days to sail here and longer to locate us in these blasted mountains."

The healer released a dejected breath. "Fine. I will stay out of your way. I can keep watch and alert you if anyone approaches, but I will take no direct part in this."

"I suggest you leave, then," Graham said. "You won't want to witness what comes next."

Help me!

I wanted to scream, but the words remained nothing more than a silent plea trapped in my head. I tried to look back over my shoulder, to force Ami to see me, but Graham blocked her view of me as he swaggered closer.

His lip curled viciously, and he slowly leaned down until his eyes were level with mine.

"Hear that, general? Your mate lives. Think she'll come for you?"

Pulling in a painful breath, I moved to speak, but nothing but wordless air pushed through my lips.

"What was that?" Graham asked, putting a hand behind his ear.

I inched my face closer to his and forced the words out, gravelly and broken. "She's...going...to end...you."

Graham's face blanched, the corners of his eyes and mouth twitching nervously. He abruptly straightened.

"Better not delay, then." He walked around me and bent low to pick up the tool he'd dropped earlier. Taking his place in front of me once more, he grabbed my chin and jerked my face forward. When he leaned in again, he sneered. "We may have less time together than planned, but don't expect any mercy. Your death may come sooner, but it will be far from quick and not at all painless."

Squeezing my jaw, he worked to pry my mouth open—an easy task, with how weak I'd become. Before I could even think to bite down on his fingers, he thrust the metal between my lips. Growling, I attempted to pull my head away from his grasp, using whatever energy I could muster to loosen his hold on either the tool or me. With my wrists and ankles bound to the chair, though, every twist of my battered body only served to drain me quicker, not force him away.

As he clamped the pliers down on one of my back teeth, my breaths quickened until he tore his hand away from me, ripping out my tooth and my screams together in one swift motion.

CHAPTER 83

CALLA

My legs itched to move, tingling uncontrollably as if a million spiders crawled through my veins. Pushing myself up from the velvet chaise, I attempted to ease the sensation by shaking them and stomping my feet against the thin rug that covered the stone floor. The Vranićs had directed us to a sitting room to await further instruction, promising to have a final decision to us before night fell. While searching the Muratch Mountains in the dark was less than ideal, I didn't know if I could handle sitting still, knowing my mate was somewhere on this island.

Once again, my torturous mind dared to pull up images of the torment Graham might be inflicting on Matthias. No matter how many times I pushed the horror away, it continued to creep back to the forefront. Pulling my shadows from my palms, I flexed them in the air in front of me, testing my control over them as I sent them dancing, swirling, and slicing through the dim light of the parlor.

"It's nice to see you finally accepting your gift," Asher noted from where he lounged in a high-backed armchair set in front of the small fireplace carved into the mountain wall. The flames—along with those of the lanterns placed throughout the large room

—cast an eerie, melancholy glow, creating their own shifting shadows on my friend's face.

"Sometimes seems like a bit of a curse still," I whispered, slipping my power back into my veins and fisting my hands.

"Who knew about your shadows anyway? Isa, obviously," he said, nodding to the general pacing at the far end of the room.

"Obviously how?" Kai asked, leaning forward in the chair opposite Asher's. The brothers had agreed to shift into their human forms as long as the nightwalkers kept their distance. It always fascinated me how the shifters' two forms complemented each other so well. Asher's scales, a lighter bronze and gold, matched his dark blond hair and sun-kissed complexion. His brothers, however, barely looked related to my friend with their dark hair and eyes that resembled their darker jewel-toned scales.

Isa didn't slow her pace. "I can sense powers in others. Can't tell what they are specifically, but I know if someone's blood contains abilities or not."

"Did Graham know?" Asher asked, quickly adding, "Not that it matters."

"I never told him, if that's what you mean, but I could tell he knew I was hiding something," I said. Pressing my fingers hard to my temples, I closed my eyes and tried to take a calming breath. Everything was a stars-damned mess, and I was here, stuck in this room, waiting for someone else's consent before I could do anything.

"Something bothering you, Isa?" Dax asked from where he leaned against the wall behind Asher.

Maintaining her pace, she shook her head, her expression tightening with concern.

"What is it?" I asked.

Still treading the invisible line in the rug, Isa pushed out a heavy breath. "Do we know for sure this is going to work?"

All three brothers chuckled, which seemed like the last reaction my friend had hoped to get. Stopping short, she pivoted and turned to us. She lifted her hands to her hips and frowned when her fingers didn't find the comfort of her sword.

"There are no guarantees, general," Asher offered casually.

"Of course not, but—"

"It worked in the forest," I reminded her.

Isa's shoulders slumped. "Yes, but that was in a smaller area and without massive black stone everywhere."

Kai eyed each of his brothers in turn. "She has quite the confidence in us, doesn't she?"

Isa swept an apologetic look among the men. "If we were simply searching for gold—even in the mountains—I'd have fewer concerns. But the stakes are rather high here."

Dax shrugged his broad shoulders. "We're mercenaries. We're used to high stakes."

"And we are expert treasure hunters," Kai chimed in, flashing his dashing smile.

Rubbing a hand at the back of her neck, Isa drew in a deep breath. I moved to stand in front of her. I'd never seen her this nervous. Her dark eyes met mine, and I counted it a small blessing that there seemed no fear there, only uncertainty. Uncertainty, we could handle. Fear would have been trickier.

"How are you so calm, Calla?" she asked. "We don't even know if he still has his ring. Graham could have easily taken it and thrown it into the Laraburn."

"Conserving energy, I guess. No point in getting worked up until I need to be," I suggested as lightheartedly as I could. "But yes, I know. There's always the chance that this won't work, that they"—I swung my glance to the brothers behind me—"won't be able to track his ring, but the alternative is to wander aimlessly through the mountains."

Asher rose and strode up beside me. "Plus, even if his ring has been taken or lost or what-have-you, there's a good chance the humans have gold of their own. We find the humans; we find him."

The door slid open, drawing all our attention to Niko and Sasha. My pulse quickened.

"We will allow you to hunt for your mate," Niko said, though he seemed to be hesitating with his next words.

"And?" I said, anxious to get underway.

"The man we have working with the humans—you'll know him by the ink on his hands and neck. You must spare his life and the life of the woman he guards."

"What of the others?" Asher asked, a hint of excitement in his tone.

Sasha bared her teeth and snarled, "Kill them all."

CHAPTER 84

MATTHIAS

While Graham no longer afforded me any rest, he took his time, seemingly savoring every pained roar and hollow scream that escaped me. Three of my teeth lay on the stone floor amidst the fingernails he'd already torn away, and blood pooled in my mouth, which was too dry to make spitting it out—or swallowing it—an easy task. My head lolled to the side when he finally released my chin and stepped back. Watching my chest rise and fall with my labored yet shallow breaths, I tried to distract myself from the pain by imagining what Calla would do to Graham when she eventually arrived.

If *she arrives...*

Without fail, my mind slipped into that pit of despair, struggling to hold onto the few lingering, strained threads of hope.

"Perhaps I should take a few of your front teeth," Graham mused. "They won't hurt quite as much, but that cocky smile of yours—wherever it's hiding—could stand to be impaired a little."

My mind blanked on a response. He might as well be talking to himself with how little I cared about anything he had to say. Chained to this stars-damned chair and weakened by poison and pain, I had no chance of freeing myself. The only way I was getting out of here was if Calla arrived. Or if the humans found it in their hearts to help me out, but that was as unlikely as Graham sparing me.

"Lucky for you, though, my arms are a little sore from yanking those teeth from your head. Plus, there are better ways to harm that pretty face of yours," he muttered, though I couldn't tell if he was actually speaking softly or if my ears were simply trying to tune him out, focusing instead on the weak yet steady thumping of my pulse.

A blade slid against leather, creating a sound that sliced straight through my consciousness and pulled my attention back to my captor. I tilted my head slightly to shift my gaze up to Graham as he approached, but his eyes weren't on mine. He seemed to be looking past me.

"Did you ever wonder why Emeryn had all the issues with the rebel humans while Arenysen didn't?"

I remained still, staring back at him without blinking or shifting any muscle of my sore face. He studied me with a raised brow.

"I almost miss your feisty responses. Almost." He took a small step forward, his knees smacking into mine. "It was rather brilliant, honestly. I brokered a deal with the rebels in our kingdom: we help ship the poison in from Dolobare and guarantee safe transport of it on the roads, and they don't attack within our borders. Not that it worked out all that great for the rebels in Emeryn. How are human-fae relations there anyway? Did they get any better after your prince married the human? Or are they still hoping for peace?"

The mention of Connor and Lieke sent an ache through my chest, my failure as palpable as the blood in my mouth.

"I assume, since your sister remains in hiding in those woods, the fae aren't too keen on welcoming humans back, no? Funny how something as inconsequential as ear shape could make or break someone's place in their own society."

He leaned in, resting his empty hand on his leg as he studied me. Once again, he grabbed my chin and forced my head up to stare at him, but this time he didn't wrench my mouth open. He turned my head to one side and then the other, and I gritted my aching teeth as realization of his plans lit in my head, sending my gut writhing with horror.

Graham continued yammering on. "I wonder if the Emerynians would welcome you back...if you looked more like the people they despise."

His hand flew to my ear, gripping it so tightly I worried if I jerked away it would rip the entire thing off, so I remained still—apart from my eyes squeezing closed, bracing for the heat of the blade. With my lips pressed together, I tried to contain my scream as he sliced slowly through the top of my ear, my howl coming out more like a muffled roar in the back of my throat. The longer he took, the less control I had, and before he'd even finished, my wail broke free and echoed off the stone walls.

I clamped my mouth shut again when his knife broke through the last of my cartilage.

"Look, *general*," Graham growled. When I refused, he screamed. "Open your eyes!"

Not sure what he'd do if I still declined, I pried my eyelids open to glare at him. He dangled the bloody piece of my ear in front of my face before dropping it into my lap, grinning the entire time.

"Other side," he commanded. "I'd hate for you to be left uneven."

"Stars forbid," I choked out. Setting my jaw, I turned my face —pushing against his hand that still gripped my chin—to offer him my intact ear. Fury raged in his eyes as I stole back the control he thought he'd gained.

Growling, he forced my head down at an angle and swiped his knife quickly through the other ear. My inevitable anguish bubbled up, but instead of coming out a scream or a groan, it manifested as a defiant laugh right in Graham's face, earning me a swift blow to my temple that sent me into a welcome world of dark emptiness.

CHAPTER 85

CALLA

We wasted no time. Once we were back out on the terrace—with Niko, Sasha, and several of their family watching—the Starck brothers shifted into their dragon forms. Isa and I worked together to get their saddles in place. My gut twinged uncomfortably at the memory of Matthias mocking Asher, goading him over whether he gave rides. When Asher had chased headlong into the forest after him, I'd thought surely that would be the end of the mouthy male suitor. Somehow, though, he had won over my dragon friend to the point he'd carried him through the forest and hunted down a gold coin to save not only his life but also his place in the tournament.

And now he was here, risking his own life to save him again.

Not only that, but he'd convinced his brothers to join in the danger.

Asher raised his foot to give me a lift into the saddle, and as I settled into place, wrapping the harness around my waist, I wondered what I'd do if any of them fell tonight. Could I survive that guilt?

Don't think about that.

Save Matthias.

That's all you need to worry about.

They know the risks.

My blood churned in my veins, a tempest of nervous anticipation and foolish hope, when Asher ran to the edge of the terrace and launched us into the air. Beating his wings, he took us higher, following the rise of the mountain slopes around us. For a moment after we slipped into the gray clouds that hovered around the peaks, I wondered if I'd put too much faith into these dragons' abilities to hunt gold. We couldn't see more than a few meters in front of us. How would we even be able to avoid flying straight into the other mountains?

The dragons flew slowly at first with Asher in the lead, his head turning this way and that, pausing every so often before shaking his head again and looking elsewhere. Craggy spires of black rock appeared seemingly out of nowhere, stealing my breath and holding my lungs hostage until Asher soared by each.

The sun's light began to fade, and hope of finding Matthias today waned with the wind rushing past me, like a mountain eroded by centuries of storms. In the growing darkness, I could barely make out Isa atop Dax. Leaning forward, I rapped my hand against Asher's neck to get his attention.

He had half-turned to peer back at me when he abruptly stopped, his snout dipping down toward the ground hidden far below us. Beneath me, every muscle in his back tensed. He didn't bother to confer with his brothers before sending us into a steep dive. The cold air stung my face and hands, and I shifted as best I could, trying to turn my cheek to lay against his scales and guard my eyes from the frigid gale. Looking back, I realized Dax and Kai had changed course along with us, holding their tight formation.

When we dropped out of the clouds, my heart sank.

Dark canyons and crevices wove an intricate web of rock. The humans were here. Somewhere. I couldn't sense them physically, but somehow I knew.

We drifted downward on silent wings, gliding through the unnervingly still air.

My nerves had already started to fray with worry when a scream rent the silence.

Agonizingly horrible, it stabbed my heart, freezing the blood in my veins.

My mate.

My mate was dying.

I couldn't breathe.

I couldn't move.

He roared another scream, this time stronger, defiant, like he was daring to call out to me, to pull me toward him, to beg me to slaughter everyone who tried to keep us apart any longer.

CHAPTER 86

MATTHIAS

Graham violently stole the control back from me with his blade, rousing me by once again flaying the skin where my tattoo had been—the skin he'd taken such care and time to heal with that salve—digging his knife in deeper than he had the first time.

There was no silencing my torment now, no hiding it under forced laughter. It poured out of me in a long, sustained wail as he buried his knife under my skin and peeled it away to expose the flesh beneath. My body silently screamed through my nerves, so loud in my head I *almost* didn't hear the sickening slap of my severed skin being thrown to the ground at my feet.

In the brief reprieve Graham granted me, my lungs pulled short, desperate gasps as shock overwhelmed my body. Pulse quickening, I couldn't still my limbs from trembling against the chair I was still confined to. My head bobbed like the raggedy doll my niece used to carry with her everywhere growing up.

"Deep breaths," Graham said with mock tenderness, his breath grating over my maimed ear. "It will do you no good to get all worked up."

Instinctively my hands curled into fists, and I winced as my mangled fingertips smarted at the pressure against them.

"Careful," he said again. "You don't want to hurt yourself."

I slid a rage-fueled glare his way, and he laughed.

"Only I get to hurt you," he charged. "Speaking of which."

In one swift movement, he thrust his hand into my gut, forcing a groan out of me. It wasn't until he pulled away, dragging his hand across my belly, that I realized he'd been holding his knife. The metallic fragrance of fresh blood overwhelmed me as moist heat spilled into my lap. The incision he'd made was small, but enough for my entrails to start spilling out.

A scream ripped from my chest, spurred on as much by the sight as the pain. Graham started to laugh once more. Lifting my gaze to his, I pushed my scream louder, drowning out his amusement. But something—someone—responded with a roar outside, a menacing and terrifying growl that seemed to shake the mountain, quieting us both.

"What was that?" Graham mumbled, his hands shaking as he spun his head around toward the doorway.

I let out one excruciating breath of a laugh before answering him.

"Sounds like my mate."

My shadows billowed from my hands, as strong as the battle cry erupting from my chest, and then Asher, Dax, and Kai added their voices to mine, filling the mountain range with the deafening boom that only three dragons could make. My own shouts shifted into a string of maniacal laughter. When their roar subsided, leaving my amusement dancing through the air, I was struck by an eerie reminder of how I'd laughed like this upon killing those first humans in my court.

Isa peered at me from where she waited on Dax's back, horror flashing in her eyes briefly before she blinked it away. Clamping my mouth shut, I waited for her chastisement, but instead she lifted a shoulder and pulled her lips into a crooked smile.

"So much for the element of surprise," she said.

"Better not give them any chance to muster weapons then," I noted, and without warning Asher threw his head down and dove toward the black rocks below. I scrambled for a handhold, my laughter bubbling back up. Concentrating, I forced my shadows away from me until they engulfed all five of us in darkness without obstructing our own visibility.

Asher weaved around the thin spires, and I turned back to make sure his brothers—and Isa—were staying with us. Trusting my friend's golden nose to know where my mate was in this dark labyrinth, I focused solely on holding my shadows steady and keeping my hands tight on the saddle.

Careening down into a narrow canyon that was barely wide enough for the dragons' wings, my heartbeat racing with excitement and anticipation, I dared peek around Asher's head. I could see nothing but rock, could hear nothing but the rush of air and the steady beat of his wings.

I was starting to grow nervous that perhaps Asher had gotten it wrong when my pulse shuddered for just a moment. My shadows snapped back into my hands, as if my heart had pulled back on the reins and frightened my powers like a skittish horse. I jerked upright, throwing my hand to my chest, confusion swirling in my mind. I hadn't relaxed at all. The thrill of my coming vengeance still burned hot in my veins. My heartbeat was racing again, but now there was more than revenge filling my chest.

Nervous fear, with the tiniest sliver of hope embedded in a suffering that wasn't mine.

Matthias was near.

These had to be his emotions through the bond, coming through as strongly as they had during our shared dream.

Before I could tap on Asher's shoulder, though, a new sound split the air—like a large arrow whizzing by. I craned my neck to peer behind us in time to see Kai tumbling in mid-flight, his body rolling to the side as his wings crumpled around him. He crashed into the mountainside with a loud growl that brought his brothers to a halt, their wings twisting to slow them down and their claws scraping against the ground.

"What was that?" Isa asked, already fumbling with her harness, but she stopped as Dax pivoted around and took off on foot to check on his brother who lay against the steep wall.

"Is he okay? Is he going to be okay?" I asked even though Asher couldn't answer in this form. My friend wasn't watching after his brothers, though. He was peering up the mountain, shifting his head this way and that as his nostrils flared. Something moved against the gray clouds that hid the peaks, pulling my attention, but whatever it was—whoever it was—had disappeared.

I leaned toward Asher's head. "We need to find Matthias."

He twisted his head around, and I followed his gaze to see Kai had shifted back into his human form, blood visible on his skin even from here, though he didn't appear to have any noticeable wounds. Isa, having dismounted now, knelt beside him, cradling his face in her hands and tapping his cheek.

Panic took hold. If we stayed here—if we delayed any longer—Graham could move Matthias.

"Please, Asher," I begged, hating that I was even daring to ask him to leave his brothers behind for me. My friend had lost nearly as much as I had, and I was here trying to pull him away from another loved one who could be dying.

Snorting out a breath, Asher sent a growl echoing down the canyon, and Dax's head snapped up to face us. They stared at each other for a long, gut-wrenching moment. Dipping their chins sharply at each other—seemingly coming to an agreement—they both turned, and Asher launched forward, leaving Dax and Isa to care for Kai.

The gray clouds descended into the canyon, making it difficult to see where we were going, but Asher barely slowed.

"That's far enough," a smooth, deep voice called from the mist in front of us, and Asher locked his knees, rearing back to stop quickly. Asher huffed out an irritated snort, and I quickly undid the harness and slipped down to the ground. As I strolled in front of my friend, my shadows crept from my palms to pool around my legs and swirl around my torso, ready to strike should I need them.

Asher gazed down at me, a gleam of mischief in his bronze eyes as he discretely nudged his snout toward the man standing before us. He must have been over two meters tall, as he could nearly look the dragon beside me in the eye, but then I noticed what must have caught Asher's eye. The man's hands, clasped casually in front of him, were covered in tattoos. His head angled slightly as if he found us more curious than a threat, giving a clear view of the tattoos that crept up out of his collar and around to the back of his neck. This had to be the nightwalker Niko and Sasha had mentioned.

"Our fight is not with you," I said, silently commanding my shadows to hold back and wait.

The man's resulting smile seemed almost genuine—and human, with the fangless row of teeth he flashed. Niko hadn't mentioned him being human, but then again, he also hadn't confirmed he was a nightwalker. If only there was a way to let this man know that we were truly allies.

"You're right," he said, his eyes narrowing as he spread his arms out to his sides. "Your fight is with all of us."

CHAPTER 88

MATTHIAS

Graham's nervous pacing echoed off the walls as if the room had its own manic heartbeat. As much as I relished in his rising fear, my body seemed more focused on keeping me alive than letting me gloat—pulling my eyes closed and slowing my breaths. I just needed to hold on until Calla found me here.

Soon. She'd be here soon.

She was close.

That unforgettable roar had signaled her arrival. As if I didn't already owe Asher for saving my life once, his bringing my mate here to save me again would leave me in his debt for the rest of my life––which hopefully wasn't going to be nearly as short as I'd assumed mere moments ago.

The battle cry of the dragon had certainly breathed new life into my dimming hope, but now I discovered something else swirling in my chest—something not from myself, but through the bond: the excited buzz of energy that always managed to hit before a battle, like our minds knew exactly what we needed to drive us forward.

"I should kill you right now," Graham seethed quietly, though his menacing words couldn't quite hide his growing uncertainty.

Sliding my eyes open, I forced my words out on a strained breath. "Your funeral."

"She's going to kill me anyway," he argued, shoving his blade into my face. "At least killing you would ensure she suffers even after she gets her revenge."

"Perhaps. Or she might show mercy like she did to the Assembly," I offered as my head lolled to the side again, my energy depleting quickly with the effort of speaking.

"After she slaughtered two of them, you mean," he corrected me. I tried to shrug, but I couldn't quite tell if my muscles cooperated or not.

"Kill me and you guarantee a nasty death for yourself." My voice was barely more than a whisper now. "Or let me live and buy yourself time to beg for clemency."

Growling, he spun away from me and resumed his pacing. Whether I'd convinced him one way or the other, I couldn't tell, but I was still breathing for the time being, which was good enough for me...for now.

CHAPTER 89

CALLA

Behind the man, a dozen people—men and women of varying heights, brandishing blades and bows—stepped out of the mist. A warning growl rumbled in Asher's chest as he brought his front leg protectively in front of me.

"You know why I'm here," I guessed, watching to see how the man reacted. He didn't move, but there, a tiny shift in his chin, a slight tightening at the corners of his eyes. "Why protect a fae?"

"The chained one means nothing to us."

"No, the one who brought him. Why—"

The man lifted a single brow. "Graham?" My lips pressed together at the name, and Asher snarled again quietly. A single, hollow laugh echoed off the walls, and the man waved a flippant hand in the air. "He's only half-fae."

Graham? Half-human? How?

My mind swirled with questions.

"With all due respect, you can't win this fight," the tall man continued. "You've seen on the mainland what our weapons can do to your kind, yes? How do you think that beast of yours will fare after we hit him?"

I scoffed. "With all due respect to *you*, you don't know what we're capable of."

The man laughed softly. He opened his mouth to say something, but another voice shouted in the distance, muffled by thick rock, but still clear enough to pierce my heart.

"Calla!"

Matthias.

Asher's head shot up, his snout pointing beyond the group of people barring our way. Desperate hope bloomed in my chest, and I couldn't tell if it was coming from me or Matthias, possibly both. Either way, he needed me. Keeping my hands hidden, I stretched my fingers wide, and with the silent order to spare the tall guard in front, I let loose the reins on my power and propelled my shadows away from me and toward the humans.

Chaos unfolded before us as darkness engulfed the entire force. Screams escaped the dark cloud, choked off by shadow. Men spun around in futile attempts to fend off their phantom attackers. Blades clattered to the ground, followed by the satisfying thumps of bodies dropping. The tall man hadn't turned but continued to stare at us, seemingly unfazed by the slaughter occurring behind him. Dropping his head to one side, he studied me curiously, and I could have sworn a smirk was attempting to pull through his stern expression.

An arrow escaped my shadows, whirring over the tall man's shoulder, narrowly missing his ear as it arced straight toward me. Asher shifted his body to protect me, and the steel tip skidded off his scales and careened off to the side. I pulled my shadows back to give Asher a clear view, and more arrows and blades came flying at us. He swung his tail forward and wrapped it in front of us. He didn't waste any time, immediately redirecting the spikes that lined the tip of his tail back toward our assailants.

The man stepped over the thrashing limb as if he were taking a leisurely stroll, a move so smooth and effortless—so inhuman—it distracted me long enough I didn't notice another attacker rushing forward, dropping to the ground, and barely avoiding having his head lopped off by Asher's tail. But it didn't stop him from sending a blade whirling end over end toward my friend's head.

I threw my hands forward, directing my shadows at this new target. Reacting instantly, the dark tendrils wound around the attacker's head and yanked it from his body. Asher groaned painfully, but thankfully the dagger had merely grazed his eye, leaving a bloody gash from cheek to brow. Despite the blood pouring from his wound, he released a deafening roar and charged forward at the last remaining humans. Crushing the fallen humans under his taloned feet, he attacked those still standing. One man attempted to flee, but my shadows caught him, holding him still while Asher's spiked tail sank deep into his chest. A pair of women lowered themselves into a crouch, their swords and spears readied as if they stood any chance against a dragon—injured or not. Asher lowered his head toward them. When he came within range, one threw her spear toward his good eye, but they had underestimated how quickly he could move despite his size.

The shaft had barely left her hand when Asher lashed out, his horned head darting forward and snatching both women up in his jaws. Their screams echoed through the canyon as he clamped his teeth down on them—crushing bones and severing limbs—before flinging them into the far wall.

I pulled my shadows back in just enough to see if any humans still breathed, but scanning the canyon—both in front and behind—I found no one, not even the man who had initially greeted us. Where had he gone? To call in reinforcements? To help Graham escape?

"Cal—" Matthias's strained scream was cut short.

Without a second thought, I took off toward the sound, leaping over the dead, but my heart jolted as if I'd just been kicked hard in the sternum. Skidding to a stop, I doubled over, my hand clutched to my chest. Where there had been a spark of hope in my veins, now lay a disheartened misery, an empty resignation.

Lifting my head, I peered ahead into the mist, to where my mate waited for me, dying.

He couldn't die, not when I was this close.

With tears pricking my eyes, I pulled in a steadying breath and charged forward.

CALLA

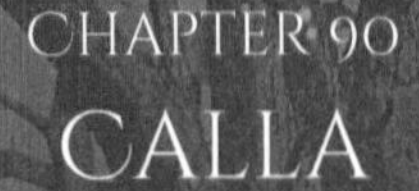

Thick, cold fog pressed in on all sides, but still I pushed on, albeit slower than I preferred. Behind me claws scraped against the ground and a ragged breath matched my pace. Risking a glance over my shoulder, I calmed slightly at the sight of Asher chasing after me with his wounded brow already starting to heal and dried blood clinging to his scales.

A heartbeat, frantic but faint, caught my ear from somewhere to my left, and I skidded to a stop, craning my head to locate the source. Asher pulled up alongside me, snorting out a breath when I raised my hand in command to hold. A rumble of thunder thrummed in his chest, his nostrils flaring and lips pulling back over jagged teeth. He'd caught a scent. I nodded to him to take the lead. Crouched low to the ground with his wings folded tightly to his body, he crept forward, sniffing along like a hound. With another irritable snort, he swung his head back to me and gestured for me to catch up.

Nudging me with his snout, he thrust me through the mist, nearly running me face first into the black stone of the mountain that seemed to swallow up what little sunlight made it into this canyon. Gingerly I ran my fingers along the rock. What had Asher discovered? What was I missing?

I steadied myself, letting my eyelids droop so I could focus on the pulse I'd heard earlier. Ignoring my own pounding heart and the low growl still brewing within Asher, I listened for that rapid beat, but it had gone silent. Slamming my palm against the rock, I dropped my chin to my chest. I hadn't come all this way and faced a horde of poison-wielding humans to wind up at a dead end.

An icy cold spread through my hand, caressing my fingers, as my shadows slipped free of their own accord. Glancing up, I struggled to make them out against the dark wall, but as they skimmed over the surface, I was able to track their movement enough to note when they disappeared behind an otherwise unnoticeable edge. Quickly, I scrambled to follow them, tripping over my own toes. Asher's tail whipped around to catch me and help right me.

"Thanks," I muttered, patting his scales as he pulled back.

My shadows led me into a narrow crevice in the mountainside where I caught the pulse I'd noted earlier. I started to dart into the opening, when Asher's growl faded, replaced by a frustrated sigh. Turning back to him, I realized the issue: he couldn't follow me while in his dragon form.

"Would you rather stand guard out here like this?" I asked. "Or shift and come with me?"

He answered by first shoving his snout into the fissure and sniffing quietly. When he emerged, he pivoted around, planted his feet, and scanned the surrounding fog. Without another word, I pulled my shadows back into my hands—not wanting to risk them giving away my presence any more than my pulse and scent might—and slipped into the mountain. The path twisted and turned a couple times before opening into a cave with sparse furnishings. The scent of leather, trees, and blood overwhelmed me.

Matthias.

He'd been here. Or he was here.

No sooner had I taken one step toward the doorway on the far wall than someone barreled into me from the left, sending me careening to the floor with a groan. My hip hit hard before I was rolled onto my back by a slight figure who quickly straddled my abdomen, pinning my arms down along my sides with their knees. Strong hands slammed into my shoulders, holding them tightly against the uneven floor.

"Ami?" I huffed out breathlessly. "Why—"

The healer smiled darkly and squeezed her legs tighter around me as she curled her fingers painfully into my flesh. "Did you honestly think no one knew of your powers all these years? You think no one knew of your cursed blood? The queen should have listened to me and rid the world of you and your evil when it was first discovered. How many would still be alive if she had?"

My mind churned, mirroring my shadows as they swirled under my palms that rested against my thighs.

"You've wanted me dead my whole life?" I asked, my confusion twisting around my swelling wrath and pulling my brows low.

"The magic you harbor is pure evil that can do nothing but destroy and maim. You know this. It's why you tried to hide it for so long. It wasn't until you lost your stars-damned mind—"

"Because I lost my entire family!" I growled, squirming my hips under her, but she was surprisingly strong and held firm.

Ignoring my outburst, she spoke over me. "I'd warned your foolish parents time and time again."

Fuck this.

I'd heard enough, and she was keeping me from getting to Matthias.

"My parents were fools indeed to keep a bitter bitch like you at the castle," I said. Not the most original words I could spit at her, admittedly, but any distraction would do. Calling to my shadows, I held Ami's stare in a silent dare to try something, but after a few moments—why, I couldn't tell—she tore her eyes from mine, flicking them to the far doorway. Her grip loosened slightly, my signal to unleash my wickedness.

Before she could bring her gaze back to me, my shadows took

hold of her neck, wrenching her head back at a grotesque angle that forced her hands to release my shoulders and her whole body to slacken in surrender. Tossing my chin up, I sent my shadows—with the healer in their powerful grasp—to the wall behind me where they twisted her around and slammed her back against the rock, holding her firmly while I stood up. Her feet scrambled to find the floor, but it was a good half-meter below her as my darkness held her by the throat and pressed her wrists into the stone. Fear flared in her eyes, her lungs frantically gasping for air.

Had I been in this position a week ago, I would have already killed her, but despite my earlier words, my parents weren't fools. They believed in mercy, forgiveness, and justice. While justice sometimes had to be dealt on swift, murderous wings, other circumstances warranted a more judicious approach.

"Get it over with," Ami rasped out, a flicker of courage briefly gleaming in her expression before it was replaced instantly by panic.

"I'm not going to kill you," I said. "Not yet, anyway. I think you deserve to come home and stand trial before the kingdom you tried to destroy."

"I was trying to *save* the kingdom," she hissed, her worried look shifting once again into bitter resistance.

Sighing, I twirled a finger in the air, and my shadows tightened around her throat, squeezing until she slipped into unconsciousness. Sure she was still alive, I ordered my shadows to carry her back out to the canyon where Asher could guard over her.

"When did Calla Vael learn mercy?" Graham's voice, its familiarity worn ragged by his betrayal, seared my heart like a branding iron. I said nothing as I slowly turned to face him. His haggard look and slumped shoulders sparked both delight and dread in my gut. On one hand, if he was as stressed and exhausted as he appeared, he'd be easier to defeat. On the other, if he looked this bad, I couldn't bear to imagine Matthias's state.

"Where is he?" I demanded. Stalking toward him, I noted

how his brow lifted slightly in surprise when I tucked my shadows back into my palms.

"He's still alive," Graham said, leaning casually in the doorway.

Pressing my tongue hard against the roof my mouth, I restrained my fury and continued to approach. "Not what I asked. Is he back there?" I indicated to the room behind him.

"Don't you want to know why?"

"Nothing you say can undo what you've done, and I'm in no mood to endure your gloating over all you've *accomplished*."

"What if I could tell you who killed Brennan?" He cocked a brow, as if he were offering an enticing dessert.

"Doesn't matter," I said, shrugging casually as I stopped a couple meters away from him and clasped my hands behind my back, if only to prevent my shadows from lunging out and ending him before I was ready.

"No shadows for me?" He flashed me that boyish grin he used to give me back when the worst I expected from him was unwanted infatuation. Now it turned my insides with disgust.

Shaking my head, I pulled the corners of my lips down, mimicking the upside down smile my mate often wore. "This is something I prefer to do with my own hands."

"Lucky me, though I admit I had hoped to have your hands on me under better circumstances." My nose wrinkled before I could suppress the reaction, and Graham's eyes darkened. "It's funny how fae and humans each think themselves superior to each other, when both are little more than self-centered, high-and-mighty bastards, too good for those who just want to be wanted."

Pushing away from the wall, he stepped toward me and shoved his hands into his pockets. I lifted my chin. He wouldn't intimidate me. I wouldn't back away from him.

"Your family saw me as nothing but a charity case—the poor bastard son of a female you couldn't even bother to protect during the damned war started by that family you chose to marry

528

into. My own father couldn't risk his crown or his reputation to admit he'd bedded that female, because if his kingdom knew he'd slept with the enemy, a fae, they would have strung him up on his own ramparts."

Wait. Was his father...

Trying to piece together all he'd said, my eyes darted away from him for one moment too long. I didn't notice he'd slipped his hand from his pocket—didn't recognize the weapon in his hand—until it was too late, the blade driving into my side, sending me stumbling into the wall.

CHAPTER 91
CALLA

My eyes squeezed shut.

I started to slide down the wall, as if my body insisted I sit and rest, but Graham's fingers wrapped around my neck under my jaw. His hot breath hovered over my ear, the scent of blood and sweat and betrayal pulling bile up into my throat.

"The King of Wrenwick may have been the one to order Brennan's death," he said slowly, taunting me as if he were dangling a treat before a hound. "But I'm the one who forced him to—a little blackmail over infidelity can accomplish a lot, even the assassination of a king." He squeezed my jaw harder. "I will have a crown one way or the other, Calla. Brennan would still be alive if you had simply chosen me instead of him. And now Matthias will die unnecessarily—along with all the other pitiful males in these trials—because you could never accept my hand."

Sliding my eyes open, I shifted my chin toward him and pressed into his grip.

"Let me see my mate," I commanded.

His eyes narrowed slightly, and I half-expected him to deny my request out of spite, but as I'd hoped, his need to boast won out. Sighing deeply, he pulled me away from the wall and dragged me into the other room. My legs nearly gave out at the sight of Matthias chained to a metal chair in the center, a large chunk of skin missing from between his shoulders—his tattoo, the one honoring his family, gone. More bile gathered when I realized it was his skin—and were those his fingernails?—on the ground near his feet.

"What did you do to him?" I whimpered, but my heart lit up when Matthias shifted and uttered a quiet groan.

Graham chuckled darkly in my ear. "You haven't even seen the worst of it." He shoved me away from him, and I barely kept from tumbling to the blood-splattered floor before I made it around to face my mate.

Dropping to my knees, my hands hovered over Matthias's knees as I surveyed his injuries. Tears welled in my eyes, making it difficult to assess his condition. Below his swollen jawline, his chest rose and fell with slow, shallow breaths. My gaze trailed down his chest, and I nearly fell backwards in horror at the sight of blood still flowing from the wound in his gut.

Reaching for his face, I stroked his cheeks with my thumbs. "Matthias, I need you to wake up now. I need you to hold on, to stay with me." His eyelids fluttered weakly but remained closed. Slowly, he leaned into one of my hands and released a hum of a sigh. "I hate you, general. Remember? You promised to take all of my hate, and I refuse to let you go back on your word."

Matthias still didn't look at me, but deep in my chest a wave of comforting love and refreshed hope poured in from our bond. Wincing as I lifted onto my knees, I pulled his head forward as far as I dared and pressed a kiss to his forehead.

Graham's slow footsteps grated on my nerves, poking holes in my heart. "As sweet as this is, I'm afraid that's all the time you'll get together." He paused, and in my periphery I noticed him wave his fingers in the air. Behind him, Ami walked in, dwarfed by the tall man from earlier standing beside her, dropping an unconscious Asher—now in his human form—to the ground.

CHAPTER 92

MATTHIAS

The scent of sugared berries and purple blooms slowly pulled me out of the darkness, though I still couldn't open my eyes to find her.

"I hate you, general."

Most would have found such words to be daggers to the heart, but for me they were a stars-blessed balm to my battered soul—a lifeline cast out to me on four simple words. I tried to move, but pain stilled me once more.

Don't leave me, I silently begged her as I leaned into her palms and cherished the softness of her lips against my skin. Her warmth fell away too soon, leaving my skin cold and lonely.

Come back!

She couldn't hear me.

I tried to pry my eyelids open, desperate to see her, hopeful that perhaps the sight of her might give my body the boost it needed to help us survive these damned mountains. They refused, though, remaining tightly closed.

"Alek," Graham's voice pierced my consciousness—the last voice I wanted to hear. "Where are the others? She wouldn't have come with just him."

"We shot one of the dragons down in the canyon. The other

two stayed with him, but we managed to secure them easily enough."

"Hear that, Calla?" Graham hissed at my mate. "You've lost. Your friends have been captured. Your mate's at death's door. You came all this way, only to fail at the last moment."

"Until I stop breathing, I have not lost," Calla seethed.

If there were more words exchanged, I didn't know, as a bolt of pain shot through me—but it wasn't mine. It was Calla's.

The tightness around my ankles and wrists eased, though. The pain subsided as quickly as it had come on, replaced with that same burst of excited anticipation I'd experienced before. Testing my restraints, I shifted one of my legs as far as I dared.

The chains no longer held.

I was freed, but how?

This time when I tried to open my eyes, I managed to lift my lids enough to see my mate's shadows slipping away from the chains. Raising my chin a bit—and swallowing hard against the resulting twinge in my back—I found her staring past me, but her eyes slid quickly to mine.

I yearned to brush her tears away, but not yet. There would be time for that.

"Take her to the humans, Alek," Graham commanded, and my heart stopped. I finally had her back, and they were going to steal her from me again.

Alek laughed darkly. "I don't answer to you, Mr. Harrison. They aren't particularly happy that you brought dragons to their doorstep. I'm not sure they'd accept any gift you offered."

Graham scoffed. "I admit he's worthless, but his mate? Have you not seen her powers? They could be of great use to the humans' cause. With their penchant for extracting and harnessing power, imagine what they could do with her shadows...or the dragons' shifting abilities?"

A soft hum filled the cave, and then Alek spoke again. "Don't let this go to your head, but you do make some good points."

Light footsteps approached, and Calla growled. "I'll end you before you can even lay a hand on me."

"I don't think so," Alek said. "You do that, and there will be no one to advocate for the release of your friends or your mate."

He stepped closer still, and Calla crawled away from him, circling around the chair and staying as close to me as she could. Leaning over her, Alek's hand shot out and grabbed her by the hair, yanking her to her feet. Shadows sprang from her palms and darted for the man, but he clicked his tongue.

"If you want them to live, you'll put the darkness away."

He started to drag her away from me, to take her to the humans, to put her through unimaginable pain.

She had come to save me, and there was no stars-damned way I was going to sit here and let her go this easily.

Roaring from both the agony and rage, I launched myself up from the chair with every drop of remaining energy in my body and—clutching one hand to my gut to keep my insides in place— barreled into him as hard as I could.

CHAPTER 93

CALLA

In a matter of seconds, the cave devolved into pure chaos. Matthias sprang from his chair and tackled the man— Alek—with one arm, working to hold his gut together with the other. Alek flung me back to the floor to fend off my feral mate. In an effort to avoid landing on my injured side, I fell onto my hands, which still ached from the intense pain of unlocking Matthias's iron chains with my shadows. Climbing to my feet, I moved to help Matthias, but Graham—his wild and murderous eyes trained on me—lunged around the chair, sending Ami scurrying backwards until she landed on her backside beside Asher.

"You can't save him this time, Calla," Graham hissed, pointing his blade at me.

"Graham, don't!" Ami yelled at him, but he ignored her.

A blaze of rage ripped through me.

"Maybe not, but I can kill you," I seethed, uncurling my fingers and yanking my shadows from my palms. They hovered in the air, heeding my command to wait.

"Thought you wanted to use your hands," he mocked around his sneer.

"I changed my mind," I said, and without warning, I sent my power soaring toward him.

Graham screamed as tendrils of darkness latched onto his fingertips, burrowing under his fingernails even as he tried to shake them free. So focused on those shadows, he didn't seem to notice the other dark ribbon aimed at his abdomen. It reared back slightly, still unseen by him until it struck, stabbing him in the gut. His eyes bulged and his mouth fell open as his lungs sucked down a loud gasp of air. Instinctively he tried to retreat, rounding his back to pull his bleeding abdomen away from his attacker, but my shadows held on. Lifting my hands, I grinned when he met my gaze.

"Please," he begged. "Have mercy."

A giggle exploded from my chest, and I shook my head. When I snapped my hands closed into tight fists, Graham doubled over, his arms fighting to wrap around his middle, where my shadows wreaked havoc on his organs—twisting, tightening, severing. My shadows released his bloody fingers and slithered up his arms, snapping his bones as they traveled up. His screams filled the cave, echoing off the walls and filling my ears with the sweet sound of overdue revenge.

"Enough," Alek commanded, and I tore my eyes away from my prey to my mate, still bleeding and now semi-conscious on the floor, the man's boot resting on his chest.

Meeting the man's cold gaze, I contemplated sending my shadows after him, remembering only at the last moment that he had my friends held captive somewhere in these mountains.

"End him already," he said.

"He hasn't suffered enough," I hissed through clenched teeth.

"His suffering will not bring healing."

"Perhaps not, but satisfaction is an acceptable substitute."

The man said nothing but lifted a brow. Pressing his foot down, he forced a groan from Matthias, and my heart jolted.

A flash of movement to my left pulled my attention as a deafening roar erupted. Ami shrieked only to be silenced almost instantly as Asher's shifting back to his dragon form sent her flying several meters away, her head hitting the stone wall. Asher's scaled body filled up a third of the room, blocking the only exit. Huffing out a breath, he glared past me to Alek who merely sighed. A snarl rumbled in Asher's throat as he pulled his lips back to bare his teeth.

Alek—unfazed by the sudden presence of a dragon—slowly lifted his boot from Matthias's chest and clasped his hands behind his back, but his calm expression did little to put me at ease. "It's time," he said. "Kill him."

"I don't answer to you." I repeated his earlier words back to him.

"If you don't, I will. We're running out of time."

Narrowing my eyes at him, I squeezed my fists tighter, drawing another delightful squeal of pain from Graham.

"Time for what?" I asked.

"To get you out of these mountains and away from here."

Matthias groaned on the floor beside the man's feet, perspiration beading his forehead despite the cold air inside this cave. Asher growled, though it was hard to tell whether he was issuing a warning to Alek or guidance to me. Regardless, Matthias needed help. Alek was right. It was time.

Keeping my hand tightly closed, I twisted my wrist around, a silent order to my shadows to crush Graham's heart. His eyes—unfocused and dull—briefly widened again as he choked on one final breath. He crumpled to the ground, his innards spilling from the gash in his gut as my shadows pulled free, leaving him in a lifeless, bloody heap beside the chair where he'd tortured my mate for days.

Once Graham's body hit the floor, I rushed to Matthias, kneeling on the hard ground beside him. I didn't look up at Alek as I asked, "Do you have any way of healing him?"

"Unfortunately, no. We create poison to kill fae, not save them. If he were human—even one able to shift like your friend here—then we could."

"Matthias?" I asked quietly, sweeping sweat-logged strands of hair off his forehead. "Can you hear me? You're going to be okay.

I'll fix this. I just need you to hold on a little longer while I figure out how."

A weak hum was his only response, but it would have to do.

"You will need to shift back if you're going to get out of here," Alek said to Asher, who snarled back at him. "If you don't, I'll have to force you to again."

Asher's growl seemed to vibrate the stone floor, but a moment later, he had transformed back to his human form.

"How did you force it anyway?" Asher asked, stepping forward to stand beside me.

"Lucky guess, actually. When we hit the other dragon—"

"You mean my brother," Asher corrected harshly.

"We learned you weren't fae shifters, because the poison should have killed him. It wasn't until we saw him shift a few moments later that we discovered you're actually human."

Asher scoffed. "You could have simply asked."

"Yes," Alek said. "I'm sure that would have gone well. Regardless, I took a chance and tried it on you while you stood guard outside. A poisoned barb shot into the soft underside of your massive head was enough to force you back to human form, and a bit of sleeping tonic laced in with it had you out rather quickly."

"But then why didn't the blade to my eye not—"

"Not a deep enough cut. Not enough poison on the blade. Any number of reasons," Alek explained.

"Well, thanks for not killing me, I suppose," Asher said. "Though don't expect any favors in return."

"Of course not."

I cleared my throat impatiently, pulling their gazes down to where I still knelt beside my unconscious mate. "If you're done bonding up there, I could use your help. Where are the others?"

Alek lowered into a crouch across from me on the other side of Matthias. "I had them taken to another detaining area further down the canyon."

"Are they okay?" Asher asked, his arms crossed tightly in front of him.

Alek nodded. "I will help get you—"

"Why? Why help us?" I asked, not sure whether to tell him about our meeting with Niko and Sasha. I couldn't risk divulging the presence of a spy among the humans if Alek turned out to not be their contact.

He angled his head at me and flashed me an incredulous look like I had just asked a ridiculous question. "You didn't attack me. A bit too obviously, if I'm being honest. Should have at least given me a scratch or a broken bone if you wanted to avoid raising suspicions."

"You wanted me to hurt you?"

"Not my preferred source of pleasure, so no. Your shadows bypassing me made it clear you knew who I was and knew not to harm me, which means you were sent by Niko. I can't risk my cover being blown, though. They cannot know who I am or why I am here."

Despite all the questions this conjured in my head, I had no time to ask any of them. Matthias needed to get help, and he wouldn't get that here.

"How do we get out of here without endangering you and your mission?"

Alek opened his mouth to answer, but Asher chimed in first. "And without getting ourselves killed."

"You have trust issues, don't you?" Alek asked, turning a bored eye to my friend. He didn't wait for a response, though. "First thing you learn about living in the mountains: you never want to be trapped. We ensure every cave has a secondary exit at least."

I looked around but saw nothing but solid walls peppered with anchor points and dangling chains.

Alek chuckled quietly. "Second thing you learn is to not make them obvious."

At this he straightened up and strolled over to a pair of empty anchors in the corner. Gripping them with both hands, he turned them—one clockwise, the other counter. The wall let out an airy hissing noise as hidden seams in the rock opened. With far less effort than expected, Alek pulled the section of the wall toward him and slid it to the side.

He turned and motioned toward the gaping hole, which was big enough for us to walk through. "This tunnel will lead you to a narrow mountain pass that we no longer use. Your friends will meet you there."

"But how will you explain our escape?" I asked, more to save my own skin when I faced the nightwalker rulers again.

"Not your problem. I'll take care of that on my end. You just need to get out and soon. Wait too long and you'll lose the cover of nightfall."

Nodding, I gestured for Asher to help me lift Matthias, but a voice stopped us short.

"You shouldn't move him like that," Ami said, pressing her fingertips to her temple as she slowly pushed to her feet, using the wall for support. "It's too risky with his injuries."

"Can you heal him?" I asked.

"Not without supplies or something to close up the wounds."

"I might be able to help," Asher said.

MATTHIAS

I didn't remember much after I tackled Alek and nearly burst my abdomen open—more open, anyway. Sliding in and out of consciousness, I heard bits and pieces of their conversation. Talking was usually more ideal than fighting, so we must not have lost. At one point the ground seemed to vibrate, sending stabbing pain through my upper back and down to my gut.

"Scales?"

That word pierced the darkness around me. I wanted to ask what that was about, but my body refused to let me open my eyes again, conserving my energy. I supposed not dying was more important than seeking clarification. I found enough energy, though, to bellow out a groan when something pressed hard against my belly.

Make it stop.

Just leave them hanging out.

I'll find a way to live with my innards on the outside.

Once the pain subsided, my world tilted, forcing a grunt from my chest, and the same pressure—though thankfully less agonizing—settled on my back, and warmth wrapped around my torso. The rock floor floated away from me, replaced by firm grips on my legs and arms as I slipped back into a peaceful, dreamless sleep.

※

Darkness enveloped me—so dark I was nearly convinced I'd lost control of my eyelids. Or I'd gone blind. At least I was out of that chair and seemed to be lying down. I shifted, surprised to find a luxurious, warm bed beneath me instead of the rough, unforgiving rock. Moving, though—even that small amount—seemed to tug at my larger wounds, not painfully, but noticeably enough. In fact, the pain had all but disappeared, and only a faint itch nagged at the two spots. My fingertips throbbed minimally, a blessing compared to the flames that had ripped through them before.

"Are you there, Killer?" I croaked out the words, my eyes searching the blackness for her.

Silence.

I took another breath, and as I exhaled, a flicker of hope lit in my chest, not from me, but from the bond.

The scratch and hiss of a match lighting warned me to close my eyes against the oncoming light. A warm glow breached the darkness, but I didn't open them yet, waiting for her to answer.

Another breath passed and then fingers—smooth and warm—clutched my hand where it lay beside me.

"I'm here," she finally said, her voice lacking the relief I'd hoped to hear.

My mind plummeted into a sea of speculation. Had someone died? Had we not escaped? Had Graham somehow won?

"Where is here, exactly?" I asked.

Her hand rested on my shoulder, but when she said nothing, I opened my eyes and turned my head to look at her. The lantern on the table beside her cast eerie shadows across her face.

Calla's eyes searched mine, but for what I couldn't fathom.

Averting her eyes, she sighed. "Still on Dolobare, with the night-walkers."

"How did we get away? Is everyone okay?"

"We're all fine, aside from some minor cuts, bruises, and a fractured rib or two. None as injured as you. Alek helped us out."

"And Graham?"

"Dead." The word fell heavily from her lips like a lifeless body.

"Only dead? Not burned, maimed, dismembered, and tossed into a sea of ravenous sharks?"

Calla shrugged and pulled her lips back into a smirk. "Perhaps a little maimed. Would have been worse, but"—she swallowed hard—"there was no time for all he deserved."

"I'm sorry," I whispered.

Her brows shot up. "Why? Because I didn't get to torture the villain more?"

I swallowed the chuckle her words incited. "For all the times you had to save my ass."

"It's an ass worth saving."

Sighing loudly, I lifted my hand to her face and tucked a strand of hair behind her ear. "Just don't tell Connor how many times I nearly died? It's somewhat embarrassing."

"Well, I cannot make any promises there, especially if he inquires about your performance in the competition. After all, it's ill form to lie to an ally."

"Even when it's to protect your mate?" I asked, immediately regretting using the word. We hadn't talked since that first dream, and even though she'd traveled over an entire sea for me, I couldn't quite tell how she felt about the bond.

"Perhaps I can make an exception for that—perhaps," she said, tapping her finger to her chin. "But only if you promise me something in return?"

"What's that?" My throat constricted, as if afraid I wouldn't be able to swallow whatever she was about to request.

Dropping her eyes down to our clasped hands, she said, "Promise you'll return to me after you go home."

A hint of worry sparked in my veins, shared over the bond. For a moment I watched Calla curiously, wishing I could lean forward and kiss away the tension in her lips. "Why would I go back to Emeryn without you?"

She lifted her gaze, and her features twisted, as if questioning my sanity. "Because I can't? I'm still queen of—"

"And last I checked, you were still in need of a king." My palms were actually sweating, like an adolescent male asking his first female out to dinner.

Calla's eyes narrowed for a moment. Her lips twitched at the corners, but I couldn't tell if she was trying to fight back a smile or a grimace. My insides were such a chaotic jumble of nervousness, excitement, worry, fear, and something else I couldn't pinpoint that made it nearly impossible to tell which emotions were mine and which might be hers. That fear and worry grew, though, when she pulled her hands slowly away from me and folded them in her lap. Her stony expression betrayed none of her thoughts as she studied me. I itched under her scrutiny—or maybe that was simply my healing wounds.

Behind her, a door opened, sending a beam of soft light shining into my darkened room. The air seemed to chill—even through the lush blanket tucked around me—as someone entered on near-silent footsteps.

"General Orelian," came a voice smooth as silk but with a deadly edge. A male and female drifted into focus, both with complexions so light they seemed to be glowing faintly. "How nice it is to see you're awake."

Pushing up onto my elbows, I winced as the movement pulled at my injuries. Calla hurriedly moved some pillows into place behind me, taking my arm to help me sit up.

"Thank you?" It came out a question despite my better judgment—offending a pair of nightwalkers was probably not the best idea—but they didn't seem to mind.

"We do hope the accommodations have been satisfactory," the female said. Her voice held a more subtle hint of danger to it than her companion's, though it still made me uneasy. Not that fae and nightwalkers were enemies by any means––mostly due to fae blood being lethal to vampires. They were also notorious hermits who preferred to remain neutral in most conflicts, hence why they had fled to this dreary island when Connor's uncle had inadvertently started the war all those decades ago.

I offered them as easy a smile as I could under their disconcerting stares. "I was unconscious until just a moment ago, but the last several minutes have been a significant improvement over my most recent lodgings. May I ask who healed me, though?"

"Not one of our kind, if that's your concern," the female said.

"Seems like that would be more a concern for you than for me," I noted, earning me a dry, humorless laugh from the male.

Calla lighted her hand on my arm. "It was Ami. With the help of Asher and his brothers."

"Ami? As in the healer-turned-traitor? You didn't—" Her quick shake of her head stopped me short, and I pulled my lips into a surprised frown. "Since when is Asher a healer though? Or are his brothers?"

"They helped in a slightly different sort of way, you could say," Calla said around a sheepish smile.

"Why all the mystery? Nervous I'll be mad that they saved my life?"

"No," she said quickly, her eyes darting away.

"Well, that was downright unconvincing, Killer. What did they do exactly?"

Pursing her lips, she slowly lifted her shoulders into an apologetic shrug before pulling the blankets back to reveal my abdomen. Where my guts had once been leaking out of my body, they were now—presumably, since I was still alive and felt relatively normal—stuffed back inside, with the wound covered by gold, bronze, blue, and purple scales. But they weren't simply laying atop my skin; they were embedded into me, as if my skin had merely been peeled back to reveal a layer of dragon armor beneath.

Reaching my hand behind my neck, I crept my fingers toward the space between my shoulder blades. Sure enough, instead of a bloody section of skin missing, I found a set of scales fused to my body.

"Well, that explains the itching as these heal," I muttered. Shooting a sideways look at my mate, I asked, "And they offered these pieces of themselves willingly?"

Another shrug. "It was Asher's idea. They have to remain in their dragon forms until the scales grow back. We couldn't use them on your ears, unfortunately, but Ami assures me those will heal easily on their own and don't carry the same risk of infection as the other wounds. They'll forever be rounded though."

The male cleared his throat, drawing our attention to him. "Queen Vael, we wanted to once again extend our deepest thanks to you for sparing our man."

"Of course, Niko," Calla said with a dip of her chin. "I know having us here isn't ideal for you, so we will be heading home as soon as Matthias feels healed enough to fly."

With quick nods, the pair gave a crisp turn on their heels. As they exited, I leaned toward Calla's ear and whispered, "I know a way we could test to see if I'm fit enough to ride a dragon."

I half-expected her to scoff and swat at me with the back of her hand, but instead she peaked a brow, her eyes falling to rest on my mouth. Tucking her bottom lip between her teeth, she rose from her chair and slid up onto the bed, gracefully lifting her leg to straddle me, careful not to lower her whole weight. My body reacted at once despite the layers of bed linens separating us, and my hands found their way to her hips as if they'd been called there by some beacon.

Fisting the edges of her tunic, I kept my eyes locked on hers. "You're not going to break me, you know."

"You were nearly gutted, general."

"Key word, *nearly*."

She rolled her eyes and sighed. Cupping my jaw in her palms, she drew out her shadows to caress my face and move my hair from my forehead. They traveled lower, over my bare chest and down across the new scaly addition to my midsection, before slipping beneath the blanket that sat between us. I tensed in the best possible way at the feel of her cold magic against my skin, which made it difficult to get my words out without gasping.

"Do you treat everyone you hate to this...torture?" I asked, barely able to finish the thought with how her shadows pressed along my length.

Calla wet her lips and donned a fiendish smile as she leaned forward. "I hate no one like I hate you, Matthias."

"I—"

Her lips pressed to mine, cutting off my words and transforming my voice into a low growl. Whether her shadows stilled or not, I didn't know—my full attention focused on the taste of her tongue as it swept across mine.

This was no mere kiss. I'd had my share of kisses, many good ones, in fact, but all faded from memory as Calla—my mate—led me in a new stars-blessed dance where our delight and wonder and desire crashed together along the bond.

CALLA

Reluctantly, I retreated, slipping away from Matthias but remaining close enough to feel the warmth of his breath upon my lips.

"Well, that certainly beats our first kiss," I said, breathily.

Matthias placed a kiss on the tip of my nose. "I should hope so. I mean, you were unconscious for that one."

Sitting back, I regarded him with an annoyed glare. "As if I could ever forget."

"But the question remains," he started, darting his tongue out to wet his lips, which sent a flash of desire surging through my core. When he didn't finish his thought, a questioning hum thrummed in my throat. His hands shifted to the front of my hips so that his thumbs drifted lower to the seam of my pants. Why in the stars did I have to be wearing pants? Though he seemed intent on not letting poor wardrobe choices wreck his plans to undo me. Expertly finding that sensitive bit of nerves, he pressed against me in slow circles until my chest heaved with quickening breaths.

"What question is that?" I asked amidst shallow gasps, echoed by his own as my shadows continued to stroke him under the blankets.

"Do you think I can beat my previous attempts at pleasing you?"

Flashing him a glare of challenge, I pursed my lips as if seriously contemplating his query. "I don't know, general."

"Hard to imagine I could be any better?" he offered, brow rising, his thumbs continuing their mischievous movements.

Angling my hips, I pressed into his hands. He smiled when a rogue moan escaped my chest.

Lifting one shoulder, I said, "We do need to see if you're healed enough to make the journey home after all."

His hands slipped away from me, and I nearly whimpered in protest until I realized he was merely shifting to lift my tunic up over my head. If sitting up caused him any pain, he didn't show it as he eagerly brought his lips to one peaked breast and then the other, giving each one the attention they craved—replacing his tongue with sweeps of his thumb when he switched sides. My head fell back as my eyes closed and my hips rolled against him, letting his hardened length press into the aching spot he'd abandoned.

Everything burned with need.

Every inch of me cried out for release.

Slipping my fingers into his hair I pulled his head back and claimed his lips once more. Whether he could read my mind or sense my desire through our bond, I didn't care. All that mattered was that his hands were slipping under my waistband and—with a few less-than-graceful maneuvers—removing my irksome clothing. All the while, my shadows did their part to shift the blankets out of our way and reveal his eagerness.

He had been remarkable before, but having him melt into me now was a whole new realm of pleasure I never knew existed. I closed my eyes on burgeoning tears. I'd known even the first times we were together that something was different with him, something magnificently and confusingly different, and now I knew why. He was my mate. I was his. The stars had formed us for each other, bound us to each other. Meant for us to be one, in every way possible.

Pushing him back down to the bed, I braced myself with hands on his chest as I moved my hips with his, relishing in how we fit so perfectly together.

"Look at me, Killer," he whispered around ragged breaths, and I obliged at once, knowing I'd find nothing but acceptance and understanding in his eyes.

He lifted a hand to my cheek, stroking his thumb against my skin—not once losing the rhythm of his body with mine.

"There she is," he said, and I couldn't fight back the smile that tugged at my open lips.

"I hate you, general," I said, a tear slipping out to greet his calloused fingertip.

"I want all your hate," he said and tugged my face down to meet his, kissing me once before he whispered against my lips. "Give me all your hate, Killer."

The command in his tone was like a breath blown on hot embers, sending fresh flames to roar inside me and pushing me harder and faster against him. Up and up we climbed together with heaving breaths and tear-stained kisses. Pausing briefly at the peak, I marveled at the gift the stars had given me in my mate. Smiling up at me, he sealed his lips to mine once more, leading us off that precipice and catching me in his arms with trembling contentment and pure fated bliss.

CHAPTER 96

CALLA

Even with everything Niko and Sasha had done for us, allowing us to remain for a few more days until Asher and his brothers' scales had regenerated, we all seemed more than eager to leave Dolobare and the nightwalkers behind us. We landed back at my castle in Arenysen just as the sun was slipping over the edge of the forest. My guards greeted us, promptly taking Ami to the dungeons to await her trial. My stablehands helped us remove the harnesses and saddles from the dragons' backs, but to my surprise, only Asher shifted into his human form.

Matthias reluctantly released my hand as I stepped forward to speak to my friend.

"Leaving so soon?" I asked, my gaze flitting to his two brothers briefly.

Asher dipped his chin low. "Afraid so. I need to get back to this job in Wrenwick."

Matthias rushed to my side, but aimed his question at the dragon shifter. "Wrenwick?" Again Asher nodded, and my mate shot me a sideways glance, lowering his voice. "Think his job has anything to do with a certain curse?"

At this Asher's eyes widened, his chin jutting forward.

"Excuse me?" His eyes darted from Matthias to me. "What curse?"

I stilled except to wring my hands together nervously. Pursing my lips, I caught Matthias's eye and gestured toward our friend. "Could you tell him?"

Confusion pulled his expression tight, but it shifted quickly with understanding. "Right," he whispered before looking to Asher. "Calla can't speak of it herself, but she might have hired a certain mage to punish those responsible for Brennan's death."

"*Might* have," Asher repeated, skeptically.

"Meaning she did," Matthias admitted. Anticipating Asher's next question, he quickly added, "The Olanders."

Isa's hand landed lightly on my arm. "I thought it was Graham."

Nodding, I explained. "Ultimately it was, but—" My voice gave out as soon as I tried to speak of the Olanders' role, but Matthias offered the words I couldn't utter.

"He may have orchestrated it, but apparently the Olanders carried it out."

Behind Asher, his brothers exchanged a glance. Asher pressed his thumb to his temple, his fingers grazing lightly over the fresh but faint scar that bisected his brow. "And what was this curse, exactly?"

"Don't know," Matthias answered for me. "Killer, here, was understandably in no mood to ask at the time, but—"

"We need to get going," Asher interrupted, tossing an anxious glance over his shoulder to his brothers, who both gave crisp nods.

"What is it, Asher? Is it something I can help with?" I asked, reaching a hand out to my friend.

"No, there's nothing more you can do," he said, stepping forward quickly to wrap me in a strong yet brief hug. Extending a hand to Matthias, he added, "I'm glad I was able to help you out."

"Me too," Matthias said, clasping hands with Asher. "If you ever need our help—"

"I know where to find you," Asher said, but his smile—

though genuine—was short-lived, slipping into a frown that seemed almost nervous. Without another word, he offered a quick nod to Isa and spun away from us, shifting mid-stride into his dragon form and leaping up into the air, his brothers following close behind.

Isa stepped cautiously up to my side and leaned around me to peer at Matthias and me both. "Either of you catch what he just said?"

I stared up to the point where the dragons had disappeared over the treetops. "You mean the *nothing more* I could do part?"

Isa nodded as Matthias asked, "Think he's helping the Olanders with your curse?"

"Fuck." The swear fell from my lips on a sigh.

Matthias planted a kiss to my temple. "Don't worry about it, Killer. If anyone can handle a curse, it's Asher."

❧

"You know, Killer, we should have asked for some more brandy while we were with the Vranićs," Matthias said, pouring a small amount into two glasses and walking over to the sofa where I sat waiting for him.

Accepting the glass, I lifted a brow. "You really think I'd waste such an opportunity?" I asked. "Don't you know me at all, general?"

"I should never underestimate you," he said around a laugh.

As he settled down beside me, the door to the solar opened, and Isa entered with Phillip close behind. Matthias was on his feet at once, bounding around the sitting room to greet the other male, asking, "You okay? Can I get you a drink?"

A low growl rumbled in my throat. He couldn't possibly be offering my brandy. Matthias spun his head around to look at me and lowered his voice. "Don't worry, Killer. I know you don't like to share."

Phillip's eyes shifted nervously between us. "I'm fine, thanks," he muttered, following Isa over to sit in the pair of chairs opposite me.

"You might want to sit down, Matthias," Isa said, her voice somber. She lifted an ominous piece of paper and nodded to where I sat.

Matthias obliged, grabbing my hand. "Who died?" When I eyed him disapprovingly, he shrugged and asked, "What?"

"Actually," Isa said, and we both snapped our attention to her. "It's King Durand."

"Oh, shit." The words fell from Matthias atop a heavy sigh, and he downed the last of his brandy before pointing to the message in Isa's hand. "Is that from Connor?"

Isa nodded, and though she offered it to Matthias, she relayed its message to me. "He died a couple days ago, while we were on Dolobare. Message was delivered this afternoon just before we arrived. The burial is at the end of the week, and—"

"I need to be there," Matthias said, refolding the message and tucking it into his pocket. Isa nodded slowly, and Matthias squeezed my hand. "I missed Brennan's, and I can't do that to Connor again."

My chest tightened at the sound of Brennan's name, though not as strongly as it once would have. "We will be there for him," I said.

Isa glanced to Phillip for a second, nodded, and turned back to Matthias and me. "That means we'll need to leave in two days, giving us little time—"

"Little time for what?" I asked. Had I missed something? I hadn't taken more than a sip of my brandy, so it couldn't be the drink's fault for my confusion.

Isa drew in a deep breath. "We still need to announce the winner of the tournament. Given all that has transpired, I would like to forego the final trial if that is acceptable to all of you." She glanced around at each of us, and we nodded in turn. "As Phillip did not complete the third trial, his points remain at one hundred. Matthias found the correct antidote, and even though he didn't have enough left to actually heal you, Calla, I think this warrants granting him at least ten points, making him the winner."

Phillip didn't balk at this pronouncement, but smiled genuinely at Matthias, who cocked his head, his brows knitting together. "Thank you, general. But can I ask why the official announcement requires time? Don't you simply draw up a memo or declaration of some sort?"

Leaning forward, Isa dropped her forearms to her knees. "Given all of the...drama...over the last few weeks and months, it may be best to do so publicly."

"How long would it take to inform the villages?" Matthias asked.

Isa noted, "Not long for the closer villages, but the further ones would never be able to travel in time to attend."

"Would those further away feel slighted if we were to send a declaration instead of an invitation?" I asked, looking to Isa, but Phillip chimed in first.

"If I may..." he started, waiting for me to invite him to continue. "As a citizen and not someone on the royal staff, I recommend inviting who you can. The distant villages will understand, especially if you were to explain all that has happened and why your presence is required in Emeryn on such short notice. Despite what you might fear, we aren't all so hardhearted."

The three of us all stared in silence at the male for several breaths after he finished speaking.

"What?" he asked, shifting nervously under our scrutiny.

Matthias pursed his lips and cast a sideways look my way. "Does Arenysen have an official order of succession for royal appointments?"

Isa was already shaking her head, so I didn't bother answering him with more than a slight smile before I turned back to Phillip.

"While you came here vying for the crown," I said, "I wonder if you might consider accepting a different position, Phillip."

"You mean, like on the Assembly?" he asked, his brow

collapsing low over his eyes, which lowered to the ground immediately. "I'd never considered it, but perhaps—"

"Think bigger, friend," Matthias whispered across the sitting area, and Phillip's eyes darted up to meet his.

Before he could misunderstand again, I asked more directly. "Would you be willing to serve as royal advisor? While you'd be a part of the Assembly, you'd permanently live here at the castle and work directly for—"

"Yes," Phillip interrupted, his face reddening as if he realized a moment too late that he had interrupted his queen. "Of course, Your Majesty. I'd be honored."

Nodding, I smiled. "In that case, your first order of business will be to help Isa draft the necessary messages to the villages and get those sent out as soon as possible."

CHAPTER 97

MATTHIAS

Two days later, I followed Calla onto the dais in the Great Hall with Isa and Phillip on either side of me.

Given the short notice, we had expected the crowd to be lighter than typical citizens' forums, but Calla's disappointment flowed freely across the bond. She shot a look over her shoulder at me, and I offered as reassuring a smile as I could muster, relieved when her nerves calmed. Turning back to the crowd, she folded her hands lightly in front of her and lifted her chin.

"Our kingdom has suffered much this past year," Calla said, her voice strong and unwavering. "The killing of first our king and queen and then my husband"—she paused briefly, inhaling slowly before she continued—"left us deep in grief, uncertain about our future, and—at least for me—in search of answers. Some of those answers have recently been uncovered, and while they have brought some much-needed peace and healing, they have also left us with some unexpected vacancies to fill here at the castle. Today, before you all, we will be announcing the successors for two of these prominent roles."

Whispers spread among the gathered fae, but it was impossible to determine how they were receiving her words. She ushered

Isa forward, and I swallowed hard, as if my heart had actually leapt into my throat. Isa's head slowly swiveled as she gazed out at the crowd, one hand held behind her back while the other rested on her sword. Every fae in the room lifted their eyes to her, leaning forward as if her words were a whisper instead of the natural boom of a leader.

"As you all know, these past weeks we have hosted a tournament to select our next king. Despite the risks of these games, twelve males from both Arenysen and Emeryn stepped forward to test their strength, courage, and wisdom. Two proved their abilities to act both swiftly and admirably, showing not only the fortitude to rule but also the heart to do what is right when others wouldn't. Of those twelve, two consistently displayed the necessary qualities, placing them at the top of the ranks. In the end, though, only one could be crowned the victor and the new king. That male is General Matthias Orelian of Emeryn!"

Phillip's elbow nudged mine, and he offered me a warm smile. Though he'd been unconscious when the bond had formed between Calla and me, he'd quickly learned of it from the staff during his healing. While Calla had been okay with introducing me as her mate, Isa had insisted it better to focus on my winning the tournament.

"Congratulations," Phillip whispered out of the corner of his mouth as he turned forward.

My heart hammered away behind my sternum. I'd faced evil forests and deadly monsters—I'd fought in battles and stood up to mobs—yet my nerves refused to calm until I caught Calla's wry smile. With a steadying breath, I stepped forward. As I made my way around the throne, my footsteps echoed through the quiet room, as heavy and loud as my pulse in my ears. I stopped to face Isa and Calla, wondering what everyone must have been thinking.

Isa continued. "General Orelian, upon arrival, you swore an oath, pledging your loyalty to our kingdom and our queen. You have shown—throughout every trial, and beyond—that you should be the next king of Arenysen. Are you prepared to fulfill your oath and rule beside Her Majesty, Calla Vael?"

"I am," I said, sending my voice echoing off the high ceilings. The crowd released a collective sigh, and a few individuals started to clap, but Isa quieted them with a placating wave of her hand.

"Queen Vael," she said, turning to Calla, who stepped forward slightly. "You, too, swore an oath, pledging your loyalty to the victor of the tournament. Are you prepared to fulfill your oath and accept Matthias Orelian as your king?"

Calla hesitated, and those gathered leaned forward even more, a hush falling over them as they waited. Slowly her shadows slipped from her palms. Someone gasped, which nearly made me chuckle, but the dark tendrils floated to me, wrapping around my hands to lure me to her. Slipping her hands into mine, she pulled her shadows tightly around our entwined fingers and whispered, "I am."

Applause swept through the crowd. Someone whistled.

Leaning toward Isa, I whispered, "Are we supposed to kiss or something?"

Isa shrugged. "You're our future king. I'm pretty sure that means you get to do whatever you want."

Calla clicked her tongue. "Nope. Only once he's officially king. In the meantime, *I* get to do whatever I want."

I didn't get a chance to utter my brilliant retort, because she was already yanking me to her and pressing her lips to mine in a respectable yet somehow still sensual kiss.

CHAPTER 98

CALLA

Returning to my throne with Matthias standing to my right, I was so focused on the peace swimming in my veins—a peace I'd never thought possible again—I didn't hear Isa name Phillip as Graham's successor as royal advisor, and only mildly registered the light applause that followed. It wasn't until a door slammed closed and a heavy silence fell over the room that I blinked out of my own thoughts and back to the present.

A guard approached the dais with Raven and Sera still bound in chains, and Isa and Phillip each slipped behind Matthias and me. When they stopped before me, I rose from my seat and dipped my chin to each of them in greeting. Raven donned a kind smile, and even Sera didn't look like she hated me quite as much as she once did.

Peering over their heads, I first addressed the entire room. "Due to recent events, I have decided to renounce the law which exiled all humans from Arenysen."

The silence seemed to intensify somehow, and wary stares greeted me. Panic struck, a heavy weight dropping into my empty stomach. My shadows, still relaxed by Jocelyn's tonic but roused by the sudden anxiety, thankfully remained settled. Drawing in a slow breath, I shifted my gaze to the women before me.

I can do this.

I'm the queen. I can do anything.

"Raven Keen. Sera Hawthorne. With this change in the laws, I—with those gathered as my witnesses—pardon you both. All charges are dropped. You are free to go."

Two guards stepped forward to remove their chains. While Raven approached and offered me her hand—which I gratefully accepted—Sera maintained her distance, remaining guarded, but at least she wasn't glowering at me.

"Thank you," Raven said before skirting off to greet Matthias with a hug.

Sera merely nodded in silent appreciation. When she didn't move to leave, Matthias stepped past me and bounded down the steps to wrap his sister in a tight hug. He whispered something in her ear, and I could have sworn I detected tears in her resulting laughter. Holding her at arm's length, he angled his head at her and said, "I will stop by to visit. Promise."

"Are you sure you don't want me to come with you?" Isa asked, dropping her hand to my mount's neck as she handed me my reins.

"Yes, Isa. We have so much to do here. I need you to help Phillip get settled so he can help coordinate the trials for the former Assembly members and the healer. Plus, I'm traveling with Emeryn's own esteemed general—"

"Former general," Matthias clarified, bringing his horse up alongside mine and flashing his too-charming smile at both of us.

"They don't know that yet, though," I noted, but then a thought struck me, and I swung back to look at Isa. "Or do they? Did we send word to them about the tournament outcome?"

Isa nodded. "We did, along with our condolences for King Nevan."

Matthias leaned over his horse's neck to speak around me. "And did we happen to mention the bond or—"

Shaking her head, Isa laughed quietly. "No, I left the story of this"—she waved her hand between us—"for you to share yourselves."

"Excellent," Matthias whispered as he settled back in his saddle, a mischievous smile on his face.

As we neared the gate, the pair of guards straightened at their posts, stern looks plastered to their faces. Their expressions shifted, though, when they recognized Matthias. They greeted him with beaming smiles, and I marveled at just how loved he was here in Emeryn and here I was, stealing him away from them.

It's not stealing if he willingly agrees to leave.

"Has the ceremony started?" Matthias asked one of the guards. He reached back for my hand while the male answered.

"Not yet. Another hour, I believe."

"Good," he said and nodded to the guards as he led the way through the gate and up the familiar gravel driveway.

I tried not to think about the last time I'd been here, and how I'd fled without saying goodbye. Would Lieke be cross with me? Would Connor welcome me back here? Would I be able to handle seeing Brennan's grave?

Matthias squeezed my hand and leaned toward me. "Don't worry, Killer," he said. "I've got you."

CHAPTER 99

MATTHIAS

Brushing aside the eerie sense of deja vu, I gave the back of Calla's hands a kiss only to have her shadows sneak out to caress my cheek when I started to pull away.

"Tell your shadows to save that for later," I said with a wag of my brow. Calla rolled her eyes, but her laughter warmed the space between us.

We had barely ridden out of the trees and into the front courtyard when Connor's voice called out. "There he is...and on time!"

Reluctantly I slipped my hand from Calla's to slide down from my saddle, clasping my best friend's hand and yanking him into an embrace. I smiled over his shoulder to where Lieke stood waiting patiently.

"It's good to see you," I said, releasing him, but he didn't let go of my hand even when I gently pulled back.

He squeezed my hand tighter and scrutinized me for a breath, his eyes narrowing when they landed on my now rounded ears. Frowning, he said, "You seem to be missing something."

"More than a few somethings," I explained. "But that unpleasantness can wait for a future conversation."

"Of course," Connor said as he slid his gaze up to Calla, but his head snapped back to me at once. Understanding flashed in his eyes. "Stars be damned," he uttered, his jaw falling open.

Ripping my hand from his grip, I offered Calla help as she dismounted.

"What is it, Wolfie?" Lieke asked, slipping her hand into Connor's and stepping up beside him.

"Matthias—" he started to say, but I wasn't about to let him steal my thunder.

Wrapping my arm around Calla's back, I finished his sentence for him. "—would like to introduce you to my wife."

"Your what?!" Lieke blurted out, but Connor was shaking his head.

"That's not what I—"

This time Calla interrupted him with a smile. "I'm also his mate."

Lieke's eyes went as wide as her mouth, and it might have been the first time I'd ever seen the woman speechless.

"Funny," Connor said, dropping his head to the side, eyeing me in that obnoxious way he did whenever he was right about something. "You never believed in mates, and now you've found yours."

"Smugness isn't a good look on you, Your High—" I cleared my throat. "I guess it's Your Majesty now, isn't it."

"Suppose so," Connor said. "But no need to tiptoe around us here. You know his health was fading fast after Brennan..."

He shifted his eyes to Calla, his features tightening with regret.

Lieke, finally finding her voice, broke through the awkward silence. "I'm so glad to see you, Calla," she said, approaching cautiously, as if she were afraid my mate might run off as she had the last time she had visited.

"Me too, friend," Calla said, and slipping her hand from mine, she threaded her arm through Lieke's and started to lead her toward the house. "Would you help me get ready?"

"Of course," Lieke said. As they walked away, she sneaked a

glance at me and whispered to Calla. "As long as you tell me every-thing that's happened between you two."

Nudging Connor with my elbow, I pulled my mouth into a lopsided grin. "Lieke still hasn't learned that we can hear her whis-pers, has she?"

Connor uttered a single laugh. "No, she just gave up trying to speak that quietly."

We started to follow our wives back to the palace when Connor stopped abruptly.

"What is it?" I asked, foolishly thinking it was something serious that had given him pause.

His features tightened, and he seemed to be searching the air for something. "You got married," he started.

"I did."

"Without me."

"If it makes you feel any better, my sister wasn't there either," I said, frowning. "Is it that big of a deal?"

Connor shook his head slowly. "No, it's not. I just would have liked to say I told you so."

CHAPTER 100
CALLA

King Durand's burial service was a beautiful, intimate affair, with only close friends in attendance. The last of the guests, having offered their condolences to Connor and Lieke, strode away through the garden gate and back to their waiting carriages and horses. Connor, tucking Lieke's hand into the crook of his arm, nodded toward the palace. Matthias started to follow them but stopped when my feet refused to move.

"You okay, Killer?" he asked, turning to face me fully and stroking the back of my hand with his thumb.

I offered a few slight nods and glanced down to where Brennan's grave sat nearby. Matthias smiled gently, saying nothing as he leaned in close and feathered a kiss to my forehead. Finding my eyes again, he whispered, "I'll be inside."

I didn't move until Matthias disappeared through the back door of the palace. Brushing away a stray tear, I made my way slowly across the garden to the simple gray stone marked with Brennan's name and the words "Beloved brother, son, and husband. Always missed. Never forgotten."

Crumpling to the ground, I ignored the wave of pain that shot through my knees as they landed heavily. With light fingers, I traced the letters of his name etched in the stone. Pulling in the garden air—the smell of freshly turned dirt and fallen leaves filling my lungs and calming my nerves—I exhaled slowly, trying to find the words I needed to say.

With a quick glance over my shoulder to ensure I was alone, I bent my head low and stared at the grass around my knees. I didn't stop my shadows as they spilled out of my hands to gather around the stone, as if saying farewell to the male who never knew of this power I possessed.

"I should have told you, Brennan," I whispered. "I should have trusted you with this piece of me."

My shadows weaved their way around me, wrapping me in their cool embrace.

"I miss you. I miss you so much. I want you to know, though, that I'm okay now. Not perfect...but better."

Maybe this was stupid, thinking he could hear me.

Does he need to hear me for these words to matter?

I shook my head at myself. No. These words were as much for me as they were for Brennan, and they deserved a voice.

"I found my mate. And part of me..." I paused to swallow back a sob. "Part of me is so furious with the stars for insisting I lose you in order to find him. But immortal as we may be, death has shown me just how fragile and precious our time here is. I don't want to waste it being angry anymore. I choose to be thankful for the time we had, because you taught me how to love, how to keep going, and how to laugh even through the hard times."

A tear-soaked giggle tumbled from my lips as Brennan's mischievous smile popped into my thoughts, quickly shifting into Matthias's equally wicked grin and a twinge of guilt sparked in my chest.

"He makes me laugh," I said, wiping away more tears. "And he saw me—all of me—and accepted me, darkness and all. He made me want to be better. He reminded me that there is good in this world, and that I am allowed to have some of that goodness."

Lowering my forehead to the cold stone, I closed my eyes tightly on the next wave of tears.

"I have to say goodbye now, but I will always love and miss you, Brennan." Sitting back, I placed a kiss to my fingertips and pressed them against his etched name.

With each step back to the palace, another piece of my grief fell away, little by little, uncovering bits of my heart that finally seemed healed. While some remained—and likely always would—I stepped into the palace unafraid and unburdened.

Matthias waited for me just inside the door, holding two glasses of brandy and pulling a wide smile across my lips.

"I thought you might need this," he said, stepping forward, but instead of reaching for the glass, I lifted my hands to his face, cradling his jaw in my palms.

"I need you more, general," I said as I lifted my lips to meet his.

But he paused and pulled back slightly, his eyes searching mine. "You'll need a new nickname for me now, Killer."

Shaking my head, I smirked up at him. "I love you, Matthias."

I braced myself for whatever snarky comment he was about to make, but he simply shifted his lips to hover over my ear and whispered, "There she is."

THE END

SPICE RACK

Please review this list if you would like to be aware of the chapters
with intimate content prior to reading.

46 - one scene
47 - one brief scene
48 - one scene
49 - one scene
95 - one scene

ANKARA ART

UP NEXT

Watch for the next book in the Immortal Reveries series

BEFORE THE SUN SETS
*A fated mates tale of a cursed princess and the dragon shifter
mercenary hired to protect her.*

Coming Fall 2026

ACKNOWLEDGMENTS

This book nearly broke me.

I'm not sure why this story was so difficult, but I have to give a sincere heartfelt thanks to those who helped see me through it from beginning to end.

Jourdan: You're hands down one of my best friends, and Calla wouldn't exist on the page as clearly or as authentically without your help. You understood her when I couldn't, and she will always and forever be a character I wrote for you. I don't deserve you, your friendship, your insight, but I'm so crazy thankful for you. Love you, friend.

To my other alpha and beta readers, Megs, Alexandria, Lauren, Tiffany, Erika, Valerie, Kaitlin, Candace, Robin, Fedy, April, Shannon: You guys were so incredibly patient with me as I had to push my deadline out time after time. Thank you for the incredible feedback, for reading this book (sometimes twice?!?), and for truly falling in love with these characters as I have.

To my street team, Candace, Frankie, Ivana, Janene, Jenn, Kerry, Lindsey, Megan, Megs, Paige, Robin, Sierra, and Veraya: Thank you for all your hard work and enthusiasm as we worked to get this book ready for launch. I hope you know how much I appreciate you and all you have done!

To my patreon members (as of my writing this out), Bee, Heidi, Valerie, Ashley, Mary Ann, Megan, Diantha, Talia, Sarah, Candace, Katie, Emily, Stephanie, Christine, Katie, Caitlin, and Leigha: Thank you for your continued and generous support in this way. I hope you know just how much it means to me to have you as part of this little corner of the internet!

To my publishing team: Noah, my editor; Rachel, my proofreader; Gerralt, my cartographer; Fran, my cover designer; and all of the artists who have painted art for this project, thank you for lending your talents to this book!

To you, the readers: Thank you for picking this book up, for loving these characters, for supporting me and my writing. I could not do this job without you.

Saving the best for last...

Joel: You're my better half and the one who kept me going when I felt like I'd never finish. You picked up the slack so often when I needed to buckle down. You have always supported this weird career of mine, and I'm beyond grateful for all you do for me and for our family. I know you don't always see the good in yourself, but you are the best person I know. I love you more than I can ever express in words.

Kids: Thank you for all the times you've encouraged me and tried to hawk my books to your teachers and friends' parents even though you aren't old enough to read them yourself. You each have such unique personalities and talents, and I'm in awe every day that God chose me to be your mother. Thank you for being patient and understanding as I spend so many hours working.

My husband, church family, and our pastors: Thank you for keeping me rooted in our Christian faith, nudging me whenever my eyes stray from what really matters. There are so many temptations in the world and in this industry, and I could not do this job without you as my rock and foundation. The Lord has granted me an often confusing talent/gift/ability, but I am beyond blessed to get to create worlds and design stories that can bring a sliver of earthly joy to my neighbors.

And finally, to my Lord and Savior, Jesus Christ: Your love surpasses all of my understanding, and I am eternally grateful for this saving grace You grant me, though I do not deserve it.

ABOUT THE AUTHOR

Vanessa Rasanen is a former engineer turned fantasy romance author of emotionally charged stories full of love, adventure, and a bit of spice. When she's not writing swoony tension and broody good guys, she and her pilot husband can be found explaining to their four extroverted children why they have to live out in the middle of nowhere. Vanessa is a morning person who lives on coffee, potatoes, and gin (not at the same time) and could watch The Mummy and New Girl on repeat. Check out her website at: vanessarasanen.com